EMM

Infamy & Ecstasy

EMMA
Infamy & Ecstasy

Peggy Savage Baumgardner

TATE PUBLISHING
AND ENTERPRISES, LLC

Published by Tate Publishing & Enterprises, LLC
127 E. Trade Center Terrace | Mustang, Oklahoma 73064 USA
1.888.361.9473 | www.tatepublishing.com

Tate Publishing is committed to excellence in the publishing industry. The company reflects the philosophy established by the founders, based on Psalm 68:11,
"The Lord gave the word and great was the company of those who published it."

Book design copyright © 2016 by Tate Publishing, LLC. All rights reserved.
Cover design by Joana Quilantang
Interior design by Richell Balansag

Published in the United States of America

ISBN: 978-1-68187-470-8
Fiction / Family Life
15.10.19

Contents

1. Nightmare of Horrors 9
2. Tora! Tora! Tora! 17
3. Children Were Caring for Children 28
4. The Intruder 32
5. She Held Her Baby One Last Time 39
6. She Left the Bank With All the Dignity
   She Could Muster 43
7. Den of Iniquity 48
8. How Could She Be So Lucky? 55
9. Her Family Was Slowly Disappearing 58
10. Bugs 62
11. She Lay Down Beside His Cold Body 67
12. Kind Words from a Stranger 72
13. Everyone Has a Few Skeletons in Their Closet 76
14. He Was Too Strict and Legalistic 87
15. What Would Misty Think If She Knew the Truth? 92
16. Why Were They Talking About the Germans? 97
17. Devil's Trash 100
18. I Could Have Danced All Night 106
19. Terminations 111
20. Private Signals 115
21. Reverend Michael Charles 121
22. Orientation 125
23. Questions 128
24. Emotions 131
25. Women in Combat 134
26. Assignments 136
27. Knight in a White Sailor's Uniform 143

28. Victory Garden 150
29. Is She Emma's Daughter? 156
30. Operation Pied Piper 159
31. Rowdy Sailors 163
32. Riverview Beach Park 168
33. Who Was That Sailor on the Steps? 173
34. He Ran Like a Coward 177
35. What Was the Accident's Name? 182
36. Who Caused the Accidents? 186
37. He Killed the Dog 189
38. Lieutenant Zane Skylur 193
39. Police Officers Were on Duty 196
40. The Children Knew Everything 198
41. Too Much Drama in Her Life 200
42. Questioning All Sailors 203
43. Imperial Japanese Navy 206
44. Turning Him Over to the Naval Authorities 209
45. She Finally Gets to See Patrick 214
46. The Snake 221
47. Hitler Is One Bad Dude 224
48. Rat's Tail 226
49. Lorenda Collingwood 230
50. The Fort 234
51. Wine and Cigarettes 237
52. Vodka 241
53. The Slap 245
54. Hot Biscuits with Peanut Butter and Honey 249
55. Christmas 251
56. The Hatchet 256
57. Boots 261
58. Terminally Ill 265
59. USS Brooklyn 269
60. Sly Comes Home! 272
61. The Proposal 275

62. Frederick Meets the Intruder 279
63. Are the Russians Coming to Get Us? 283
64. Divorce Papers 286
65. Very Cruel Person 288
66. Do Not Answer the Door 290
67. Way to Go, Sailor! 295
68. The Question 299
69. Child Support 302
70. She Loved Him Enough to Let Him Go 306
71. Life-Changing Situation 311
72. Reverend Dolan and Reverend Charles 313
73. God Works in Mysterious Ways 317
74. Hair Loss 321
75. The Divorce Was Final 324
76. They Saluted the Dead Soldiers 326
77. I Love You Truly 330
78. Battle of the Bulge 334
79. Hitler Commits Suicide 338
80. Spiteful Jealousy Brings Consequences 342
81. Last Hired, First Fired 356
82. President Franklin Delano Roosevelt Dies 358
83. Surprise Visitor 361
84. Miss Emma 364
85. Tony Lost a Leg in the War 368
86. Harry and Lorenda's Wedding 374
87. Sly and Emma's Wedding 377

1

Nightmare of Horrors

Even though they had only dated a few times, Harry Carswell proposed to Emma Patton immediately after she graduated from high school. Emma accepted his marriage proposal without giving it a second thought, because she was very infatuated with his charm and good looks.

Their grandparents raised both Emma and her cousin Margaret, but they were never close. After hearing about Harry and Emma's engagement, the possibility of any future relationship between the cousins ended that day. There was only a year difference in their ages, but they each had their own circle of friends and never did anything together. They never talked about what was going on in their lives, so Emma had no idea that her cousin had a crush on Harry.

Emma was excited about their upcoming marriage and immediately began making plans for their wedding and choosing a style for her wedding gown. She was so excited, that she refused to pay any attention to her cousin's negative behavior, nor Harry's.

Emma wanted to have a beautiful wedding as well as a storybook marriage. She had no idea that her marriage to Harry would become a nightmare of horrors.

Their first baby was born nine months after they were married. Emma gained a lot of weight with the baby and had great difficulty losing it. Harry shamed her by saying that she was fat and that he could not stand how she smelled when she was breast feeding the baby. He totally avoided her and began making nasty remarks about her weight, how she looked, and the way she smelled. He also began accusing her of doing things that she had never even thought of doing.

Harry was not intimate with Emma for a very long time after the baby was born, but one Saturday morning out of desperation, he reached over and touched Emma on her waist as she was getting out of bed. She immediately turned around, looked at him, and then lay back down. As if on cue, the baby began crying. It was so annoying that Harry could not concentrate on what he was doing. He became so angry that he kicked Emma out of the bed. He then yelled at her and told her to go take care of her brat and to shut her up.

Emma got up from the floor and went to check on the baby. Harry turned over and went back to sleep because the baby was her responsibility, not his.

Emma understood how frustrating it must be for a man like Harry. He told her when they were first married that he had certain needs that he expected her to take care of, or he would become very agitated and angry. He was honest with her from the beginning, and she knew that she would have to do better with how she looked and smelled. She was very lucky to be married to Harry, and she should try harder to do everything she could to please him.

She changed the baby's diaper, fed her, and then put her back in her bed for her morning nap. She quietly opened the bedroom door and saw that Harry was still sleeping, so she closed the door and went to take a quick bath and freshen up. After bathing, she opened the door to the bedroom just as Harry was waking up. As she slid under the covers, he said, "Now that is what I am talking about. When you come to bed with me, I want you to smell like a real woman, not like a nurse maid."

For about six months, things began improving in their relationship. Emma was back to her average weight, looking good and preparing Harry's favorite meals. While he ate, she would feed the baby and put her back in her bed. She would then do the dishes, clean the kitchen, and take a bath. Afterward she would join Harry either in the living room or the bedroom.

There were many times when Emma wished that she could occasionally have a night when she did not have to cook, clean the kitchen, give the baby a bath, feed her and put her to bed, take a bath, and put on clean nightclothes, all to please Harry. She would like to just lay back on the sofa or the bed, in the clothes that she had on, close her eyes, and sleep until she woke up naturally. However, that was not to be, and she knew that she would have to accept things as they were.

One month, Emma was late with her monthly cycle. She knew that she was probably pregnant, because she was having the same symptoms that she had with her first pregnancy. Harry was happy, passionate, and loving, as long as he was getting most of her attention, but she knew that when she told him that she might be pregnant, it would ruin everything between them again, so she kept quiet and said nothing.

While they were cuddling one night, Harry rubbed his hand over her stomach and asked her if she was gaining weight. If she was, he said, she should start watching what she ate, because he did not want her getting fat and ugly, the way she did when she was pregnant.

Emma began wearing loose clothing to hide her swelling abdomen but thought it best not to wear any of her old maternity clothes. One evening just as she was going to sit on the sofa beside Harry, he playfully grabbed the tie of her wrap around dress and told her to get rid of that thing. When she took it off, Emma immediately saw anger rising in his face. He grabbed her by the arm and literally threw her across the room and said, "Don't try to pull that trick on me again." She had suspected that he would not like having another child to compete with, but she had no idea that he would be so violent with her.

After that night, Harry began acting angry and ignoring her. It was as if he ignored her, the baby would go away. Just the thought of her being fat with all of those brown spots on her face was repulsive to him. He had heard men talk about their wives having a glow while being pregnant. Emma sure missed the boat with that one.

Emma would never do anything to harm the baby she was carrying, but she knew by having it, there were going to be problems between her and Harry. He would not touch her and spoke very little to her when he was at home, which was not very often. Most of the time, he would come home very late. When he did come home, he would expect his dinner to be ready regardless of the time, which added more stress for Emma.

Harry came home from work one day in one of his nasty moods and found Emma's grandmother sitting on the front porch holding a baby. He had a feeling lately that it was probably about time for Emma to have her baby. She was so big that she looked like she waddled when she walked. She must have popped the baby out as soon as he walked out the door that morning. However, he was thankful that it happened after he left for work.

For some reason, Mary Byrd had been worried about her granddaughter and came down for a visit. As soon as she walked in the door, she realized that Emma was in labor. Her water had broken, and she was ready to deliver her baby. Mary did not even know that her granddaughter was pregnant again.

Emma was screaming out with labor pains, and the baby was crying, probably from being hungry or needing her diaper changed.

Mary ran to the bedroom and picked up the baby, then went to Emma. She changed Henrietta's diaper and put her down on the bed beside Emma. She then helped Emma get into position to give birth to her baby. She found a rubber doormat, wrapped it in an old sheet, and put it under Emma to keep from messing up her bed. She barely got everything ready when the baby popped his head out. Not long after that, he opened his mouth and let the world know that he had arrived.

Henrietta lay on the bed beside Emma and did not make a sound the entire time her mother was giving birth to her baby brother.

After Mary got Emma and the baby cleaned up, she was very tired. When she saw that Emma was resting and Henrietta was sleeping by her side, she wrapped the baby in a warm blanket and went out on the screened-in porch so that she could sit down and rest. She was in her late sixties, and this had been a very tiring day, to say the least.

She had been sitting there for only a short time when Harry came home. He immediately demanded to know why she was there and wanted to know whose baby she was holding. He did not give her time to answer before he asked if his dinner was ready. He did not even ask about Emma or the baby.

Mary told him that he knew very well whose baby she was holding and if he wanted something to eat, he could pull up his big boy's britches and fix it himself, because she sure was not going to cater to him, not after the day she had.

Harry stomped out of the house and went to a restaurant to get something to eat. The whole time he was eating, he thought about everything that was happening to him. He could not understand why Emma and her grandmother had to continuously mess with his life. He wanted his life to be as it was when he and Emma were first married, not as it was now.

After he ate, he went home and stomped back into the house, pulled his arm back, and made a fist and shook it at Mary. He told her that she was to have his dinner prepared when he got home every night, or she could get out of his house.

Mary stood up, looked him in the eye, and said, "I am not afraid of you, and I will cook when I get ready to cook, but it will not be for you. I will take care of my granddaughter and her babies, but I will do nothing for you. Act like a man and quit acting like a baby." She then glared her eyes at him as though daring him to hit her and said, "If you ever lay one finger on me, you will either find yourself dead or sitting in a jail."

That did not go over well with Harry. It was all that he could do, not to hit that woman. She could get under his skin faster than anyone he had ever known, other than his own father.

Harry began eating breakfast, lunch, and dinner at the restaurant every day. It was his choice to go there to eat and not because he was afraid of Mary Byrd.

He brought no groceries home for her to cook and neither did he bring anything from the restaurant for them to eat. He did not care if they all starved; in fact, he wished they would.

About two weeks after the baby was born, Harry came home and found Emma in the kitchen cooking. He looked around, saw that her grandmother was not there and could not believe his good fortune. He was getting sick of eating out, but he was not going to lower himself to do a woman's work in the kitchen. Whatever Emma was cooking sure smelled great.

Not only was Emma cooking, she had already fed both babies and got them ready for bed. She was very tired because it was her first day without her grandmother. She was also thankful that her grandmother had gone shopping for food before she left. If not, she would not have had anything to prepare for dinner. She had to smile with that thought, because she knew that her grandmother had not purchased the groceries just so she would have something to cook for Harry.

Her grandmother was a strong woman, and Emma wished that she could be more like her. She could only imagine what Harry would do, if she stood up to him as her grandmother had. He would probably leave her and their babies. What would she do then? If he did leave them, she knew that she still had the remainder of her inheritance deposited in the bank, and that would probably take care of them for a while. They had no house payment or rent to pay, and all that she should have to worry about would be food, utilities, and taking care of her babies. That gave her some peace of mind.

Harry was very hungry and anxious to eat because he had not eaten a home-cooked meal in weeks. He opened the lid on the pot of green beans that was cooking in order to savor the smell. He slammed the lid on the pot, grabbed Emma by the arm, jerked her around, and wanted to know why she did not have new potatoes and onions in the green beans the way he liked.

When she told him that they were out of potatoes and onions, he became angrier, because he remembered Mary cooking potatoes and using onions and eggs to make potato salad for them to eat. It had looked and smelled good, but there was no way that he would eat anything that woman cooked. Not after the way she treated him.

Harry shook Emma and then threw her against the wall. He dumped all of the food on the floor and told her that she looked like a pig, so if she was hungry, she could eat like a pig. He then left and went to the restaurant to eat.

As he sat eating at the restaurant, he realized that name-calling and accusations were no longer working with Emma. If it was the last thing that he ever did, he was going to teach that woman how she was supposed to treat him.

When he walked in the back door, he saw that she had already cleaned the kitchen. That was good because it would have probably made him even angrier if he had to walk through the mess he left in the floor.

He went in search of Emma and found her propped up against the bed nursing one baby and trying to change the diaper on the other. He grabbed her by the arm and jerked her up from the bed, causing the baby to fall out of her arms. Luckily, it landed on the bed. Her arms and back were still painful from where he had thrown her against the wall earlier, and the only way she could sit and feed the baby was to support her back against the bed. When Harry let go of her, she immediately fell to the floor, because she had no strength to stand on her own.

Harry jerked his belt off and grabbed her up again. He whipped Emma with the belt, the way his father whipped him when he was a young boy and did not do what his father told him to do. While whipping her, he called her every ugly name he could think of.

Each stroke he delivered was more intense, and he had to admit that it was also very enjoyable. He could not believe how relaxed he felt after whipping Emma.

Emma was not feeling or thinking anything, because she lay unconscious at his feet. Harry went to their bedroom, lay down across the bed, and immediately went to sleep, without guilt or worry. His anger had totally dissipated. It had been a long time since he had been that relaxed.

It was over an hour before Emma was alert and able to pull herself up. She knew what Harry did was inexcusable and unbelievable. She also knew that it was something that she would never forget.

Henrietta was holding the baby as though she was holding a doll or a security blanket. The baby lay sleeping in the comfort of her small arms

Emma finally got her wish. She crawled up on the bed and put her arms across both of her babies and went to sleep, fully clothed.

2

Tora! Tora! Tora!

Harry had wished many times that he had not married Emma. She was beneath him, and they both knew it. Even though they were both now in their twenties, she looked much older than he did. He could have gotten almost any girl that he wanted in high school. The only problem was that none of those girls received a large inheritance as Emma did. She did not have very much left in her inheritance fund, but he had to admit that he had a good time with what he had spent, plus it helped him put up with her. If it were not for her money, he would have been gone a long time ago.

He had never been as peaceful and relaxed as he was that night when he gave Emma her first whipping with his belt. The whippings and the beatings he gave her with his fists were the only things he enjoyed doing with her now. It made him sick at the thought of touching her in an intimate way, and it was a long time before he finally gave in, and then it was only because he could not find any one else. When he was with her, he was very rough because that was the only way he could stand touching her. He enjoyed it like that, but he mostly wanted her to feel like he was punishing her.

Harry had been seeing three other women since he and Emma were married. Emma had never found out about them, at least he did not think so. Of course, if she did, she would never say anything to him about it, because she was too afraid of him now, and that made him feel even more powerful and deserving.

He had gotten involved with Rebecca Mason, a teller at the bank where Emma had deposited her money. He mostly did it because it would be easier for him to get money out of Emma's trust account. One day Rebecca threatened to break it off with him if he did not leave Emma. That did not go over well with Harry. The next time they were together, she hugged up to him and told him that they could be together all of the time, if he would leave Emma. She then said, "I should go to your house and tell her about us."

That did it! Harry had his fill of her attitude. He grabbed Rebecca by the shoulders and banged her head against the wall. She looked dazed as though she was about to faint, and it left a bloody mess on the wall and on her clothes.

Harry could not believe how excited he became by just looking at her injuries and the blood. It was a real turn on for him. He grabbed hold of her chin, kissed her, and then hit her on her jaw with his fist. The blow actually knocked her out. He looked down at her as she lay on the floor and said, "I bet you will not try that stunt again." He then stepped over her and left. He did not even wait to see if she was going to be okay. He actually did not care.

Rebecca survived the attack, and she never said anything to Harry again about leaving Emma. She took Harry's punishment the way he told her that a woman should if she really loved her man.

Harry could not believe his newfound lust. He loved seeing passion in a woman's eyes when he was with them, but he loved seeing fear in their eyes even more.

When Harry was in one of his moods, he would attack whoever was close to him, and Emma was usually his closest target. Being a good wife, she always took the beatings and never said a word. Not one time since they were married had she ever accused him of anything or told him that he hurt her feelings over something he may have said. The other women he was seeing did not appreciate his new behavior. One woman left town and with no forwarding address and the other looked and dressed like someone suffering from some type of mental disability. She was always walking around with her hair uncombed, looking down at the ground, and literally running every time he came near her. What was wrong with those women?

Harry was afraid to be with Emma thinking she might get pregnant again, but there were times when he did not have a choice. When he was at home, all he could smell was messy diapers and soured breast milk, and you could always bet that one of her kids would be crying.

He could not believe that Emma actually asked him to hold one of those kids. He worked hard all day long, and the last thing he needed or wanted was to go home and have to hold a crying kid. Especially one that needed its diaper changed. Why would she even consider asking him to do such a thing?

Thankfully, he had met a few women on his route with whom he became friendly. Donna Peterson, a cute little blonde-haired woman, seemed to appreciate the fact that he tried to keep himself looking good. Not too many men that drove a truck delivering coal could dress that well.

Harry often gave Donna a little extra coal because she was always flirting with him and inviting him to come in and have some tea or coffee with her. After having a glass of tea with a woman like Donna, it sure made him hate to go home to a woman like Emma.

One morning while he was drinking coffee with Donna, she turned around, and her robe fell open. It was just enough to tease him, but it was very difficult to walk out of her house that day. He was going to have to find out what time her husband came home from work. Maybe he and Donna could become friends with benefits. He hoped that it would happen soon, which it did.

Harry had to go back by his house one morning because he had forgotten to take his delivery list with him. When he walked in the house, the kids were crying, and Emma had her head over a bucket throwing up. He knew what that meant! He walked over to the bucket and kicked it as hard as he could and vomit splattered everywhere!

He looked at Emma with total disgust and started calling her a lazy, good-for-nothing slut. He could not believe that she was pulling that trick on him again. He told her that there was no way she could be pregnant, certainly not by him. He grabbed her by the hair, yanked her head up, and forced her to look at him. He told her that she had better take care of this situation before it became a baby. One of the men that he worked with had used an ice pick on his wife, and he heard of another one making his girlfriend drink kerosene. He told her there were ways of getting rid of it, and she had better decide which way she was going to do it, or he would decide for her.

Emma looked at him as though she could not believe what he was saying. Harry did not have the stomach to use an ice pick on her, but he did make her drink a cup of kerosene. After she finished drinking it, he hit her in the stomach so many times that she nearly passed out. Afterward, Harry walked out of the house, waved to his neighbor Charles who was working in his yard, got into his truck, and drove away.

Harry smiled to himself because he had accused Emma of being with Charles, but he was almost positive that Charles was not the baby's daddy, not with a good-looking wife like Sara. If you had a wife that looked that good, a man would have to be out of his mind to consider touching a woman that looked like Emma.

He knew that he was probably the father, whether he wanted to be or not, because he knew Emma would never cheat on him.

If she had not let all of this stuff happen, they may have even been able to be like husband and wife again. Of course, that would have to be after he got his fill of Donna Peterson. He grinned and doubted that he would ever get tired of that little darling. He had grown quite fond of her and was now stopping by her house almost every day, which he would be doing in a couple of hours. He did not need to be with Emma or any other woman since he had met her.

Six months later, Donald was born. Much to Emma's surprise, it appeared that there was nothing wrong with him. After the way Harry hit her in the stomach when he found out she was pregnant, she was surprised that she did not miscarry. Her grandmother had come down a few days before the delivery, but almost as soon as the baby was born, Harry insisted that she leave, which her grandmother did. She did not want to be around Harry any more than he wanted to be around her.

After Mary left, Harry told Emma that he did not want that woman back in his house ever again and then told her that she did not need anyone there to help her. All she had to do was take care of her three kids and have his dinner prepared every night when he got home. He had to work hard all day delivering coal, and that was the very least she could do.

Harry had a good arrangement with Donna Peterson. He sometimes felt that he might actually be falling in love with her. When he could not see her on the weekends, he felt lonesome and missed her. He had never laid a finger on that woman in a harmful way, and he never had a desire to do so. He would not want to put a blemish on her gorgeous body. Just being with her relieved him of all his frustrations and stress. It was a shame that he did not meet her, before he met Emma. If he had, he was sure that his life would have been much better than it was now.

He was not going to cry over past mistakes because he had it made now. That is until Pete Peterson came home early one day and saw his coal truck parked in front of the house. He had to jump out the window to keep Pete from seeing him. As he left, he heard Pete ask Donna why she was having coal delivered again. He also wanted to know why she was so scantly dressed in the middle of the day.

That was a close one! Harry had to pull into a wooded area a couple of blocks away and straighten his clothes. He would have to take a little time off before going to see Donna again. He could see how his coal truck parked in front of a house with a large coal pile in the back could draw attention.

The two older kids were getting to where they were not much trouble because they knew if they got in their daddy's way, he would lay a good whipping on them. They had learned that when he was home, they had to stay in their room. The only time he permitted them to come out of their room was after he had finished eating. The rule in his house was that he ate first, regardless of the time he came home. Emma could feed her kids after he ate. The next rule was that after they ate, they were to go straight to bed. After they were in bed, Emma was to clean the kitchen and then take a bath before coming to bed. He told her if she was too tired to take a bath, she could sleep on the sofa.

There were times when he would sit at the table drinking his tea or coffee after he had eaten, hoping the kids would get hungry and fussy. He especially liked to rile Frederick. All he had to do in front of him was to say something bad about his mother, and the little tyke would actually come at him, knowing what it would cause him to get. The boy would always try to take up for his mother. When he came at him, Harry would jerk his belt off, grab Frederick by the arm, and give him a good whipping. By now, that boy should know not to do that. He knew that he would get a beating if he came in between him and his mother.

Harry always used his belt on the kids. He did not get the pleasure out of using his fist on them as he did when he beat Emma, but it still helped him to get rid of some of his stress and frustrations.

However, it did bother him a little when he would whip Donald or Henrietta. Donald looked just like he did at his age, and it would make him remember all the beatings his father had given him. Henrietta favored his mother who was the only stable person he ever had in his life. However, she could not, or would not, protect him from his father. She always acted a little afraid of him also, but he knew that she loved him, regardless of what he did to her or anyone else.

One night Emma was looking good. When she came into the living room after doing dishes, Harry asked her why she was so dressed up. She smiled and said that she was dressed up for him. He was the only person that mattered to her. She came over and started massaging his shoulders the way she did before the kids came along. Afterward, she very lovingly kissed him on the top of his head.

Harry immediately pulled her from behind the chair and made her sit on his lap. She smelled good, and it felt good having her sit there. He had to admit that she was still a good-looking woman when she was not pregnant or had her head stuck in a bucket vomiting. One thing led to another, and he took her right there on the living room floor. He did not care if the kids came in or if someone walked past the window or walked through the front door. In fact, that made it a little more enticing. After all, it was his house, and he was the master of his domain.

When everything was over, Emma looked like a wrinkled mess, and her hair was sticking out all over her head. Harry could not believe that he had actually been attracted to her a few minutes prior. He looked at Emma and said, "Don't ever try to seduce me like that again. If you do, you are going to be sorry." He kicked her out of the way and then went to take a bath to wash off her smell.

Emma sat in the floor in front of the sofa with her knees drawn up to her chest, and she put her head down on her knees. The pain was so deep that she could not even cry anymore.

The only time Harry came home after that was to eat and sleep. He would cringe if Emma even came near him. He had given her orders to feed her kids leftovers from the night before and have them in bed before he came home and he did not want her in the kitchen while he ate. After she put his food on the table, she was not to come back into the kitchen unless he called her to get something for him. After he ate, he would tell her to get in the kitchen and wash the dishes and not make any noise because he was going to bed. She was already sleeping on the couch because he only permitted her inside the bedroom to bring in his clean laundry and put it away.

If he happened to be in the bedroom when she came in, he would not even speak to her. He would act as if he did not see her. He no longer permitted her to put her clothes in the same closet with his. She had to hang them on a rope on the back porch.

Emma could not believe that one night of total humiliation was bringing her so much grief. About six to eight weeks after that night, she realized that she was pregnant again. She was lucky because she did not have morning sickness this time, and she was trying not to gain any weight because she feared what Harry would do when he found out.

When she was about seven months pregnant, Harry came home from work, turned on the radio, and lay down on the couch to take a nap. When he heard Donald crying, he yelled out at him to suck it up because he was tired of hearing him whine.

Emma dried her hands with a kitchen towel, walked over to the door between the kitchen and the living room, and told him that she thought Donald was sick and may have a fever because he felt hot. Harry jumped up, knocked Emma against a wall in the kitchen, and said, "How dare you talk back to me that way?" The blow was so forceful that she just slid down to the floor after hitting the wall. He walked over to her, put his foot on her stomach and then started kicking her. With each blow, he felt more powerful. He literally felt like he hated this woman now.

As he was kicking Emma, he was also cursing her and accusing her of cheating on him, and he told her that he knew that none of her brats belonged to him. All of a sudden, Harry paused from kicking her and just stood there looking at her. When he saw the small bump on Emma's stomach, he got so angry that he actually stood on her stomach trying to kill the unborn child that he knew was inside her.

Emma was so weak that she did not even try to fight back. She knew that it would only make him worse if she did. With one final kick to the right side of her abdomen, Emma passed out. Harry left her on the kitchen floor, went to the living room and turned up the volume on the radio, trying to block out any sound that may come from the kitchen.

Henrietta and Frederick sneaked into the kitchen to check on their mother when they saw that their father had gone to his bedroom and closed the door. For the remainder of their lives they would never forget what their mother looked like as she lay on the floor that day. She was lying in a pool of blood and wetness because her water had broken during the beating. Emma was alert when they sat down beside her. She put her finger to her mouth motioning for them to be quiet. She was afraid that Harry had killed the baby inside her, and she knew he was capable of doing the same thing to them.

Emma was unable to sit up because the baby's head was coming out. She was in a tremendous amount of pain and told Frederick to go to the drawer where she kept her scissors and bring them and some matches and alcohol to her. She told Henrietta to bring her some old towels and warm water. Both of the children immediately ran to get the things she had asked for. Emma, with the help of her children, delivered baby Patrick. They cut and tied the umbilical cord, and Henrietta lifted the lifeless baby to her mother's arms.

Emma sat with her back braced against the kitchen wall feeling that she may pass out any minute, but she continued working with her baby trying to get him to breathe. Finally, she heard a tiny noise, and it sounded like the baby sneezed. Frederick heard it also and laughed.

When Harry heard Frederick laugh, he hollered from the bedroom asking him if he wanted some of the same thing that he had just given his mama.

They could hear Harry as he stomped out of the bedroom toward the kitchen. The sound frightened Frederick and he grabbed Emma's arm and accidentally bumped the baby. The baby immediately let out a cry and so did Frederick because he thought he had hurt the baby.

As soon as Harry heard the sound of the crying baby, he stopped, turned around, and went back into the bedroom. He grabbed a bag out of the closet and started packing his clothes.

Harry and Emma had a favorite song when they were first married. Every time they heard "The Tennessee Waltz," he would hold her close and kiss her passionately as they danced to the music. Their song was playing on the radio as he left, but no song, anything, or anyone was going to get him to go back inside that house ever again. He hoped the beating he just gave her would kill her and the baby.

Emma also heard the song as it was playing on the radio. She also heard the door when Harry slammed it shut.

She had suffered many beatings from Harry, but none was as violent as this. As she sat bracing herself against the wall, she could feel the dampness of her blood under her legs. She could not move without excruciating pain because there was not a single part of her body that Harry had not kicked.

Halfway through the song, an announcement came over the radio, saying, "We interrupt this morning broadcast to bring you this important message. Today, December 7, 1941, at 7:55 a.m., Japanese aircraft carriers crept to within striking distance of Hawaii and launched a deadly attack on Pearl Harbor.

"Two waves of 354 Japanese bombers, dive-bombers, torpedo bombers, and fighters decimated an unprepared United States Pacific Fleet. They sank four battleships and two destroyers and heavily damaged eleven other ships.

"Around 8:10 a.m., an armor-piercing bomb penetrated the USS Arizona's forward magazine. The explosion sank the ship and killed 1,177 men. There were approximately 2,500 service members and civilians killed, and another estimated 1,200 injured. Thankfully, all aircraft carriers remained unscathed.

"Some have speculated that the Japanese were tired of negotiations with the United States. They wanted to continue their expansion within Asia, but the United States placed an extremely restrictive embargo on Japan, in hopes of curbing their aggression. Rather than giving in to the United States's demands, the Japanese launched a surprise attack against the United States in an attempt to destroy the US naval power.

"As the first bombs dropped on Pearl Harbor, Commander Mitsuo Fuchida, leader of the air attack, called out, "Tora! Tora! Tora! (Tiger! Tiger! Tiger!), a coded message, that told the entire Japanese navy that they had caught the Americans totally by surprise. By 9:45 a.m., just less than two hours after the attack began; the Japanese planes left Pearl Harbor and headed back to their aircraft carriers. It is expected that within the next twenty-four hours, President Franklin D. Roosevelt will declare war on Japan."

As Emma lay on the floor listening to the broadcast, she realized that her attack and Patrick's birth was on the same date that the Japanese attacked Pearl Harbor. The only difference was that her attacker was not her enemy; he was the man she loved.

3

Children Were Caring for Children

After receiving the almost fatal beating from Harry and then delivering her baby on the kitchen floor, Emma was weak and in so much pain that she could barely move. She was almost positive that she had broken ribs and a possible concussion. Her rib area hurt with the slightest movement or deep breathing. She also had blurred vision and was very nauseous.

Henrietta and Frederick brought things that would help her be a little more comfortable as she lay on the kitchen floor. She remained there, with her children by her side, until around noon the next day. Henrietta carried the baby to the boys' bedroom and put him in Donald's crib. Donald climbed in the crib and lay down beside his baby brother. Henrietta then went back to the kitchen and got on one side of her mother, and Frederick got on the other. Together they helped their mother get up from the floor.

Emma sat down on Frederick's bed and lay back on the pillows. Her children stood watch over her and their new baby brother. When the baby would wake up and need to have his diaper changed, Henrietta would change his diaper and then bring him to her mother so that she could feed him. Children were caring for children.

One time after Emma fed the baby, Donald crawled up beside her and wanted her to breast-feed him. It had not been that long since she had stopped breast-feeding him, and he was probably feeling a little insecure about everything that was going on, so she let him nurse from her other breast, and afterward, he went to sleep in her arms. Emma pulled him close and went to sleep also.

Henrietta found some cold biscuits and put jam on them, and that was their meal. For their young ages, they really did a lot to help their mother. They were in the kitchen washing dishes and cleaning up the floor later that day, and Emma could hear them laughing as they worked. Laughter was something rarely heard around their house, especially when Harry was home. The children now seemed happy and acted as though they did not miss their father. To be truthful, neither did Emma!

One thing she was sure of was that she would have to go to work somewhere. They would run out of food soon, and she would have to go to the store. Harry did not stock their cabinets with any food before he left. Week to week, he only bought what he wanted prepared, and he bought no extra. Harry never let her see the bankbook, so she had no idea how much money she had left. When she said anything to him about the money, he would just act defensive and tell her not to worry about it. He told her that he was taking good care of their money by investing it. If she looked at the bankbook, she would only see the small amount he kept there for emergencies. He told her that all the banking information stayed in the bank for safekeeping because you could not trust people these days. He feared someone might break into their house and steal all of their money and important papers, so he thought it was best to let the bank keep it in their vault.

Emma had never believed everything Harry told her, but she never questioned him either. Because she did not believe everything he said, she took money out of his wallet when she knew that he would not see her. She would only take a few dollars at a time, but she had a strong feeling that she and her children may need a real emergency fund some day, and she was right. She did not have much money saved, but she hoped it would last until she could get to the bank or find a job.

About a week later, she knew that she had no other choice but to go to the store to purchase things they needed. They had very little in the house in the way of food products. She had made them gravy that morning for breakfast. All she had was about a half cup of flour, and she used that with a little shortening, salt, pepper, and water to make the gravy. Harry had stopped their milk delivery, so there was no milk to put in the gravy or for the children to drink. The poor children were so hungry; they ate the gravy and old bread without any complaints.

While at the grocery store, Emma overheard a woman saying that she was going to be quitting her job as a waiter and wanted to know if anyone needed a job. Emma walked over and introduced herself, and the girl told her that her name was Jewel. Emma told her that she was looking for a job.

Jewel said that she and her husband Bill were expecting a baby, and it was due on May 18. She was going to work for a few more weeks to get more money saved; then, she would be leaving and the restaurant would need someone to replace her.

Emma asked her what the hours would be. Jewel told her that she worked from two o'clock in the afternoon until ten o'clock at night, but she thought that the girl that worked the night shift wanted to switch to the day shift, so the hours would probably be from ten o'clock at night until six o'clock in the morning.

Jewel told her that the pay per hour was not that great, but most of the people that came in were good tippers. She said that the only thing she did not like about the job was when someone was out, she had to do a double shift, and most of the people that came in later in the evening were heavy drinkers, and they could get a little rowdy at times. Her husband did not like anything about the job and did not like her working there. After the baby was born, she was not going back to work for at least a year.

When she did go back to work, she was going to try to find a job with better hours because of the baby. Bill wanted her home at night and told her that he did not marry her so that he could spend his nights alone. He wanted her to be there with him and their baby.

Jewel offered to walk with her over to the restaurant and introduce her to the owners if she liked. Emma told her that she felt that she was not dressed appropriately to go on a job interview. Jewel told her not to worry because Brice and Karen were wonderful people and great to work with, and they were very good to all of their employees.

The owners were nice, and they seemed pleased with Emma. They told her when Jewel decided to leave that they would love to have her come to work for them. If she liked, she could come in a few days before Jewel left and learn what all was involved with the job. They would pay her an hourly wage, but it was up to Jewel to decide if she wanted to split the tips with her. They asked her if she had children, and she told them yes. They hesitated for a minute and then asked her if she had someone to take care of them while she worked. Emma did not know what to say, so she lied and said, "Yes, I have a sitter." She would have to call Henrietta her sitter.

4

The Intruder

As soon as Jewel decided that she would quit work in February, she asked Emma if she could handle the shift by herself. Emma told her that she thought she could and asked Jewel if her hours would be from ten o'clock at night until six o'clock in the morning. When Jewel said yes, Emma felt as though she had a great weight lifted off her shoulders. The hours were perfect. She could be with the kids all day and then put them to bed around 8:30 p.m. After they were in bed, she could get dressed and be at work by 10:00 p.m. When she came home the next morning, she could get them up and feed them breakfast.

Emma had never worked outside her home before, and it was going to be a new adventure for her, especially with four children. She knew that she would have to take all precautions to keep her children safe while she worked.

Everything worked out great for a few months. She was actually bringing home more money than Harry said that he did driving the coal truck. Her only problem was leaving her children home alone. Every night when she left them, she would almost feel sick from worrying that something may happen to them while she was gone.

One night, Emma fed Patrick, then read Donald a bedtime story, and put them to bed. Henrietta was putting on her gown, getting ready for bed, and Frederick was already in his bed. Henrietta slept with Donald in the big bed, and the baby slept in his crib on the other side of the room. At first, Frederick slept at the foot of their bed, but after a few nights of Henrietta kicking him when she would turn over, he decided he would go back to his own bed.

As Emma was getting dressed, she heard a noise that sounded like a muffled scream. She grabbed her robe and quickly ran to Henrietta's bedroom. The first thing she saw was Donald lying on the floor, and his arm was bleeding. She saw movement and immediately turned her head to the left. Headed toward the window was a large man with a knife in his hand. She reached out to grab Frederick as he ran past her, because she did not want the man to hurt him also, but he was too fast.

Frederick woke up when he heard the scream. Henrietta and Donald were always fighting, so their sounds were nothing new to him, so he laid his head back down on his pillow. He knew if he went to them, both would beg him to choose sides. He did not like getting into the middle of their fights. Their fights usually started when Henrietta was trying to go to sleep. Donald would lie on the bed close beside her, sucking his thumb with his feet dangling up in the air and would constantly reach over and touch her on the arm and say, "Poke." This drove Henrietta crazy, and every time he did it, the battle would begin. Henrietta would cry out, saying, "Donald, would you please stop poking me." Donald would just lie there either sucking his thumb or laughing.

Frederick was almost back to sleep when he heard his mother as she ran down the hallway. He immediately jumped out of bed and ran after her. When he got to the door of the bedroom, he saw a man heading toward the window with a knife in his hand and saw that his brother was bleeding. It only took the four-year-old a couple of seconds to realize that something was wrong.

Because of his protective instincts, Frederick ran past his mother toward the man and hit him behind his knees.

The man lost his balance and Frederick then pushed him as hard as he could, which was not very hard for a child of his size, but it was hard enough to cause the man to lose his balance and fall. As the man fell, he hit his head on the iron headboard of the bed. He lay on the floor not moving, and it looked as though he was not breathing, and blood was seeping out from under his head.

Donald had a bad cut on his arm, so Emma pulled the sash from her robe and tied it around his arm to stop the bleeding. She asked Donald if he was hurt anywhere else, and when he shook his head no, she checked to see if Henrietta was okay.

Emma told Frederick to go get his baseball bat. When he came back with the bat, she told him to stand behind the man, and if he moved, she wanted him to hit the man on the head as hard as he could.

Frederick did exactly as his mother told him to do. He got behind the man's head, spread his legs, and raised the bat. He intended to take him out if he made a move or opened an eye.

Emma walked over to the window, and it looked as though the intruder had cut the screen with the knife, broke the glass, unlocked the window, and climbed in. She looked out the window and could not see anything because it was so dark. They lived in an area that had no outside lights other than what was on their porches, and there were not many houses on their street at that time of night with their porch lights on. When Harry was with them at night, it did not seem as scary, but now that it was just Emma and the children, it could be scary during the day, but especially so at nighttime. This type of incident was what Emma feared most when she left her children alone at night. She wondered if the man broke in because he thought the children were alone.

After she took care of Donald, she told Frederick and Henrietta that she was going to go next door to get some help and told Frederick to keep guard over the intruder until she got back. When she opened the door to leave, she told them not let anyone into the house until she got back. She then ran barefoot to Charles and Sarah's house.

When she knocked on their door, Sara answered almost immediately. As soon as she saw Emma, she knew something was wrong. She told her daughter Brittany to run and get her father.

After Emma told them what happened, Charles told Sara and the kids to stay in the house with the doors locked. He also told his wife to get his shotgun and aim it at the door. If anyone tried to break in, he told her to pull the trigger. He then picked up a club that he kept behind his back door and grabbed Emma by the arm, and they ran to her house.

As soon as they got to the house, Charles told Emma to let him go in first. He said that he would check everything out, and then he would let her know when it would be safe for her to come in. She said. "No way, Charles, I have to get to my children." She ran past him to Henrietta's room. As soon as she reached the door to the bedroom, she saw that the whole scenario had changed since she left just minutes before.

Henrietta was sitting in the middle of the bed holding Patrick, and Donald was peeking out from under the bed. Frederick lay against the wall under the window looking dazed and the window was open, and the man was gone.

Emma immediately said, "What happened?"

Henrietta told them that Patrick had started crying as soon as she left, and she and Donald were afraid to walk around the man lying on the floor, so Frederick left the man long enough to get Patrick and take him over to Henrietta. Because the man was not moving, Frederick thought that either he was out cold or dead, so he felt that it was safe to lay his bat down and take Patrick to Henrietta.

As soon as Frederick handed Patrick to Henrietta, the intruder rolled over, jumped up, knocking Frederick down, and started climbing out the window. Just as he had his head and one foot out the window, Frederick grabbed his bat and hit the man on the leg that was still inside the room, causing the man to grab his leg, lose his balance, and fall out the window.

Frederick looked up at his mother and his neighbor and did his best not to cry, because he let the man get away, but he did not succeed. Emma went to him, and Charles ran outside to try to catch the intruder, but there was no sign of him, so he came back inside the house.

When Charles got back to Henrietta's room, Emma was sitting in the floor with her arm around Fredrick, Donald was on her lap sucking his thumb, and Henrietta was sitting beside her, holding baby Patrick. It broke Charles's heart to see the fear in their eyes.

The kids looked okay except for being scared, but Emma was literally skin and bones. He walked over to where they were sitting and asked Emma if he could get the police, her husband, or anyone else. He told her that he would stay with them, but he was concerned with the safety of his own family with someone like that in their neighborhood and wanted to get back home and make sure they were okay. He told Emma that they had an extra bedroom, and they were welcome to come to stay at their house if they liked.

Emma and the children looked up at their neighbor with fear and gratitude in their eyes. Frederick spoke and said, "You can't get in touch with our dad because he left us! He beat our mom and made baby Patrick come out of her stomach. We are glad he is gone! We don't miss him at all, and we do not want him here now."

Charles did not know what to say. He had heard some of the neighbors say that they thought Harry might have joined the military after the bombing of Pearl Harbor because no one in the neighborhood had seen him since then. When he thought about it, Sara had been listening to the radio and came out to the yard where he was working and told him the news about the Japanese bombing Pearl Harbor. He was going back inside the house with her to listen to the broadcast as Harry was leaving his house. Harry smiled and waved at them and drove off in his truck. Charles did however remember that he was carrying a bag.

Charles could not remember the last baby being born. In fact, he did not even know that Emma was expecting again, but the baby must have been born sometime around the time that they saw Harry leave. He could not believe that any branch of the military would accept a married man with four children. In addition, why would he want to leave his family, with no one to look after them?

Emma told Charles that she did not have anyone who could come and stay with them. She then told him that she was supposed to be leaving for work soon, but she did not want to leave her children alone after what had just happened. She asked him if he could possibly go to the restaurant and let them know that she would not be at work. She asked him not tell her boss that she did not have a sitter to leave her children with.

Charles did not question her. He told her that he would go to the restaurant after he checked on his family and that he would tell them about the intruder and about her son and that she would not be able to come to work. He promised Emma that he would not tell them that she did not have a sitter, which was something that he could not believe, because of the ages of the children and especially with the baby being so young. Had she been leaving her children home alone at night? He hated to think of what may have happened if she had not been at home. What kind of a mother would do a thing like that? As he thought about it, he knew that this mother was probably doing all that she could possibly do to help her family survive.

Before Charles left, he walked over to the window and looked out. A chair was directly under the window. He could see where the intruder had cut the screen with the knife. The glass was broken on the window near the lock. The nails that Emma had put above the window were small, and it looked as though they had probably popped out or bent allowing the window to be raised, giving the intruder a way in.

All of this made Charles a little concerned for his own family because he sometimes had to work nights, and he did not want anything like this to happen to them. He made a mental note to ask other neighbors if they had seen anyone in the neighborhood that should not have been there, and he was going to ask his family to stay more alert. If they saw anyone who did not belong in the neighborhood, they should tell him or someone else immediately

Emma thanked Charles and told him that she appreciated all of his help. He said, "That is what neighbors are for. We are more than happy to help any way that we can." Before going home, he closed the window and put the chair on the porch. He would come back later, fix the window, and make sure all of their windows were more secure.

5

She Held Her Baby One Last Time

Charles and Sara met an older couple who had been trying to have children for years but had never succeeded. The woman said that she would love to have a child around even if it were not her own. On many occasions, they had talked about adopting but had never actually checked into it. Sara told her that if she would like to babysit children, she knew a woman who could really use their help. She then told the couple about Emma and her children. The woman said that she would love to take care of the baby while the mother worked, but she did not think that she was up to taking care of all four children. The woman looked up at her husband and said, "This could be the answer to our prayers."

The next time Sara saw Emma, she told her about the couple. Emma's immediate answer was no and told Sara that she appreciated the woman's offer, but she did not want to separate her children.

One Sunday morning after working the late shift, Emma had to walk home in freezing rain because she did not have the money to ride a bus. She barely had enough money to buy a few groceries, which she had to carry as she walked home in the horrible weather.

She heated their house by burning coal in a fireplace. Harry would sometimes bring home coal home that he held back from a delivery, and he would add it to the coal pile behind their house. There was probably enough coal to last a couple of winters if they were careful.

At night when she left, she had to let the fire burn down because she was afraid to have it burning while she was away. The house was old, and she knew that it would only take a spark and the house would burn down with her children in it. One of her fears was that they would freeze or burn up in a house fire while she was at work.

Emma had been giving some serious thought about the woman's offer to babysit Patrick while she worked. Sara had told her that she had asked the woman how much she would charge, and the woman told her that she would not charge Emma anything; she would consider it an honor to help her.

One afternoon, Emma went over to Charles and Sara's house and asked them if the couple was serious about their offer to babysit with Patrick while she worked. Charles told her that he thought they were, and if she were interested in accepting their offer, he would try to get in touch with the couple and let them know.

Emma asked every question about the couple that she could think of, and Charles and Sara told her all that they knew about the couple, which was actually very little. After talking with them, the offer did appear to be the answer to one of her prayers. Emma told Charles and Sara that it would only be a temporary arrangement, but it would really help if they could watch the baby. Sara offered to let the other three children sleep at their house at night while she worked, but Emma told her that it would be asking too much of them, but she appreciated their offer.

The next day Charles and Sara brought Mr. and Mrs. Timmons to meet Emma. They were very well dressed, and Patrick immediately took to them. They told Emma that they would be delighted to help with the baby. One thing they would like for Emma to do was to sign a paper giving them temporary custody of Patrick just in case he got sick and they had to take him to the doctor. They did not want any doctor thinking they had kidnapped him.

The couple had a very distinguished-looking man with them that had the paperwork ready for her to sign. The man folded some papers back and told Emma to sign on the line where he had placed an X. He told her there was no need for her to worry about reading everything written on the papers, because it was just a bunch of legal terminology. Emma signed the papers, and the man left, but the couple stayed with her for a while longer.

Emma held her baby to her breasts as she fed him one last time. When it came time for the couple to leave, it broke Emma's heart to part with her baby, but she felt that it was best for him.

The couple told her that since the weather was so bad, they would be more than happy to keep Patrick during the day also. As Emma thought about their offer, she agreed that it would be very difficult for her to take the baby to them every night before she went to work and then have to walk to their house to pick him up and take him home with her the next morning. She could barely make the walk home, especially if she had to carry a bag of groceries. Just the thought of having her baby out in the weather they had been having lately was of great concern to Emma.

She finally agreed that the couple could keep Patrick during the day also but assured them that it would only be temporary until she could make other arrangements. Mrs. Timmons smiled as she took Patrick in her arms. She reassured Emma that she would take very good care of the baby.

Patrick could actually be their child if Emma did not make contact with them within ninety days. It was all written in the folded over pages the lawyer gave Emma to sign without reading.

Frederick and Henrietta saw the couple as they carried baby Patrick out of the house, and they ran to the living room wanting to know where the people were taking their baby brother.

Emma said, "Those nice people are going to babysit baby Patrick for a little while. When things get better for us, we will go get Patrick, or they couple will bring him home." Neither of them liked the idea of strangers taking their baby brother, but neither of them said anything else.

Donald had been playing in another room when he heard Frederick and Henrietta talking to his mother about the couple taking his baby brother. He immediately came into the living room and crawled up on his mother's lap. He had a small piece of his blankie in one hand, stuck his thumb from his other hand into his mouth, and laid his head back against his mother.

Emma had not gotten any sleep that day because of spending so much time with the couple. She was very tired and knew that she needed to get some sleep, or she would not be able to work that night. She stood up; still holding Donald in her arms, laid him down on the bed, and then curled up beside him. When she woke up about five hours later, he was still lying there with her. He was not sleeping; he was just lying there looking at her, with his thumb still in his mouth, and holding the little piece of his old blanket. She reached over, kissed him on the forehead, and pulled him up close. She knew that Donald had been feeling very insecure, and now with the couple taking Patrick, he was probably feeling even more so. The thought brought tears to her eyes. Donald reached up with his blankie to wipe her tears away.

6

She Left the Bank With All the Dignity She Could Muster

O ne night Emma had to walk to work in extremely bad weather. It had turned very cold, and the wind was blowing so hard that she had difficulty walking and had to stop periodically to rest, usually in the doorway of a building. In all probability, there would not be many people who would come to the restaurant in weather like this, but she knew if she wanted to keep her job, she would have to go to work, regardless of what the weather conditions were.

As she was resting in one of the doorways, she read some of the notes taped to the window. One note said there was an apartment for rent. It only had one bedroom, one bathroom with a living room, dinning room, and kitchen combination, but it was close to where she worked, and it was also in a much better location than where they now lived. If they could move there, she would not have as far to walk to work or to the grocery store. It was not so bad when the weather was nice, but when it was cold or raining, it could be a very miserable walk.

She could probably make the one bedroom work for them because she could sleep in the bed during the day, and the children could sleep there during the night. On the nights that she did not work, either she or Frederick could sleep on the sofa. Another option would be to put Frederick's smaller bed in the sitting area instead of a sofa. She could put it up against the wall and place the pillows long ways at the back of the bed. They could sit on it during the day and sleep on it at night.

Harry and Emma bought their house with money that her parents left her, and she never thought about making a house payment. That is until she received a foreclosure notice from the bank the next day.

The bank was foreclosing on their house because there had not been a payment on the mortgage in six months. She knew that someone must have made a mistake. She had inherited enough money for them to pay cash for their house and buy what they needed to furnish it and still had five thousand dollars left to put in a savings account.

When Emma left work that day, she walked all the way uptown to the bank where they had deposited the five thousand dollars and asked to speak to the person in charge of the bank. When the girl asked why she wanted to speak to the president of the bank, Emma showed her the foreclosure notice. The girl asked Emma to wait a moment and she would see if the president of the lending division was available. When she came back, she asked Emma to follow her, and she took her to an office upstairs and introduced her to Mr. Jeremiah Kistner.

Mr. Kistner asked Emma what he could do for her, and she handed him the foreclosure notice on their home. She explained to him that she and her husband bought the house with money from a trust fund her parents had left her and they did not have to make mortgage payments. She told him that after purchasing the house, they had five thousand dollars left, and they put it into a savings account in his bank.

Mr. Kistner asked Emma to wait until he could pull her file. When he came back, he asked how long it had been since she had seen the deed to their house or their savings balance. She was embarrassed but said that she had not seen anything since the day they bought the house and opened the savings account, because her husband always managed her inheritance after they were married.

Mr. Kistner said, "Shortly after you deposited the five thousand dollars into a savings account with our bank, either you or your husband started making frequent withdrawals from the account. A couple of years later, you and your husband applied for a mortgage loan on your home. The monthly payments were always made when due until the last six months when no payments have been made on the mortgage."

Emma sat down in a chair beside the bank president's desk. It was more as though she dropped into the chair from shock. To herself she thought, *What in the world did Harry do with all that money?* She felt bad when she would take a few dollars out of his wallet, but this went way beyond anything she would have ever considered doing without him knowing about it, and it was her money

She looked at Mr. Kistner and told him that she had not been in the bank since the day she deposited the five thousand dollars.

Mr. Kistner told her that there was always identification required with any activity to any bank accounts, and they would not have loaned them money on their house had their identification not been verified. Emma told him that she had used her birth certificate. Harry used his birth certificate and driver's license, and they both used their marriage license for identification when they bought the house. They used the same documentation when they deposited the five thousand dollars into the bank.

Mr. Kistner pulled out the file on Emma and Harry and showed her where both their birth certificates were checked before approving the mortgage loan, and it was processed by Ms. Rebecca Mason, one of their best associates. He told her that he would bring Ms. Mason to his office to confirm the transactions.

Just a couple of minutes after Mr. Kistner asked his secretary to bring the associate to his office, Rebecca Mason walked through the door. She had never seen Emma, and Emma had never seen her before. When Mr. Kistner asked Ms. Mason about the mortgage transaction for Harry Carswell and his wife, Emma Patton Carswell, she looked very pale and almost lost her voice at first but quickly regained her composure. She looked at Mr. Kistner and then to Emma and said that she remembered Mrs. Carswell and her husband coming into the bank to apply for a mortgage for their home. She said that it was a simple transaction because they had a previous good history of a savings deposit account with their bank, no liens against the property, and they had all the proper identification required for the loan.

Emma could not believe what she was hearing. She knew the girl was telling a lie because she had never seen the girl before, and she had not been in the bank since the day they opened their savings account. Nevertheless, why was she telling the lie?

After recovering her own composure, Emma stood up, looked at Mr. Kistner, and said, "Sir, I have never been in this bank except for the one time that I was in with my husband when we opened our savings account. In addition, Ms. Mason, you are not being truthful and for what reason I do not know, but I would like to withdraw the five thousand dollars that was deposited in this bank and close out the savings account."

Mr. Kistner told her that all of the late payments would have to be paid. She would receive any savings left in her account.

Emma said, "Even though I do not agree with what you are saying, please take out the amount of money that you say that I owe the bank and give me the remaining money in my savings account, and I will gladly leave your bank."

Mr. Kistner was looking at Emma's savings account information as she spoke. He dreaded what he was going to have to tell the poor woman. He looked at Emma and said, "Mrs. Carswell, there is no money in your savings account. About six months ago, your husband came into the bank and withdrew all of the money in your account. That was also the date that the last payment was made on your mortgage."

Emma could not believe what she was hearing. She said, "Sir, you must be mistaken. Surely if my husband had drawn out that much money, he would have said something to me about it. Mr. Kistner, you look like an honest man, but I think someone from your bank has stolen all of my money, as well as trying to foreclose on my home. I think you should be more aware of what is going on in your bank. I don't know how, but I definitely feel that Ms. Mason is somehow involved with those transactions, and I feel that you should investigate the situation thoroughly."

Emma then told Mr. Kistner that she would look for an apartment for her family and they would be out of their home as soon as possible, because there was no way she could pay the amount of money he said that she owed the bank for the mortgage or the overdue payments. She looked at Mr. Kistner and then to Ms. Mason but did not say anything else. She turned around and walked out of Mr. Kistner's office and then out of the bank, with all the dignity she could muster.

As she was walking out of Mr. Kistner's office, Emma heard Mr. Kistner tell Ms. Mason that he would like to have a talk with her, and then she heard his door close.

7

Den of Iniquity

Emma went to check on the apartment that was for rent. Bob Frasier, who managed the apartments, said she could rent the apartment and move in that day if she liked. She could live there and the first month rent was free, and she could start paying rent the next month. That was wonderful news for Emma. Where the apartment was located, she would be able to get to her children faster if something was to happen to them, and it was in a much safer area of town.

When she got home, she tried to act excited about the move. She did not want her children to know that they had to move out of their home. She wanted them to think that she was moving them to a better and safer location.

Emma and her children packed up their things, and Charles came over in his truck and helped them move. All of Harry's things and everything else that would not fit in their new apartment, Emma left behind. She told Charles, if there was anything in the house that he may want, he was more than welcome to take it. Everything else, the bank or the new owners could either keep or throw away.

The apartment was actually much nicer than their home. It was small, but they could manage. She was also not as tired when she got home from work each morning, because she did not have as far to walk. As soon as she got home, she would prepare breakfast for the children, and they would all eat together. After cleaning up the kitchen, she would tell the children not to go out of the apartment while she was asleep, and if they needed her for anything, all they had to do was wake her up. She would then go to bed and actually sleep for maybe four to six hours, which was something she had not done in a long while.

When she got up, she would prepare their evening meal, and they would all eat together again. When the weather was good, she would take them outside for a short walk, because she knew they needed to get out for fresh air as often as possible.

One day a man who called himself The Preacher came by to visit with them. He introduced himself telling them that his name was Reverend Dolan, but everyone called him The Preacher, and he would like to extend to them an invitation to visit his church. Emma told him that she was always busy on Saturday night and was just too tired to go anywhere early on Sunday. The Preacher told her that he could come by each Sunday and take her children to church if she liked. Emma asked the kids if they would like to go to church with him and the boys said yes but Henrietta said that she did not want to go without her mother.

Sunday as soon as they had eaten breakfast, The Preacher came by and picked up the boys and Emma went straight to bed. She was now able to sleep a little longer at least one day a week.

When The Preacher brought the boys home one Sunday, about a month after they had been going to church with him, he asked Emma if he could come in and talk with her. He began by saying how sorry he felt for her, having to work and take care of her three children. He told her that he would like to help if she would let him. He offered to let Donald and Frederick stay with him for a while. He said that he had plenty of room for them because he had converted an old school building into a home and church office. The first floor was for the children who came to

Sunday school, and the rooms on the second floor were bedrooms and storage for the church. He said that the boys would have their own bedrooms, and he would look after them as if they were his own. There was plenty around the church to keep them busy, and they could earn a little money helping him. He promised her that they would be in church every time the church doors were open, and he would help mold them into great young men that would make her proud.

Emma did not think that her little boys were old enough to do any manual labor because they were so young. She hoped the work he was talking about was just a figure of speech. He was probably talking about them picking up after themselves, and he would give them an allowance, which was something that she could not afford to do. She was not earning the money that she did when she first took the job at the restaurant because many of the young men that came in late at night were now in the military fighting in the war. The ones that did come in were mostly heavy drinkers and could barely pay their bar bill, much less leave her a tip.

Emma asked the boys if they would like to go stay with The Preacher for a while, and they both said sure. They told their mother that The Preacher was good to them, and they had lots of good food and desserts to eat on Sundays after they went to church.

She finally gave in, packed the boys clothes, and gave them hugs. Seeing them leave with The Preacher gave Emma a very sad feeling. She let them go with him because she thought things would be better for them at The Preacher's big house than it was in their little two-room apartment.

When Emma came home from work a couple of days later, she found Frederick sitting outside, beside the door of the apartment, with his head bowed over his knees. The poor child was cold and stiff, because the weather had gotten down in the thirties during the night. She picked him up, carried him into the apartment and put him in bed with Henrietta. She watched as he snuggled down into the warm bed. Later in the day when he woke up, she asked him why he had come home. He told her that he did not like The Preacher at home as much as he liked him at church, and he was not going back to stay with him. He said The Preacher was creepy. Emma had no idea what he could be talking about but felt that he was possibly exaggerating the situation just to get to come back home. There had always been a strong bond between her and Frederick, but he definitely was not a mama's boy, but he did think of himself as her protector.

Later that day, The Preacher discovered that Frederick was missing and came looking for him. He tried to drag Frederick out of the apartment to take him back to his house. He jerked off his belt as though he was going to whip Frederick. When he did that, Emma had flashbacks about Harry when he would jerk his belt off and whip her or one of the children, and it did not go well with her. She disciplined her children, but she had never beaten them. They had already endured too much discipline from their own father to last a lifetime, and she was not going to allow anyone to hurt them again.

She said to The Preacher, "Don't you dare lay one finger on my son. You are supposed to be a minister. Someone, with whom children can feel safe. If this is what you and your church represent, I am not sure if I want either of my boys staying with you."

Emma did not have a good feeling about the whole situation now.

When The Preacher boldly said, "To spare the rod is to spoil the child." Emma told him to turn lose of Frederick immediately because he was not going with him. If Donald did not want to stay with him, he was to bring him home also. If he did not do as she said, she would report him to the police for kidnapping her children.

The Preacher turned and looked at Emma and in the same bold voice said, "Home! You mean this Den of Iniquity?"

Emma was speechless! Frederick grabbed her around the legs and would not let go. She put her arm on his shoulder and told him that he did not have to go with The Preacher. She then asked Frederick and Henrietta to go into the bedroom while she talked with The Preacher.

After they left, Emma asked The Preacher why he made such a nasty remark by calling their home a Den of Iniquity.

He told her that he knew what was going on there. Some of the people in his church saw her walking into town every night, leaving her poor little children at home alone, to fend for themselves. He let her know that he had asked Frederick and Donald if they knew why their mother went out every night. He asked them if she had a boyfriend that she was going out to see, or if she was out hunting a boyfriend. They gave him the name Charles, but they did not know his last name. Donald said that sometimes Charles took her places in his truck. When The Preacher asked Donald what Charles's last name was, he just shrugged his shoulders and said that he did not know his last name.

The Preacher then said, "I can't believe that any true mother would have a man coming in and out of her house and her children not even know his name. That is no way to raise children, and you should be ashamed of yourself. Your children need to live in a safe God-fearing home, not in a place like this. Children raised, or should I say grow up, in an environment like this usually follow a wayward path and wind up dead or in jail."

Emma could not believe what was happening. All she wanted was for her children to be safe and feel loved, and that was the only reason she let him take her boys home with him. She told him that she needed to talk to Donald to find out if he wanted to stay with him or if he wanted to come home. After a lot of discussions and disagreements, The Preacher finally agreed to bring Donald over.

The next day, The Preacher was true to his word and brought Donald home. When they arrived, Emma and Henrietta went out to meet them. Frederick stayed behind watching from a window. He was taking no chances of being sent back to live with that man.

Donald told his mother and sister that he loved them, but he liked being at The Preacher's house better. There are always other boys there to play with. The house is always warm, there is always good food to eat, and everyone has a piece of cake or pie to eat for dessert after lunch and dinner.

He also told her that he wished that Frederick would go back with him because it would be nice to have his big brother with him.

He bowed his head as though in serious thought and said, "Even if Frederick doesn't want to come with me, I want to go live with The Preacher." He told her that The Preacher was good to him and treated him more special than the other boys that lived there. He said, "He even lets me sleep in the same bed with him and told me that he would adopt me and let me be his son, if you would sign the papers. I wish you would sign those papers, because I do not want to come back to live with you, because we were always cold, hungry, and afraid because you left us alone all of the time. The Preacher is good to me and never leaves me alone.

"He is going to take me with him, everywhere he goes. Yesterday he bought me a nice, warm coat and new clothes to wear instead of the patched clothes we had to wear. You made us stay inside all of the time while you slept. You never allowed us to go outside to play, even in the summertime. The only time we got to go outside was when you would walk with us up the sidewalk, turn around, and walk back to the apartment. When we took those walks during the winter, we had to wrap our blankets around us because we did not have coats to wear."

Shocked by what Donald said, Emma told him in a tearful voice that he could go with The Preacher, if that was what he truly wanted to do.

When she saw Donald leave with The Preacher, she had the same sick feeling she had when Mr. and Mrs. Timmons left with Patrick.

Guilt and loneliness was now consuming her. She needed to think of some way to get her family back together. What could she do to make that happen?

8

How Could She Be So Lucky?

After The Preacher left with Donald, Frederick crawled up on Emma's lap, and Henrietta stood beside her mother with one arm around her mother's shoulder and the other on Frederick's knee. Both children were shaking and so was Emma. No one said anything for a long while. No words could ever express how all three of them felt.

When Emma had a day off, she told Henrietta and Frederick they were going to go by train to her grandparents' house. She knew it would take all the money that she had to buy the tickets, but they needed to get away from there for at least for a few hours, and she knew that Henrietta and Frederick both enjoyed going to see their grandparents. She also needed to talk with her grandmother about something. She had to find a way to protect her children.

Her grandparents were getting old and had already raised Emma's mother as well as Emma and her cousin, but she was hoping they would allow Henrietta and Frederick to stay with them for a while. Her rent was due, and she was behind in her utility bills. It took all the money she had to buy the train tickets. If they cut off their utilities, the children would have no electricity, and she would not be able to prepare meals or have lights on in the evening. She would somehow manage by herself, but she did not want her children to suffer because of her inabilities to handle their situation. She would do whatever she had to do to keep her children safe and warm, even if it meant giving them up. She had never dreamed that she would have even thought about giving her children to someone else, but she was in a desperate situation and had to make drastic choices.

Emma had never had to pay bills before because her grandparents paid them when she lived with them, and Harry had always paid them after they were married. She was very naïve about everything other than cleaning house and taking care of children.

After she purchased their tickets, they got on the train. Henrietta and Frederick sat very solemnly looking out the window. As of late, neither of them ever smiled, and she could certainly understand why.

Emma stored the big bag that she had brought with her under her seat. When she sat down, she probably had the same look on her face that the children had on theirs, because she was going to ask her grandmother if Henrietta and Frederick could stay with her for a while. She had so many things happening at one time that she could not concentrate on solving any of her problems and did not feel capable of taking care of herself or her children. She would love to have a nice home where her children could grow up happy and safe. Because of the decrease in her income, she could not pay her rent and utilities or buy enough groceries for them to eat.

Her grandparents had never approved of Harry, even after they were married. Her grandfather warned her that he had heard that Harry had a very cruel disposition. Of course, she did not believe him, because she thought that Harry was perfect. From the time her problems started, neither of her grandparents had ever said, "I told you so."

They had never taken one dime of her inheritance. They used their own money to pay for everything they did for her. In fact, she did not even know about the inheritance until she was ready to graduate from high school. They told her then because they wanted her to know that she had enough money to go to college if she wanted to. On her next date with Harry, she told him about her inheritance, and he proposed to her on their next date.

Emma was in love with love and was excited about marrying Harry. She dreamed they would have a big house and have many children, and they would live happily ever after. She felt that by her inheriting the money, they would never have to worry about money issues, like other young couples.

At first, Harry said they should forget about a big wedding and elope. He told her that the sooner they were married, the sooner they could start their lives together, and he thought it was foolish to waste a lot of money on a lavish wedding.

When she told him that her grandparents were paying for the wedding, Harry backed off and told her to go ahead with her plans. He told her that he would like to get married as soon as possible, because he did not want another man trying to take her away from him.

His remark really made Emma feel good. The best-looking person from her school was jealous and feared that someone may try to take her away from him.

How could she be so lucky?

9

Her Family Was Slowly Disappearing

Mary Byrd was preparing the midday meal and did not know that her granddaughter and her great-grandchildren were there until they walked into her kitchen. When she turned around and saw them, tears came to her eyes, and she grabbed all three of them in a big hug.

After they ate, Frederick and Henrietta went outside with their grandfather to watch him chop wood. He was a cheerful old man but could seem a little gruff sometimes, but they loved him and their grandmother.

While the children were out of the house, Emma told her grandmother about Harry leaving, the home invasion, and the couple that was keeping Patrick and about Donald choosing to live with The Preacher.

Her grandmother stopped what she was doing and sat down in a chair. She said that she had been afraid that something like that would happen one day. She told Emma to go get Donald and Patrick and all five of them come and live with her and their grandfather. They had plenty of room, and she and their grandfather would love having them live with them.

Emma knew that her grandparents could not handle all of them living there. They were not poor, but it would probably put a big financial strain on them taking care of her family.

She did however ask her grandmother if Henrietta and Frederick could stay with her for a little while. She told her about her rent being due and that the utilities were overdue. Another big snowstorm was headed their way and she did not want them staying in the apartment without heat or electricity. She told her grandmother that it would not be for a long time. She just needed some time to get things taken care of and hopefully to find a better-paying job with better working hours. She wanted to get all of her children back together so that they could be a family again. She hoped that she could do it by spring.

Her grandmother did not like the idea of Emma's children living in different homes. She told Emma that she should get them back as soon as possible. Mary knew that it would be difficult caring for an infant plus three other children while Emma worked, but she would be willing to try.

Mary hugged Emma and told her that they would do whatever they could to help. When her grandfather came back into the house with the kids, her grandmother asked Henrietta and Frederick if they would like to stay with her and their grandfather for a while. Henrietta jumped at the idea, but Frederick was very adamant about not staying. He needed to go home with his mother so that he could protect her if they had another intruder. His grandmother assured him that it would only be until his mother could get a better job and place to live. He told her that he would not stay anywhere without his mother. If his mother stayed, he would. If she went back to their apartment, he would go back to the apartment with her.

With a very sad look on his face, Frederick said, "Could we all live with you, Grandma? Mom could get a job here, and we could all live together in your house. It is warm and always smells like fresh bread baking in the oven. I promise that I will help Grandpa cut the wood and bring it into the house and anything else you want me to do."

Mary hugged her grandson and told him that they were always welcome in their home.

Frederick said, "When Mom gets another job, can we get baby Patrick and Donald back and all of us come to live with you?"

His grandmother gave him another hug and said, "You sure can."

Frederick said, "That sounds great, Grandma. When Mom gets a new job, we will all come back and live with you, but I am going home with Mom until she does find that job."

On the way home on the train that night, Frederick sat beside Emma and laid his head on her shoulder and went to sleep. Emma tried to go to sleep, but her heart was breaking because of her situation, and sleep would not come. In the quiet times like this, her mind would wonder back to when they were still a family. She still could not come to terms as to why Harry would treat her and their children so cruel and why he would leave them in such a bad situation. He could have left them if he had not wanted to be there, but he could have at least provided some means of support for his children, and they were his children. Why would he take all of her money, mortgage their house, and leave them without a place to live or food to eat?

Emma had heard rumors of Harry seeing other women, but in the situation she had always been in, she was afraid to say anything. As the saying goes, "He literally kept her barefoot and pregnant." He blamed her for each pregnancy and told her that he was tired of seeing her fat and ugly with all those brown spots on her face. He told her that she was beautiful when he married her, but she had let herself go. He said that she looked like she never washed her hair and smelled as if she never bathed. He even accused her of having lovers. She had to laugh about that, because she would have never had the time to have a lover. If she looked and smelled as bad as he said she did, who would want her.

Emma thought back to what The Preacher said. Did people really think that she was like that? Why would they make such false accusations without even knowing her? She wondered if The Preacher was just making it up so that he could keep Donald.

She did not want to judge, but she did not feel comfortable with her son living with The Preacher. She needed to get her son away from him as soon as possible. She hoped and prayed that The Preacher was not a pedophile. What would she do if something like that happened to Donald, or any of her children?

Frederick was still asleep when the train stopped, so Emma carried him to their apartment. It was only a few blocks, but she was only four feet and eleven inches tall and weighed around a hundred pounds, and Frederick weighed about thirty-five pounds. When they got to the apartment, she carried him up two flights of stairs.

When she got to the door of their apartment, she saw a note that had been left by the utilities department telling her that her utilities would be turned off in ten days if payment was not received, and there would be a five-dollar reconnection fee to have the service turned back on.

Emma sat down on the bed with Frederick still in her arms. She took off his jacket and shoes and tucked him into bed with his clothes on. She was so tired that she did not change into her nightclothes either. She lay down on the bed beside Frederick and pulled him up close. It was just the two of them now. Her family was slowly disappearing. She lay there with her son in her arms and cried herself to sleep.

10

Bugs

Sometime during the night, Emma heard Frederick screaming and trying to get out of the bed. She thought he was probably having a bad dream because of everything that had been happening lately. She got up and turned the light on.

What she saw was the most disgusting thing she could have ever imagined. There were bugs crawling all in their bed, and some of them were crawling on Frederick. He had brought a piece of cake from her grandmother's house, and she thought that must have been what they were after. She had dropped everything on the foot of the bed when they came in, because she had been too tired to put anything away.

There was a homeless shelter down the street from where they lived, so she grabbed Frederick and a change of clothes for both of them and headed to the shelter. The shelter was full because it was so cold outside, but since it was a mother and a child, they made room for them but told them that they would have to sleep on the floor.

The next morning when they woke up, all of their things were missing, including Emma's handbag. She went to the woman that ran the shelter and asked her if she had seen anyone bothering her things, and the woman told her no. The woman that she was talking to was actually the person who had stolen everything. Emma thought it was possible that one of the homeless people stole their things.

What was she going to do now? Her grandparents had given her enough money to pay the rent and utilities and buy some groceries, but now she had nothing. She could not ask them for more money. She knew they would give it to her, but she also knew that they could not afford to do so.

For now, she and Frederick would have to go back to their bug-infested apartment. She was afraid to ask the apartment manager to spray their apartment for bugs, because she wanted to bring as little attention to them as possible. She hoped that they would not evict them for at least a week or so. If the weather would take a turn for the better and more people would come to the restaurant, she would make more money with their tips. The meager amount they paid her per hour would not pay the rent or the utilities, but it would at least keep them from going hungry.

She had noticed a few bugs in their tiny kitchen before but nothing as they had in their bed. It made her skin crawl just thinking about them.

When they got near the apartment, Emma started talking to Frederick and said, "We are not going to be afraid of those nasty bugs. Let's go in and see how many we can get rid of." Frederick did not know if he liked that idea, and it did not sound like fun, but he told her that he would try. He would much rather get rid of them than have them crawling on him while he was sleeping. He had seen a couple of the bugs on the floor at times, but they were not crawling on him at night. He would make sure that he left no food anywhere except in the kitchen from now on.

Frederick had not liked sleeping on the floor at the shelter either. He would rather catch bugs than smell dirty feet all night again. He had curled up on the floor at the shelter right beside his mother. There was a man sleeping on a cot near where their heads were. The man was so tall that his feet hung over the end of the cot, and his feet smelled awful, and he snored all night. He did not know which was worse the man or the bugs. He really did not like either, but he thought he could handle the bugs better than stinking feet. At least he hoped so.

When they got to the apartment, Emma acted as though she was going to try to scare the bugs when she opened the door. Frederick fell right into the game. They did catch a lot of them, but by the time they went to bed, they did not see any crawling around, especially in the bedroom.

The next day, they heard that the neighbors in the apartment next door to theirs had a bad problem with bugs, and the property manager had sprayed their apartment. All of the bugs probably came over to their apartment after he sprayed

Emma finally got up enough courage to go see the property manager that afternoon. She would tell him about their bug problem and how they had to stay in a shelter for the homeless, and while they were there, someone stole her handbag and all of her money, and she would be late paying her rent and utility bill.

The property manager had heard all types of stories from his tenants, but Emma was different. He especially liked her and told her to forget about the rent for this month. She could pay a couple dollars extra each month to reimburse him. He also said that he would take care of her utility bill to keep them from turning off her electricity and water. He told her that he was sure they could work something out between them to pay him back; he then winked at Emma.

She thanked the manager, but she did not feel comfortable with his wink. He had never said anything out of the way to her before, but she did not like the suggestive look on his face when he winked. Many men had done that at night at the restaurant, and she knew that the wink meant more than just a teasing wink to be cute or funny.

When she left the property manager's apartment, she and Frederick walked down to the small grocery story that was down the street from the apartments. She had heard from one of the other employees at the restaurant that the store would let people buy groceries on credit, and he would let them pay him when they received their weekly pay.

When she walked into the store, she asked to speak to the owner. The man that she had spoken to told her that he was the owner. He told her that he was helping another customer, but he could talk with her shortly, if that was okay.

A few minutes later, he came back over and asked how he could be of help. She told him that she had heard that he let customer buy groceries on credit. He told her that he would, if they had a steady job. He said that he would let them have a certain amount of groceries, and if they paid for them by a set date, they could charge more groceries, and if they kept paying, as they should, they could buy their groceries when they needed them and pay him at the end of each week or when they received their paychecks. He asked her if that would be an arrangement, she would be interested in.

Emma told him that it sure would be. She told him where she worked and when she received her pay. She told him that she did not need many things. They made an agreement, and Emma established credit at the grocery store. She walked out of the store with food and a feeling that she had made a great accomplishment by working out a deal with a reputable store, and she did it on her own.

That night when she got ready for work, Frederick was looking at her in a very odd way. She went over to him and asked him what was wrong. He told her that he had never stayed by himself before, and it was a little scary, but he assured her that he would be okay.

It was very difficult for Emma to leave him that night, but she had no other choice. After she left, Frederick went to the window in order to watch his mother as she walked down the street. As she was leaving, he saw the property manager take hold of his mother's arm. He saw her shake his hand loose and say something to him. She then continued walking down the street.

Frederick did not like what he had just seen happen. All night long he sat by the window watching for his mother to come home. He could sleep during the day when she slept, and that way, he would be awake just in case something happened and she would need him. He mostly wanted to make sure that the property manager did not bother his mother again. He still had his bat that he had intended to use on the intruder, and he would not hesitate using it on the apartment manager if he did anything to hurt his mother.

It was just the two of them now, and he would probably be afraid every time she left him alone. Even though he was afraid of staying alone, he was more worried that something might happen to his mother and he would never see her again. He did not know anyone at the apartment complex other than the apartment manager. He could probably go live with his grandparents, but he did not know where they lived or how to get there. He also did not know their last name. He had always just called them grandma and grandpa.

Frederick decided that the first thing he was going to do was to get his mother to write down his grandparents' names and directions to their house and also find out which bus and train to ride to go to their house. He would also need money for the bus and the train. He had seen his mother drop nickels into a little machine when they got on the bus, but he could not remember how many nickels she dropped. When they rode the train, she had to pay a whole dollar and some change. He would try to save enough money so that he could get to his grandparents' home if something did happen to his mother. The only problem was that he did not get an allowance, and his mother never had any extra money, but he knew where she always kept the bill money hidden, because she never carried it in her handbag anymore. The next time they went to see their grandparents, he would ask his mom to let him pay. That way he would know exactly how much it cost. He had a plan, and it gave him a more comfortable feeling.

11

She Lay Down Beside His Cold Body

Emma tried to keep her mind on her work, but her homelife stayed on her mind all of the time and was controlling all of her emotions. She had not seen baby Patrick since the day the couple left with him. It would be great if she could see him occasionally, but she knew that it would probably be worse seeing him and then having to part with him again. She wondered if he was bonding with Mrs. Timmons. It would probably be best if he was, but it made her feel sad at the thought of him putting his tiny arms around another woman's neck and feeling safe in the warmth of her arms.

What would she do if they were not okay? Donald had made it clear to her, that he was not coming back to live with her. He liked living with The Preacher much better than having to live with her, never having enough to eat, and being cold and afraid all of the time. Every time she had seen him since he left, he seemed to be okay and was always very well dressed. In fact, she thought him overdressed for his age, and he and The Preacher always wore matching suits. It was as though The Preacher was grooming Donald to be just like him. She had not seen a smile on Donald's face in a very long time, so she did not know if he was happy or not. In fact, his face showed no emotions.

Emma shut her eyes because she knew the tears were going to start flowing if she kept dwelling on her children.

At least there was not really anything to worry about with Henrietta because she was with her grandparents. She knew they would treat her with love and a lot of spoiling. She had wished so many times that Frederick had stayed with them. He felt that he had to take care of her, and there was no way that he would stay anywhere without her. She was very concerned because she knew that no child his age should be home alone every night. The look he gave her when she left for work let her know that he was afraid, even though he said that he was not.

Emma knew that she was going to have to find a different job. In another year, Frederick would be starting school. Maybe she could change shifts and work while he was in school. The only problem with that would be that he would probably have to get himself dressed for school and walk to the bus stop alone, or he would have to walk home from the bus stop alone. Either way, it was not safe for a first grade student alone. It would be better if the bus stopped in front of the apartments, but it did not. The bus stop was about two blocks away.

Emma was always anxious to get home to Frederick, but she also dreaded going home. The property manager was acting very strange. He was now making unwanted advances toward her. He was always standing at the entrance door to the apartment building every morning when she got home and every night when she left. He had been making very suggestive remarks as to how she could repay him. She not only owed him back rent, but she now owed him for the utility bills that he had paid for her, and she had no way to pay him anytime in the near future. She was barely making enough money to pay her current rent and utilities and buy food. She brushed off his advancements and comments by pretending that she thought he was just teasing with her and that she did not know what he was actually hinting about, but she was becoming very afraid of him. She knew well what an angry man could be like.

One day Emma overheard some of the customers talking about a sewing mill needing help, and from the way they talked, the pay was much better than what she was making now even with tips. When she had first started working at the restaurant, her tips was sometimes triple what she made per hour, and it made it easier for her to meet her obligation, but she was not able to do so now.

She thought that the job at the sewing mill might be worth looking into. She was now working from ten o'clock at night until eight o'clock in the morning because the other waiter did not want to work the breakfast shift. She wanted the lunch and dinner shift when most of the big tippers ate. Emma now had to work twelve-hour days. Her hours would be from eight o'clock at night until eight o'clock in the morning. If she took a regular job, she would only be working eight hours per day instead of twelve.

At least with a job like that, she would know how much money she would make every week, and she would not have to put up with a bunch of drunk men making passes at her every night. It seemed that when they found out that she no longer had a husband, they became worse than they had been in the beginning.

She would at least like to find out more about the job at the mill, but she knew that she should get home to Frederick as soon as possible because she knew that he was not sleeping at night. He was always sitting at the window every morning when she came home. She had to smile because she knew that he felt like he was her protector. A child that young should not have to live with that type of responsibility, whether it was real or not. He should be sleeping instead of sitting up all night waiting for his mother to come home.

There was a back fire escape to their apartment building. Emma decided that she would enter the apartment building that way instead of going through the front entrance. Frederick was not expecting her to come in that way. When she passed the window, she saw him sitting in the window and looked as though he had been crying. She knew if she asked him if he had been crying, he would be embarrassed and say no. She just gave him a hug, and they ate breakfast and then set the clock for eight hours of sleep, and they both went to bed.

That night she decided to leave by the fire escape, and the next morning, she came back the same way. When she arrived home the next morning, there was a note from the utilities company telling her that her power was off. Had the apartment manager lied to her about paying the bill for her?

Frederick was sitting in the window with several blankets around him. When she got inside the apartment, it seemed colder than it did outside, plus there was no water or electricity, and there was no heat in the apartment.

Even though Frederick was getting almost as tall as she was, she still bent down picked him up and carried him to the bedroom. She pulled the covers back and put him in the bed. She lay down beside his cold body trying to get him warm. He was shivering so much that she was concerned that he may be suffering from hypothermia.

She knew that she should go talk to the property manager, but every time she tried to leave, Frederick would hold onto her. Finally, she just pulled him close, and they both went to sleep. She woke up about three in the afternoon and realized that the heat was on, but they still had no electricity.

She could hear the property manager arguing with the people in the apartment below them. Evidently, he had been cutting the heat off at night to save money. He knew that Frederick was there at night by himself because she had asked him when she first moved in if he could keep an eye on him. She did not expect him to babysit Frederick, just to be alert in case there was some type of emergency. It took a very cold-hearted person to do something like that to a child, but she knew the responsibility was hers and not the property manager's, so she could not blame him. She was the person responsible for taking care of her child.

She should have been a better wife to Harry, and he might still been with them. She should have tried to be more careful and not get pregnant so many times. She should have listened to her grandfather when he told her about Harry. She should have paid her rent instead of going to her grandparents' house. When her grandmother gave her money to pay the utilities and rent, she should not have left her handbag out where someone could steal her money. She realized that she could think about all the things she should have done, but it was not going to change her situation. She was going to have to make the changes, or their situation would never change. The main thing on her agenda was to do a better job of taking care of Frederick.

Having made almost no money in tips the night before, Emma decided to go to the sewing mill and see if they had any jobs open. She bathed and dressed and then woke Frederick and dressed him. She told him that they were going to eat at the restaurant where she worked and then they were going to take the bus on a little trip, because it was too cold to walk that day. Frederick was ready to leave the apartment before she could put on her coat and get her handbag.

12

Kind Words from a Stranger

The bus ride to Upland was uneventful. Frederick did not look out the window as he usually did. Instead, he just laid his head on his mother's shoulder and slept all the way to their stop.

As soon as they walked through the door at the sewing mill, the woman behind the desk asked Emma if she was there for a job. When Emma said yes, the woman gave her an application form and then asked her to have a seat and fill out the form and sign it and bring it back to her. When Emma took the forms back to the woman, she looked over them and then introduced herself to Emma. She said, "My name is Misty McMenus."

Misty asked Emma if she had any sewing experience. Emma told her that she made all of her clothes, and sometimes she would make curtains and scarves for her home. Misty asked her if she made the dress that she was wearing, and Emma told her that she had. Misty told her that she was very impressed because the dress looked very well made. She then told Emma that she saw no reason why she would not qualify for the job and asked her when she could start to work.

She told Emma that there were jobs available on all three shifts. First shift 6:00 a.m. until 5:00 p.m., second shift 2:00 p.m. until 10:00 p.m. and third shift 10:00 p.m. until 6:00 a.m.

When Misty saw the address where Emma lived, she looked at her and raised one of her eyebrows. When Emma asked her what was wrong, Misty said, "Is Bob Frasier still the manager of those apartments?"

Emma said, "Yes, why do you ask?"

Misty asked her if she had ever had problems with him. Emma did not answer but instead looked over at Frederick. When Misty saw her look toward her son, she immediately said, "We need to get you out of that place. That guy is a sex offender, and neither you nor your son should be living anywhere near that pervert."

Emma was not surprised, but she did not know what to say. She knew that she had no other option besides staying in the apartment, at least until she was able to save some money.

She told Misty that she would love to move to a different apartment, but she did not have any money for moving expenses. She then told Misty about her experience at the homeless shelter and the situation that it put her in with the apartment manager and the utility company.

Misty told her not to worry. Her husband was the manager of the apartments across the street. They were rent-subsidized, and she knew there was a two-bedroom apartment available. In her situation, Misty knew that Emma would probably qualify for reduced rent without any problems.

Emma was astonished! She had no idea that there were such places available. If she had known, she would still have all of her children together, and they would have been living in one of them.

They walked across the street to the office for the apartments, and Misty introduced Emma to her husband, John, and then proceeded to tell him about Emma's predicament. Emma did not have to say anything to John about her issues. It was almost as though Misty had remembered everything she had told her, and she was now relaying it to John, exactly the same way that she had told her, word for word.

John told Emma to fill out a registration form, and he would see what he could do for her. While Emma was filling out the form, Misty took John out to the hallway to talk to him. They were talking quietly, but Emma still heard Misty when she asked John to try to get her and Frederick into an apartment that day if possible. She also told him where she and her son were living. Of course, Emma could not hear John nod his head yes in affirmation of what Misty was telling him, but she hoped that he agreed with her.

After Emma handed the form back to John, he told her that he would like to show her and her son a vacant apartment. Misty told them all bye and walked back across the street to her office at the sewing mill. She was feeling more comfortable about her new employee and her child knowing that John would take care of them.

The apartment had two bedrooms, it was new, and no one had ever lived in it. John told her that the two-bedroom apartment rented for twenty dollars a month. If she wanted to wait on a one bedroom, he knew of one that may come empty in about a month or so, and it would only be fifteen dollars per month. Emma instantly said no and told him that the two-bedroom would be wonderful because they only had one bedroom where they now lived.

The next surprise came when Emma found out that the twenty dollars also included utilities. She would not have to pay for electric, water, or heating. She could not believe her good fortune. The apartment was small, but it would be perfect for her and Frederick.

She asked Frederick if he would like to move to the new apartment, and he smiled for the first time in a long time and said, "You bet. This is much nicer than our apartment that we live in now. Plus, we will not have to put up with Mr. Frasier bothering you."

John said, "Misty told me where you live, and she also told me to get you out of that place as soon as possible. Are you ready to move today?" Frederick was jumping up and down begging her to say yes.

Emma said, "John, I don't think that I have any other choice but to say yes."

He said, "Let me get my truck, and I will meet you out front in just a few minutes, and we will get you moved in by bedtime."

Emma could not believe all that was transpiring. It would be wonderful not to have to see Mr. Frasier's face again or have to contend with his advances and suggestions.

True to his word, they only had to stand out front for a few minutes until John drove up in his truck. Frederick wanted to ride on the back, but John said that it was too cold, but the first warm day, they would take ride, and he could sit in the back of the truck if he liked. The smile that came over Frederick's face was worth a million dollars. It only took a few kind words from a stranger to bring a smile to her son's face.

13

Everyone Has a Few Skeletons in Their Closet

John and Misty were take-charge-type people. Emma could not believe how fast John got all of their things out of the old apartment and into the new one. Misty had called Bob Frasier before they got to the old apartment. Emma did not know what she said to him, but he did not come out of his apartment on either trip they made to move their things out of the apartment. Normally, every time the door opened to the entrance, he would check to see who was entering. She feared that he would make trouble for her because she owed him for the current rent plus what she owed on her previous months' rent and the utility bill that he paid for her, if he paid it. She could not believe it when he did not say anything to her. She felt guilty about owing him the money but knew that she would pay him what she owed him as soon as she had the money.

When they returned with the last load, John told Emma that Misty wanted her to come to her office so that she could give her a copy of her work schedule. Frederick asked her if he had to go with her, and she told him no. When she came back, Frederick had already made a friend, and they were passing a ball back and forth in front of the apartments.

Frederick introduced his new friend to his mother. He said, "Mom, this is my new friend Dave Spencer." Dave stuck out his hand for a handshake, and Emma shook his hand.

Dave said, "Nice to meet you, Mrs. Carswell." When Frederick asked if he could stay outside with Dave for a little while, Emma told him that he could, but she wanted him to stay where she could see him. She was not familiar with the neighborhood, and she did not know what type of people lived there, but of course, she did not voice her fears in front of Frederick's new friend.

She only said, "Have fun!" After she said that, she thought to herself, *Frederick had not been outside to play in a very long time.* When they lived at their house, she would take her children outside sometimes while Harry was at work, but that had been a long time ago. All she had been worrying about were her other three children when Frederick actually had worse living conditions.

Misty had told her that many of the people that had come to work for the sewing mill lived in the apartments. Because of the war, many people were without jobs and had to sell their homes and move into something less expensive. She told her that they were all good people and that she was sure that she and Frederick both would make many new friends. Emma said to herself, *It seems like we have already made three good friends.* It almost made her cry because she was so happy.

It was Thursday, and Misty told her not to worry about coming to work until Monday. She also told her that she knew the owner of the restaurant where she had worked and that she had talked with him and told him that she had moved and would not be able to come back to work there because she was coming to work at the sewing mill.

Misty did not tell Emma that Brice and Karen, who owned the restaurant where she had worked, were also one of the owners of the sewing mill. They actually had business interests in many areas in the city. They told Misty that Emma was a very good worker, and they would highly recommend her for the job. They also told her that they were not having many customers coming in during the night shift, and they had been talking about closing the restaurant earlier and not have the night shift, but knowing the job was probably Emma's only source of income, they had continued to stay open. They felt bad about her working all night because they were sure she was not making very much in tips. After paying for a babysitter, she probably did not have very much left over. Brice told her that he knew the job in the mill would be better for her and her children."

Misty only saw the one son that came in with her when she applied for the job. She looked at her application again to see how many children Emma actually had. On her application for the job, she stated that she had four children.

Misty called John and asked him if he knew how many children Emma had. John pulled the application and told her that Emma stated that she and her son would be the only people living in the apartment.

Misty decided that she was going to mind her own business with this one. She was not going to make an issue out of this unless it became necessary. She just said, "Thanks, John, I was just making sure." She did not even tell John about the other children. She may later, but for some reason, she felt like it was not something they should talk about right now.

Emma had three days before going to her new job. By evening, she had everything placed where she wanted it. Frederick had actually fallen asleep on the sofa right after dinner the first night. She had not seen him that relaxed in a very long time. She put a blanket over him and let him sleep there. She also had no problem falling asleep. She was very thankful that Misty had allowed her to wait until Monday before coming to work because she was very tired from the moving. Saturday morning, Dave knocked on their apartment door. By habit, Emma went to the door because she had never allowed Frederick or any of her children to open a door without her with them.

Dave wanted to know if Frederick could come out and play. Frederick looked up at her with a very excited look on his face, and there was no way she could tell him no. She smiled at him and told him to go and have fun. That was the first time in Frederick's life that someone had wanted him to come out and play.

At lunchtime, Emma went out to call Frederick inside to eat. She asked Dave if he would like to eat lunch with them. It was just soup and crackers, but he was welcome to eat with them. He said, "Thank you, but my mother has already called me to come in to eat." He then told Frederick that he sure was glad that they moved in and he would see him later. Frederick sat at the table and ate with a very hearty appetite. That was the first time Emma had seen him eat like that. Most of the time when they were all together, he would wait until everyone had food before he would eat anything. He would never overeat, because he knew they might not have enough food for another meal if he did.

Their new apartment was located near The Preacher's church. Emma wondered if maybe they should visit the church so that they could see Donald. When she asked Frederick if he would like to go, he said, "Are you going to try to make me stay with The Preacher again?" Emma told him no, that she thought it would be a chance for them to see Donald.

Sunday morning Emma got out the best clothes that she and Frederick had. They were clean and pressed, but there were three patches on the front of Frederick's pants and two on the sleeves of his shirt. Her clothes were not much better, but she decided they would go to church anyway. Surely, people at the church would not shun them because of the way they were dressed. They walked to the church because it was only about five blocks away. The weather was warm, and a light jacket was all they needed.

When they opened the door to go into the church, they could hear that the service had already started. The Preacher was talking and welcoming all the people. When he saw her and Frederick, he paused for a moment and frowned. Some of the members turned around to see what had caught his attention. All they saw was a very poorly dressed woman with a young boy that was dressed about the same way sitting at the back of the church. They turned back around very attentive to their minister and totally ignored them.

The church service was nice. Emma had not been to church since her wedding day, and Frederick had only been in there a few times when he went with The Preacher. After the service was over, The Preacher walked to the back of the church and stood at the door while someone prayed. Since they were at the back, they were the first to get to the door.

To Emma's astonishment, Donald was standing beside The Preacher at the door. Neither Donald nor The Preacher acted as though they knew her or Frederick. The Preacher put out his hand, gave her a quick handshake, and actually put his left hand on her arm with a movement that told her that he wanted them to move along. When they got to Donald, he stuck out his hand to shake theirs, pretending that he did not know them. Frederick said, "Donald, don't you remember me? I am Frederick, your brother."

Donald looked very embarrassed by Frederick's question and looked up at The Preacher. The Preacher told Donald that he should walk the new people outside. Donald looked at The Preacher as if he could not believe that he was asking him to do such a thing. He walked outside with Emma and Frederick looking as though he wanted them to walk away and not say anything. When they were out of range for anyone hearing them, he asked them why they came to the church.

He also told them that they both looked awful and that he was ashamed of them. He then asked Frederick not to call him brother because he was not his brother anymore. When Emma reached over to give Donald a hug, he stepped back avoiding her touch.

She was devastated that he would treat her and Frederick that way. She looked away for a couple of seconds so that no one would see her tears. When she turned her face back to where her two boys were standing side by side, she felt embarrassed for Frederick. Donald had on a suit and tie, and Frederick's clothes looked like they were ready for the ragbag, but he stood tall with pride. He would not dignify his brother's actions by acting as if he was any less dressed than he was. The whole scenario broke Emma's heart. She tearfully told Donald good-bye, but he said nothing back to her. He merely walked away and took his place beside him. The Preacher glanced up at them and then put his hand on Donald's shoulder as though he was drawing him into a conversation with the people he was talking with. Emma and Frederick both saw what he did. Emma gently touched Frederick's shoulder and told him that they should go, so they began their sad walk home.

Frederick did not say a word all the way home and neither did Emma. What they thought was going to be a joyous reunion turned out to be another big heartache for both of them. Emma wondered what had happened to Donald. He had always been so sweet and gave her hugs so easily. How could a child change so fast?

Neither she nor Frederick wanted anything to eat for lunch. She was happy when Dave knocked on their door wanting Frederick to come out and play. It was just what Frederick needed after the sad incident at the church.

Later Sunday afternoon, The Preacher went to Emma's old apartment trying to find her. The apartment manager told him that he did not know for sure, but someone had told him that she had moved to the apartment complex that was across the street from the new sewing mill, but he had no idea as to what the apartment number was.

The Preacher was familiar with the apartment complex, and he had recently met John and Misty while knocking on the apartment doors inviting people to come to his church. He went to their house that was beside the apartment complex and asked where Emma Carswell lived. He told them that Mrs. Carswell and her child had visited his church that morning and he wanted to thank them personally for visiting with them. Misty did not particularly like The Preacher, but she had no reason as of yet not to trust him, so she gave him Emma's apartment number.

When he knocked on the door, Emma opened it and was surprised to find him and Donald at their door. The Preacher did not ask to come in; he just pushed her to the side and walked in as though he owned the place. Donald did not go inside with him. Instead, he walked over to where Dave and Frederick were shooting marbles and watched them play. Frederick looked up, and both he and Dave said hi, but Donald said nothing. Neither Frederick nor Dave said anything else and neither asked Donald to play. Donald was a little jealous because he had never been able to get down on the dirt to play since he went to live with The Preacher. The Preacher always made him stay clean and neat, telling him that it was a bad reflection on him if people saw his son dirty.

Donald looked up when he heard The Preacher say, "Well, this place is a little nicer than the dump you were living in. Did you find yourself a new boyfriend to pay for this apartment?"

Donald was embarrassed and hurt by the remark The Preacher made, but as usual, he just pretended that he did not hear anything. Things seemed to go better for him when he did that. Sometimes in his dreams, he would see his mother, as she would kiss him on the top of his head. In other dreams, her face would be all swollen and bruised, and there would be a man standing over her looking mean. Another dream he had was of a man standing over him with a big knife, and he would wake up crying. When he did, he would take the tiny piece of his blanket that he kept hidden, hold it tight and put his thumb in his mouth.

He knew that people would make fun of him if they knew he still sucked his thumb, but that was the only thing that calmed his beating heart, enough to go back to sleep. Sometimes he did not want to go back to sleep. He would lay there thinking about his mother and did not want her to be hurt again. He knew that he still loved her, but he also knew that he never wanted to live the way they had to live ever again. He was young and did not remember too much of his young life, but he did remember always being either hot or so cold that you thought your fingers were going to break off and always being hungry and scared.

After The Preacher forced his way in, he asked Emma what she was trying to prove by coming to his church. He demanded to know if she was going to try to take Donald away from him. When she said that Donald was her son, not his, he got red in the face, and you could tell that he was very angry. He walked over to the window and told her to look at the boys. When she walked over to the window, she could see Frederick and Dave playing, and Donald was standing near them. Dave was dressed pretty much like Frederick, but Donald had on the same suit and tie that he had on at church that morning. Dave and Frederick were down on the ground on their knees laughing and shooting marbles, but Donald was standing over them with no emotions on his face.

The Preacher asked Emma if she truly loved Donald. She told him that he knew that she loved her son. He said, "If you truly loved him, you would leave him alone. Don't you think that he is much better off where he is than to be back living in a place like this?" She asked him what was wrong with their apartment. It was new, and she was very proud of it.

He said, "Nothing but low life's lived in a place like this, and Donald deserve better." He did not say anything about Frederick deserving better.

She looked up at him and said, "You self-centered hypocrite. You stood up there Sunday preaching about love and forgiveness and being good to your neighbor, but then you come to our home and talk to me like that. This is the second time you have talked to me that way. I promise you, the next time you say something as you have today, to either Frederick or me, I will make you sorry that you every laid eyes upon either of us. I will become your worst nightmare, and you will curse the day you were born." All of the hurt and pain from Emma's past came out in those few words, and she looked as though she would follow up on her promise.

She actually scared The Preacher, and he stepped back a little. He had never had anyone to talk back to him before. Emma only came up to his chest, but she stood there with a force that he had never seen before in a man or a woman.

People had always looked up to him, and no one had ever talked to him the way that little woman was doing. The look in her eyes would make anyone fear for their lives. He believed that she might actually do something to hurt him or try to take Donald away from him. In his entire life, he had never cowered down to anyone, mostly because of his height and size and the sound of his deep voice. However, he had to admit, that little woman scared him. He had no idea as to what she might say about him, and he could not afford to have any gossip spread around, whether it was true or not. Everyone had a few skeletons in their closet, and he did not want anyone hunting one of his because he did have a few from his younger days, and he would prefer to let a sleeping dog lie.

When The Preacher regained his composure, he said, "I did not mean for things to sound so harsh. I was merely asking you to look at Donald. He is very well dressed and has everything that he needs. I feel certain that he will grow up to be an honorable person, whom many people will admire. If you really loved your son, why would you want him to give all of that up and come back to live with you?"

Emma walked over to the window and watched as Donald stood beside Frederick and Dave. It was true; he did not look like he belonged with them. She turned around and looked at The Preacher. He did not know what she was going to say or do, but he did not want her to get upset with him again. If people heard the way she was talking to him, they might think that he had done something to her. He could not afford anyone hearing anything bad about him. That would cause people to start gossiping about him and possibly ruin the reputation that he had built in this community.

When Emma spoke, she said, "Take Donald and leave. If he ever does want to come home and I find out that you will not let him, I will follow through on my threat. I will hunt you down like a dog, and when I find you, I will be your worst nightmare." She knew that she sounded like Harry, but she did not care.

The Preacher believed her and said nothing else. He bowed his head, turned, and walked out the door. If anyone heard any of their conversation, he would rather people think that he had been the victim, not her.

After he walked out the door, he called to Donald in a very meek voice and said, "Come along, son, we need to go." That remark was as if someone plunged a knife in Emma's heart. He called Donald son, as though he was Donald's father.

Because there were some people outside their apartments, The Preacher added, "Tell your new friends good-bye." Donald told them good-bye and walked over to where The Preacher was standing. The Preacher put a protective arm over his shoulders, and they left.

When Emma looked out the window again, Frederick and Dave were playing as though nothing had happened. She smiled to herself. She might be small, but The Preacher knew that she would live up to her promise. For some reason, all of this gave Emma a sense of empowerment that she had never felt before because she had given all of her power to Harry when they were married. It was the first time in a very long time that she felt good about herself.

85

Emma would have to reconcile to the fact that Donald may never come back to her. At least she knew that he seemed happy with The Preacher, and that was the only thing that was important to her. Whatever it took, she wanted her children to feel safe and loved.

14

He Was Too Strict and Legalistic

Emma chose the first shift at the sewing mill. With her hours being from 6:00 a.m. until 2:00 p.m. she was able be at home with Frederick every afternoon and especially at night. They did not have to waste their whole day sleeping. She would fix his breakfast before she left for work. When she took her break, she could walk across the street and check on him. A number of the employees that lived in the apartments did the same thing. When the whistle blew telling them it was time to go back to work, all they had to do was walk back across the street.

Emma and Frederick made many new friends, and all of the neighbors were very nice and looked out for one another. Sophia and Vera were Emma's new friends from the sewing mill. They were single and still lived at home with their parents, but the three of them became friends almost immediately, and both of them adored Frederick.

One day Vera and Sophia were talking about how they would like to meet some nice-looking men, but the pickings were slim because most of them were away fighting in the war. They talked about going to a bar later that night to see if any single men were there. They thought if they were old enough to work, they should be old enough to go out and have fun. Sophia sniffed and said, "If we go to a bar, I sure hope The Preacher doesn't find out."

Emma looked at Sophia and asked, "What is the name of your minister?" Sophia answered and said that his name was Reverend Dolan, but everyone calls him The Preacher.

Sophia then said, "We like most of the people that go to the church, but we don't particularly care for The Preacher, because he is too strict and legalistic. It seems as if we are attending an occult meeting rather than going to church because he is so controlling."

Vera frowned and told Emma that one Saturday afternoon, she and Sophia caught the bus and went to town to shop at the five-and-dime. When they came out of the store, they decided to go to see a picture show because they had never seen one before. They went to the cheapest one because it only cost a nickel to get in. You had to read everything they were saying because it did not have any sound. They called it a silent movie. However, they still enjoyed it because it was their first movie, and they had never done anything so exciting before.

When they came out, The Preacher was standing outside the theater near the exit door. He was carrying a sign that said if you went inside the house of the devil, you would bust hell wide open. He did not say anything to them when he saw them come out the door. However the next Sunday, he came back to where they were sitting and took them both by the hand and literally dragged them down to the front of the church. He told the whole congregation that he had caught them exiting a place where they, good young Christian women, should not have been. He demanded that they pray and ask God's forgiveness. After they prayed, he said that he knew that God had forgiven them if they had been sincere with their prayers, and now they should pledge to God and all the members of the church that they would never step foot in a place like that again.

Sophia mischievously raised her eyebrows and glared her eyes. She said, "He turned around and said that God had probably forgiven us, but they, as members, were human and may have a little more trouble believing that we were sincere. He told them to watch out for us, and if they caught us going down that wayward path again, they should come to him immediately. He said it was their responsibility to watch over us. If we ever went there again, they would all know that we were not truthful when we prayed, and they may have to ex-communicate us, and possibly our families, from the church because it would show them that we were children of the devil and not of God."

Sophia said, "When we were leaving the church, The Preacher shook our hands and said, 'Everyone sins, even me, if you can believe it, but as I did, you must also ask for forgiveness.'"

Vera chimed in and said, "He asked us to go to his office because he would like to counsel us. When we met him in his office, he wanted to know every little detail about the movie. We have been afraid to do anything since then because The Preacher told us if we had died in our sleep after going to that place, we would have gone straight to hell. He told us that we should be thankful that he caught us and made us repent and that we should be more careful about our sinning ways. Every time I look at a good-looking person, gossip about someone, or just tell a joke, I feel guilty. It is a great burden thinking that everything that you say or do may send you to hell."

Both girls immediately noticed the expression on Emma's face, and Vera said, "If we have said anything that offended you, Emma, we are sorry."

Emma shook her head and told them that they had not offended her. She told them that she had some personal issues that she was dealing with and assured them that it was not because of anything they did or said.

After Emma left work, she was feeling very sad. It was weighing heavily on her heart as to whether The Preacher or Mr. and Mrs. Timmons may be abusing her babies. She did not even know where the Timmonses lived now. She heard that they had moved shortly after taking Patrick home with them, but she thought that they would at least come by and let her know where they had moved. When she asked Charles and Sara, they said that they did not know either. They told Emma that they automatically took it for granted, that she and Mr. and Mrs. Timmons would have stayed in touch because of Patrick.

Charles said, "They seem like very nice people, and we don't think they would ever do anything to hurt Patrick. Every time we saw them with the baby, before they moved, he was happy and healthy, and they doted on him. You could tell that they were taking very good care of him. But I do have to admit that we were very surprised to hear that you had not had any contact with Patrick since they took him home with them."

Charles's comment cut through to Emma's heart because she was constantly struggling with guilt over her children. She knew that Henrietta was doing great with her grandparents. Frederick was changing daily and was becoming a happy young boy. She did not think that she had ever seen him so happy. He and Dave spent almost every waking hour playing together. They also spent the night with each other several times a week. Having Dave as a friend was one of the best things that could have ever happened to Frederick.

She had seen Donald and The Preacher visiting people in their apartment complex. The first time she saw them, she was outside hanging clothes on a line. It was good to see Donald. He walked proud and a little cocky, just like The Preacher. He might live with The Preacher, dress like The Preacher, and act like The Preacher, but he would always be her child. She gave birth to him, and she would always be his mother.

She naïvely left her clothes and walked around to the front of the apartment building, just in case The Preacher was bringing Donald to see her. They both pretended that they did not see her and walked past her to another apartment, without acknowledging that she was there. When her new neighbors opened their door,

The Preacher shook their hand and started talking to them in a very nice manner. The neighbors invited them in and then shut the door. Frederick had witnessed the whole incident. He and Dave were coming around the corner of the apartment building, just as The Preacher and Donald knocked on their neighbor's door. Dave could sense that there was a problem between Frederick and his mother and The Preacher and his son, but being the good friend that he was, he did exactly as Frederick did and acted as if they had not seen them either.

The next time Emma saw Donald and The Preacher, they were walking toward another apartment in the complex. Frederick and Dave also saw them and turned their backs to Donald and The Preacher as though they had no idea who they were. She saw Donald as he watched Frederick and Dave play with their friends, and her heart felt so bad because she thought she saw a look of sadness on Donald's face.

Every time she saw Donald and The Preacher together, they both had on suits. She wondered if The Preacher ever permitted Donald to play or wear clothes that he could play in. He always looked like a little soldier walking beside The Preacher. In fact, he looked like a miniature version of The Preacher. Both of them usually wore similar suits, white shirts, and a black tie. They looked as if they were going to a funeral by the way they were dressed and the looks on their faces.

Emma tried to buy Frederick a suit, and he wanted to know why. He told her that it was more fun playing in his dungarees than it would be wearing a suit all of the time.

15

What Would Misty Think If She Knew the Truth?

One evening Vera and Sophia came over and told Emma that they were going out and wanted to know if she would like to join them. When Emma asked where they were going Sophia said that they were going to catch the bus, go uptown and walk around.

Frederick was spending the night with Dave so Emma said that it would be nice to get out for a change. They told her to go change and they would wait on her. Emma asked what they wanted her to change into and all three of them started laughing. It looked like it was going to be a fun night.

When they got off the bus, they first went into the five-and-dime to see what they could find. It was the first time Emma had ever been out with girlfriends or with a date that she did not have a curfew and the freedom to do as she pleased. Before she was married, her grandparents would not let her go out with what they called "a gang of girls looking for trouble." Harry had been the only person she had ever dated seriously, and her grandparents set her curfew to 10:00 p.m. when they went out.

They told her that they trusted her, but her grandfather said that he did not trust Harry.

When they passed one store window, Emma saw a beautiful blue dress. Vera also saw it and said, "Emma, why don't we go inside and try it on?"

Inside they went! They were trying on everything in the store and a sales clerk asked Sophia, in a very nasty tone of voice, if they were there just to try on clothes, or did they intend to purchase anything.

Sophia told her that she had intended to buy dresses for her maid of honor and bridesmaid, but with her attitude, she would take her business elsewhere. The three of them put their clothes back on and left the store immediately. They could barely keep from laughing as they headed for the door. When they looked back inside the store, they saw the poor sales clerk gathering all the dresses they had tried on and hanging them back up on the racks.

Emma said, "We should have hung the dresses back up before leaving?"

Vera responded, "We should have, and would have, had the sales clerk not been so nasty to us."

Their next stop was at a café where they had a sandwich and tea. There were three good-looking men sitting on stools at the counter. One of the men looked around, saw them, and then whispered to his friends. The other two men turned around, and all three propped their elbows on their knees and just sat there looking at them.

All three girls knew the men were looking at them, and it was all they could do to eat their sandwich. Finally, one of men got up with enough nerve to come over and ask them if they could sit with them.

Vera said, "Sure, come on over."

The men introduced themselves as Brian, Erik, and Ryan. They said that they were from out of town and did not know anyone, and they were hunting for a place to go have fun and asked the girls if they knew of a place.

The girls told them that they had no idea where to go.

The men asked them if they could find a place, would they like to go with them. Vera and Sophia were delighted, but Emma did not know if it was proper for her to go to a place like that since she was still legally married to Harry and had four children. She told the men that she had a little boy at home and maybe she should not go with them.

Erik asked her if she had a husband at home with the little boy, and she told him no. He said, "Well, doesn't that make you single also?"

Emma smiled and said, "I suppose it does, but I am a few years older than Vera and Sophia." The men shrugged as though stating that it did not matter. They paired off, and the three couples went on a hunt for a place to go dancing.

They finally found a place just outside of town, and it was full of sailors in uniform. Sophia leaned over and whispered to Emma and Vera, "I think we just died and arrived in heaven. Just look at all those good-looking men in uniforms. Please help me remember how we got to this place."

The men were very nice to them. They bought them sodas to drink and then ordered beer for themselves. They asked the girls if they would prefer a beer, but Vera and Sophia thought they had already sinned enough for one night by just by going dancing, and Vera told them, "Thanks, but we really should be leaving." And then she told them how much they had enjoyed coming to the dance with them. Vera did not want to tell them that she and Sophia had curfews and needed to go home. The men walked them to the bus stop and waited with them until the bus came. Sophia all dreamy eyed turned to see if the men were still standing there watching their bus go up the road. Of course, they were not! They were going back inside to the dance.

It was close to midnight by they time the bus dropped Emma off, and it was about ten minutes later when Sophia and Vera got home. Both of them were able to sneak in without their parents catching them.

As Emma started to open her door, she saw a note under her door, so she picked it up and read it. "Reverend Dolan came by for a visit at *10:45 p.*m." There was no signature on the note, so she did not know if The Preacher had put it under her door or if one of the neighbors had put it there.

The time was underlined. If it was The Preacher, what was he doing there at that time of the night? She did not know what to do. She did not get very much sleep that night because she was worried that there may be something wrong with Donald.

The next day as she was walking down the street to work, she saw The Preacher walking up the street, and Donald was right beside him. Both of them were dressed in suits, which seemed to be their normal daily attire. When they saw her, The Preacher immediately took Donald's arm. As they crossed the road, she heard The Preacher say, "Can you believe the trash on those sidewalks?" and they walked all the way to the apartment complex in the high weeds. Emma was so embarrassed that she could feel herself turning red. She just stood there watching them as they walked. Donald's back was straight, and he was keeping step with The Preacher.

Misty was coming up behind Emma, and she heard the remark made by The Preacher, and for some reason she knew that he was referring to Emma. In a very professional and loud voice, she said, "Good morning, Ms. Carswell, how are you doing today?" She addressed Emma as most people would address the CEO of a company if they just happened to walk up to them. Misty looked at The Preacher and then at Donald and knew they had heard her. She smiled as she made a decision. The Preacher had best not come to her office again wanting a donation for his church.

95

Misty got in step with Emma and walked inside the building with her. When they were inside, Misty made a nasty comment about The Preacher, saying that she had come under an attack by that man because she would not give him information about an employee. She went home that night and told John. He went to The Preacher's house and had a talk with him, and The Preacher had not spoken to her since.

Misty laughed and said, "He is some piece of work, and his son is a miniature of him. Lord only knows what that boy is going to be like when he is grown."

Emma did not know how to reply to Misty's remark. Donald was her child, not The Preacher's, and it hurt to hear anything negative said about him. She wished that she could go back in time and do things differently with all of her children. She felt so much guilt that it was almost impossible not to cry. What would Misty think of her if she knew the truth?

Misty saw the tears forming in Emma's eyes however; she pretended that she did not.

16

Why Were They Talking About the Germans?

Frederick came up to his mother and asked her if she would mind if Dave called him Freddie. When she asked why, he told her that was what Dave was calling him. Emma totally understood what he was saying without asking him for further explanation. She told him that it was up to him as to what he wanted his friends to call him.

One day when Emma was not working, she asked Frederick and Dave if they would like to take the bus and go to town. The boys were excited because they had heard some of the older kids talk about going to town. They did not actually know where town was, but they were anxious to go find out.

Emma told Dave to run home and ask his mother if it was okay. He was back in just a few minutes with his face washed and his clothes changed. They boys were ready to go before she was.

They walked up the street to the bus stop. It was a beautiful day, and Emma hoped that it would be a new beginning for her and Frederick because they had never been able to do things like this. The boys could not sit still during the bus ride. They were entertaining everyone on the bus with their stories. One older woman told them that she wished they were on the bus every time she had to go to town because they made the ride seem shorter and much more interesting.

When they got off the bus, Emma gave Frederick a dollar because that was what Dave's mother gave him to spend. She took them to the five-and-dime, and they started going up and down the aisles looking at everything. They had a whole dollar, and they did not know what they wanted to buy.

When they walked over to the section where the radios were playing, Emma started having flashbacks to the day she heard the romantic song playing, the door slamming, and the announcement about the attack on Pearl Harbor. The reason she had given their radio to Charles when he moved them was that there were too many memories involving it. There were times when she would move a certain way that she still had pain in her back because of the brutal assault by Harry.

The store had one of their radios playing, and they were talking about the war. The newscaster was talking about the children who were suffering during the war. No one knew what permanent damage the war may be doing to the children who may survive.

They were saying that the physical damage to the children would be obvious, but the psychological damage would be much deeper. Some of the occupying troops had been very brutal to the children. The Nazi Party was using young boys for soldiers, and Hitler pinned Iron Crosses onto their uniforms while in the garden of his bunker in Berlin.

Emma was wondering why they were talking about Germany. She thought that only the Japanese and the United States were at war. What has been happening? She had seen newspaper headlines, and they were telling about the war, but she never had extra money that she could spend to buy a newspaper. She had also seen signs in windows, and people were always talking about the war, but she never really knew what was happening.

She had to admit that she had not given the war much thought. She was too busy trying to survive. Everyone in their area seemed to be going about their business as they always had. She had heard Vera and Sophia talking about how all the men had gone to war, but she thought they were just exaggerating. However, from the time she went to work in the restaurant, there was a steady decline of younger men coming in. That was the main reason her income had dropped so dramatically.

There were nearly two million children evacuated since the start of World War II, and those children had accounted for one in ten of the deaths from 1940 to 1941.

Emma thought the war had just begun on that awful day, December 7, 1941. Patrick would probably never know how his birth took, place and for that, she was thankful, but the poor thing would always be celebrating his birthday as people memorialized the attack. She knew that Frederick and Henrietta had memories of what happened. Donald said that he had a lot of bad memories, but she did not know what they were about.

Frederick and Dave were getting anxious to go outside and see the city, so Emma took them through the checkout counter. On her way out, she picked up a newspaper and planned to read it when they got home. She wanted to know more about what was happening outside her small world. She needed to be thankful for everything they had now and forget about dwelling on what could have been or should have been. Both of the boys did not like it, but they let her take their hand as they crossed the street.

It was wonderful watching the two boys see the city for the first time. They were amazed with the tall buildings. They were counting the taxis going up and down the street either picking up passengers or letting them off at their destination. What they could not understand was why everyone was blowing their horns.

Frederick and Dave were very tired from their trip, and they both slept all the way home on the bus. Emma nodded off a few times also, but she knew that she couldn't go to sleep because they may miss their stop, and she did not have enough money left to pay for them to ride the bus again.

17

Devil's Trash

Emma read the newspaper all weekend. She read it once and then went back and then read it again. When she went to work on Monday, she told Sophia and Vera about everything that she had read in the newspaper, and they seemed to be as oblivious as she was about the war. They had heard their parents and some neighbors talking about how bad it was getting, but neither paid much attention to what they were saying. Sophia said that she did remember hearing them say that they may start rationing out food and other items.

The three women began that day, trying to find out what was going on and what they could do to help. The first thing they were going to do was to talk to other people about the war and find out exactly what was going on.

Sophia said, "We are working women now, so I guess we need to act like adults." Emma and Vera both looked at Sophia and could not believe she was saying that because they both thought that she would always be forever young, happy-go-lucky, enjoying every day, and not worrying about tomorrow. She was always in a good mood every day.

It was not long after Emma shared what she had read about the war that Misty told them that they were going to start sewing military uniforms instead of regular clothing. They were going to have to switch off and learn other sewing methods. She wanted them to be the first to learn the new method because all three of them were fast learners.

The problem was, all three of them had grown very comfortable with what they were doing, and it was a little more difficult learning to make the durable military uniforms than it was making shirts and blouses. Nevertheless, as usual, they were quick to learn, and in just a few weeks, they were training other women how to cut and sew the uniforms. No one complained! Most of them were happy because they had a job and their working conditions were great.

Emma and Frederick had both changed since moving into the new apartment. The apartments may be government subsidized but almost everyone there was good, hard working people. Many of her neighbors had sons or other family members that were serving in the military, some killed in action.

Everyone there was like family to Emma and Frederick. Working so many days per week, they did not get to go see their grandparents and Henrietta very often. When they did go, it was a good reunion. Frederick loved to go for a visit, but there was no way he was going to stay anywhere except with her. When it became time to go home, he would always stay close to Emma because he was afraid she would try to sneak off and leave him.

Henrietta had visited them a couple of times, but the apartment was so small, and she was so used to the big house that she would not stay more than a night or two. She had stopped trying to get Frederick to stay with her at their grandparents' home. She understood because she wanted to stay with her grandparents and go to the school with all of her neighborhood friends and classmates. She loved her mother and her brother, but she did not want to go back and live with them again. The thought actually scared her.

Frederick and Dave had become almost inseparable. They were both getting ready to start school in the fall, and that was all they were talking about every day. They were scared and anxious at the same time.

Emma was now taking the boys into town at least once a month. She had promised them that she would take them to the picture show sometime soon, but every time she even thought about going, she could just see The Preacher standing outside when they came out, so she would distract them with the option of doing something else.

The Preacher did not come around as often as he did when everyone was new in the complex. She certainly did not miss seeing him, but she did miss seeing Donald.

Frederick finally let Emma buy him a suit if she promised that she did not buy it because she wanted him to go stay with The Preacher. She promised him that she would not, so he was okay with it. He just did not like trying them on. After he got his suit, Dave's mom bought him one also. They both put on their suits one day and let their parents take pictures of them. When Emma and Frederick were looking at pictures after they were developed, Frederick said, "Mom, do you think that I look just as good in my suit as Donald does in his?"

Emma smiled and said, "Yes, Frederick, you sure do."

Shortly after they bought the suit, Emma received word that her grandfather had passed away. Misty let her take some time off so that she could go to his funeral. She stayed a couple of days longer than she intended because she wanted to make sure that her grandmother was okay.

Her uncle Charlie came to the funeral. He was her mother's brother and her grandmother's only son. He told her grandmother that he would come and live with her if she liked. His wife, Michelle, had run off with a guy in the military, and he was now living by himself. He was not interested in finding another wife because he was still in love with Michelle and hoped that one day she would wake up and realize that she had made a mistake and come home to him.

Her grandmother told Charlie that he was a hopeless romantic, but he was more than welcome to stay with her. She told him that he would have to sleep upstairs because she had one of the two bedrooms downstairs and Henrietta had the other.

When Charlie started acting as though he was complaining about walking up the stairs, Mary said, "Charlie, are you telling me that you are getting too old to climb stairs? You are only fifty, and you have always told me that you had super human strength, and now you are telling me that you can't climb those stairs."

Henrietta had walked into the kitchen just as her grandmother was talking to Charlie. She had never heard her grandmother tease anyone like that. She was always so serious with everything she said. She looked at her mother and raised an eyebrow. When Emma smiled, Henrietta sat down and listened to the humorous banter between her grandmother and her uncle.

Later her mother told her than her uncle had always had a great sense of humor and most of the time would get the best of his mother, but it was all in fun between them.

After laughing so much her mouth hurt to grin, Henrietta asked Frederick if he would like to go for a walk with her. She told him that she would like to show him off to her friends. As they walked, she told him all about going to school and told him how nice the people were. Frederick said, "Henrietta, don't even think about trying to talk me into staying up here. I like where we live, and you know how close Dave and I are. We will both start first grade in a few weeks. We are going to walk to school together. We play with each other every day."

He stopped and said, "Henrietta, are you walking with me just to get me away from the house so that Mom can leave me? I love Grandma and Uncle Charlie, but I want to stay with Mom."

Henrietta laughed and told him that it was not a trick. She wanted him to walk with her because she was proud of him.

With the exception of his mother, no one had ever told Frederick they were proud of him before. He held his shoulders higher, and he and Henrietta walked around two more blocks. When they would get to a house where one of Henrietta's friends lived, they would stop, and she would introduce them to her brother Frederick.

When they got back to the house, his mother told him they should get their things and start home. Frederick immediately ran into the house and got his things ready. He asked his mother if he could wear his suit going home. She told him that he could, but as soon as he got home, he should take it off and hang it up so that it would not get dirty.

On the bus trip home, Frederick sat a little taller in his seat. Emma told him that he should take his hat off in the presence of women. He did not like it, but he took it off and held it on his lap, but as soon as the bus stopped and they got off, he put his hat back on.

Emma knew they were both dressed nice, and it made her feel proud. Before she made enough money to buy them new clothes, her clothes looked like sacks on her and poor Frederick's shirts, pants, and even his underwear had patches on them. She felt herself standing a little straighter and her head held higher because she was proud of how far she had come from the days when they lived with Harry, and Frederick seemed to feel the same way.

Emma was happy that she was finally making more money, and she could finally pay Mr. Frasier the money she owed him. She did not send it to him anonymously as she intended. She went to the bank and got a check for the full amount. She then took the bus down to the apartments. When she got to the door, she started to turn around and leave, but she did not. She knocked on the door, and when he came to the door, he looked as though he had just seen a ghost. To him, she probably was a ghost from his past. She merely handed him the check and told him that it was for the money she owed him for helping her with her rent and utilities. She smiled and thanked him for his help and then turned around before he had a chance to say anything and walked back to the bus stop to catch the bus back home.

Frederick met Emma at the bus station because she told him that she would only be gone about an hour, and he wanted to make sure that she got home safe. As they started down the street to their apartment, Donald and The Preacher crossed the street right in front of them. It startled Emma, but she tried not to let it show. She could see they were not going to speak to them, so she and Frederick did not speak either. Just as The Preacher and Donald passed them, Frederick said, "Devil's trash."

After they got far enough away from The Preacher and Donald and he knew they could not hear him, Frederick said, "Mom, I know that I probably should not have said that, but I am hurt and angry toward The Preacher. He took Donald away from us, and now they both act as though they are better than we are. I was beside our apartment building the day The Preacher and Donald crossed the street, and I heard him say that there was too much trash on those sidewalks, and I know he was talking about you. I swore that one day that I would get even with him, and now I have."

Emma said, "Frederick, I understand how you feel, and please always remember that we are just as good as anyone else is. We just had a few problems that we had to work out. Nevertheless, we are okay now. You hold your head high and be proud of who you are. Don't stoop to their level by saying nasty things to them or other people."

Frederick said, "I know that I shouldn't have said what I did, Mom, and I am sorry for saying it, but I am glad that I had on my suit today. I think I look just as good in my suit as The Preacher and Donald look in theirs."

Emma patted Frederick on the back and said, "You sure do, Frederick. I can't think of anyone that I have seen that looks better in a suit than you do."

With that comment, Frederick held his shoulders high and cocked his hat on his head the way his uncle Charlie did.

18

I Could Have Danced All Night

On her first morning back to work, many of the other employees came to Emma and told her how sorry they were for her loss. Most of them wanted to know if there was something they could do for her. Some of them said, "If you need my help in any way, please let me know." Emma thanked them for their kindness but had to smile to herself. Now that she did not need anything, everyone was offering to help her.

One day after work, Sophia and Vera asked Emma if she would like to go dancing at the place they found when they were with the men they met at the café. Emma was a little hesitant, but she said she would see if Frederick could stay with Dave for the night. Vera said, "Great, we will see you around six."

When Vera and Sophia got to Emma's apartment, they found that she had already washed and styled her hair, polished her shoes, and had one of her new dresses on. She even sprayed some of the Evening in Paris, which she had bought in the five-and-dime store, behind her ears and at her wrist.

Vera whistled! Emma considered the whistle as an indication that Vera thought she looked good. Sophia said, "Emma, you clean up pretty good, and you smell great. We could not tell how pretty you were underneath all those big floppy dresses you wear to work. You make me feel underdressed. Maybe I should go back home and change into prettier clothes."

They all three laughed at the remark. Emma had never had any close friends that she could talk, have fun, and go places with. After they were married, Harry would not take her anywhere with him, especially after she got pregnant. Occasionally when she would have the children out in the yard playing while Harry was at work, Sara or Charles would come over and speak to her, but they were the only friends she had until she met Vera and Sophia.

One day Harry came home early in the afternoon, and she was still outside with Henrietta and Frederick. She had been talking to Sara and Charles, and Sara had to go inside for something. Harry pulled into the yard and saw her talking with Charles. He just sat in his truck and stared at them, and she could tell that he was getting angry. She told Charles that she had best be getting back inside so that she could start dinner. Charles just nodded his head, and they both walked back to their homes.

Just as soon as she walked into the house, Harry jumped out of his truck and stomped into the house. He immediately started accusing her of every nasty thing he could think of, things she did not even know about, much less would do.

All of that stuff was behind her now, and she was going to try to leave it there. She was going to go out with her two best friends and have fun.

When they got to the dance, many people were standing around waiting for the doors to open. A couple of men came up to them and asked them if they would like to sit with them. Sophia said, "No thank you, but we would like to dance with you when we get inside." The man tipped his hat and told them that they would check them out when they got inside.

After the dance opened, everyone crowded in and chose tables or seats around the wall. If you sat at a table, you had to order a drink. It did not matter if it was alcohol, coffee, or just a glass of water; you still had to be a paying customer. Emma ordered coffee, and Sophia and Vera ordered beer. They had heard, if you drink beer, you would have more fun, and they intended to have a lot of fun. Emma's coffee only cost a nickel, but their beer cost twenty-five cents each. Vera said, "At that price, they may not be having too much fun if it took beer to make the fun happen." In addition, the girl that brought their drinks stood around until they each pulled out money and tipped her.

No one asked them to dance the first couple of songs, and then finally someone asked Sophia to dance. While they were dancing, the person told her that his name was Rodney Glen. He told her that his friends were Dalton and Braydon, and they wanted to ask one of her friends to dance, but they would be embarrassed if they turned them down. Sophia told him that they were not there to find husbands; they were there to have fun and dance. Rodney smiled and told her that he would tell his friends that the girls would dance with them. When the dance was over, Rodney walked Sophia back to her table. You could tell that he wanted her to ask him to sit with them, but she did not, so he left and joined Dalton and Braydon.

When the band played the next song, three good-looking fellows whose names were Ben, Jeremy, and James came over and asked them if they would like to dance. All three immediately said yes. When that song ended, the band took a break. After they came back in and started playing, no one asked them to dance for the next three songs. Sophia said, "What do you say we leave this place? Evidently, no one wants to dance with us."

Rodney, the person Sophia danced with, was now dancing with a very pretty blonde whose name was Ashley. They knew Ashley because she worked with them at the sewing mill. Evidently, Rodney's friends did not want to dance with them either because they saw the two of them over in a corner talking with Addison and Kaylee, two other girls that they worked with at the mill. All of the men who worked in the factory, and evidently the ones at the dance, seemed too swoon over all three of those women.

Tonight was just not their night to have fun. They wasted their money buying the beer. For one thing, it tasted nasty, and it definitely was not creating any fun for them. Feeling as though they could not compete with the women there, they decided to call it a night and go home.

Just as they got up to leave, three marines in uniform came in, grabbed them by the hand, and twirled them onto the dance floor. All three were a bit cocky and very good-looking, and all three of them were great dancers. Neither of marines asked the girls if they could sit with them after they danced. They automatically assumed that they were welcome and pulled up three chairs and made themselves comfortable. They immediately started a conversation by telling them their names. The marine that was talking with Emma said that his name was Casey Campbell, and his friends were Edward Brice and Levi Brice, who were brothers.

Emma, Sophia, and Vera told them their names.

When it was time for them to go home, they hated to leave. The three marines asked if they could escort them to the bus stop. As they were walking to the bus stop, Emma told Casey that she had never had so much fun in her life. She said, "I could have danced all night." Casey took her hand, twirled her around, and danced up the sidewalk with her. When they got to the bus stop, Casey kissed Emma on the cheek and told her that he had a great time.

After the marines left them, Vera said, "I sure hope they are at the dance the next time we go."

Emma said, "Casey told me that they were with a unit that stood guard at a funeral for one of their comrades who was killed in action. They had to spend the night here and then go back tomorrow. Someone told them if they wanted something to do and scare some sailors in the process, they should go to the dance. Casey is very good friends with a girl named Carol Ann. She told them that he showed her a picture of them together, and the girl was beautiful. Casey also told her that Edward was in a relationship with a girl named Kim, and Levi was head over heels for a girl named Cheryl."

Sophia said, "We still had a good time, and all three of them were gentlemen. Just think, if we had left five minutes earlier, we would have missed those good-looking marines, and we would be riding the bus home complaining about being ignored by the sailors."

19

Terminations

When they got to work on Monday, Misty came to Vera, Sophia, and Emma and asked if she could see them in her office. Misty had always been good to all three of them, especially Emma, but all three felt as though she was going to tell them something that neither of them wanted to hear.

When Misty began talking, she told them that since they were the last three hired, she had no other choice but to let them go first. Sophia said, "Last hired and the first fired." Misty smiled at her humor and then told them how sorry she was, but if the work was not there, they could not afford to keep everyone.

She said, "Girls, I am really sorry to tell you, but today will be your last day on the job. You can pick up your last check in my office this afternoon when your shift ends."

Vera and Sophia did not like it, but they did not have too much to worry about because they still lived at home with their parents. Emma on the other hand was devastated. She could barely keep focused on her job the rest of the day. When it came time to go home, she went by Misty's office to pick up her check. She felt as though she was hyperventilating as she walked into her office.

Vera and Sophia had already picked up their checks and had gone home. Misty asked Emma to come in. When she did, Misty got up and shut the door. She told Emma how sorry she was about everything, but she had no other choice. She felt sure that more people would also be losing their jobs and then said, "This war is really hurting everyone."

With her next statement, Misty surprised Emma and said, "John has something that he would like to talk with you about. He wants you to stop by his office on your way home."

When Emma left to go to John's office, she had no idea what he wanted to tell her. She supposed he was going to tell her she would have to move if she did not find another job soon. She braved herself for more bad news.

John was with someone when she walked into his office. He told her to have a seat and he would be with her shortly. Emma was shaking because she was so nervous. She had the sinking feeling that she and Frederick would wind up in their old situation again. They had just started feeling comfortable and safe, and now this. Frederick was going to start first grade soon, and he told her a couple of days ago that he hoped that he and Dave could walk to school together. Dave had been so good for Frederick, and she hated to separate them by having to move away.

When John asked her to come into his office, Emma could feel the heavy weight creeping up her back as she walked into his office.

John started the conversation by asking her how she and Frederick were doing. She said, "John, you can cut it with the small talk. Just tell me what you want me to do."

John laughed and said, "Misty told me that she was going to have to let you and two of your friends go, and she really feels bad about it, but I think I have some information that maybe will solve all of your problems." Emma was all ears because John sounded positive.

He told her that a munitions plant was hiring women. Most of the young men are off fighting for their country, so they are going to hire women to take their places. It would probably be much heavier and more dangerous work than the women were used to, but the pay is much higher. It is not as much as the men were making when they did the work, but it will be much more than they would ever make at the sewing mill.

Emma breathed slowly, sat back in her chair, and asked him where the munitions plant was. When he told her, Emma had a sick feeling that she might have to go through exactly what she had to go through when she had to work nights leaving Frederick alone.

John told her that he also managed some apartments near a little town called Garden City. "You could walk to work, or you could take a bus when the weather was bad. There is a bus stop beside the apartments, and it would only cost a nickel a day to ride the bus over to the plant because it is not that far away, and the bus ran on a schedule that coincided with the shift changes at the plant." He told her that he was going over to the apartment complex that afternoon. "Mr. Spencer is going to work in the plant as a supervisor, and he and his family is in the process of moving into one of the apartments."

Emma did not know of any Spencers that lived in the apartment complex except for Dave's family. She asked John if they were Dave Spencer's parents. John told her yes, and Emma felt her load lighten. That would mean that Frederick and Dave would still be able to be friends.

Emma told John that she really appreciated all that he and Misty had done for her and Frederick. John smiled and said, "Hey, Freddie and Dave are my buddies. I have to keep them on to do odd jobs for me."

Emma smiled at what John said. He had been giving Frederick and Dave a nickel or dime to clean up trash that people would drop in the parking lot of the complex. Frederick was saving most of his money that he earned, and she thought that Dave was saving his also. They wanted new clothes for school and a few other things, but they would not tell her what they were.

John told Emma that he would be ready to go in about thirty minutes. He told her that Frederick rode over earlier with the Spencer family since he was staying with them while she worked.

Emma told John that she would be back within thirty minutes. She then went home and changed from her old baggy working dress to one of her new ones. She thought if she was going to go apply for a job, she wanted to look her best.

John was standing at his truck when Emma came down. He said, "Wow, Emma, you look great." His comment embarrassed Emma, but it also made her feel good.

20

Private Signals

As soon as Frederick saw John's truck and realized that his mother was with John, he ran over to greet them. He said, "Hi, Mom, I hope you did not mind me coming over with Dave and his parents. They needed to move some of their things and did not want to leave me alone at the apartment. John said that he would come and get me later if the Spencers could not make it back before you came home."

Emma told him that it was okay as long as he was with Dave's parents or John. Frederick then said, "Come on, Mom! You have to see their new apartment. It is so nice. I wish we could move here."

John looked at Emma with a look that said, "I told you so."

When they entered the apartment, Emma was astonished as to how big it was. She would love to have an apartment like this one. She was becoming as excited about it as Frederick was.

John told Emma to come with him. He went to the next apartment and opened the door. Frederick was right behind them. When they were inside the apartment, Fredrick grabbed his mother's hand and pulled her to a room that he would like to be his. He told her that Dave's room was on the other side of the wall. There was a sign already on the door that said, "Freddie's

Room." Emma could not help but laugh. It looked like the new apartment was a done deal.

Dave and Frederick already had it all figured out. Their bedrooms would be back to back to each other, and they could make up signals that they could tap on the wall to let each other know what they wanted to do. It would almost be like living together.

When Emma told John that she did not know if she could afford an apartment like this one, he told her that it would only be thirty dollars per month, and that included electric, water, and heating just like the other apartment.

Emma could not believe that they could have the apartment for only ten dollars more per month. She then received another surprise. John said that Dave Spencer's father was going to be a supervisor in the munitions plant and that he had already talked to Mr. Spencer about hiring her. He told Emma that all she had to do was to go over to their personnel office and complete the paperwork, and she would have a job.

Emma was finally starting to relax a little. She knew that she would miss what she had at the sewing mill, and she would miss the new friends that she had made there, but she felt like things were changing, and she would have to change according to her situation. She hoped that Vera and Sophia would apply for a job there also, but that would be a long distance for them to travel back and forth each day from their parents' homes.

Mr. Spencer drove Emma over to the personnel office of the munitions plant in his truck. The first people Emma saw were Vera and Sophia. They had come to apply for jobs also. One of Sophia's neighbors had told her about the job openings, and she immediately went to tell Vera. They told Emma that they had stopped by her apartment to see if she would like to come with them to apply for one of the jobs, but she had not been at home.

Emma introduced Sophia and Vera to Mr. Spencer. He shook the girls' hands and then said, "Stay right here, girls, I have an idea." When he came back, he had applications for all three of them. When they looked at the job openings, all three looked at each other. One opening was for someone to paint radium on tiny measurements so that pilots could see their instrument panels in the dark. The others were to operate massive hydraulic presses that cut metal parts and for a crane operator to move bulky plane parts from one end of the factory to the other. If you had experience, there were openings for inspectors that checked all necessary adjustments before either the large bombers or the small fighter planes left for the war zone.

Sophia asked Mr. Spencer about what they made at that plant. Mr. Spencer told her that they made airplanes, tanks, large caliber guns, warships, and artillery ammunition.

He told them not to be afraid of the jobs. They had found that most often women were proving they could not only do the job, but in some instances they did it better than their male counterparts, because they paid more attention to detail. He said that there were many women already working in these positions while the war was going on. Other jobs would be coming available if they were not interested in any of these jobs.

All of the women hired that day were to start the next Monday. They would find out what their jobs would be when they came to work Monday morning.

Mr. Spencer told them that probably by church time Sunday, everyone would be in their new apartments. He had already talked to John about it, and they would both use their trucks and move everyone to their new apartments.

Sophia and Vera decided they were going to talk to John about an apartment. If they could move out of their parents' homes and move into one of the apartments, they could share expenses. Vera said, "Yes, and we could share all of the housework also." You could tell that they both were excited at the idea of being out on their own, especially since all of them would be living door to door with each other, creating a safer environment.

Things moved at a very fast pace over the next couple of days. By Saturday afternoon, they were all in their new apartments.

Frederick and Dave were all set to start the new chapter in their lives. The first thing they did was to make up their secret codes.

Dave said, "Freddie, do you suppose it would be okay if we drilled a little hole through the wall? If we did that, we could talk, and not have to remember all of these codes." Frederick told him that they should not do anything to damage the walls. He knew that neither John nor their parents would not appreciate having holes in the new walls. Dave agreed, so they continued making up their codes.

The next Saturday, Sophia and Vera came by to ask Emma if she would like to go out and do something with them. From talking with some of their neighbors, they discovered the dance they had gone to was just a few blocks away, and they had heard that there had been many sailors coming there on Saturday nights.

Emma told them that she would some other time, but the past week had been hectic for her, so she thought she would stay home and relax for a while. They told her that they would miss having her with them. Emma said, "Maybe next time."

After Emma prepared dinner, she and Frederick walked around the neighborhood trying to get to know the area. There was a large grocery store just up the street from them, so they walked through it to see what all they had in it. It was ten times larger than the little grocery store where Emma shopped in Upland. They had everything that you would need in your kitchen.

When they came out of the grocery store, they walked up the street a little further and saw a church. The minister was out front painting a sign announcing all of the services they were having there. He immediately said hello and stuck his hand out to shake theirs. Emma and Frederick both were a little skittish of preachers. He introduced himself to them and told that he was Reverend Michael Charles and the little woman coming up behind them was his wife, Kedra, and the little boy his wife was holding was their son, Blake.

Emma and Frederick both turned around to see whom he was referring to. A woman walked up behind them, and her smile would light up the sky. She extended her hand to shake theirs and said, "Hello, my name is Kedra, and that wonderful man is my husband." Emma and Frederick both told her their names at the same time. Kedra and Reverend Charles both laughed at their nervous behavior. This had happened many times with people who were not regular churchgoers.

Kedra said, "My husband and I would like to invite you to come to our church tomorrow." Emma and Frederick both looked a little hesitant because of their bad experiences with The Preacher, but after talking with them a little longer, they told them that they would love to visit with them.

When they got back to their apartment, Dave and his parents were sitting outside. Frederick immediately ran over to where they were. Dave asked him where they had been, and he told Dave that they had visited the grocery store and the church that was just up the street. Mrs. Spencer told Frederick that she knew about the church. They had some friends who attended the church, and they had visited the church with them a couple of times. She also told him that they were planning to go visit the church on Sunday. Dave said, "Great, Freddie, we can put on our suits and walk to church together." The boys were then off to scout out the apartment complex and find out whom else lived there.

Emma heard everything that the Spencers were saying about the church. She told them that she and Frederick liked the minister and his wife. She asked them what they called the minister. Mrs. Spencer told her they either called him Reverend Charles or Pastor. Emma said, "Thank you. I just wanted to make sure."

Mrs. Spencer asked Emma if she was comparing him to Reverend Dolan, The Preacher. Emma glanced down not wanting Mrs. Spencer to see any emotions in her eyes. Mrs. Spencer told Emma that she had seen him bothering her and other people in the complex. He was going around asking about all the boys in the complex to see if they would like to visit his church. He evidently has some type of farm, and he gets young boys to come and help him with the farming. He takes in young boys and says that he is teaching them how to work the land. She said that she thought that he was just trying to get cheap labor. All of the boys that work around the farm wear old clothes with patches on them, but he and his son wear suits every day. He walks the streets daily trying to get people to come to his church, especially if they have young boys.

Emma was looking embarrassed and told Mr. and Mrs. Spencer that she should be going. Mrs. Spencer asked her if she had offended her about something, and Emma told her no, that everything was fine. She just had some things that she needed to do.

She was not ready to talk with anyone about her son and The Preacher.

21

Reverend Michael Charles

Sunday morning after breakfast, Emma dressed in her best dress, and Frederick wore his suit. Emma was glad that she had left a big hem in Frederick's pants and sleeves because she could tell that he had already grown about an inch since they bought the suit.

Emma's grandparents had always taken her and her cousin to church when they were little. They always went to Sunday school and then to the worship service. She actually enjoyed going to church then, but after she and Harry were married, he never wanted them to go anywhere together, especially to church. He said that he had no desire to mingle with a bunch of Holy Rollers, so she had no experience in going to church as an adult, except for the Sunday she and Frederick visited The Preacher's church. She sure did not want to go through that experience again.

When they heard the tap on the door, Frederick said, "It's Dave!" When he opened the door, Dave and his parents were standing outside ready to go to church.

As they walked to the church, Mrs. Spencer told Emma that she was going to love the church. Had it not been so far from their other apartment complex, they would have already been attending service there.

When they got to the church, the bells were ringing. It was a signal that church would be starting in five minutes. Dave and Frederick ran up the steps to the door and opened it for their parents.

Standing immediately inside the door was a very friendly couple that greeted them as they came in. They shook their hands, told them that their names were Joann and Jim, and welcomed them to the church. The man told Dave and Frederick if they were not over twelve, they could go to the children's church if they liked, or they could stay with their parents. Frederick said, "Do you think that we look old enough to be over twelve?"

The man laughed and said, "You sure look mature in those suits."

Dave and Frederick both held their shoulders up high and said that they would stay with their parents this Sunday; then, Frederic said, "If we come back again, maybe we can go to the children's church."

The man told them if they did, they might want to wear comfortable clothes that they could play in, because after their children's service, the teachers took them outside to play and gave them snacks to eat. "When you come to the worship service with your parents, you can wear your suits." Frederick asked the man if they served snacks in the big church. The man laughed and said, "Only when we have communion." He then opened the door for them to go into the sanctuary. Emma had been in other churches before, but none had ever been as beautiful as this church was.

Almost as soon as they sat down, someone started playing a piano and then someone started playing an organ and the choir entered the church in beautiful robes. They remained standing until Reverend Charles came forward and welcomed everyone to their church and asked them to please turn to their neighbors and greet them. "If you do not know them, introduce yourselves," he said. After everyone greeted one another, Reverend Charles said a prayer. Everyone sat back down, and the music started again, and the choir began to sing. Frederick had never heard a choir sing. He thought that it was the most beautiful sound he had ever heard.

The order of service was also beautiful and very spiritual. When they passed the offering plate, Emma put in a dollar, and Frederick put a dime in the plate. He was not going to be too generous until he found out if John was going to let him and Dave work around the new apartment complex. His mother told him to take some of his money to church to put in the offering plate. He asked her how much it cost to go to church. She told him that it did not cost anything to go to church, but the church helped many people in the community, and it cost money for the upkeep on the church and all the buildings and grounds around it, so everyone gives an offering when they go to church. He asked how much should he put in the plate, and she told him that was between him and God.

Frederick looked at his mother and said, "How do we ask God how much we should put in?" Emma told him to listen to his heart. After he debated on that for a while, he remembered when they were at The Preacher's church; Reverend Dolan said that every person should give at least 10 percent of everything they owned to the church. Frederick decided to put a dime in the plate.

After the benediction, Reverend Charles stood at the door, bidding everyone a good day and shaking everyone's hands. Emma told him that she really appreciated him inviting them to church. She told him that she enjoyed every minute of the service and he would definitely be seeing her and Frederick again. Emma thought that Reverend Charles was nice and was thankful that he was nothing like The Preacher.

When they got outside, people that had not shook their hands during the service came up to them, introduced themselves, welcomed them to the church, and told them that they hoped they would come back again. Emma had never shaken so many hands in her life.

All the way home, everyone was talking about the church. Everyone loved it, and Dave told Frederick that he had been to the Sunday school before, and he really liked it. If Frederick wanted to, they would go to the children's church instead of going to the big people's service the next time they went. Frederick agreed that it was a little difficult to sit still for a whole hour, so the boys started making their plans for the next Sunday.

While they were eating lunch, Frederick said to his mother, "Mom, Reverend Charles's church is sure not anything similar The Preacher's church. I really enjoyed going to church today." Emma patted him on the head and told him that she had enjoyed it also and was looking forward to going again next Sunday.

22

Orientation

Before the women could go to work, they would have to go through an orientation program. Monday morning when the women came for the orientation, most of them were nervous because of the type of work that would be involved.

Mr. Brian Woodie introduced himself as the personnel director for the munitions plant. He first told the women about jobs that were available and the pay they would receive per hour worked and the shifts where there were openings.

Mr. Woodie said, "First let me tell you women how much we appreciate you coming to our company seeking employment, while our men are at war. We know that most of you are not accustomed to performing work outside your traditional gender expectation. We know that it is going to be a great sacrifice for all of you because you may have homes to maintain and children to take care of as well as being out in the workplace now."

He paused and then said, "In addition, we hope that you understand that you will not earn the salary normally paid to the men, who previously held these positions. As you know, these jobs are only temporary because you will only be filling in for the men until they return from the war. If the men are willing to risk their lives for our country, the least we can do is to assure them that their jobs will be waiting for them when they return home."

Mr. Wood proceeded to tell them that some of the jobs available were in areas such as metals, chemicals, munitions, shipbuilding, and engineering. "There would be different steps assigned to some of the jobs. Some will be putting the cordite into the shells and another group will put together the fuses. It is very repetitive work, and it will demand your attention the entire time you are working. It is very important that you do not talk while working, unless it is necessary or if there is an emergency."

"Gun shells, explosives, and other materials are needed to fight the war, so you need to learn quickly and efficiently so that the weapons will be ready when needed. You have to be very careful when handling the explosives because unexpected gunfire will put you at great risk."

He also told them that not only was the work dangerous, it was also very stressful, and they may be required to work long hours, six or seven days per week, and many times, the job would require them to work double time.

"It gets hot inside the buildings because the machines put off an enormous amount of heat. It is noisy, and there will be noxious fumes and possibly other dangers involved, such as shells exploding or firearms that will shoot when not expected. If you become drowsy, you have headaches, eczema, loss of appetite, and shortness of breath, you feel like vomiting, your heart is beating fast, you find your urine is not the same color, you are turning yellow, or you have a lot of pain in your arms or legs, you should let your supervisor know immediately."

One last thing Mr. Woodie said, "We do not allow propaganda of any kind in or on the grounds of this establishment, whether it is for the war or against the war. If you are caught doing this, you will be terminated immediately."

Mr. Woodie paused and then said, "I am sure that you women will appreciate what our men have to go through, once you start your employment here. If you feel that you cannot do these jobs, you may want to apply at the knitting plant down the street. In that plant, they knit socks for the military. If you are more interested in knitting instead of working in this factory, please feel free to leave now."

Five women left.

Mr. Woodie said, "If you are trained in nursing or wish to train in nursing, they could use you in the military. There are also other military jobs available. If any of you women would like to sign up for any of those positions, there is an office just down the street that will help you enlist. Please do not enlist in search of a husband, enlist to serve your country."

Two very homely women left.

Emma, Sophia, and Vera stayed put as well as about twenty-five other women. Vera whispered to Sophia and Emma, "Are we crazy or something for staying here?"

Sophia rolled her eyes as though she was having that same thought. Emma knew that she would do whatever she had to do in order to survive because she had no other choice.

23

Questions

At the end of the orientation, Mr. Woodie asked the women if they had any questions. There were plenty of hands raised. He told the women that he would try to answer as many of their questions as he possibly could, within the time that he had allotted for the orientation.

Sophia asked the first question wanting to know exactly when the war started and why.

This was not they type of question Mr. Woodie anticipated, but he answered it anyway and said, "The beginning of World War II goes back as far back as 1931 when Japan invaded Manchuria. Between 1931 up to December 1941 there were many wars going on involving Germany, Italy, China, France, Great Britain, Soviet Union, Poland, Greece, Hungary, but the United States was not involved in any of them until the Japanese bombed Pearl Harbor on December 7, 1941. December 8, 1941 is when President Franklin D. Roosevelt declared war on Japan in retaliation."

He asked the women if they had heard the news announcement on the radio about the attack on Pearl Harbor. He told them that he would never forget that day. He and his wife were listening to the radio. All of a sudden, the music stopped playing. The announcer said that Japanese aircraft carriers launched a deadly attack on

Pearl Harbor. They hit the USS Arizona with an armor-piercing bomb that sunk the battleship and killed over one thousand men. Off and on they continued interrupting the broadcasting the entire day, and the bombing was all they talked about.

Vera raised her hand, and Mr. Woodie pointed to her. Vera said, "If the United States was not involved in the war at that time, why did the Japanese bomb Pearl Harbor?"

Mr. Woodie told her that the Japanese were tired of negotiations with the United States. Japan wanted to continue their expansion within Asia, but the United States placed an extremely restrictive embargo on them in hopes of curbing their aggression. Rather than giving in to the United States, they launched a surprise attack in an attempt to destroy all of the United States Naval power.

He said, "I have heard that Commander Mitsuo Fuchida, leader of the air attack, called out 'Tora, Tora, Tora,' meaning 'Tiger, Tiger, Tiger,' a coded message that told the entire Japanese navy that they had caught the Americans totally by surprise."

When he finished talking, another woman raised her hand and asked, "As smart as the United States is, why did they not know of the attack, and how long did the attack last?

Mr. Woodie said, "By 9:45 a.m., less than two hours after the attack had begun, the Japanese planes left Pearl Harbor and headed back to their aircraft carriers."

There were hands popping up all over the room wanting to ask questions and Mr. Woodie could see that the questions were starting to affect some of the women. When he saw Emma Carswell wiping tears from her eyes, he knew that it was possible that her husband may have been one of the men killed during that attack. Whatever the reason, he could tell that it was greatly affecting her when he saw her silently leave the room.

Mr. Woodie felt that he needed to close the meeting because it was turning into more of a discussion about the war than about the job openings. He excused himself to the women and told them that he did not have any more time and that he needed to get back to his office. Before leaving, he told the women they would receive a half a day's pay for attending the orientation and told the women if they had any more questions involving employment, he would try to schedule another meeting with them later.

On the way back to his office, Mr. Woodie just shook his head. Women were good workers, but they just took up too much time and ask too many questions that did not pertain to any of the jobs, and they were getting too emotional about his answers. He could not believe how little they knew about the war, and he did not have the time or the patience to give them all the information they were seeking. Had these women been wearing blindfolds? Did they never read a newspaper?

There was a nasty war going on and most of those women did not know anything about what was going on beyond the confines of their homes. If they were going to be good workers, he knew they needed to be completely knowledgeable as to what they were doing and why they were doing it.

This was not normal work for women, and Mr. Woodie hated hiring them to do the jobs, but he had no other choice. Other countries had begun doing the same thing. There were so many men all over the world fighting, and the only people left to do the work were these dainty little women and in some cases young children.

24

Emotions

Vera followed Emma outside and could tell that she was still crying. She walked over to her and put her arms around her. Just the gentle touch of someone who genuinely cared meant a lot to Emma. Vera listened to the heart-wrenching sobs from Emma and knew that she needed to let out whatever it was that was affecting her, and Vera was not going to leave her alone until she knew that she was going to be okay.

Sophia and some of the other women were leaving the building getting ready to go home. When they saw what was happening to Emma, they all walked over to where she and Vera were standing. Mr. Woodie's car was in the parking lot outside the plant, and they all stood around it in support of Emma. Some of them were whispering, and some of them thought they were feeling some of the same sadness that Emma was feeling. Some of them had tears in their eyes. Most of them had lost someone who was either a friend, family member, or someone they loved in the war, and they thought they could feel Emma's pain. None of them could have ever imagined the real reason that caused Emma to be so emotional.

Finally, when Emma quit crying, they all gathered around her, giving her hugs and saying words of comfort. Emma had never felt as welcomed to a group of friends as she was with these women. She was not ready to tell anyone about the things that happened to her, but she knew that if the time ever came that she felt comfortable talking, she would have a wonderful support group.

Most of the things that happened to Emma would be almost unbelievable by most of those women. She knew that she had many people to be thankful for in her life. She was very thankful for her grandparents most of all, for loving and raising her and her cousin and always being there when she needed them. Sara and Charles helped her as much as they possibly could. The first chance she got, she was going to take the bus and go talk to them. Surely, by now they have found out something about the couple that has Patrick. She felt comfort in knowing that he was safe and cared for. Nevertheless, he was still her child, and she grieved over him.

Someday she hoped that Donald would know how much she loved him and would eventually come back to her. If not, she knew that he was where he wanted to be.

Speaking of friends, Misty and John saved her and Frederick from possible harm. She knew there was something wrong with Bob Frasier when she first met him, but she did not figure it out until he had tried to force her to do something against her will. He thought he had her in a position that she could not say no. She was so thankful that Misty and John took control of the situation. She could only imagine what may have happened, if they had not.

She was sorry that her job at the sewing mill had to end, but she understood what Misty had to do. She hoped that the job at the munitions plant would work out just as well. She would give them her best work and hope they would want to keep her if they had any jobs available after the war.

Then she thought to herself, *If they did keep me and some of the other women, it would probably mean that some soldiers probably lost their lives while fighting in the war or came home wounded and not able to work.* It did not matter how the war ended; Emma knew that she would have to find work somewhere.

Having a job and a steady income would give her more of a felling of security for her and Frederick. It is a terrible feeling when you do not have enough food in your house to feed your children.

While growing up in her grandmother's house, you could always smell fresh bread baking with at least one meal, and sometimes, it would be twice a day. During those days, she would have never dreamed that her life would have taken such a drastic turn.

25

Women in Combat

Mr. Woodie felt that everyone should take part in the war effort. Political and social leaders agreed that both women and men would have to change their perceptions of gender rolls. At least as long as there was a national emergency. Women were going to have to contribute in a variety of ways, but he would have never dreamed that he would see them working in a place like the munitions factory. He was concerned about them, but if he intended to fill the government work orders that were now coming in, he had no other choice. Instead of being just a locomotive plant, they were now building fighter and bomber planes and the ammunition for them. These women should not being doing manual labor working in plants like this.

There were a lot of political posters and subway cards portraying women in uniform putting on lipstick in a very provocative pose. The last poster he saw was a woman in full uniform, getting into a fighter plane. What was the world coming to?

Maybe he was from the old school, but women just did not belong in those types of jobs. They were too delicate, and they should be home baking cookies and taking care of their homes and their children. But he knew that it would be best if he kept those opinions to himself, especially during this war.

He felt that he had just witnessed what the war could do to women. All the information about the war was probably more than Emma Carswell could handle. He hoped that it did not scare any more of the women away from the jobs.

26

Assignments

After gathering all the women in the conference room, Mr. Woodie called out their names and jobs and told them who would be their immediate supervisor and what shift they would work. There was not enough time to allow the women to choose where they would like to work, so he chose for them.

Emma Patton Carswell, crane operator

Krista Smith, sheet metal mechanic

Kendall Campbell, machinist second class

Melinda Moody, radio mechanic

Chloe Matthew, grinder finisher

Cheryl Peppers, hair and clothing inspector

Brandy Wynn, metal and nail technician

LeeAnn Beckham, personnel assistant

Morgan Smith, riveter

Amanda Ryan, radio installer

Brook Erikson, airplane mechanic

Debby Waldrop Strait, journeyman welder

Clair Bailey, grinder finisher

Lorenda Collingwood, riveter

Judy Hornet, crane operator

Gail Snowman, crane operator

Carol Ann Friday, mechanical parts supervisor

Zoë Adele, riveter

Geneses Jonah, hydraulic inspection

Kaylee Nikolas, media support

Maria Grace, control panel assembly

Addison Moody, technical mechanic

Vera Neese, radium painter

Ashley McFallen, emergency equipment

Sophia Kennedy, hydraulic press

Kimberly Edwards, brake assembly

Ann Mackenzie, communications technician

Lillian Orion, riveter

Mr. Woodie walked back into his office after giving out the job assignments. He hoped that he was not going to regret hiring those women. Not giving them a choice as to where they would work was not something he normally did. Usually if there were vacancies, men would come in fill out an application for whatever job they had been seeking. They would interview them for the job, and if they were hired, they would meet their supervisors and assigned a shift. These women did not have any of those options.

As he looked at the women, you could tell they were frightened, and they had a right to be. He hoped that they would get more comfortable as each day passed. He watched as Emma Carswell tried to climb the ladder to the crane. The dress she had on was about two or three sizes too big for her. If she bought it to fit, she must have lost a lot of weight because it hung on her like a sack even with the belt she wore.

The next thing he saw was Sophia Kennedy standing near a machine. It would be very easy for that beautiful long hair to be sucked into the in the machine. If that happened, she would probably receive serious injuries.

There were some rules that he knew he would have to implement immediately, and he knew it would not go over well with some of the women because of their religious beliefs or social standing. The women would have to wear pants. He knew that it was not socially acceptable for women to wear pants in public, but he knew they would have to be a requirement for these jobs.

The next day he put out an addendum to the job descriptions. All women were to wear pants and flat shoes. No high heels would be acceptable even if they were the type that had the low heel and laced up the front. They would also have to wrap their hair in scarves and tie the scarves tightly to their heads.

When he told the women they would have to wear pants, scarves, and no high heels, you could have heard a pin drop in the room. He had already prepared himself for that response.

He told the women that he was going to make a room called the water house, and he would install little lockers for each of them. If they did not want to wear pants on their way to work, they could wear a dress and then change into pants in the water house before going into the plant. They would also have a seating area put in there where they could go and eat or rest during their breaks.

He told them that he was open for further suggestions if any of them had any.

One of the women asked if they could wait until after they received their first week's pay before they had to wear pants. She told him that she did not have any pants, and her husband's pants would be too large for her. She said that she would be very grateful if he would.

Mr. Woodie told the women that they could have a week before he would enforce the clothing requirement, but low heels and a scarf for their hair was a mandatory requirement and enforced immediately. Regardless as to how it looked, they were also required to wear all safety gear to prevent accidents from happening.

The next day when they came to work, about half of the women were wearing pants. Some of them looked like they may have on their husband's pants because they were so baggy. Even a large belt holding them up could not camouflage the fact that they were men's pants. He had to smile when he looked at them. At least they were trying. He did not know of a single store that sold women's pants, and he knew that the women would have to wear men's pants or make their own. He did not shop in the women's departments in stores, but he would make a point of asking his wife, Stacy, if they sold women's pants in any of the stores where she shopped.

Emma Carswell wore her big dress the next day, but she had it cut from the hem to above her knees, and it looked like maybe she had hand stitched it together. He would consider that acceptable attire until she was able to get some pants that would fit her. She was so tiny she would probably have to shop in the boys department for pants. If any of the other women asked to do their dresses like that, he would accept it as long as there was not a lot of material flowing around the bottom.

Within about a month, most of the women were comfortable with their assignments. Most of them wore their pants to work, but a few of them wore their dresses and then changed after they got to work.

He walked by their water house one day, and he could hear a lot of laughter. He considered himself lucky that he was able to hire a group of women who got along well with each other and worked well together. That had been one of his biggest concerns.

The women also proved that they could not only do the job well, but in some instances, they were doing them better than the men did. They were so careful that nothing got by them unless it was right.

The women earned a much lower salary than the men who did the same job. However, they were still making more money than they would have been making in sewing mills or housekeeping for someone, and that made all of them happy.

It was dirty work, and the women were glad that pants were required because it was almost impossible to keep their laundry caught up with the hours they had to work.

The men who were training the women seemed amazed that the women were capable of do the jobs so efficiently.

Mr. Woodie recently read a story in the paper about a woman who died in a munitions plant when some shells exploded unintentionally. A slight slip of the hand when drilling into a shell or the simple misplacement of a fuse could have drastic and deadly consequences

It seemed that most women had excitable temperaments and lacked technical instincts and he was afraid they would wind up causing accidents. He was impressed as to how well the women were able to handle the guns.

He and some men at the mill had been talking about how many women were joining the military. In many countries involved in the war, they allowed the women to serve but restricted them from killing anyone, and the women could not be court marshaled. They also could not receive medals of valor or recognized for their service in the military, and Brian thought that was wrong.

From what he had heard, about fifty Japanese American and Chinese American women worked in the Intelligence Service Language School. Twenty-one women were in the Pacific

Military Intelligence Research, and they were working with captured Japanese. The navy, however, refused to accept any Japanese women even if they were Japanese American.

Mr. Woodie had some married women in his newly hired employees, but most of them were single, hard working, and very physically fit. They probably built muscle sweeping, mopping, cooking, picking up after their family, and carrying children around all day, plus digging and working in their yards or gardens.

As Brian sat at his desk, he thought, *The women have to be very tired when they go home. It is amazing as to how proficient they are at getting their work done.*

Most days I am so tired that all I want to do when I go home is to sit down, read the newspaper, eat dinner, and then go to bed.

He could only imagine what these poor women had to go through, working such long, strenuous hours and then have to go home and do everything alone. Sometimes they also had to work double shifts.

Stacy was able to sleep until about 6:00 a.m. every morning. She then gets dressed and makes breakfast, and while they were eating, she made the beds. When the kids were are all dressed, she walked them to school. She gets to her classroom around 7:45 a.m. She greets her classroom of about thirty, fourth-graders students and teaches them from 8:00 a.m. to 3:00 p.m., After school, she walks home with the kids. If she needs anything for dinner, she has the time to stop at the grocery store to get it. When she gets home, she gets the kids started on their homework and then starts dinner. After dinner, she cleans up the kitchen, washes a load of clothes, makes sure all homework is finished; then, baths are given and children put in bed and the laundry is dried and put away. She then does her lesson plan for the next day. When she finally came to bed, Brian would try to let her know how much he appreciated her by snuggling up close and putting his arm around her. Many times, she removed it and scooted over to the edge of the bed. He had to admit that he was a little hurt when she did that but would not dare say anything. He was too good of a husband to do that.

He had told Stacy on numerous occasions that she needed to come to bed earlier or take a nap during the day the way he did. At night when they were in bed together was the only time they had a chance to be alone without the kids. When he reminded her of that, she would sometimes give him that cute little sweet puckered smile, her eyes would squint, and wrinkles appeared on her forehead. He was so thankful that Stacy got a good education, enabling her to have a better career, and only has to work seven hours per day and not have to do men's work as those women did.

Brian had no idea as to how tired Stacey really was by the time she was able to go to bed at night. She was too good of a wife to say anything.

27

Knight in a White Sailor's Uniform

The women had now been working in the munitions plant for several months. They sometimes had to work on weekends in order to fill the orders coming in from the government, so they really did not have a lot of time to socialize outside of work and family.

Several of the single women were talking about how they would still like to go out and meet some men. Vera told them about a place where sailors go when they are docked in the Naval Basin. If you just wanted to dance and have fun, it was a good place to go, but if you were looking for a husband, they would probably have to wait until the war was over. Most of the sailors they met either were married or had a girlfriend back home waiting for them. They are only there to have a good time.

Most of the women only wanted a break from their monotonous jobs, so Vera told them where the dance was located and said that she and Sophia would probably see them there. They tried to talk Emma into going with them, and she told them that she might, if Frederick could spend the night with Dave but could not if he wanted to stay home.

Early Saturday morning, Frederick and Dave were busy cleaning up trash in the parking areas and along the road. She wondered if John only hired them because he knew the boys needed the money. John swore to her one day that it was because they did a good job.

When she asked Frederick if he had plans for the evening, he told her that Dave wanted him to spend the night at his apartment. They were building something, and Dave's father was helping them. She did not ask him what it was because she knew that if Frederick did not tell her something, it was because he did not want her to know about it. He would be with Dave and his father, so she knew that he would be okay.

Emma washed and rolled her hair and took a bath before preparing Frederick's dinner. When he came in, she was just going into the kitchen to start the meal. He told her that Dave's mom had invited him to eat dinner with them, and he wanted to know if it was okay. She told him that it was okay. That worked for Emma also because she would be able to take a short nap before going out with the girls.

The short nap turned into three hours. Vera and Sophia woke her up when they knocked on her apartment door. When she went to the door in her robe, they thought that she was not going to go with them. When she told them what happened, they started helping her to get dressed for the evening.

Emma had several new dresses now, and they helped her to choose one to wear. It felt great to be in a dress and heels again because they were tired of wearing pants all of the time. With their hair pulled up under a scarf and no lipstick on, they felt that they looked like men.

Sophia was good with hair, so she took the pins out of Emma's hair and pulled it up from around her neck and pinned it up with hairpins. She did the sides the same way, and the style looked great on her. Before she quit, Sophia made two kiss curls beside her ears and two on her forehead. Emma had never felt so beautiful before.

When they got to the dance, she was the first one asked to dance.

Sophia sniffed and said she was not going to make Emma look so good the next time, because she was attracting all of the men. Vera elbowed her and laughed.

When the next song started playing, a sailor walked toward their table. Vera got up and stood in front of Emma. The sailor smiled and looked around her to Emma. Vera got a bit hurt this time, but not for long. By the time the sailor got Emma to the dance floor, other sailors were coming over and asking all of them to dance also.

The sailor that Emma was dancing with told her that his name was Sylvester Bandowski, but his father called him Sly, and now almost everyone called him that. The only person that called him Sylvester was his mother and his officers. He laughed and said that he did not care what they called him, as long as they called him to dinner.

They danced almost every dance that night. When they were not dancing, they were either sitting at the table talking or standing at the edge of the dance floor talking. Sly told Emma that he really enjoyed dancing with her and talking with her and wished that he could see her again before he left, but they were pulling out the next day, and he did not know when or if he would be back because they were going to very dangerous territory.

That night after the last song played, Sly asked Emma if she walked home or if she rode the bus. She told him that she and some of her friends walked together. He asked if he could walk with them. Emma told him that she would like that.

Vera and Sophia had also met sailors that wanted to walk them home also. The six of them walked and talked all the way to Emma's apartment complex. Sophia and Vera told Emma good night and told her that they would see her on Monday. Sly walked Emma to her door, and the other two sailors walked Sophia and Vera to their apartment.

As they stood at her door talking, he told her that he would really like to see her again. She smiled and told him that he knew where she lived; she also told him where she worked. He was a little amazed when she told him that she was a crane operator. He thought it was funny because she was such a tiny little thing to be working with such a large piece of equipment. He said, "I have always heard that good things always come in small packages, and you prove that to be true."

Emma did not invite him in as he had hoped that she would, but they did stand at her door talking for a long time. When they heard laughter, they looked to where the laughter was coming from. They saw two small heads peaking out of a window. Frederick was waiting up for her just as he always did at the other apartment. Instead of staying the night at Dave's apartment, he and Dave decided to stay at Frederick's apartment so that he would be there to make sure his mother got home okay. Mr. Spencer was okay with that because he would be next door if the boys needed him.

Sly laughed and asked who the two boys were. She looked up at him and said, "One of them is my neighbor's son and the other is my son Frederick."

Sly was startled because he thought that Emma was single.

About that time she heard Frederick say, "Well, are you going to kiss her good night or what?"

Emma laughed and said, "That is Frederick, my son!"

Sly said, "Well, I don't think that we should disappoint the young man." He then kissed Emma.

Emma was embarrassed, but as soon as Sly put his arms around her and kissed her, the embarrassment was forgotten. As he tightened his hold and kissed her more passionately, Emma responded the same way. Sly was stirring emotions that Emma had never felt before in her life, and she was enjoying it.

Sly did not want to let Emma go, and it appeared that she felt the same way. Not only did Sly stir emotions in Emma, she was having quite an affect on him also. He could feel how nervous she was when he first took her into his arms, but she just seemed to melt as soon as he started kissing her.

When Sly pulled away from Emma, he knew that he wanted to know everything about this beautiful woman. They stood there holding each other, looking into each other's eyes, as though they were looking into each other's souls.

Frederick and Dave interrupted their thoughts when they heard the boys laughing. Emma laughed and said, "I would like to introduce you to my son, Frederick, and his best friend, Dave Spencer. And, boys, this is Sylvester Bandowski"

Frederick looked at Sly and said, "Glad to meet cha...sir." He couldn't figure out how to pronounce Sylvester or Bandowski so he just said sir. He then put out his hand to shake Sly's and so did Dave.

Sly said, "It is nice to meet you, Frederick, and you also, Dave."

Frederick looked at Sly and said, "Everyone calls me Freddie or Fred. Only my mom calls me Frederick.

Sly said, "Fred, my name is Sylvester, and everyone calls me Sly except for my mother, and she always calls me Sylvester." Sly was very impressed with both Frederick and Dave, and the boys liked him immediately.

When Emma walked Sly out, the boys had their heads back in the window.

Sly told her that he was serious about wanting to see her again. He said that after just one evening together, he was not going to be ridiculous and ask her to wait on him.

He asked her, if he made it back, would she allow him to call on her again?

Emma was so impressed with Sly because she had never met anyone with such good manners. The way Sly treated her made her feel special. The way he treated the boys made him even more special to her.

She asked Sly how old was he, and he told her that he was twenty-four years old. She said, "Sly, I am almost thirty years old and have a son."

He looked at her and said, "I don't care if you are fifty. I am still attracted to you."

Emma smiled at his remark and said, "Sly, if you are serious, I would love to see you when you get back." She was careful not to say *if*. He told her that if he made it through the war, he definitely would be back to see her. She told him that she would be praying that he would make it through the war safe and would be anxiously awaiting his return. He gave her an address where she could write to him, and he wrote down her address.

Sly then pulled her into him arms, looked into her eyes, and then kissed her with the same sweet passion as before. When he pulled away, he said, "Emma Patton Carswell, I think I have just fallen in love tonight. I have danced with many girls but never enjoyed it as much as I did when I danced with you tonight. There was just a very special feeling when we would hold each other close and dance together. Also, I have never felt this way when I have kissed someone before."

Sly was looking straight into Emma's eyes when he said those words. Before he left, he pulled her into his arms one last time, and the boys were enjoying every moment watching Emma and Sly.

Sly slowly slid his head down Emma's arm to her hand and then kissed her hand before walking away.

Emma pulled her hand to her mouth as though kissing her hand where he had kissed it and watched as Sly walked down the street and until he turned the corner to catch the bus to take him back to his ship.

Emma stood outside her apartment, hoping the bus would pass her apartment as it normally did. Sure enough, in just a few minutes, the bus passed. Sly waved and threw her a kiss as the bus passed. Emma's heart was pounding, and she knew that she felt a very special connection to Sly. She did not want to put the word *love* to the feeling, but it was a feeling that she had never experienced in her almost thirty years of life.

When Emma walked back inside the apartment, the boys were laughing and cheering. Dave said, "When I grow up, I want to be a sailor, and I am going to kiss a girl just like that.

Frederick said, "Me too, but I don't want to do it until I do grow up though." The boys then ran to Frederick's room and went to bed.

Emma went to sleep that night with a very good feeling. She could not believe that Sly told her that he thought that he had already fallen in love with her. She was not sure that it was love, but it sure gave her a good feeling knowing that someone cared enough about her to treat her the way Sly treated her and could stir feelings in her that she had never felt before. It would be wonderful if he would be her knight in a white sailor's uniform, and they would live happily ever after. She had a similar dream once before with Harry, but he had never held her and looked into her eyes the way Sly did, not even after they were married, and he certainly did not make her tingle when he kissed her. Of course, he never kissed her the way Sly did either. She shivered at the thoughts of those kisses.

28

Victory Garden

Sunday morning Frederick and Dave were awake and out of bed before Emma. They woke her up with their laughing and talking. Frederick had changed so much and was now a happy boy, and he was friendly with everyone. When he saw something that he could do for someone, he was right there to help. Everyone in the apartment complex liked him and Dave.

Emma had to give a lot of credit to Dave for bringing Frederick out of his shell. The Spencers had suffered greatly because of the war, but thankfully, Mr. Spencer now had a good job as a supervisor at the munitions plant, and Mrs. Spencer worked from home knitting socks for the military so that she could be home with Dave. She told Emma that it would be great if she would allow Frederick to stay with her while she worked. It would give Dave someone to play with.

After breakfast, Emma and Frederick walked to church with the Spencers. They all had grown to love the church. They were especially fond of Reverend Michael Charles and his wife, Kedra, and their two-year-old son, Blake, was very adorable with his million-dollar smile.

Frederick and Dave were now going to Sunday school with the younger children. They said that the teachers always gave them snacks to eat that were very tasty. The snacks had tasted better when they first started going to church, but since they were rationing sugar, the snacks weren't quite as sweet, but they still tasted good.

As they were walking home from church, Mr. Spencer told his wife that he would join her later at home. He said that he needed to take a walk behind the apartment complex to check on something. The boys looked at each other, and Dave told his father that there was nothing out there except for tall weeds.

Mr. Spencer told them that he knew there were high weeds, but John had told him that there was a vacant lot behind the apartments where they had intended to build another apartment building. When the war began, the building project had to be put on hold. Mr. Spencer said that he and some of the other tenants in the apartment complex asked John if they could clear the lot and plant a garden. Everyone was planting what he or she called Victory Gardens. With everything rationed, it could help greatly as a source of food. John told them that he would talk to the managers, and he would let them know if it would be okay with them. He came back to them a few days later and told them go ahead with their garden, but he wanted to make sure that everyone was in on it so that there would be no major conflicts among the tenants.

Mr. Spencer helped plan the garden and how they all could share in making and maintaining it. Every day you could see people out there working, clearing the brush and tall grass. Some were burning debris, and others had shovels or hoes turning up the soil. The bad thing was that Frederick and Dave would have to build another fort to play in because their fort had been in a big oak tree right in the middle of where everyone was going to plant the garden. They knew they could not have any fun if adults were working around the tree, so they decided to scout for another location for their fort.

The first Monday after Labor Day, Emma and Mrs. Spencer took Frederick and Dave to register them for the first grade in the Garden City Elementary School. The boys were beside themselves with the excitement.

The school was only a few blocks from the apartment complex, and the boys would be able to walk to and from school. There were other children in the complex going to the same school, so they had a large group that would be walking every day. Parents formed a group, and they would take turns walking with the children every morning and back home in the afternoon.

The first day of school, the boys were full of excitement. They both had belts which they were going to loop and buckle around their books so that they could sling them over their shoulders and carry them as the older boys did.

Frederick and Dave had the same first grade teacher, and that made it even better. They went to school together and then did their homework together after school. To their parents' amazement, the boys never had any serious disagreements. They did not always agree on everything, but they always worked it out between themselves, and none of their disagreements seemed serious.

On the Monday before Thanksgiving, Emma told Frederick that she would have Thanksgiving Day off and asked him if he would like to go see his sister and his grandmother and eat Thanksgiving dinner with them. He said that he would really like to see them but wanted to know if Dave could go with them because he had never taken a long bus trip before.

Emma told him that Dave could go with them if it was okay with his parents. When Dave asked his mother if he could go, she did not agree at first, but after Dave and Frederick persisted and Emma told her that she would love to have him to go with them, she eventually gave in and told him that he could go. She even gave them a pumpkin pie to take with them.

It was starting to get cool outside. The coat that Emma bought for Frederick the year before would barely close, and the sleeves were getting too short. They had a switch program going on in the apartment complex. You could swap your child's clothing that was too small for larger clothing that was too small for an older child. Sometimes the adults would swap, if they had lost or gained weight. It kept them from having to go out and buy new clothes, which most of them could not afford. Emma needed to check with them to see if anyone had a coat that would fit Frederick.

Frederick and Dave talked and laughed the entire trip. Emma laid her head back listening to them and then let her mind wander back to the delicious kisses Sly gave her before he left. She had written him almost weekly, but she had never received a letter back from him. She feared for the worst. She also knew that he could have found someone else that he may have fallen for who was more his age and did not have a son. She was trying to decide if perhaps she should stop writing to him. She did not want to be embarrassed if she ever ran into him sometime and him be with someone else. In every letter that she wrote, she told him about everything that was happening and about other things that involved her and Frederick. However, she never mentioned her pre-sewing plant era or her husband.

She knew that if she ever wanted to get married again, she would have to get a divorce from Harry, but she had no idea as to how she should go about doing that. She had never known anyone personally who had ever gotten a divorce. When everyone in her family and circle of friends were married, they stayed married, unless one of them passed away. She decided that she would cross that bridge when she came to it. For now, she was just going to enjoy being happy for a change.

Frederick never mentioned anything about their past and had quit asking questions about Patrick or Donald. It was as if he had just accepted everything as it was. Emma hoped that by him having the life he had now, he would forget all the bad things that had happened to them. Even with the war going on, she and Frederick were in a much better place in life than they had ever been. They no longer had to live in fear, as they once did.

Just thinking about everything that had happened to her and her children made Emma want to cry, but she would not let that happen now. Today they would go to her grandmother's house and enjoy spending time with her daughter and her grandmother and, of course, Uncle Charlie.

You could smell the aroma of food cooking when they were walking up the sidewalk. When Mary Byrd saw them, she called Henrietta, they ran out to meet them, and it was a wonderful homecoming. When Emma looked up, she saw her uncle Charlie standing on the porch with that same humorous look on his face. She sometimes wondered what he had been like as a child.

They were not able to get a turkey for the Thanksgiving meal, but they did have a large hen, and everything tasted wonderful. Emma thought that it always tasted better when you did not have to prepare it yourself. It had been a long time since she had cooked a big meal. After the meal, Uncle Charlie took the boys out to help him cut wood, the way Grandpa always did.

After helping her grandmother and her mother clean up the kitchen, Henrietta asked her mother if she would like to see her room, and Emma said that she sure would.

Uncle Charlie had built shelves for Henrietta, and she had put all of her toys and all of Emma's old toys on the shelves. When her grandmother asked Henrietta if she would like to go through some of her mother's and her aunt's toys, Henrietta said that she would love to go through the ones that her mother had played with. She told her mother that they always made her feel good when she played with them, knowing that she had played with the same toys when she was a young girl.

Emma told Henrietta that she was welcome to come and visit them or come and live with them if she liked. Henrietta said, "Mom, I have made a lot of friends here, and I don't mean to hurt your feelings, but I would much rather live here with Grandma instead of living in those places where we lived and be scared all the time and not ever having enough to eat."

Emma was startled because Henrietta had never said anything like that before. It was almost verbatim to what Donald had said. She had always been so worried about them that she never though at the time as to how her children felt living in that situation.

She had no idea that Henrietta still thought about how their life once was because she always seemed so happy when she saw her. She was thankful that Henrietta was now settled into a lifestyle with her grandmother and her uncle, but at the same time, she grieved over the fact that her daughter did not want to live with her. She reached over and put her arms around her daughter, and they sat on the bed hugging each other for several minutes. It was all that Emma could do not to cry.

29

Is She Emma's Daughter?

After everyone was out of the house, Emma's grandmother told her that she had some information that she would like to share with her. She told her that she had found out that Harry had joined the navy.

She and Henrietta had been out shopping for school clothing when they ran into Harry's parents. Henrietta did not know who they were and asked her grandmother why they were staring at her. Finally, they came over and wanted to know if the beautiful young woman with her was possibly Emma's daughter. Mary said, "Of course I told her that she was, so Mrs. Carswell proceeded to ask me if there were other children."

She said that she told them in her very haughty voice that all the children were well; no thanks to Harry. Mr. Carswell barked and said, "I'll have you to know, woman, my son is in the navy fighting for his country."

Mary said that she stood there looking at him for a long time trying to make him feel uncomfortable, and then she said, "Mr. Carswell, I think the truth is that your son left his family and ran off and joined the navy to keep from supporting them."

Thankfully, Henrietta was looking at dresses and was not paying any attention to them. She told Henrietta to try on some of the dresses. Henrietta was excited because she had already chosen three that she wanted to try on.

The next thing her grandmother told her shocked her even more. Mary said, "Henrietta and Donald are going to the same school. Can you believe that The Preacher sends Donald to school in suits? Henrietta came home one day and told me that she thought she saw her brother at school, and he was wearing a suit, and the other kids were dressed in regular school clothes, and it made him stand out, and he acted as though he was someone special as he strutted around looking down on everyone else."

Henrietta told her that she thought about speaking to him when she saw him looking at her, but she decided if he wanted to talk to her, he would have to initiate the conversation. She was not going to allow him to embarrass her by pretending that he did not know her, the way he did her mother and brother.

Her grandmother said that Henrietta told her that after a few weeks, Donald finally came to her and told her that he was her brother. Henrietta told him that she knew that he was her brother, but after the way he acted after going to live with The Preacher, she was not sure that she wanted anyone to know that she and Donald were brother and sister.

Mary said, "Henrietta is becoming a very strong young lady. She is very different than she was when she first came to live with us. She has no problem standing up for herself"

Little by little, she and Donald have begun to be a little friendlier with each other. She still does not tell anyone that he is her brother, and as far as she knows, he has not told anyone that she is his sister. In fact, some of her girlfriends think that Donald is sweet on her. Henrietta lets them think what they want because she is actually smitten with a good-looking young fellow named Pete Fleenor. She thinks he likes her too, but he has not said anything to her. She says that he is always doing things to try to get her attention. He acts as if he is a little jealous of Donald because he is always wearing suits. She says if he would just let her know that he likes her, she would let him think he took her away from Donald. Mary shook her head and said, "Kids, I will never understand them."

Emma told her grandmother that she realized that Henrietta was becoming a very strong young woman, and she gave her full credit for molding her into the person she had become.

Mary thanked her and told her that she was trying and then gave Emma a big hug, letting her know that she was also special to her.

When it came time to go, none of them wanted to leave. It did not bother Frederick to say that he did not want to leave this time because Dave was with him, and he knew that his mother would not leave without Dave. It had been a nice visit, and Emma was feeling better about everything.

When they got to the corner to catch the bus, Frederick and Dave looked like they were both ready for bed, and they slept all the way home.

When they got home, both of the boys had no desire to stay up playing and went straight to bed. Emma had to work the next day, but Frederick could sleep in if he wanted to because Mrs. Spencer always made sure that he had breakfast, and if he had to go to school, she made sure that he was dressed properly.

Even though her job was hard, it was still a much better situation for her and Frederick, and they were both happy.

30

Operation Pied Piper

When Emma got to work on Friday morning, Sophia and Vera were anxious to talk to her. They wanted to plan to do something on Saturday night. They had rested up over Thanksgiving and were ready to get away from their jobs and have fun. Emma was not quite as rested as they were, but she did feel that a night out with her girlfriends would be fun.

When Emma got home from work, Mr. Spencer brought her the newspaper. Every time he bought one, he would pass it around to the other tenants after reading it. She decided to take a break and sit down and read it.

The headline news was about evacuating children. Some were now living with strangers.

The impact of the evacuation depended on your social status. Parents who had money made their own arrangements, but the other children were not as lucky. They gathered them at the train station, and neither the child nor their parents knew where they were going.

They were calling the evacuation Operation Pied Piper. The intentions were to save the children from the risks associated with aerial bombing of cities by moving them to areas thought to be less at risk. There were over three million people displaced, with around a third of their entire population experiencing some effects of the evacuation.

Over twenty thousand civil servants took their paperwork and were now working in hotels in the better coastal resorts and spa towns. They called it Plan Yellow.

Emma felt that her children had experienced similar trauma in their young lives. They were probably just as scared as the children in Europe who were in the middle of a war zone.

She remembered the day when Henrietta was just a tiny baby about three months old. Harry had always wanted his food prepared and hot the minute he walked in the door in the evening. If it was not ready and be exactly what he wanted to eat, he would get extremely angry.

One day in particular he was in one of his moods. He did not get what he wanted for dinner, so he did not eat. Instead, he dumped all the food in the garbage so that no one else could eat it either and then went to bed. Just as he was going to sleep, Henrietta started crying. He yelled out wanting to know what was wrong with that brat and then laid his head back down on the pillow and smiled. He hoped that she was crying because she was hungry. If Emma fed her, she would have to scoop the food out of the garbage can. He had actually eaten at the restaurant down the street before coming home, and that was why he did not want the food she had prepared. There was nothing wrong with the food; he just wanted to belittle Emma.

Emma was not able to calm Henrietta as fast as Harry thought she should, so he came into the baby's room, grabbed their three-month-old baby and gave her a very harsh spanking for crying and keeping him from being able to go to sleep.

As he spanked her, Henrietta cried harder, so he spanked her harder. Finally, he tossed her into her bed and left the room. The poor thing hit the bed so hard that it appeared to knock the breath out of her. After he left the room, Emma picked her baby up and tried to comfort her.

Emma could not believe that a person could beat a baby that was only three months old. She should have known what a sick person he was then. Anyone that would take his anger out on a poor defenseless baby had to be mentally deranged. What did that make her? She did nothing to protect Henrietta.

Henrietta had bruises all over her body and cried every time she tried to pick her up or change her diaper. She feared that Harry had broken one or more of her fragile bones.

After that when Harry was home, she tried to keep Henrietta out of his sight. A couple of nights she slept out on the porch with Henrietta snuggled up close to her. As long as she held her in her arms, Henrietta would not cry, but with Harry's insistent demands, she had to juggle feeding and nap times for the baby. That would keep her safe from her own father.

She should have left Harry then before the other children were born. She let her fear of insecurity, put her and the lives of her children in jeopardy.

She was almost positive that Harry was the cause of Frederick having problem with his shoulders and spine. She remembered one time that Frederick had been playing in the middle of the floor, and for some reason, Harry got upset with him. He walked over, jerked Frederick up, and held him in the air by his arms as if he wanted everyone to look at what he was doing to Frederick. It was as though he was holding up a prize kill. When she went over to get Frederick away from him, he knocked her down and then threw Frederick on top of her.

Another time she went into the dinning room and saw Harry standing in the middle of the floor holding Frederick by his arms, daring him to cry. When she asked him to put Frederick down, he threw Frederick to the floor and then grabbed her and held her up by both of her arms. It seemed like he held her there for about five minutes before dropping her to the floor. Her arms were so sore that she could hardly pick anything up for a couple of weeks. She could only imagine how poor Frederick felt.

After that, it did not matter how severely Harry spanked Frederick; he would do his best not to cry, but Harry would keep beating him until the poor child had no other choice but to give in and cry. After one of Harry's beatings, she heard Frederick say that someday he was going to take Harry down. She feared that some day when Frederick got older that he might have so much rage built up inside him that he would actually kill Harry or possibly someone else.

What did all of this say about her as a mother? She should have stopped Harry some way. She had always heard that all good wives must be submissive to their husbands. She heard their minister preach on that subject many times when she was a young child, and it had always stuck in her mind as to how she should be as a wife. She had often wondered if there was a God. If there was, why did he not do something to stop Harry?

Her grandmother told her that if he was her husband, she would wait until he went to bed and then she would hit him over the head with her cast iron frying pay. She told Emma that she would not put up with a man like Harry. She said that she would rather eat dirt and drink pee than stay with a man like Harry.

After Harry left, she had often wondered where he went. She kept thinking that he would walk in one day, and everything would be as it had been in the beginning, but she had not seen him after that day. The only thing she wanted now was that neither she nor her children ever have to see him again.

She wished there had been a Pied Pieper that would have come in and saved her children from their Harry. Their father was their greatest enemy. In her heart, she knew that she should have played the part of Pied Pieper and saved her children. Why did she not have the courage to stand up to him? She bet that no other true parent would have allowed such things to happen to their children. What did that make her? Was she just as bad?

31

Rowdy Sailors

Frederick spent Saturday night with Dave and his parents. When Vera and Sophia found out that Emma was alone, they talked her into going to the dance with them.

They wore their best dresses and shoes. All three were upset because they had heard that women's clothing would have to make some major changes. Width and length of the sleeves on women's clothing changed, and they could not have a belt wider than two inches. All three of them had dresses and belts that did not conform to those standards. They had purchased the clothing before the rule came out, but they feared they would get in trouble if they wore them. Were they going to have clothing police?

Some families were recycling all of their clothing. Women would sew strips of fabric together from old clothing to make quilt tops. They would take an old blanket that had seen better days and tack the quilt tops over the old blanket. It was very comforting for the children because the fabric from old family clothing made the blanket even more special.

It had not been that long ago that Emma remembered sewing patches on her clothes and on her children's clothes. There was no rationing then, but Harry would not buy any new clothes for them that were not necessary. He said they stayed home all the time, and no one saw them, so there was no need in spending money on new clothes when she could patch up the old ones.

Of course, that same rule did not apply to Harry. Even though he delivered coal, he was probably one of the best-dressed people around. It seemed as though his closet kept getting larger while she only had the clothes that she had when they were married, and the only items added to it were the big maternity dresses her grandmother gave her to wear while she was expecting.

She had been sewing strips of fabric from those dresses to make a quilt for her bed. They had many good memories because the dresses were from her grandmother.

She still had the dress where Harry made black marks on it from the coal residue on his hands and clothes. She cut around the darkened spots that would not come clean, but she saved a few scraps. Sometimes when she would think about what could have been or should have been, she would look at one of those pieces of fabric and realize that what she and her children had now, regardless of where they lived, who they were with, or what they ate, was better than anything they could have ever had with Harry.

They could hear the music when they were about a block away from the dance, and it built their excitement. It sounded like the dance was already in full swing. When they walked through the door, they saw something completely different than they expected. Women were dancing with women.

There were only about four or five men at the dance, and all of them were old and would only dance the slow dances with the women. Sophia said, "What a pitiful sight. We probably should have just stayed home."

They sat around drinking coffee or tea listening to the band play. At least they were doing something besides sitting home. Just as they thought about leaving, they saw a bunch of sailors coming into the dance. Emma searched each face hoping she would see Sly in the group. He was not with them, and she was very disappointed.

They did get to dance a lot that night. The sailors had been on their ship for a very long time, and they were a rowdy bunch of sailors. Most of them were drinking heavy, and after a while, some of them became obnoxious. That was something that Emma could not tolerate. She decided that she would rather watch them dance than to be on the dance floor with a drunk, rowdy man, trying to paw all over you.

Finally a man came in that did not have a sailor's uniform on. He was just average looking, but he was dressed very nice. When he saw Emma sitting by herself, he came over and asked her to dance. When she realized that he was not drinking, she got up and danced with him.

After the dance, he sat down beside her and started talking. He said that his name was Tony. She asked him why he was not away fighting in the war. He told her that he and most of the sailors at the dance had been, but their ship was in dock for repairs. He knew that he should be in uniform as the others were, but for one night, he just wanted to be someone besides a sailor. He was proud of his country and his uniform, but he had seen so much death and destruction that he just wanted to see something different for the night.

He looked at Emma, smiled, and said, "Would your name happen to be Emma?" She looked at him in total surprise because she had no idea as to how he knew her name.

She said, "Yes, but how do you know my name?"

Tony smiled, and for some reason, he seemed familiar, but Emma knew that she did not know him, and she did not think that she had ever met him.

He told her that he was Sly's brother. That really surprised Emma. In fact, it brought tears to her eyes, but her face lit up with just the mentioning of Sly's name. Emma was anxious to find out if Sly was home and how he was doing.

Tony handed her his handkerchief to dry her eyes and then said, "A couple of days after Sly met you, his ship sailed. He came home that night after meeting you and told our parents that he had found the love of his life. He told them all about you and your son and about him dancing with you. He also told them about your son watching and cheering him on as he kissed you good night. He described you so well that it was easy to recognize you from their description."

Tony's comments brought a few more tears to Emma's eyes, but it also brought a smile to her lips.

Listening to Tony talk about Sly made Emma sad that she had not been able to get to know him better. Just the few hours she had been able to spend with him meant so much to her.

Tony looked at her and said, "Don't be sad! Let's dance this one for Sly. Do you know how to do the Lindy Hop?" Emma told him no, that she really was not a very good dancer; she just tried to follow whomever she was dancing with. Tony pulled her up anyway and was determined to teach her.

When that dance ended, the next one he tried to teach her was the East Coast Swing, and then they all got into a big circle to do The Big Apple.

Emma was very tired by the time she finally got back to their table, so Tony asked Vera and Sophia if they would like to dance. After seeing him dance with Emma, both of them jumped at the chance.

Tony kept all three of them dancing. If they were not on the dance floor dancing, Tony would be teaching them another dance step at the side of the dance floor. Thanks to Tony, all three of the girls had a ball that night, and none of them drank anything except coffee or tea. Sophia said, "We don't need beer to have fun on the dance floor. We just want men that know how to dance."

When the dance closed, Tony told them that he would like to walk them home. It seemed that Tony had an eye for Sophia. He and Sophia walked behind Emma and Vera. It appeared that Tony could talk as well as he could dance and kept them entertained all the way home.

When they got to Emma's apartment, Tony told her good night and then told her that he would be sure to tell his mother to write to Sly and tell him all about his little brother entertaining his girlfriend while he was away. Emma laughed and told Tony that she thought she would go in and write Sly a letter also and tell him about their night. It had been a couple of weeks since she had written, but she had a lot to tell him now. At least she would use that as an excuse to write him.

Sophia invited Tony to come in and have a cup of coffee with her and Vera. Emma could hear them talking and laughing until around 2:00 a.m. She knew what time it was, because she had just finished writing her letter to Sly and had looked at the clock. If he did not leave soon, he would have to spend the night or walk back to his ship because the next bus would not come by until 5:00 a.m. because it was Sunday and not many buses ran on Sunday.

She lay down on her bed and listened to them talk and laugh until she finally went to sleep, which was sometime after 3:00 a.m. She was thankful they had the last apartment.

That people in the apartment below them were away from home for the weekend, so no one else could hear their joyful chatter except Emma. She did not mind; she just wished that she and Sly were with them. That was the thought on her mind as she went to sleep with a smile on her face.

32

Riverview Beach Park

Emma wished that she could sleep late Sunday morning, but as usual, Frederick and Dave came bouncing into the apartment around 7:00 a.m.

After breakfast, they all walked to church together. This was becoming a regular routine with all of them. Sophia and Vera did not make it to church every Sunday, but when they did not work or go out on Saturday night, they would usually go. However, she did not think they would be going with them this Sunday. After the night they had with Tony, Emma could not blame them because he was very entertaining and so was his brother.

On the way home from church, Mr. Spencer asked Emma and Frederick if they would like to go with them next Saturday to the Riverview Amusement Park. Emma had heard about the park but had never been there. All Frederick needed to hear was "amusement park" and "swimming," and he was all ears.

Mr. Spencer told them that he had thought about taking them before, but it seemed that every time he had a Saturday off, the weather would be bad, or he would have too many other things to do.

As Mr. Spencer told them about the park, Emma became excited and wanted to visit it as much as Frederick and Dave did.

Neither of them had ever been to a place like that. He told them that the park had a merry-go-round that was originally horse powered, but in 1917, it was upgraded to a Dentzel carousel from the Dentzel Carousel Company out of Philadelphia.

On Decoration Day of 1922, the park became The Riverview Beach Amusement Park. They added swings, picnic area, water slide, sliding boards, an airplane ride, and a Ferris wheel. There was a Toy-Land added for the children. They also have The Old Mill, The Whip, Tilt-A-Whirl, and a small train and some scooters. He also told them all about the flowers and the trees in the park.

He saved the best for last. He told them that there was a ride called a roller coaster, and they named it The Hummingbird. It went very fast and had what they called camelback hills.

When it gets warm, they open up a huge swimming pool. It is full of beautiful clear water. You can see all the way to the bottom of the pool. People go over to the park just to swim in the pool.

The amusement rides really fascinated the boys, but the large pool with clear water where you could see bottom fascinated them more, and they were very excited about going. Their swimming hole was muddy, and you could not see your hand in front of your face because it was so dirty, but it did have the big rock where they could dive into the water. Neither of them had told their parents about learning to swim, and they could not wait to surprise them.

The next week went by way too slow for Frederick and Dave. All they talked about was going to the amusement park. Finally, it was Saturday, and it was going to be a beautiful day. Vera and Sophia decided that they would also like to go with them. It seemed to the boys that the bus would never come. When it did get there, it was packed, and they all had to stand up and hold on to a bar to keep from falling, but no one seemed to mind.

When they got to their stop, the boys saw a huge boat in the water. They thought maybe this was where they were supposed to be going, but they did not see any of the amusement rides.

Dave said, "Dad, this doesn't look the amusement park you were telling us about."

Mr. Spencer said, "No, son, this isn't the place I was telling you about. The boat ride is a surprise. We are going to ride on the big boat all the way over to the amusement park."

The boys were beside themselves with excitement. They rode across the Delaware River to the amusement park. When the boat pulled into the dock, they could see the park, and it looked like a million people were already there.

None of them, not even the adults had seen anything like this before. Riverview Beach Park was large and looked unblemished with a lot of walking paths, and every one of the paths had people walking on them. It was springtime, and everyone was excited. From the picnic area, you had panoramic views of the Delaware River. Everything that Mr. Spencer had told them about was there, and they intended to see and do everything.

When they finally got to the swimming pool, both boys started begging to go into the water. Emma did not know how to swim, and she was a little afraid to let Fredrick go in. Mr. Spencer told her that the boys could go into the shallow water and play and he would watch them.

Both boys had come prepared. After they changed their clothes, Mr. Spencer took them down to the shallow end of the pool. He said, "Boys, you should be very careful going into the pool because it might be slippery. Don't go in past your knees, and don't put both feet in at the same time to test how deep the water is." The boys looked at Mr. Spencer trying to figure out what he was saying. Mr. Spencer laughed and told the boys to go on in and have fun. He said that he was just teasing with them.

Dave and Frederick walked to one side of the shallow end of the pool and then to the other side of the shallow end, and neither were making a move to go into the water.

When both boys felt like they had teased their parents enough, they slowly walked around the pool as though they were hesitant about going in. When they got to the deep end of the pool, they looked back to see if their parents were watching. When they saw that all eyes were on them, Frederick said, "One, two, three," and both boys dived into the deepest part of the pool.

Emma thought she was going to have a heart attack, and she and Mrs. Spencer ran to where the boys had jumped into the water. When the boys surfaced, they were about ten feet away from where they went in. They began swimming to the side of the pool like young athletes. Neither mother could believe their eyes. Both wanted to know when and where did these two boys learn to swim. When Mr. Spencer joined them, he had a big smile across his face.

He told them that while working at clearing the field for the garden, he saw Dave and Frederick sneaking off into the woods. He did not want the boys to know about the close tabs that he kept on them, but he would follow them, watching from a distance. The boys had taught themselves how to swim, and they had done a very good job of it. He wanted to show them off to their mothers, and he wanted the boys to experience swimming in something besides muddy water.

Emma was still shaking all over, but she was also laughing. She could not believe her eyes! She had never heard Frederick even mention swimming before, and because he was always telling her about things that he and Dave did, she thought she knew everything about him and what he and Dave did every day. Evidently, he only told her what he wanted her to know. He was still just a baby to her, but she had to admit that he was growing up fast. She felt sure that over the years to come she would probably be surprised many more times by things that he would do.

Both mothers were very proud watching their boys swim, but as mothers usually do, they were also concerned about them being in deep water; where both of the boys wanted to stay.

When Frederick went up on a board so that he could dive into the water, Emma held her breath. He jumped up a couple of times with his arms raised above his head and then dived into the pool. He went into the water with very little splash and then came up about ten feet from where he went in. Emma held her breath the entire time that he was under water. When he came up, he had a big smile on his face and looked straight at her. She was so proud that she thought that her heart would burst.

They had a wonderful time at the park, and all of them thanked Mr. Spencer for coming up with the idea. On the way home, when both boys were out of hearing range, he told the women all about following Dave and Frederick. He told them how he stayed hidden while he watched them, but many times, he had almost blown his cover when he hid behind some trees. As a parent, his first instincts, was to run and help them if he thought they were having problems, but he learned to take their kidding in stride.

Evidently, they had been scouting around, because they found a huge rock that stuck out over the area where they went swimming. He told them that he almost stopped them when he saw them on the rock getting ready to jump into the water. He remembered as a kid that he had done the same similar thing, so he left them alone. He was worried at first that the boys might get hurt, so he tried to stay close to them just in case one of them got into trouble. However, neither of them did, so he just quit worrying about them. They eventually invited other young boys to go with them, and he felt a little better because some of those boys were older and could swim very well, and they taught Frederick and Dave more swim strokes.

When someone told him about the park, he thought that would be a great outing. The boys were constantly hearing stories about the war, and he just wanted to give them a break and a chance to show off their swimming skills.

He apologized to his wife and Emma for not saying anything to either of them about what the boys had been up to. He thought it would be a good surprise for both of them.

33

Who Was That Sailor on the Steps?

Sunday morning they were all tired, but they still went to church, because Frederick and Dave loved their Sunday school class and were excited every Sunday when it came time to go.

During the service, Reverend Charles reminded everyone that the next Sunday was homecoming, and he wanted everyone to bring food and stay for the afternoon meal. He said that he knew that many things were not available because of the rationing, so they made a menu and asked that everyone sign up for what they could bring. It did not matter how much or how little they brought or if they were able to bring anything; he wanted everyone to stay and eat together after the service.

As they were walking home, Mr. Spencer told them that he would like to get a newspaper. He would catch up with them or see everyone later at the apartment complex.

When the women turned the corner toward the complex, Emma stopped and looked like she might faint, and Mrs. Spencer asked her what was wrong. Vera and Sophia immediately stopped and turned around when they heard what Mrs. Spencer asked Emma.

Emma looked as if she was terrified of something and could not say anything. Sophia looked over to where she saw Emma looking and saw a very handsome sailor sitting on the steps that led up to her apartment. None of them could figure out why Emma had such a look of fear on her face. The sailor was very good looking, and they tried teasing her about him, but it was not getting the affect they had hoped it would get.

Vera and Sophia immediately went into a protective mode, and each put a hand on one of Emma's arms, because they felt they might have to protect her from falling.

Dave and Frederick had been walking a good distance behind their parents so that they could talk about everything they had done the day before and how they had surprised their mothers. They had also been trailing behind them because they did not want anyone else that saw them to think that they had to walk with their parents. They did not want to look like babies.

Frederick walked up to his mother and, in his protective way, wanted to know what was wrong. Vera looked at Frederick and moved her head nodding to the sailor that was sitting on the steps. When Frederick looked where she had motioned, the same look of fear came on his face.

All of them were trying to figure out what would cause Emma and Frederick both to be so afraid of someone. Normally they were easygoing and seemingly happy people, and the sailor sitting on the steps was so good looking that any woman would check him out.

Finally, Emma started walking toward the person on the steps. Frederick took his mother's hand and walked in a very protective mode right beside her.

When they started walking up the steps, the sailor stood up but did not say anything. When they got to a couple of steps from the sailor, everyone heard Frederick when he said, "What are you doing here?"

Neither of them had ever heard Frederick talk to anyone that way; it was totally out of character for Frederick.

The next thing that happened surprised them even more. Frederick ran up to the sailor and started punching him in a blind rage. The sailor grabbed Frederick by the shoulder, and it looked like he tried to push him down the steps. He then took hold of Emma's arm and jerked them both together, asking which apartment was their. Frederick was kicking and screaming like crazy, telling his mother not to tell him because he was there to kill them. Emma was not doing or saying anything, but she did look like she had the fear of death on her face and pointed to their apartment.

Mr. Spencer walked up just as this was happening, and he immediately went to Frederick and Emma's defense. The sailor did not see Mr. Spencer walk up behind him, but he saw him when as he was jerked around to face a man who was six foot, five inches tall and weighed around 225 pounds of solid muscle.

The sailor immediately let go of Emma and Frederick. The odds were not in his favor this time. Frightening a tiny little woman and a six-year-old made him feel big, but facing Mr. Spencer was another story.

The sailor told Mr. Spencer that it was none of his business. This was his wife and kid, and he would treat them as he chose to do.

Emma gently put her hand on Mr. Spencer's arm and told him that they would be okay. Emma's hand was shaking, and she did not appear to be okay. No one could believe that Emma would have been married to someone that would behave like that and in a sailor's uniform. However, no one said anything, and Mr. Spencer stepped to the side.

Emma unlocked her door, and the three of them walked into the apartment. The sailor closed the door. Mr. Spencer walked up to the railing in front of Emma's apartment and stood in front of the window. If that man even looked like he was going to attack Emma, he would be there to protect.

After about five minutes, the sailor came to the window, stared out at Mr. Spencer, and then closed the curtains so he could not look in. Mr. Spencer stood around for a little while. After not hearing any loud talking or noises, he went to his apartment.

However, he did leave the door open so that he would be able to hear if anything happened and Emma and Frederick might need him.

34

He Ran Like a Coward

After closing the curtains, Harry very quietly, with his teeth clenched, told Emma and Frederick to sit down, and they had better do it quietly. He said, "You know what will happen if you don't."

Emma and Frederick did as he said because they both did know what he was capable of doing.

In a very low voice, Harry asked Emma what she was trying to prove by going to dances and dancing with a bunch of drunken sailors. He and Tony, a sailor he met on the dock, were going to a place where Tony thought that his brother's girlfriend might be. He wanted to let her know that his brother was okay.

He told her that he stopped at a store to buy some cigarettes, and Tony went on to the dance. When he finally got there, he never dreamed that the girl Tony would be dancing with would be his wife. He told her that he started to come in then and teach her a lesson right there in front of everyone, but when he saw all of the other sailors there, out of respect for them and not wanting to ruin their weekend, he walked out of the dance and went back to his ship.

He told Emma that he knew that he had spent the night with her because Tony did not come back to the ship until Sunday morning.

Harry said that he hung around the shipyard until he saw Tony return. He told him that he apologized for cutting out on him, but he developed some kind of a stomach virus. When he saw him having such a good time, he did not want to interrupt his fun, so he left and came back to the ship.

He acted as if he was teasing Tony and asked him about the good-looking woman that he was dancing with, and Tony asked him which one.

Harry described Emma to Tony, and he told him that her name was Emma and that she was his brother's girlfriend. He also said that he had walked her and her friends home and wound up having to sleep a couch because there were no buses running that late.

When he asked Tony where they lived, he told him the name of the apartment complex, but he told him that he could not remember any of the apartment numbers. For one thing, Tony did not think that it was any of his business because Emma was his brother's girlfriend and because he liked Sophia a lot. If he did not know their names, he had no business bothering them.

Harry told her that all it took was for him to ask the first man that he saw which apartment Emma Carswell lived in. He said, "You must be very popular around here. I always knew that you were not the sweet innocent wife you pretended to be."

Neither Emma nor Frederick said anything. Harry knew that he still had them under his control. When he got through with Emma, she would think twice about going to any dance again. She ought to stay home and take care of her kids as a real mother would. After being on a ship for months, he deserved at least one night on the town before shipping out again. It was tough living on that ship with no women around.

Harry looked at Emma without saying anything. He could not believe that she actually looked better now than she did when they first got married, and she was dressing nicer than he had ever seen her dress, and it really aggravated him because she never dressed like that for him.

He asked her where she and her friends had been, but before she had a chance to answer, he said they had probably been out all night and were just coming home.

Frederick spoke up and said, "We went to church this morning with our friends." Harry snarled at Frederick and told him to shut it up; he had not asked him anything or given him permission to talk. Fredrick sat back down, wishing that he were a man. If he was, he felt like he would kill Harry. However he was not a man, and he knew that had to keep his emotions under control because he knew that Harry would possibly kill him and his mother if he did not.

When Harry put his hand around Emma's neck and started choking her, Frederick started to get up. Harry glared at him and told him to sit back down, if he did not want him to kill his mother right in front of him. Frederick eased back down into the chair.

Harry asked Emma why she left their home. He went there to get some things that he left, and the person that was living in the house told him that the bank had foreclosed on the house and the family that lived there moved out.

He wanted to know where all of his things were, and Emma told him that she left them in the house when she moved because she could not afford a place large enough to store all of his things.

As soon as she said that, he got angry and hit her on the side of the face with the back of his hand. He told her that he did not believe a word that she was saying and he wanted the rest of his things that he left in their house.

He immediately went into the bigger bedroom looking through her closet and through the dresser drawers. He then went into the small room and did the same thing.

When he did not find what he was looking for, he came back into the living room and told Emma that he would ask her once again what she did with his things, and she had better tell him the truth.

Emma told him again that she left all of his things in the house because she did not have room for them. They had to move into a smaller place and barely had room for their things.

After she said that, Harry went wild! He went back into her bedroom, took all of her clothes out of the closet, and ripped them to shreds. He broke the heels off her new shoes and destroyed all of her personal items. He then asked how it felt to have all of your things destroyed.

Emma said nothing, and she motioned for Frederick not to say anything either.

Harry got within just a few inches of Emma's head, balled his fist, and hit her straight in her face her. You could hear her nose break. He then started on Frederick. The way he was hitting them did not make a loud sound, and he told them that he would kill them if they tried to scream or make a sound. Both of them knew that he meant what he said.

Emma was bleeding from a cut on her head, from her nose, and from her ears. Frederick's nose and mouth was bleeding.

When Harry got some of the blood on his uniform, he got angry about that and said, "Just look at what you did. I will probably get in trouble over these stupid stains."

When he finally opened the door and walked out to leave, Frederick jumped up, ran after him, and gave Harry a big shove just as he got to the steps.

Harry fell down both set of steps. He lost his balance from the shove and tumbled down the steps. When he got up, his uniform had dirt from the stairs that mixed with the bloodstains. He knew that he was going to be in big trouble with his chief officer, and it made him so mad that he started back up the steps toward Frederick, yelling that he would teach him a lesson that he would never forget.

Just as he got to the top, Mr. Spencer stepped out of his apartment and in front of Frederick. That stopped Harry in his tracks, and he started backing down the steps. He did not like to cower down from anyone, but looking at the man in front of Frederick, who looked like a giant at the top of the steps, he knew that he would be the loser if he started a fight with him, so he dusted himself off and walked away. He turned around once, pointed his finger at Frederick, and yelled out that he and his mother had not seen the last of him.

Mr. Spencer did not think kindly of Harry's remarks and started down the steps after him. When Harry saw him coming after him, he took off running like the coward that he was.

Mr. Spencer asked Frederick if he was okay, and Frederick said yes, but he could already see a black eye and many bruises on his arms and face, and he figured there were probably many more on the child's body that he couldn't see.

When he walked into the apartment with Frederick, he saw Emma bending over, and he gently lifted her face. When he did, he could not believe the extent of her injuries. He could not figure out, how a beating like that took place with him being next door listening and not hear anything. He told Emma that they should tell the police about what happened, but Emma asked him not to. She told him that she did not want other people to know anything about Harry, and she was too ashamed for anyone to know that that she had ever been married to someone like him. Mr. Spencer nodded his head and then went walking in the direction that he had seen Harry going.

35

What Was the Accident's Name?

When Emma saw Frederick's black eye, nose damage, and the bruising on his arms, legs, and face, she could not help but cry. Frederick was trying his best to be strong and not cry, but when he saw his mother crying, tears started pooling in his eyes. When Emma looked in the mirror, she realized that she looked worse than Frederick did.

Was it just her and their children that Harry enjoyed abusing? What would make a man beat a woman who loved him, and why could anyone be so cruel to a child, especially their own? Emma had no answers for either question.

On Monday, Emma's face looked worse, and Mr. Spencer did not want her to go to work. He told her that he would talk to her supervisor and tell him that she was in an accident, but Emma told him no because she needed that job, and she was not going to do anything that would constitute them firing her.

When she got to work, it was all that Emma could do to climb the ladder to the crane. At least, being sixty feet up in the air, no one could see her bruises.

At their first break, Sophia and Vera came over to check on Emma. Sophia started crying as soon as she saw what Emma looked like. She had never seen anyone beaten so severely. She immediately said, "We have got to do something about that man. No one should go unpunished after doing something like that."

They caught Emma at a weak moment, and she broke began crying and told them what Harry did to her and Frederick after they went into her apartment and he closed the door.

Neither Sophia nor Vera could believe that that anyone would want to hurt someone like Emma. She was one of the kindest and sweetest persons they had every known, and Frederick was like a little brother to them.

Emma told them the whole story about Harry coming to the dance with Tony but was a little later coming because he had stopped off to get cigarettes. When he got there, she told them that Harry had seen her dancing with Tony and got upset about it.

Sophia laughed and said, "He should have seen me with Tony."

Vera punched Sophia with her elbow and said, "We know all about you and Tony. I did not go to sleep as early as you thought I did." She then laughed and so did Sophia. Emma had to smile because she knew what Vera was insinuating.

Sophia told her that Tony was supposed to come back to see her the next Saturday. She told them that he was going to get off the bus at the apartment complex and walk with all three of them to the dance. He said that it would be good for his image to be seen coming in with three gorgeous women.

Emma said, "I don't know if I will ever go there again."

"You can't let that jerk make you afraid to leave home. You should report him to the police or at least let Tony know about what he did to you and Frederick," Vera said. Emma told them that they had no idea what Harry would do to her and Frederick if he ever found out that she reported the incident to the police.

The whistle blew, and it was time for them to go back to work. It was actually harder for Emma to climb the ladder this time. The pain was getting worse, rather than better.

As Emma sat working the crane, she remembered that Harry did not even ask her about the other children.

At two o'clock, the whistle blew, signaling a shift change. It was all Emma could do to climb down from the crane. Judy Hornet took over the afternoon job as crane operator. When she saw Emma, she asked her if she had fallen off the crane. Emma smiled and told her that she had been involved in an accident. Judy said, "It must have been a bad accident. She then told Emma that she could double shift the next day for her if she liked because her husband was going to be working, and it would give Emma a chance to rest and recoup from her "accident." Emma told her that would be wonderful if it was okay with the boss. Judy told her that she and Gail Snowman, the girl on the third shift, did it all the time. As long as the crane was in operation with an experienced operator, they were fine as long as they did not have to pay anyone overtime pay. She felt sure that Gail would also double shift if she needed her.

Emma asked her if she would speak to Gail when she came to work and let her know if she did not show up at least by the time the whistle blew would she please cover for her. She was going to try to take her son to the doctor as soon as she got home if the doctor could see him, and if not, she would take him the next day.

Judy said, "Don't you worry about the job. Between me and Gail, we can keep the place running until you get over whatever accident you had."

Emma thanked her and told her that she would do the same for her anytime she needed her.

As Emma walked off, Judy thought that she had seen a couple of women who looked like they may have been involved in the same accident as Emma. She wondered what the accident's name was. She knew someone must have beaten Emma because the bruising on her neck looked like some very strong fingers had done it.

Judy knew another woman who worked with them who once looked like that. She was dating a sailor, and they were talking about getting married. Every time her fiancé came home on leave,

Lorenda would come to work looking just like Emma looked. She felt that it was a sad day when men had to take their emotional frustrations out on a woman and especially a child.

When Emma said something about taking her son to the doctor, Judy wondered if the person that did this to Emma did the same thing to her child. If so, she hoped that Emma would get her child away from them as fast as possible. She would if someone did something like that to her child. In fact, she might be the one the police would be hunting because she would probably kill the jerk. Judy just shook her head and climbed up the ladder to the crane.

36

Who Caused the Accidents?

D r. DeRand Peppers was able to see both Emma and Frederick that afternoon. When they walked into his office, the nurse was talking to the receptionist. As soon as she looked up and saw Emma and Frederick, she immediately walked over to them. With a quick visual assessment, the nurse immediately took both of them back to a room. Within minutes, the doctor came in. Emma knew there were many people in the waiting room when they got there and could not believe they would take them in first.

Dr. Peppers immediately asked Emma what happened to her and her son. She told him that they were in an accident, and Dr. Peppers immediately asked her what kind of an accident.

Emma was embarrassed to tell him, but the doctor insisted. He told her that he had seen quiet a few accidents where people looked the way she and her son looked, and the accident reports usually follow a trail that leads to a husband, father, boyfriend, or stalker. He told her that he wanted an honest answer and asked her which one caused their accident, not if one of them caused the accident.

Emma was embarrassed with his questions, and tears started forming in her eyes. The doctor turned his attention to Frederick. He put him up on the table and began examining him.

The doctor asked Frederick if his shoulder hurt, and he told him yes. Dr. Peppers was almost positive that he probably had a dislocated shoulder, and he could see large marks on the child that looked like an adult handprint. With the dislocated shoulder and the bruises on his arm, whoever did this would have had to be much larger that his mother, and he suspected the child's father or his mother's boyfriend did it.

When the doctor checked Frederick's nose and face, he saw more damage. His nose was broken, and he had bad bruising on the side of his head, hidden by his hair.

The doctor called his assistant to take Frederick into the adjoining room and told him what he wanted him to do for the child.

Dr. Peppers then turned his attention to Emma. He looked her straight in the eyes and told her that he wanted to know who beat her and her child, and he did not want any more answers about it being an accident.

Emma bowed her head going deep down inside her soul to gather courage. When she raised her head, she looked straight at the doctor and told him that her husband, Harry Carswell, Frederick's father, did it.

The doctor did not say anything else until he finished examining Emma. He was sure that she probably had a couple of fractured ribs and definitely a broken nose. The doctor told her that he could tell that her nose had been broken before, and in fact, it looked as though it had been broken several times before.

They were in the doctor's office for around three hours. The doctor's assistant helped the other patients that only needed prescriptions or had minor problems, and the doctor continuously worked with Emma and Frederick.

Finally, when they were ready to leave, the doctor told his nurse to take Frederick to her office and give him a coloring book and some crayons because he had been such a strong boy. He had a few more things to do with his mother, and then she would join him.

When the nurse left with Frederick, the doctor handed Emma a pad and a pencil and told her to write down the name of the man who hurt her and her son. He also wanted to know where he worked, where he lived, the date this happened to them, and had it ever happened before. He also wanted to know if he had threatened them in any way, if they reported him to the police.

Emma was embarrassed to put everything down on paper because there would be no covering it up once she wrote it down. She did not know where the courage came from, but she wrote down exactly what Harry did and said to her and Frederick this time. When she finished and handed the paper back to Dr. Peppers, he gave her orders as to what she could and could not do and what Frederick could and could not do. He felt that Frederick should not go back to school for the rest of the week, and she should not be working in a munitions factory in the condition that she was in until she was fully recovered. He told her that if she fell or was bumped firmly enough, one of the broken ribs could puncture her lungs, and she would be in big trouble then. He wrote notes for the school and where she worked, stating that they had been in an accident, and he had ordered bed rests for both of them for at least a week.

Emma felt that she could not be out of work that long because she needed the money, but she would let Frederick stay home from school. It would be very embarrassing for any of the kids to find out what had happened to him.

If the police arrested Harry, she knew what he would probably do once he got out of jail.

37

He Killed the Dog

When Emma and Frederick came home from the doctor's office, they both went to bed and stayed there for most of the afternoon. Her nose and Frederick's were both broken. Frederick's shoulder was bound, her ribs were bound, and Frederick's right little finger had a splint on it.

Frederick came into her room around 3:00 p.m., telling his mother that he was hungry. She had not even thought about preparing lunch, and now it was dinnertime, and neither of them had eaten anything since breakfast. Mrs. Spencer asked earlier if she would fix them something to eat or if she could do anything for them. Emma thanked her and told her that they would be fine. The Spencers had already done so many things for them that she should not ask them to do anything else for them.

By now, everyone in the complex probably knew what happened to her and Frederick, and she were too embarrassed to talk to any of them. She had decisions to make. She hoped that moving again was not one of them because she and Frederick were settled and happy. If they did move, she knew that Harry would probably find them wherever they went. She wished that he would just make a new life for himself and leave them alone. He had made it clear that he did not love her or their children.

She and Frederick went to the kitchen, and she fixed them some soup to eat. After they ate, Emma cleaned the kitchen and then sat down with Frederick and told him that they needed to talk.

The things Harry did to them could possibly leave anger and rage in Frederick, and she did not want him to be like his father. She should have had this conversation with him long before this happened. She had been so busy making a living that things like talking to him about what his father did to them were neglected, and she knew that she should do it now.

She began by telling Frederick that what his father did to them was wrong. She did not want him to grow up thinking all fathers were like Harry. She also did not want him to think that beating your wife and children was okay.

Most of the time, when someone beats the people they profess to love, they have a problem. They cannot control their anger, and they take it out on the first person that triggers their anger. Just because they have so much anger, it does not give them the right to abuse people.

Frederick said, "Mom, please stop! I know exactly what kind of person Harry is. He is a very mean, cruel person, and he should go to jail for the things that he has done to us. He beat you and me and then acted as though nothing happened, except our blood staining his uniform. No real father would do that. For a very long time, I have wished I were a grown-up so that I could go kill him for what he did to us. That was what I really wanted to do when I pushed him down the steps. When I saw the way Mr. Spencer stepped in front of me, protecting me from Harry, I knew then that he is the kind of person that I want to be, not someone like Harry."

Emma pulled Frederick close and said, "I understand how you feel. We need to find ways to help protect ourselves from Harry, but we should not think of killing him or anyone else."

Frederick looked up at his mother and said, "Mom, some of our neighbors have said that it is okay for us to kill our enemies.

Harry is our worst enemy. We should tell the police about everything that he did to us so that they can put him in jail. We should not protect him any longer. He may kill us the next time, and you know it. Why will you not do anything to protect?"

Frederick's words ripped right through Emma's heart. Her son seemed to be more of an adult than she was, and she knew that what he was saying was true. Many times, she had wished that she had followed her grandfather's advice about dumping Harry while they were dating. She now knew that she was only in love with love and really did not get to know Harry before marrying him.

She remembered seeing Harry get angry at the neighbor's dog. At the time, he convinced her that he was protecting her from the dog. They had been walking leisurely down the street holding hands when the neighbor's dog started barking and ran toward them. Just as the dog got to them, Harry took his foot and kicked the dog until it looked like it might die and then took her by the arm and told her that the dog would never bark at her again, and they continued walking to her grandparent's house as though nothing happened.

Emma felt sorry for the dog after it happened and thought about telling the neighbors about what Harry did, but the dog died the next day, and she thought it was best not to say anything because it could bring the dog back to life.

If she had left Harry, after the first or second child was born, things would have probably been better for her and the children. He told her many times if she went running to her grandmother or anyone else about anything that happened in their house, he would kill her, the kids, her grandmother, and her grandfather, and she believed him.

She knew that Harry always lived up to his threats that involved her and her family. What did she ever do to make him hate them so much? In the beginning, she actually felt that Harry loved her, especially during the time they first got married. They would listen to music, and he would pull her up close whispering things that he would like for them to do. Emma never felt comfortable when he talked like that. In her wildest imagination, would she have ever dreamed that was what married couples did? It actually made her sick to think about it.

When Sly pulled her close and kissed her on her balcony in front of her apartment that night, everything seemed wholesome and loving. At no time when she and Harry were together while they were dating, and especially after they were married, had he ever made her feel loved and wanting to melt into his arms. Harry would always pull her to him very firmly and would grope at her in places that she felt were not appropriate and were unladylike, especially before they were married. It was more like a prelude to sex rather than an act of love.

There were so many warning signs, and she ignored all of them.

38

Lieutenant Zane Skylur

Early the next morning, someone knocked on Emma's door. When she opened it, she was not surprised to see a police officer. She had a strong feeling that the doctor would report their injuries to the police; he was probably required to do so.

Emma immediately started shaking. She knew what would happen to her, Fredrick, and possibly her grandmother and Henrietta if they arrested Harry. Why would none of these people leave them alone? All of this was just going to make it worse for her and Frederick. She felt without a doubt, if they arrested him, he would be out in no time at all, and the next time they arrested him, it would probably be for murder.

The police officer bid her a good morning and introduced himself, telling her that his name was Zane Skylur, and he wanted to know if she was Emma Patton Carswell. When she answered yes, Officer Skylur asked if he could come in and speak with her. Emma opened the door wide to allow him entrance. When Officer Skylur walked inside, he could see that Emma's injuries were much greater than he had anticipated or had ever seen in this type of domestic situation, and it made him angry. When he saw that Frederick looked almost as bad as his mother did, he knew that he would do everything in his power to bring the person responsible for this to justice.

Officer Skylur asked Emma if she and her son would tell him what had happened to them.

Emma did not immediately speak, but Frederick looked straight at the police officer with tears in his eyes and said, "Officer Skylur, my father, Harry Carswell, did this to us. He is mean and cruel and hurts my mama and us. He once beat a little baby out of my mom's stomach. She probably would have died if my sister, Henrietta, and I had not taken care of her and baby Patrick."

Officer Skylur looked around and to see if other children were present. When he saw none, he immediately thought that they might be either at school or outside playing. He turned to Frederick and asked him if he could tell him all about this attack.

Frederick stood straight and said, "Sir, just what do you want to know?"

When Officer Skylur asked a question, Frederick gave vivid details about the beating in the kitchen and about Harry leaving them. He told the truth and told it very factual. He told about things that Harry did to him and his brother and sister, which she knew nothing about. He told Officer Skylur about his dad holding him up by the arms until he thought his arms were going to break off. He said that he was too scared to cry. For a long time afterward, he could hardly move his arms.

Office Skylur asked him if he told his mother or anyone else about what his father did to him and his brother and sister.

Frederick paused, bowed his head, and very meekly said, "Mom was there with us most of the time when he would do things to us.

Being very curious about his question, Officer Skylur said, "Frederick, did your mother do anything to try to stop him?"

When Frederick did not answer, Officer Skylur turned to Emma and said, "Mrs. Carswell has this really been going on that long? If so, why did you not ever do anything to stop that man from doing such things to your children?"

Emma did not know how to answer his question. If the police ever found out what she had allowed her children to go through, she was afraid that they might take the only child that she had left away from her. Everything sounded so pitiful and horrendous coming from Frederick, and she knew that she would have never told the officer about everything, but Frederick did.

When she did not answer, Officer Skylur told her not to worry about anything that she might say. They were not there to punish her; they wanted to find the man and punish him for what he did to her and her son.

Frederick sat down beside Emma and said, "Mom, please tell the police officer what he wants to know. We should not protect Harry any longer. I hope that they will put him in jail, and we will never have to see him again. Please, Mom! I never want to be beaten like this again, and I am sure that you don't want to either"

Emma sat up and looked straight at the officer and said, "Sir, if my son can be that brave, then so can I. Just tell me what you want to know."

They gave the officer all the information that he asked for. When he finished talking to them, he told them that he was going to put a police office on guard outside the apartment complex for the next few days. He suggested they not go anywhere unless it was necessary. If they did have to go anywhere, he wanted them to alert the officer as to where they were going and approximately what time they would be home. They could not allow the officer to be her personal bodyguard, but they could put a man on duty to protect the community because of the crime that was committed there, and they would stipulate that the officer always be near her apartment when on duty.

39

Police Officers Were on Duty

Frederick tapped his secret message to Dave through his bedroom wall. In just a minute, Dave knocked, and Frederick opened the door to let him in. Dave told him that there was a police officer guarding their apartment. Frederick immediately said, "Mom, come look, our police guards are here." Frederick waved at the police officer, and the officer nodded back at him and smiled.

Emma looked out at the police officer and smiled. By his size and appearance, she knew that Harry would not confront him. For the first time in a very long time, she felt safe, but she also knew that if Harry wanted to, he would figure out a way to get to them.

The next day, Officer Skylur came back to tell them that the police were late being dispatched and missed the ship that Harry was sailing on. He said, "When the ship that he is on comes back into port, we will be there waiting on him. That is if he is lucky enough to make it back. This war is more important than one man, but we will put forth our best efforts to catch him."

He then told Emma that there were going to be three police officers standing guard inside the apartment complex stationed within a visual field of her apartment. Officer Bud Harold is the officer on duty now; he nodded his head toward a police officer who was standing across the street. "Officer Harold is the biggest and strongest man we have on our force. Just looking at the size of the muscles on that man, your husband would be dumb to take him on. Officer Harold talks about as tough as he looks, and that alone will scare someone off.

"Officer Lou Henderson is slim built but has won many honors with that 9 mm. All that he needs is a target whether it is as big as the side of a barn or one small hole that you would think that only a straw could go through. I have personally seen Officer Henderson pull that 9 mm on a group of visiting Canadians who were making fun of one of the local women. When Officer Henderson pulled that 9 mm, one of the Canadians laughed and said that his bunion on his foot probably hurt worse than a bullet shot from that gun. He then took one of his feet pointing to where his bunion was on the other foot. The man stood up and started toward Officer Henderson in a very aggressive manner. The Canadian began hopping over to a bench, yelling that Officer Henderson shot him on his foot, where he had a bunion.

"Officer JM Vernon is a former military man. He was off fighting in the war and received an injury that kept him from going back to active duty. When he came to the police department seeking employment, the chief hired him on the spot. Officer Vernon may not be as big as the other two officers, but he makes up for it with his marshal arts skills. He could take your husband out before he realized that he was there.

"There are also going to be three officers on duty at the back entrance to the apartment complex, because someone could very easily come through there without unseen. Their names are Officer Patrick June, Officer Don Andreson, and Officer Frank Bomgartener. These men are also very physically fit. We want you and your son to feel safe. We are ready for Harry Carswell if he comes anywhere near you again."

40

The Children Knew Everything

Everyone was able to go about their business in the apartment complex because everyone felt safe and loved watching as the officers change shifts. All of the police officers were very impressive looking, and Emma did not think that Harry would dare confront either of them. From what she heard, Mr. Spencer went after Harry the night he beat her and Frederick, and Harry ran like a scared chicken. She hopes that he will be too afraid to come around again with Mr. Spencer and the police officers watching her apartment.

If the ship that Harry was sailing on went to war, she knew they might never see him again. She felt guilty thinking something like that, but she knew it was her true feelings.

She was going to make sure they had some type of weapons around just in case Harry did slip past the police officers. She now had two ball bats ready. One was behind the front door and the other was in her bathroom.

She told Frederick if Harry every came back again and put one finger on either of them to grab one of the bats and hit him as hard as he could, and she intended to do the same. She told him to preferably hit him in the knee or groin area. That should take him down easily. If he could not get either of those areas, she told him to go for his hands.

Emma heard Frederick tell Dave what their plan was and about the police officers standing guard. Dave said, "I hope my dad is around if he ever does come back. You and your mom will not need the police officers. I heard him tell my mom that he wished he had done it when he was here. Dad was standing just inside our apartment with our door open while he was in your apartment, and he said that he did not even hear anyone talking. My dad said that he should have heard some type of scuffle after he saw how badly you and your mom were beaten. I sure am glad my dad is not like that."

Frederick told Dave that Harry was a very mean man. He then shared details as to how his father would torture him and his mother. He even told him about having a sister that was older than he was and two brothers that were younger than he was.

He told him about Harry stealing all of his mother's money from an inheritance that she received from her parents after they died. He left them no food or money to buy food and he had not paid the mortgage payment on their house for months, and they had to move out of the house because the bank took it away from them. He said, "Mom never told me some of the things that happened, but I would listen when she would talk to Grandma. I surprised Mom with all the stuff I told the police officers, because she thought that I knew nothing about what was going on."

Dave said, "Yeah, grown-ups don't give us kids enough credit.

Before that day was over, the boys knew everything there was to know about each other. They decided to become blood brothers because one of them had heard that blood brothers were closer than friends were. Frederick took his knife out of his pocket, stuck it into his thumb, and then let Dave do the same thing to his. They pressed blood out of their thumbs and then put their thumbs together, pressing their own blood into the other's blood, and that day they formed a strong blood brothers friendship bond that would last all of their lives.

41

Too Much Drama in Her Life

Emma was tired of Harry's abuse. She intended to be fully prepared the next time he came around. She was seriously thinking about trying to find a gun to keep in her apartment for their protection. When she told Mr. Spencer about possibly getting a gun, he told her that she would probably be hurt worse than Harry would because the kick of the shotgun could injure her shoulder. He told her that it was best if she let the police handle Harry. She told him okay, but she knew in her mind that she would take whatever measures necessary to protect her son. No way was she ever going to let Harry hurt him again.

Harry always diverted the blame in order to give him an excuse to unleash his violent temper, especially during the times that Emma was pregnant. She did not want any more children after Frederick was born. She had a boy and a girl, and they were both beautiful babies. There was no way that she would have deliberately gotten pregnant again. In fact, she had prayed that she would not.

After each child, the beatings from Harry escalated. Emma did not actually believe that he had any reason for to be jealous of anything or anyone because most of the things he would accuse her of had no truth to them at all. Now that she had been away from him for a while, she could see that he was just a very angry, insecure man.

As the old saying goes, "Old too soon, and smart too late."

Harry told her that he loved her many times before they were married, but he never told her after they were married. She thought back to the times he would tell her that he loved her while he was constantly trying to fondle her, in ways that she did not think were appropriate. When she made him stop, she saw signs of that anger, but she thought that he was just frustrated. How in the world had she been that naïve?

She thanked heavens that her grandmother had been so strict. What would have happened if she had given in to Harry? She would have probably gotten pregnant, and he would have either run away or claimed that the baby was not his. She would have been embarrassed and would have had to carry the shame of being an unwed mother.

She needed to quit thinking about all of the things Harry did and start thinking about what she could do to get back to work as soon as possible. She would not receive her pay unless she worked, and she needed to make some money. She and Frederick had gotten along pretty good, and she had even managed to saved a little money, but she would need a bigger nest egg if any of her children ever wanted to come back to live with her.

Monday, Emma went back to work, and Frederick went back to school. She told Frederick that it would be okay if he told a little white lie and say that he was in an accident. She knew how embarrassing it would be for him to go to school with so many bruises and other kids find out that his father did that to him. She hated to go back to work with her bruises still showing. She would just have to deal with it. Most of the people that she worked closely with probably already knew about what happened. If they were cold enough to say anything, so be it. She was no longer going to hide.

Her main concern about her going back to work and Frederick going back to school was about security. The police officers were guarding the apartment area, but when they left the apartment, they were alone.

If Harry came back, the first place he would probably look for them would be at her apartment. She would only go to work and to the grocery store until they arrested him. No way would she go to the dance with her friends. She did miss the fun she had when they went dancing, but she was not going to take any chances of coming in contact with Harry. They told her that he had shipped out, but she was still not going to take any chances.

There was just too much drama going on in her in her life.

42

Questioning All Sailors

Things were finally getting back to normal. When Emma knew there was a police officer at the complex, she felt comfortable letting Frederick go outside to play with Dave. She told him not to go anywhere that was not within the police officer's view.

One Saturday Vera and Sophia came over and tried to talk Emma into going dancing with them, just to get her out doing something, besides staying home all of the time, but Emma was not ready to go out. Right now, she felt that she and Frederick were safe, but she did not want to push their luck.

Around midnight she heard voices outside. When she looked out her window, she saw the police officer talking to a sailor. The sailor had his back to her, but her first fear was that it was Harry. She woke Frederick and told him to tap an alert code to Dave so that his father would be on guard. She had her ball bat, Frederick had his, and they were ready for Harry if he tried to do anything to them again.

There was a knock on their door, and Emma was afraid to answer it until she heard Sophia and Vera laughing. She opened the door for them to come in, and she was surprised to see that Tony was with them.

Sophia said that she had no idea that the police officer on duty would question every sailor that came around the complex. When the officer got up close to Tony, he recognized him from seeing him with them before, but he still asked him the same questions he asked any sailor that came into the complex area.

With Tony being home, it made Emma a little nervous, because she thought that Harry could possibly be on leave also. Tony tried to reassure her that the only reason their ships were in port at the same time was because both of them were in need of repair.

Before when he met Harry, he was on the dock standing around with a bunch of sailors talking. Harry asked if anyone would like to go with him and be his wingman. Since he did not have anything else planned, he told Harry that he would go with him.

Tony wanted Emma to know that he did not condone that type of behavior. He felt somewhat responsible for what happened to her and her son, and he wanted to apologize to her.

Emma told him that she appreciated the gesture, but no apology was necessary because Harry was the villain, not him.

Tony told her that he had heard the ship that Harry was sailing on would be out for a very long time unless it received damages as his ship had. The British and the United States navies have halted the Japanese naval advancement to the central Pacific at Midway. They are stopping them from island-hopping and making advances toward Australia at Guadalcanal. He said, "I don't think that you will have to worry about him for quite a while."

Emma breathed a sign of relief. She reached over and patted Frederick on the head and told him that it was just a false alarm and that he could go back to sleep. She told him to tap his code on the wall telling Dave that they were okay.

Tony said, "I don't think he will have to tap a code on your wall. Your next-door neighbor is standing outside right now in his pajamas and in a very protective stance."

They walked over to speak with Mr. Spencer and introduced Tony to him, and they all stood outside talking until Mr. Spencer finally bid them all a good night and said that it would soon be time to get up and go to church. As they were going back to their apartments, Tony cleared his throat and asked, as though talking to the wind, "Does anyone know of a place where I can sleep tonight?"

Sophia smiled and said, "Come with us, Tony. You can sleep on our couch." Vera looked at Emma and rolled her eyes.

43

Imperial Japanese Navy

S unday morning Dave knocked on Emma's door letting them know that it was time to leave for church. When she and Fredrick walked out the door, Tony was talking with the Spencers, and Emma felt by the way they looked at her when she walked out they door, they had been talking about her.

They all walked to church together. Emma and Frederick always felt safe anytime Mr. Spencer was with them. Dave and Frederick walked over to the police officer and told him that they were going to church. The police officer told them that he would be waiting there when they got back. The boys waved bye to him, and the police officer tipped his hat in return.

When they were walking home from church, Mr. Spencer walked over to the newsstand to get a copy of the Sunday newspaper. When he walked back to where the group was waiting on him, Emma could see the headlines on the paper, and it was about the United States and British navies.

Emma had not been keeping up on the news about the war as much as she should have. There was so much going on in her life that it took precedence over everything else. She asked Mr. Spencer if he would let her read his paper after he was finished. He told her that she sure would, but he would like to have it back after she finished because he was saving all of the ones that had any information about the war in them, which was almost every day now.

Late afternoon Mr. Spencer brought the paper over to Emma, and Dave came with him wanting to know if he could play with Frederick. After Mr. Spencer left and the boys went to Frederick's room to play, she sat down on the sofa to read the newspaper.

The top news was about how the Imperial Japanese Navy was the second most powerful navy in the pacific. It was the third largest in the world, and they were dominating the Western Pacific. Their naval air service was one of the most potent in the world.

The Japanese destroyers were very formidable, and it had come as a nasty surprise to its Allies, who underestimated their technical capabilities. The Japanese had reassessed their naval needs in mid-1920 and placed an emphasis on ships and weapons technology and night fighting.

The Imperial Japanese Navy requirements gave rise to warships that were substantially larger than their European or American equivalents. Japan also had a highly competent naval air force, designed around some of the best airplanes in the world.

The A6M Zero was the best carrier aircraft. The Mitsubishi G3M bomber was remarkable for its range and speed. The Kawaniski H8K was the world's best flying boat.

The Japanese pilot corps was of higher caliber as compared to their contemporaries around the world due to their intense training and frontline experience.

The navy also had a competent tactical bombing force based around the Mitsubishi G3M and G4M bombers, which astonished the world by being the first planes to sink enemy capital ships underway.

Other countries were finding weaknesses in Japanese naval aviation. They had very little in the way of defensive armament and armor.

American aircraft was able to develop several new competitive designs, but industrial weaknesses, lack of raw materials, and disorganization due to Allied bombing raids hampered their mass production.

Millions of women are now part of the work force in the defense industry. The women have also had to perform essential civilian jobs, such as police officers, loggers, taxi driver's farmers, and chemists.

The women now have to do these jobs and take care of their homes and their children, and they are doing the jobs quite efficiently. It had once been a great concern for our country because women were not part of the labor force in the United States, but the women have stepped forward and have proven that they have the ability to keep our country running smoothly.

The article made Emma feel proud that she was part of that workforce, and reading anything about the Japanese caused her to have chills.

44

Turning Him Over to the Naval Authorities

Emma was taking one day at a time and had not given much thought as to what she would do after the war if she lost her job. She was totally dependant upon her income at the munitions factory for their survival. She had to remind herself daily that they were okay now, and she would just deal with everything as it happened one day at a time.

She decided that it would be good for her and Frederick to get away from everything for a couple of days, so she decided that they would go visit her grandmother and Henrietta for the weekend. She knew that she should first contact the police and tell them what her plans were. She felt guilty about them watching her apartment day and night and did not want to cause them to have to be there to protect her and Frederick when they were not at home.

She asked the officer on duty Tuesday morning if he would tell Officer Zane Skylur that she would like to speak with him if possible. The officer told her that he would give Lieutenant Skylur her message.

That afternoon when she came home from work, Officer Skylur was outside her apartment waiting on her. He told her that he would like to speak with her. Automatically thinking that he was there because of her request, Emma told him of her plans. He listened to her very patiently and then gave her some very disturbing news. Due to the war, they had a shortage of labor. They were no longer going to be able to keep the police officers on duty at the apartment complex any longer. They were going to have to turn everything over to the naval authorities. As soon as the ship that Harry Carswell is sailing on comes back into port, they will arrest him. He told her not to worry but to remain alert to her surroundings. He apologized for the bad news but said that he had no other choice. many of their young police officers were now serving in the military, and it had affected their budget and labor tremendously.

Emma told him that she understood his situation and thanked him for all the help they had already given them.

After he left, Emma felt sick to her stomach. It was awful to have to worry about your safety all of the time. When Frederick came home from Dave's for dinner, she told him about how they would not have the police officers watching them anymore. She immediately saw fear on Frederick's face. He said, "What will we do if Harry comes back? They will not be here to protect us from him. Maybe we should go some place and hide so that he can never find us."

Emma told him that they were not going to let Harry control their lives anymore. They would just have to be more alert to people around them. She then said that she would like them to go visit their grandmother. Frederick did not know if he liked the idea or not. He said, "I don't care whether we have a policeman watching out for us or not, don't you even think of taking me to Grandma's house and leaving me."

Emma had to chuckle a little because that thought had not entered her mind in a long time, but evidently, Frederick still harbored those fears. She told him that was not the reason she wanted to go for a visit. She told him that it would be nice to see Henrietta and her grandmother because it had been so long since they had been there for a visit.

Frederick finally agreed, if she promised that in no way would she try to talk him into staying.

Emma hugged him and told him that she would not do that to him without telling him first.

Everyone in the apartment complex had gotten so complacent seeing police officers guarding the buildings, and for some reason, they all felt a sense of fear without them.

Mr. Spencer had an idea! He went around the apartment complex asking everyone to meet him in front of his apartment at five o'clock that evening. He told them that he had something very important to talk with them about. Everyone looked up to Mr. Spencer and thought highly of him as a good neighbor or because he was their supervisor at the plant or possibly both.

That evening Mr. Spencer presented his idea to all the tenants. His suggestion was that they form their own security force. He felt that all of the men could take turns watching out for any suspicious person coming into the complex.

He said that he knew where he could get some loud whistles. If they saw anyone that they felt should not be there, they could blow their whistle. Everyone that heard the whistle would become alert and immediately go to the person who blew the whistle.

Most of the neighbors were nodding their heads in agreement, and Melinda Moody spoke up and told Mr. Spencer that she thought that was a wonderful idea. Her husband, Terry, was not able to attend the meeting, because he had to work, but she felt sure that he would go along with the idea. Before he left for work, he had told her that he did not feel good about leaving her and the children, knowing there would not be a police officer there to protect them should something happen. She then told Mr. Spencer that it made them all feel safe knowing they were out there watching out for them, especially when their children were outside playing.

211

Brian and Scott Moody, Melinda's sons, spoke up and asked if they would be carrying guns. Mr. Spencer told him no, that the only weapon they would be carrying would be a whistle, but he would not object to anyone having a big stick or a ball bat with them. He also told them that he did not want anyone putting himself in harm's way. They should always make sure that there were two of them together at all times. "Never allow your children to walk or play outside alone."

Brian Moody spoke up and said, "Our father took us hunting and taught us how to shoot a gun. Whether you tell us that we can carry a gun or not, we want everyone to know that we have our own shotguns and, we know how to use them, with or without your permission, and we intend to use them if anyone tries to hurt our family or our friends."

Most of the neighbors smiled at Brian's comment because everyone knew that Terry and his boys would be great protection for anyone in the complex and would probably be the first three chosen for the patrol unit. Terry was over six feet tall and very muscular, and his sons were following right in their father's footsteps and looked even stronger.

Before Mr. Spencer went any further with their plans, he told everyone that he would check back with all of them after he talked with John. If he got John's and the owners' approval, he would set up a schedule and work out all the details as to what everyone could or could not do and then call another meeting.

When Mr. Spencer went to John's office the next day, Eddie Maxwell, one of the owners of the apartments, was in John's office talking to him. Someone from the complex went to John the night before and told him about the meeting Mr. Spencer called, and John had contacted the owners asking them if they would approve of the idea, and that was why Mr. Maxwell was there.

When John saw Mr. Spencer come through the door, he motioned for him to come on in to his office and have a seat. After the introduction pleasantries, Mr. Spencer told John that he had something that he would like to discuss with him, but he could come back later.

John said that he already knew about him wanting to get a group of volunteers together to patrol the complex and asked him if that was what he wanted to discuss. If so, would he please tell them about his plan?

After Mr. Spencer told them what he would like to do, both John and Mr. Maxwell thought it was a good idea. After what happened to Emma Carswell, one of the neighbors was not feeling too safe, thinking Harry Carswell might come back around and attack someone else, and he also did not feel comfortable with a bunch of their neighbors armed with guns, and he was just nervous about the situation. "I, and the owners, do not want any vigilantes going around trying to scare anyone, and we do not want any heroic activities."

John told him that when he got his list together of the people who would volunteer, he would like him to come to his office. They would prepare an agreement so that all the people involved would know what they could legally do as a citizen on patrol, and he wanted everyone involved to sign the agreement and have a witness to each signature.

John told them that the incident with Emma Carswell's ex-husband was the only major problem he had encountered since becoming manager. Mr. Spencer looked at John and said, "He isn't exactly her ex-husband. They have not officially gotten a divorce, but they have been separated for a very long time, and I think it is probably because of his abusive behavior."

John told him that Harry's name was not on the lease agreement and could not live there. They did not want anyone like him in, or around, the complex, and they would never allow him to live there. He then said that he thought it would be a good idea if they kept a special watch for Emma and her son. Mr. Maxwell nodded his head in agreement.

45

She Finally Gets to See Patrick

Mr. Spencer and Dave walked Emma and Frederick to the train station and then waited until she paid for their tickets and boarded the train. They made sure that they had the exact time they would be arriving back on Sunday evening and then stood and watched the train leave the station before he and Dave left to go back home.

Emma felt bad about Mr. Spencer going to so much trouble, but it did make her feel much safer. She was so thankful that all of the people where they lived and where they worked seemed nice and protective of them. She had been lucky with Charles and Sara Mollenix when Harry first left her. If it had not been for them, she did not know what she and the children would have done. After the night the intruder got into their house, Charles constantly kept watch on them.

When they arrived to their destination, Emma and Frederick walked the six blocks to her grandmother's house. The weather was beautiful, and it would be foolish to pay for a bus ticket for six blocks. They always preferred walking when the weather was pretty.

Frederick was being very quiet and had not said anything since they got off the train and she was concerned about him. With all the things that happened to them, he might still think that she was bringing him to her grandmother's to leave him so that he would be safe from Harry.

Emma looked at Frederick and said, "I bet that Dave secretly wanted to come with us, because he had such a good time when he came before. If you like, maybe the next time we come, he can come with us." He seemed to perk up a little after her comment and started kicking stones out of their way as they walked, but he still was not talking very much.

When they were in front of the neighbor's house where Harry had beaten their dog, Emma began to feel sad. Just like everything else, she did not tell anyone about him killing the dog.

After he found out about her inheritance, he acted as though he worshiped the ground she walked on and actually proposed to her at the exact place where he kicked the dog to death. She wondered why he proposed at that spot. Was it coincidental, or was it on purpose?

He got very upset because her grandmother wanted to plan a big church wedding for them. He thought they should be married by a justice of the peace because a big wedding was so much trouble and too expensive. He said that it was not her grandmother, who was getting married; it was their wedding, and they should decide how they wanted to get married and how much they wanted to spend on a wedding. When Emma told him that she had always dreamed of a big church wedding and it was not going to cost them any money because her grandparents were paying for everything, Harry seemed to go along with everything about the wedding; he just wished they would hurry it up a bit.

Emma was thinking and almost walked past her grandmother's house. She probably would have if Frederick had not touched her arm, saying, "Mom, this is Grandma's house."

Henrietta was the first to see them and came running outside to greet them. Her grandmother came to the door to see what all the excitement was. When she saw it was Emma and Frederick, she went out to meet them also. Uncle Charlie stood at the door watching them with that same mischievous grin, which made you wonder what he was up to now. He did not run to meet them, but when Frederick saw his uncle Charlie, he ran and jumped up on him, and Uncle Charlie swung him up on his shoulders and took off around the house with Frederick.

While Mary finished cooking dinner, they all sat in the kitchen until it was ready. It seemed like her grandmother's kitchen was always the meeting place for everyone that came to visit. It was probably because she was always in the kitchen baking or cooking, and the room had a very inviting aroma.

After dinner, Charlie took Frederick out to let him help chop wood. He was quite amazed as to how strong the boy was getting. When he first saw him, he was just a skinny little runt and seemed to be afraid of his shadow. Now he was looking very healthy and was also getting good at chopping wood. Charlie realized that he was growing quite fond of Frederick. He and Michelle never had any children, so that just made Frederick even more special.

When they started to gather the wood to take it to the wood box, a little snake crawled out from under the wood. Charlie told Frederick not to be afraid of it, because the snake would not hurt him. He could tell that Frederick was afraid of the snake, so he picked it up and tossed it out into higher weeds, and then he told Frederick that it was just a little garter snake. They had a long talk afterward, and Uncle Charlie told Frederick what snakes he should be careful of and what they looked like.

When they got back to the kitchen, the first thing Frederick told them was that Uncle Charlie picked up a snake. Immediately Henrietta shivered! Emma had to admit that she did not find that idea too pleasing either, but she let Frederick tell them all about it.

That evening when it came time for bed, Charlie told Frederick if he did not want to sleep with his mother, he could sleep in his room or on the couch. The boy was growing up and should not have to sleep with his mother. That statement really made Frederick perk up. He said, "Mom, if you don't mind, I will sleep on Grandma's couch." Emma had not thought of sleeping arrangements when she decided to come for an overnight visit. She was going to have to accept the fact that Frederick was growing up, whether she wanted him to or not.

Emma's grandmother came to her room after everyone else had gone to bed and asked her if they could talk. Of Emma said yes, but she could tell that it was going to be bad news because that was the only time her grandmother would have that tone to her voice.

Her grandmother told her that she might have met the people who had Patrick. When she was out one day taking her afternoon walk, she met some new neighbors and welcomed them to the community. They were very gracious and friendly. When she asked them where they were from, they were a little hesitant with their answer. She pretended that she did not notice their behavior, but she did get a good look at their child, and she said that he looked just like Harry did when he was young. Another thing, I personally thought they looked a little old to have a child that young.

She told her that she tried not to look at the baby too much to keep from drawing attention. She would have loved to pick the child up and hold him in her arms. Of course, any grandmother would feel that way about a child that may possibly be her grandchild.

Emma asked her if she would walk with her the next morning so that she might run into them because Patrick was still her baby, and she still had legal rights to him.

Her grandmother told her that the Timmonses walked to church every Sunday, and they came right by their house. She told her that she could watch from the front window, and she could see them when they start down the street. "You can go out and approach them about the baby in a casual way as though you were headed out for a walk."

It was difficult for Emma to get any sleep that night. She was up, dressed, and was sitting at the window before anyone else was up. She wanted to make sure she saw the couple that may possibly have her baby. After she had been sitting there for a couple of hours, her grandmother brought her a cup of coffee. Emma told her grandmother that she was afraid to drink it because she might have to go to the bathroom and maybe miss the couple. Her grandmother told her to run to the bathroom now, and she would watch while she was gone.

Emma was drinking her coffee when she saw the couple turn the corner to come down the street and immediately recognized them. She walked down their sidewalk as though she was going out for a morning walk. She did not want to make a big scene because some of the other neighbors might hear them.

She stepped out just as the Timmonses got to their walkway. "You could have knocked Mrs. Timmons over with a feather." She immediately grabbed her heart, went pale, and looked like she might faint.

Mr. Timmons asked her what she wanted, and Emma said that she wanted Patrick. She told them that they could discuss this out in the open where all the neighbors could hear or they could go inside and talk. Mr. Timmons told her that there was nothing to discuss. They told Emma that she had legally signed adoption papers before their lawyer when she gave him to them that day, and she now had no legal rights to Patrick.

Patrick started crying, and Mrs. Timmons picked him up. It broke Emma's heart because she could see the bond between them as mother and child.

Emma did not know what to do about the situation. She said, "The only papers that I signed were to let you have guardianship over Patrick in case he needed medical attention. There is no way that I would have signed adoption papers giving my baby to you."

Very haughtily, Mr. Timmons said that she should have taken the time to read the papers before signing them. He said, "You were in such a hurry to get rid of him that you did not even take the time to read what you were signing."

She told them that she was not in a hurry to get rid of her baby; she just wanted to find a safe place for him to stay until she had the means to take care of him, and that is what they said that they would do until she could come and get him.

Mr. Timmons told her that she was welcome to come to their house and read the adoption papers. Patrick was now legally their child. If she tried to make a scene, they would report her to the police. He then told her that they sold their house and moved to where they thought was far enough away so that the baby would not have to deal with all the gossip around town about her and never have to know that his mother gave him away to the first couple who would take him.

Now it was Emma's time to go weak and feel lightheaded and feel as though she may faint.

Patrick started crying again, and Emma knew that she would not do anything to hurt her child. She would rather give him up than hurt him.

When she did not say anything else, the Timmonses turned and walked back up the street, taking their child home instead of continuing on to church.

Emma stood there shaking. Her grandmother came out and encouraged her to come back inside the house.

After they were inside the house, Frederick was up, dressed, and in the kitchen with Henrietta and Uncle Charlie eating breakfast. Emma went up to her room, sat down on her bed, and cried. Her grandmother came up shortly afterward and sat at her side, holding her as though she was a small child.

When they went back down to where the others were, Emma told them that she was not feeling well. Uncle Charlie told her that it was probably because she had eaten so much of her grandmother's strawberry rhubarb pie the night before, and it had made her sick. He said, "Next time, save all of us a piece."

Emma had not eaten any of the pie, and everyone thought the comment was funny because they were the ones that ate all of the pie. It was one of their grandmother's greatest creations.

When it came time for them to leave, it was sad, and everyone hated to see them go, and Frederick and Emma neither wanted to leave.

46

The Snake

One the way home on the train, Emma tried her best to keep Frederick entertained, but she was carrying such a heavy load of guilt where Donald and Patrick were concerned that it made it difficult for her to concentrate. She needed to stay focused on her only child left and not neglect him. Frederick was a real trooper. He had less, and complained the least.

As soon as the train pulled into the station, the first people they saw were Mr. Spencer and Dave standing on the platform waiting for them. Frederick was anxious to tell Dave about chopping wood and especially about his uncle picking up a snake.

Frederick did not even say hello to Dave or his father. Instead, he ran up to them breathless telling them about his uncle picking up a snake. Dave said, "No way! No one would be crazy enough to pick up a snake."

Frederick assured him that his uncle picked up the snake. He told Dave that there were non-venomous snakes, and if they did bite you, it would not kill you. His uncle Charlie had drawn him pictures of the snakes that were dangerous and the snakes that were not dangerous. Dave immediately told him that he could pick up all the snakes that he wanted to, but he sure was not going to pick one up. To him, a snake was a snake, regardless of their color, and if they bit you, you would die.

The boys walked in front, chatting and having fun all the way home. Mr. Spencer asked Emma if she was okay because she looked so pale and was quiet. She told him that she had eaten too much strawberry rhubarb pie at her grandmother's and she was not feeling too well. He told her that was one of his favorite pies, but many people did not know how to mix the ingredients together to make them taste good. His wife had tried to make one, but it did not turn out as his mother's did, so she never attempted it again.

Emma told him that she had craved the strawberry rhubarb pie when she was expecting one of her children, but she never attempted making one. She left that specialty to her grandmother. She did well with cakes, but for some reason, she had never been able to conquer making piecrusts. Her crusts always turned out thick and hard, not light and flaky as her grandmother's were.

Emma did not even realize that she had said one of her children and not her baby or Frederick. Mr. Spencer noticed the comment but said nothing. He felt that Emma was carrying around a lot of pain from her past, and he was not going to make matters worse by asking her any questions. Instead, he started telling her about how they were going to work the citizens' patrol. He told her that she did not have to be afraid because there would still be someone watching the complex day and night.

That did make Emma feel a little better and safer because she was dreading coming home without having the police there.

That evening when Dave was over at Frederick's playing, Mr. Spencer asked his wife if she knew anything about Emma having more children.

Her reply was that she had never heard Emma speak of anyone except her grandmother. After her husband caused all the commotion at the apartment complex, everyone there knew about him. Mr. Spencer nodded his head and said, "I know! It has spread all over the plant as well."

Mrs. Spencer said thoughtfully, "Do you think that monster has her other children?"

Mr. Spenser said, "I sure hope not. Hopefully they are with her grandmother or another relative."

Mrs. Spencer said, "I would hate to think that any child would have to live with him. If the timing is ever right, I will ask her. But for now, I think we should not cause her any more stress than necessary."

47

Hitler Is One Bad Dude

Monday morning came too soon for Emma. It had been great visiting with her daughter, grandmother, and uncle Charlie over the weekend. It seemed that everything was always pleasant there. She had tried to make their home like that, but when Harry came home, everything changed as fast as switching off a lightbulb.

It was sad about Patrick, but at least she was able to see him and know that he was loved and being taken good care of. He looked very healthy and happy. That is until he thought she was going to touch him. He had been with the Timmonses for a long time and knew them as his mother and father. It hurt, but she would have to learn to accept it because she knew of nothing that she could do about it.

She still could not believe that she had been so trusting when she signed those adoption papers without reading them first. She would never trust anyone like that again; she had been so naïve.

For several months afterward, everything seemed to be settling down to a normal routine again, with nothing eventful or uneventful happening. Emma no longer read the newspaper unless Mr. Spencer brought her one that he had read. There was a newspaper stand just outside the plant; she would look at the headlines each morning before entering the plant, and it seemed there was always something dramatic happening. Thankfully, there was not too much going on at the home front except for the rationing. Families had received war-rationing books dictating how much gasoline, tires, sugar, meat, silk, shoes, nylon, and other items anyone person could buy. There were even ration books for chicken wire. It was a hard time for everyone.

She heard some people in the plant talking about how the British troops had defeated the Germans and Italians at El Alamein in Egypt, sending the Axis forces in chaotic retreat across Libya to the eastern border of Tunisia.

On another day, she heard some of them talking about how United States and British troops landed at several points on the beaches of Algeria and Morocco in French North Africa, but she did not hear enough to know why they did that and what happened.

There was no more notable news discussed until one day she remembered Mr. Spencer and John discussing the war. Mr. Spencer asked John if he had seen the headlines, and John said that he sure did. They started talking about how between November 23, 1942 to February 2, 1943 Soviet troops did a counter attack, breaking through the Hungarian and Romanian lines northwest and southwest of Stalingrad and trapping the German Sixth Army in the city and how Hitler refused to allow them to retreat or try to break out of the Soviet ring. John said, "Hitler is one bad dude."

Emma could not figure out why so many countries were at war with each other. *Why could people not get along and grow their countries, instead of trying to destroy or conquer others.*

48

Rat's Tail

Frederick and Dave would be going into the second grade when school started. Frederick was changing into a well-bred young man. Emma thought that it was mostly because of the influence of Mr. Spencer and John McMenus. They both showed Frederick a lot of attention. Both men had trucks, but with the gas rationing, they were not able to drive them very often. When Mr. Spencer went into town for groceries, he would normally walk, and he would take Dave and Frederick with him. Sometimes they would take Dave's wagon so that he and Frederick could pull the groceries home in the wagon instead of having to carry them. Mr. Spencer would always buy them a piece of candy for helping him. Whatever energy they got from the sugar content would be worn off by the time they arrived back home, but it was a big treat for the boys.

Because of the rationing, everyone had to cut corners wherever possible. It was difficult to make a sweet dessert without sugar, so the women tried to be creative with desserts and other food they prepared for their families. There was one dish called Lord Woolton Pie. The recipe involved dicing and cooking potatoes (or parsnips), cauliflower, carrots, and, possibly, turnip. After stewing the vegetables, you add rolled oats and chopped spring onions to the thickened vegetable water. You then made a potato pastry to go on top of the pie and grated cheese to sprinkle over the piecrust. When the pie was golden brown on top, you took it out of the oven. Mr. Spencer told his wife that he did not think that it would ever be one of his favorite foods.

On Sunday when they got ready for church, Mrs. Spencer and Emma were planning to dress conservatively because of the posters about women's clothing.

The only clothes and shoes that Emma now had were the few things that she had purchased after Harry destroyed all of her clothes and shoes. She was only able to salvage a few dresses, but naturally, they were mostly the ones that were not very pretty.

After she went to work at the sewing factory, she was finally able to buy herself and Frederick some new clothes, but she purchased most of her clothes after she went to work in the munitions factory. After not having any new clothes for a very long time, it made her feel good just to wear something new.

After Harry destroyed her clothing, she went shopping in a secondhand store where she heard that you could get nice used clothing for very little money. In the store, she found a pair of heels that were beautiful and fit her perfectly, and they only cost a dime. She also purchased a couple of dresses for fifty cents each and their stockings were two pair for five cents, so she bought four pair.

For church, Emma put on the black dress that she had bought at the secondhand store. It had a belt about a half-inch wide, which was acceptable for women's clothing. When she put on the black shoes and looked into the mirror, she thought that she looked as if she was dressed for a funeral. She actually bought the dress to wear in case she did have to go to a funeral, but she did not like it for church.

Before changing dresses, Emma went to Frederick's closet and pulled out his white dress shirt. He was going to wear everyday clothes to church so that they could play after the children's service, so he would not need the white shirt. She put it on over the black dress. The tail of the shirt was too long to let it hang loose, so she rolled it up in the back until it was at her waist and then tied the front together but did not button it.

Her hair did not get completely dry before she went to bed the night before, and it was sticking out everywhere. She had gone to bed with pin curls on top and on the sides of her hair. It was too difficult to sleep with the pin curls all over her head. She then took the bobby pins out of the top of her hair and combed it. She then got one of her old stockings that had runs, and put some cloth scraps into it. When it was about twelve inches long and about two inches thick, she cut the two end pieces off and tied them so that the scraps would not come out. She then put it around the lower back of head and secured it with bobby pins. One end of it came to about the top of her left ear and the other end came to about a couple inches above her right ear. She then started tucking her hair over the stuffed stocking. After she did that, she secured her hair around the stuffed stocking with hairpins. She turned around and around looking at the finished look. She thought that her hair looked just like the ad on the bobby pin holder, and she felt that she looked better than she had in a very long time.

Frederick was already outside talking with Dave and Mr. Spencer when she walked out her apartment door. As she turned around from locking her door, she heard a big wolf whistle. Having no idea who did it or who it was for, she looked around at everyone standing in her group of friends. Sophia spoke up and said, "Now that is the way you should dress all of the time."

Vera asked Sophia how she learned to whistle like a man. She asked Emma which fashion magazine she had gotten her outfit from because she would like to have one just like it. Emma had never had anyone to tell her that she looked like someone from a fashion magazine before, and it made her feel good.

Frederick spoke up and said, "Mom, why are you wearing my white shirt?"

Mrs. Spencer broke into the conversation to keep Emma from having to answer Frederick's question and said, "Emma, I think you look wonderful. You have an amazing eye for fashion. I love the way you have your hair ratted. I have been thinking about getting myself a rat's tail. She then looked around at Sophia and Vera and asked them if they had one, and they each shook their heads no.

Mrs. Spencer told them that the rat's tail was the new thing in style. They made them out fabric that looks like stockings. When using it, you first take your comb and comb your hair downward toward your scalp to make it puff up and stick out. It actually looks like a rat made a nest in your hair. You then work your hair over the rat's tail. It keeps it very neat and out of your way. She then told Emma that the way she had her hair curled at the top made the style look even prettier.

Sophia laughed and said, "I am not going to go to that much trouble with my hair, unless I am going somewhere that I need to look nice or going to go somewhere to have fun and meet good-looking men. I sure would not do it just to go to work at the factory. All of those men are either married or over the hill.

Vera said, "No one would see it in the factory anyway, because we have to wear scarves over our hair."

49

Lorenda Collingwood

Monday, while on a break at work, Sophia and Vera told Emma about their weekend. They were bored after church, so they took a bus down to the docks where naval ships anchor. Sophia said, "It looked like there were a million sailors there. We are going back next Sunday. Would you like to go with us? Since we have been to church, we are already dressed nice, so we don't have to go to any trouble getting dressed and doing our hair."

Emma said that she would love to do something like that with them, but she was afraid that she might see Harry. As long as she stayed close to home, in the plant where she worked, she felt safe, especially if Mr. Spencer was around, but she would not feel comfortable going to some place like that.

Vera told her that they looked for Harry, but with so many sailors around, it would be almost impossible to find his face.

Sophia told her that she would keep an eye out for him. If they did see him, they would come back immediately and tell her so that she could be on guard, just in case he decided to pay her another visit.

Vera asked Emma if she had seen the new woman they hired not too long ago; her name is Lorenda Collingwood.

Emma said, "No, is it someone I am supposed to know?"

Vera and Sophia looked at each other trying to figure out how they could tell Emma what they knew, but they knew they needed to tell her everything.

They told her that they had tried to become friends with Lorenda, because they felt sorry for her. She came to work looking as though she had been in a bad accident. She was on the verge of tears, so they tried to talk to her and console her. It was before they saw Emma.

Finally, Sophia said, "Emma, Lorenda Collingwood and I have been talking, and I found out that she has a fiancé by the name of Harry Carswell. She moved into an apartment near here so that she could be close whenever he came home on leave. She came to work at the factory, because she could not find anything else. Evidently, her parents do not particularly care for Harry and are trying to break them up and want her to come back home and finish her education. Instead of breaking up with him, they are now engaged and supposed to get married as soon as he is discharged from the navy."

Vera waited for Sophia to pause, and then she said, "Her fiancé had not seen the apartment she rented for them, and she was really excited for him to see it and wanted to make everything special for him. The maintenance man came to fix a leaking pipe, and Harry arrived before he left. As the maintenance man was leaving, he heard Harry making accusations about her talking and flirting with him, while he was there. He even heard him say that he was going to check the bed. He said that he thought he could hear Lorenda trying to change the subject and calm Harry down and try to diffuse his anger. She told him that she had found a good job and did not need to ask for money from her parents now.

"Evidently, he got mad about that also, and told her that she should not treat her parents like that. He could not believe that she would be that cruel to them. With her parents being so wealthy, he felt sure that they would want to help her, and it probably hurt their feelings by her not accepting any money from them. He had to use the small amount of income he made in the navy to go back and forth to the ship, so he would not be able to give her any money to help with expenses, so she should let her parents help."

Sophia said, "When he found out where she was working, he really got upset. Harry told her that he has a cousin that works at the factory by the name of Emma Carswell. He told her that there was a lot of bad blood in their family, and he did not want her to have any contact with his cousin. He told her, if he ever caught her talking to her, he would break it off with her, and she would never see him again."

Vera told her that later Saturday evening they walked to the store, and he accused Lorenda of flirting with a man that lived down the street from the apartments. She said that all she did was to say hello to the man, but it made Harry so mad that he grabbed her arm and held it so tight that she thought he was going to squeeze it off. He did not speak to her the rest of the night, and he left early Sunday morning without saying good-bye. She said that she thought that he had gone back to his ship until he came running in late Sunday evening. She said that he had dirt and blood all over his uniform, and there were a couple of torn places on the left leg of his uniform. He told her to clean it up, because he could not go back on board his ship with his uniform looking like that. When she asked him what happened, he told her that no man would ever to talk to her again. She said that she was embarrassed because she knew that he had probably fought with the neighbor that he accused her of flirting with.

Sophia said, "You will never guess what happened after she got his uniform cleaned, patched, and hung in front of the fan to finish drying. Harry grabbed her by the hair and dragged her to the bedroom. At first she thought he was just playing around and trying to make up for being such a jerk, but when he got her on the bed, she said that he did things to her and made her do things to him that she would never tell anyone about."

Vera said, "Emma wasn't that the same weekend that Harry beat you and Frederick? That was probably the reason some of the men were making comments about there being a catfight over the weekend because when you both came to work, you both were all bruised with black eyes, looking as though you had been in a bad accident. We are not telling you this to make you afraid or jealous. We want to protect you."

Sophia told her that Lorenda's father had been out of town on business and stopped in to see her and her new apartment. When she opened the door to let him in, he saw what she looked like and immediately called a mover and packed up all of her things and took her home with him. Lorenda was too weak to argue with him. He told her that he was afraid when she decided to move to a big city alone something like this would happen. All she told him was that she got beat up. She did not tell him who did it.

When Emma got home, she talked to Frederick and made him promise that he would not leave the apartment unless someone was with him and never open the door when he was there by himself.

It made him a little nervous because he thought what she was talking about had something to do with the war. Frederick looked at her very seriously and asked, "Mom, will they make me go into the army and fight in the war?"

Emma said, "Heavens no, Frederick! Whatever gave you that idea?" He told her that he had overheard someone saying that the army was drafting all the young boys. Emma told him that it was the older boys, not the ones that were still in elementary school.

50

The Fort

Finally, school was out for summer vacation, and Frederick and Dave were discussing how they wanted to build their new fort. They had been making plans for it for the last few months, and now it was time to start construction.

They took their plans to Mr. Spencer and had him to go over them. He told them that he would help them build it. Dave and Frederick were excited because they knew that Mr. Spencer was great at building things. He told them that he would not build their fort for them, but he would be their worker when they needed him. This really made the boys feel proud because Mr. Spencer acted as if he had a lot of confidence in their abilities.

John had some lumber left from the construction of the apartments that he stored behind his house. He told the boys that this was probably what he was saving the lumber for and that he might be able to help them in the evenings.

Another neighbor had some nails and told the boys that they could have them. This fort was becoming a community project. At first, it made the boys a little hesitant, but then they decided that it would be great to have others helping them and possibly playing with them when the fort was finished.

Between the Victory Garden and building the fort, everyone stayed busy the first couple of weeks in June. By the third week in June, the fort was finished.

John told the boys that what they needed now was some bows and arrows so the boys started looking for small limbs on certain trees that would be flexible.

They had the bows trimmed down, and all they needed was some string. Mrs. Spencer had lots of heavy wood yarn left from making socks for the soldiers, and it worked perfectly.

Now the boys had to try to make some arrows. Mr. Spencer told them if they liked, he would help them with the arrows. It was mainly because he did not want the boys using a sharp knife by themselves.

The Fort was completed and everyone had bows and arrows; all they had to do now was enjoy it. There were two main rules. You could only shoot your bow and arrow at targets, not toward people. You also could not use tomatoes as targets.

It was a great summer. The garden they planted produced many vegetables, and all of the kids were happy and having a good time. There had been no major news in the papers about the war, so everyone seemed a little less stressed. Very few disagreements erupted among the kids, and the adults were so tired after working long hours in the plant and then working in their garden that most of them were too tired to do anything during the evenings.

There had been no sighting of Harry at the docks or anywhere around town, and this was great for Emma and Frederick. She was still afraid to let Frederick roam away from home as he once did. The only places that she went were to work, to the grocery store, and to church, and she always had people with her when she went to those places.

Sophia and Vera always walked to work with her, and they usually met up with a number of other people from the apartment complex that also walked with them.

When Emma went to the grocery story, it was usually with Mr. and Mrs. Spencer so that the boys could pull their groceries home in the wagon.

One evening when she was getting ready for bed, Emma heard a light tap on the door. She went to the window to peak out to try to see who it was before opening the door. It was Vera, so she let her in.

Vera said, "I have some interesting news. Lorenda Collingwood is pregnant. Her father came through town checking to see if Harry was home on leave. He said that he is very anxious to talk with him. If anyone sees him, he would appreciate them telling Harry that he is looking for him."

Emma had a strong gripping sensation in her chest. She feared what the poor girl would go through when she told Harry that she was expecting. However, according to Vera, Harry may be the person needing their sympathy.

51

Wine and Cigarettes

It was so hot in the plant during the month of July that some of the women were fainting from exposure to some of the fumes and material they had to work with.

Most of the men went outside to smoke. However, it was not ladylike for a woman to smoke in public.

One day when Vera thought that she could not stand the heat any longer, she walked outside. Her supervisor walked up to her and asked her why she was standing outside. She told him that she had gotten so hot that she felt like she was going to faint and thought that maybe a breath of fresh air would help. He asked her if the fresh air had helped, and she said yes. He told her to get back to work then. That did not go over very well with Vera. When they took their meal break, she told Emma, Sophia, and some other women about what her supervisor said. Several of the women decided that they would buy some cigarettes so that they could take smoking breaks.

That afternoon, Sophia and Vera went by a store on the way home and bought a pack of cigarettes. They tried smoking, but they found it disgusting. They went over to Emma's to let her try one. After smoking about three cigarettes, she told them that it did ease some of the tension that she was feeling, so they gave the cigarettes to her.

After finishing that pack of cigarettes, Emma bought more. If she were nervous, she would smoke a cigarette. It gave her something to do with her hands, and for some reason, smoking did seem to relax her.

One evening while Vera and Sophia were visiting with Emma, they decided to try to smoke a cigarette again. Emma told them that she had seen the men suck the smoke back into their lungs before they blew it out, and she was trying to learn to do that.

When Vera tried to suck the smoke back in, she started coughing. When Sophia tried it, she was a little better at it than Vera was. The three women sat there smoking cigarette after cigarette until they had smoked two packs. They realized that they had smoked all of Emma's cigarettes. Vera told Emma that they would go to the store and get her more cigarettes.

While they were gone, Emma fixed Frederick his evening meal, called him in to eat, and then got him ready for bed. Just as she was walking out of his room, Frederick rose up and said, "Mom, it sure smelled a lot better in the apartment when you and your friends did not smoke."

Emma laughed and said, "I am sure it did, Frederick. If it bothers you, too much I will not smoke inside." He told her that it was okay , but maybe she could keep his door closed while she was smoking, so that the smell would not get into his room.

About fifteen minutes later, Sophia and Vera knocked on the door. Emma knew who it was because they had also made up a secret knock so that she would not have to look out the window to find out who it was before she opened the door. Anyone standing at the door knocking could see when you peaked out the window. If it were someone she did not want to open the door for, the person would have already seen her looking out the window and would know that she was at home.

When Emma let them in, she could see that Vera was carrying something in a bag that was bigger than cigarettes should be. After placing the bag on the table, Vera pulled out a whole carton of cigarettes and a bottle.

Sophia laughed when she saw Emma look at the bottle. Neither of them had ever drunk very much alcohol, so Emma was wondering why they had bought it.

Vera said that Emma had told them that she wished that she had less tension in her life, so they bought something that would make them all less tense.

Sophia walked over to the cabinets, pulled out three glasses, and poured about an ounce in each glass. She said, "On three, drink it and see what happens." On three, they all put the glasses to their lips and sipped the wine, and all three of them found it to be very tasty.

The three of them sat there for about two hours smoking and drinking wine. After they drank all of the wine, they decided to call it a night.

Sophia had drunk more of the wine than Emma or Vera, and she was acting a little tipsy. She said that she felt as if she was walking on clouds when she walked them to the door. When they left the apartment, Sophia and Vera were both singing and walked as though maybe they may have drunk a little too much wine also.

Emma sat by herself with the lights off for about another hour smoking cigarettes, drinking the remainder of the wine while she looked out the window. She was feeling more relaxed than she had in a long time. She lay over on the couch and pulled up the afghan that she kept on the back of the couch and covered herself up. The next thing she knew, it was morning, and Frederick was tapping her on the shoulder telling her that she was going to be late going to work if she did not get up.

Emma could not believe that she had slept so long. Normally she only slept about three or four hours per night. She really had to hustle to change and get to work on time. She did not even have time for a bath. Just a quick change and ran a comb through her hair.

When she met up with Sophia and Vera, they were bright-eyed and cheery. They probably went straight home to bed whereas Emma had stayed up smoking and drinking.

As they walked with a group of women through the door of the plant, one of the women spoke up and said that someone smelled like a smoke stack.

Emma ignored the woman and glanced over at the newspaper stand as she did almost every morning for the last month or so. She could read part of the story, and it said that the Germans launched a massive tank offensive near Kursh in the Soviet Union. The Soviets blunted the attack and had now begun an offensive initiation of their own. The United States and British troops landed in Sicily. The Fascist Grand Council would depose Benito Mussolini to enable Marshal Pictro Badoglio to form a new government.

It all meant nothing to Emma, and she soon forgot the headlines because Sophia had put a pack of cigarettes in her shirt pocket where the men could see them. Some of the women gasped in horror, and some of the men glared their eyes. Sophia just walked past them with a smile on her face, and Vera called her a daredevil.

Sophia could not wait until she saw a bunch of men standing around smoking. She fully intended to join them, mostly just to see what they would do, because she still had not acquired a taste for smoking cigarettes.

52

Vodka

By August 1, it was so hot inside the plant that a couple of the men fainted. Now that it was the men fainting, instead of the women, the plant manager decided that he needed to try to do something about the heat. He had considered women to be weaker and not cut out for these jobs and did not want to go to any added expense, because he knew they would all be leaving when the men came home from the war.

After they opened the windows and placed blowers in front of some them, it made it a little more bearable, but it was still very hot.

Everyone in the apartment complex was trying to keep the garden watered. The kids loved going out with buckets of water. Of course, they got more on themselves than they did the plants, but as long as they did not injure the plants, no one cared. They were a lot cooler wet than they were dry.

It had been so hot that neither Sophia nor Vera wanted to go to the dance. There had not been any younger men there lately because most of them were away fighting in the war, and all that was there were older men, married men, or men that were so sweaty that they smelled like skunks. They would rather stay home, get them a bottle of wine, and keep as cool as possible.

The nightly drinking was becoming a habit with the three of them. It seemed there was nothing else to do. They could not go anywhere unless they walked because there were fewer bussing running because of the gas rationing, and they were not going to walk in the heat to go anywhere. By the time they got home each day the first thing they wanted to do was take a bath and find some place to cool to sit for a while.

One evening Sophia and Vera brought a different type of drink called Vodka. They had heard other people talking about it and decided they would try it by themselves before ordering any of it when they went to the dance. They really did not need alcohol to have a good time but Sophia had heard that it made the ugly men more handsome when you drunk it.

Sophia bought a cigarette holder that looked like it was at least eight inches long. When she put her cigarette into the holder, it made it all look like it was about a foot long. She thought she really looked sophisticated smoking her cigarette like that.

She told Emma and Vera that by the time the smoke came through the pipe holder that it did not taste as bad and she thought it looked much better than sticking a cigarette into your mouth puffing on it.

The cigarette holders become a fad. Most of the women that smoked were now using the cigarette holder because they felt like it made it look more ladylike than holding a cigarette between your fingers.

When they went outside to sit under the tree, they each took a full glass of vodka with them. Neither of them had tasted it yet, but they thought it looked like water especially with the ice cubes in it. Sophia said that it was vodka on the rocks. People would probably think that they were just sitting under the tree cooling off with a glass of water.

At the first sip, Sophia gasped, and Vera coughed, but Emma liked the taste. She also like the way she felt with just a few sips from her glass. After only a few sips, Sophia and Vera were ready to call it quits and poured the rest of what was in their glass into Emma's glass.

When they left for home, they told Emma that she could have the bottle of vodka because they could not handle that stuff. They would go back to drinking wine or try beer.

Emma actually liked the taste of wine best because it made her feel relaxed and want to have fun, but one glass of vodka equaled the effects of a couple of bottles of wine. The only difference, vodka made her feel angry, and for some reason, she liked feeling angry for a change. She did not feel like a little scared kitten; she felt like a lion that was ready to roar and could take on the world. She was ready for a fight. She wondered if this was what Harry drank when he went out every night. Maybe that was why he always wanted to fight with her when he came home. She wondered what would have happened if both of them had drunk vodka.

That night Emma drank about half of the bottle of vodka before going to sleep. The next day, she was late getting to work. She did not even have time to change her clothes or comb her hair. When she walked into the plant, her supervisor asked her what in the world was wrong with her. He told her that she looked hungover from a binge. She told him that she felt like she had a stomach virus but came to work anyway. He told her that maybe she should go back home so that none of the other workers would catch whatever it was that she had. Going home was fine with her because she had a headache so bad that she thought someone could hit it with a brick, and it would not make any difference.

As soon as she got home, Emma went back to bed. Frederick had already eaten some old biscuits with jam and was outside at their fort. When he saw her come home, he went straight to the apartment and asked her what was wrong. She told him that she was sick and had to come home from work early.

Frederick did not feel good about the situation with his mother. He knew if his mother did not work, they would have no money coming in, and they may have to move back to one of the old places they lived or either move in with their grandmother. Neither of those scenarios was pleasing to him. He had gotten used to their life there, and he loved having Dave around to play with. He left her alone until she had slept for a few hours before he came back into the house.

Emma looked terrible when Frederick came back in. Her hair was a tussled up, and she smelled terrible. He knew something was different, but he could not figure out exactly what was happening with his mother.

When Frederick said something to Emma, she shouted at him and told him to go outside and play with Dave. He told her that Dave had gone in for lunch, and he had thought that maybe she would have had his lunch prepared also. She said, "Well, I don't, so go in there and fix yourself something eat."

Frederick walked into the kitchen and scourged around for some food. He found some peanut butter and crackers and ate them. Normally his mother would have tea or iced water for him to drink, but she had made no tea, and she had sat the water pitcher on the counter and did not put it back inside the icebox to stay cool. He poured some water from the pitcher into a glass and the put the water pitcher back where it should be and went back outside to play with Dave.

When he got outside, Frederick asks Dave if he knew, what vodka was. Dave told him that he thought it was liquor. He said that he had heard his dad talk about a man that drank vodka, and it caused him to lose his job. His dad said that the man stayed hungover all the time and was always trying to start fights at work.

Frederick asked him what hungover was, and Dave just shrugged because he did not know the answer for that question.

53

The Slap

Emma sat on the sofa sipping vodka, and it seemed like it was making her feel better. She had thought that maybe the vodka was what made her sick the night before, but she was not sure now; it may be just what she needed.

When Frederick came in for supper, his mother was singing and dancing around while she cooked. Frederick said, "Wow, Mom, you sure made a speedy recovery." Emma danced over to where her son was and started trying to dance with him. Frederick thought it was funny the way she was acting, but he really did not like her acting this way.

When the meal was ready, Frederick sat down to eat. Emma sat with him, but she did not put any food in her plate; she sat drinking her water.

Frederick looked over to where the bottle of vodka was and noticed that it was almost empty. It had been about half full when he saw it that morning.

He asked his mother what she was drinking, and she told him that it was water, and he told her that he did not believe her. Emma got angry and asked him just who had nominated him as her keeper and then walked over and slapped Frederick in the face. Frederick was startled, to say the least, by his mother's actions and did not make a move. When he did talk, he said, "Mom, please don't be like Harry."

Emma was feeling so angry that she told him to shut his mouth and eat his supper.

She then walked over to the bottle of vodka and started to pour more of it into her glass. When she did, Frederick ran over, took the bottle away from her, and poured it down the sink. When he did that, she got so angry that she took the back of her hand and slapped Frederick across the face. When he started crying, Emma walked away and went into the bedroom, fell across the bed, and passed out.

Frederick did not know what was happening to his mother, but he did not like it. He went into her bedroom, pulled the covers up over her, and then went to his room, lay down on his bed, and cried. He had not done that in a very long time. He was afraid of what was happening to his mother and afraid of what would happen to both of them if she kept acting this way. He had always felt that as long as he had his mother, he would be okay, regardless of their circumstances.

Frederick cried himself to sleep. When he woke up, it was about 4:00 a.m., and he could hear his mother crying, so he went to her. When he asked her what was wrong, she told him that she had a terrible headache. She looked up at Frederick and asked him what had happened to his face and he said, "Mom, you hit me." Emma started crying then because she could not remember hitting her baby. She would never hit him in the face. She would not hit him anywhere that hard.

Frederick sat down beside his mother on her bed. He said, "Mom, I think you got drunk on vodka. A man that Mr. Spencer knows drinks vodka, and it caused him to lose his job. If you drink it again, you might lose your job."

Emma could not believe what her son was telling her. Had the vodka affected her that way? She did fine when she drank wine, but she knew that something was happening to her when she drank the vodka because there were times that she could not remember things that happened, and she definitely did not remember hitting Frederick.

Frederick lay his head over on his mother's shoulder. She put her arm around him and promised him that she would never take another drink of Vodka.

It seemed like an escape from reality while she was drinking vodka. She did not worry about anything and felt like she did not have a worry in the world. She hoped it could help her to forget about all the bad stuff she and her children had been through.

Frederick interrupted her thoughts and said, "It really hurts to watch you like that, Mom! Do you remember the way Harry would act some nights when he had been out late and how he would always beat you and whip us? That was the way you acted last night."

Emma did not know what to say. She was so hungover from the vodka that she felt like she was going to throw up any minute, and she wished that she had never touched that stuff. It was poison for her. She could not solve her problems by drinking alcohol. She had to keep her promise that she would never drink again.

Frederick told his mother to go back to bed and then told her that before Mr. Spencer left for work he would go over and tell him that she was too sick to go to work and ask him to tell her boss.

Frederick stood outside and watched for Mr. Spencer to come out of his apartment. When he did, he walked over to him and told him that his mother was still sick and could not go to work and wanted to know if he would tell her boss.

Mr. Spencer saw the bruise across Frederick's face and asked him what had happened. His first thought was that Harry was back, but he had not heard anything, and he knew that the men were keeping a special watch for Emma's apartment and felt they would have seen him had he been there.

Frederick told him that he got up during the night to go to the bathroom and get a drink of water and ran into the wall. It was a lie, but he would do anything to protect his mother.

Mr. Spencer did not really believe him because he could see a handprint on his cheek and bruising on the other, but he did not say anything. The only answer he could come up with was that he must have gotten into a fight or his mother had slapped him. The handprint was not very large, so it could have been from a young person. He did not say anything further to Frederick because he did not want to embarrass him. He told him not to worry that he would tell Emma's boss that she was still sick. He then told Frederick to take care of his mother while she was sick.

Frederick thanked him and then walked back into his apartment.

About 9:00 a.m., Emma came walking into Frederick's room. She said, "Frederick, I don't know what all happened last night, but I am sorry for hurting you, and I promise that I will never do anything to ever hurt you like that again."

Frederick went over to his mother, put his arms around her, and told her that he loved her. Emma kissed the top of his head and told him that she loved him too. She then made a pot of very strong coffee and started their breakfast.

As Mr. Spencer had asked him to do, Frederick stayed home from school to take care of his mother. He was also staying home because he was ashamed of the bruises on his face.

54

Hot Biscuits with Peanut Butter and Honey

It was around noon the next day when Emma started feeling as if she may live. The coffee and the aspirin helped greatly. When she looked around her apartment, it looked awful, so she immediately started cleaning.

Shortly afterward, Frederick walked in. He did not ask for lunch, but she knew that he had probably come in because Dave's mother had called him in for lunch.

She asked him if he was hungry, and Frederick said that he was, but he could eat some crackers and peanut butter.

Emma told him that she was fine and that she would have him something fixed shortly. Preparing the food still made her a little queasy on her stomach.

When the food was ready, they sat down to their meal. Frederick reached over, took his mother's hand, and said, "This is the way I like you, Mom."

Tears came to Emma's eyes, but she brushed them away and gave her son a big hug, and they ate lunch together. She did not think she was going to be able to keep it down, but after she ate, she started feeling better.

That evening, Emma took some vegetables from the garden and cut a tiny piece of the meat they were rationed and fixed them a good meal.

She had hot biscuits to go with the meal, and Frederick ate as though he was starving. He told her that he loved her biscuits especially when she put butter and honey on them. She told him that she did not have any butter, so she mixed a little peanut butter with the honey for him to eat.

Working long hours in the plant and then having to walk everywhere they went was very tiring. Emma realized that she was going to have to make more time for Frederick because he was all she had left.

55

Christmas

On September 3, all the children in the apartment complex had to go back to school. It had been a great summer; it just did not last long enough.

Frederick and Dave were lucky because they had the same teacher, and they both loved her. It seemed like it was going to be another good year for Frederick.

A few weeks later, Emma glanced at the newspaper headlines as she was walking into the plant. She always hoped that one day she would see a headline story about the war ending. However, if that did happen, she would probably be out of a job and so would many other women. It would not be so bad for the ones that were married, but for the single mothers and other single women, it would probably be very difficult for them.

She bent over the newspaper stand trying to read the front-page news. There were several stories with big bold print. The first was about Badoglio government surrendering unconditionally to the Allies. The second said that under Mussolini's command, on September 12, the Germans immediately seized control of Rome, and on September 9, Allied troops landed successfully near Anzio, just south of Rome.

Emma had no idea who Mussolini was or where any of the areas were that they were talking about. She wondered if any other Americans were as confused as she was about the war. Occasionally she would overhear the men in the plant and around the apartment complex talking about things that were happening with the war. It was as if they were speaking in a foreign language.

The weekend before Thanksgiving, some of the men went wild turkey hunting, and Mr. Spencer brought home a big one. Mrs. Spencer invited Emma and Frederick to have Thanksgiving dinner with them.

It was the best meal that any of them had eaten in a very long time. Lard, butter, eggs, and grain were part of the things rationed, but between the two families, they had enough breadcrumbs and cornmeal to make stuffing for the big bird.

Emma was good at making biscuits and mashed potatoes and gravy, so that was what she prepared. She poured the potato broth over her flour mixture instead of water to make gravy. Mr. Spencer told her that he could make a meal off nothing but her gravy and biscuits.

The coolness in the air felt good after the hot summer months. That did not last long because shortly after Thanksgiving, they had almost twelve inches of snow, which the kids loved because the schools were closed, and they were able to make some snow ice cream with honey and milk. It would have tasted better if they had more sugar and some vanilla to put in it.

The first Saturday in December, Mr. Spencer took Dave and Frederick out to hunt for Christmas trees. While they were out, Mrs. Spencer and Emma popped corn for them to string and put on the tree. Mrs. Spencer gave Emma a string of lights, and the boys had made some angels at school, and with the other Christmas ornaments they made, both families had beautiful Christmas trees.

Emma had not had a Christmas tree since she married Harry. He told her that it was just a waste of money to buy toys and junk to put under a tree. Frederick had never had a Christmas tree or received a Christmas gift.

When Emma went Christmas shopping, she bought Frederick a Brownie camera. She knew that he would like to have one because Dave had one, and they loved taking and looking at the pictures.

Emma and Mrs. Spencer did not know it, but Mr. Spencer had the boys out making special cutting boards for them for Christmas. They sanded them so smooth that when you rubbed your hand over them, they felt as smooth as glass.

With the money Frederick and Dave made helping John and Misty, they bought small Christmas presents for their parents and some film for Dave's Brownie camera.

Christmas was going to be great this year.

In the past when Frederick would hear other kids talking about what they got for Christmas, he would lie and tell all the kids that he got the same thing.

They did not have any wrapping paper, but Emma and Mrs. Spencer had sewed squares together to make quilts, and they let the boys use some of the squares to wrap their gifts in so they would look pretty under the tree. She gave them some yarn to make bows for their packages. She told the boys to be careful with the yarn and squares after opening their packages because it had to go back into the sewing boxes for quilts and socks.

Dave and Frederick made up a little jingle for their mothers because they sewed scraps together for quilts. "The two Mrs. Sew and Sews makes our quilts from our old clothes." When they came up behind their mothers while they were talking, they would say, "Hello, Mrs. Sew and Sew."

This year Frederick and Dave both had parts in a Christmas play at church. They both played the part of shepherds. After the play was over, everyone got a bag of fruit and a small toy from under the tree.

Reverend Charles told them when they gave each other gifts at Christmas to be sure to do it out of love not as a show. He told them that when they gave someone a gift at Christmas, it was like giving Jesus a birthday present. Jesus loved us, and we should love each other. A good way to show that love was to give gifts to those we love.

When they got home that night, Frederick went to his mother and gave her a big hug. When she asked him what was the hug for, he looked up at her and told her that he was giving her a gift of a hug because he loved her. That was what Reverend Charles told them they should do.

Emma thought her heart would burst with pride. She gave Frederick back a hug and told him that she loved him too.

Christmas morning, Frederick was up before Emma. He got her gift from under their tree and placed it on the kitchen counter. When Emma came into the kitchen, the first thing she saw was the gift. When she looked over at Frederick, he was sitting on the floor right beside his gift. She immediately went over to the tree, got his gift, and handed it to him. She could not believe how excited he was as he opened it.

After he opened his package, he held it close to his chest smiling very sheepishly. Emma asked him why he was smiling. Frederick told her that he was so excited about receiving his first gift that he had sneaked into the living room and opened it one night after she went to bed early. He told her that that he was so excited about it being a Brownie camera that he spent some of the money that John had paid him to buy film for the camera, and he wanted the first picture to be of her when she opened her present.

Emma fluffed her hair as though trying to look prettier for a picture and then went over to the counter and got her gift. She could not believe her eyes when she opened it. It was the nicest cutting board she had ever seen. When she asked Frederick how in the world he had been able to buy such a nice cutting board.

He smiled and told her that Mr. Spencer taught him and Dave how to make one for her and Mrs. Spencer.

Emma told him that the cutting board was so nice that she did not want to use it and mess it up. Frederick told her that Mr. Spencer said to tell her that when she washed it to put a tiny bit of lard on it and grease it well and the wood would not split.

Emma smiled and held the cutting board up so that Frederick could take his first picture with his camera. Frederick hugged his mother and said, "Mom, this is the best Christmas anyone could have."

56

The Hatchet

Emma put all the gifts together for her grandmother and Henrietta, and she and Frederick walked to the station to catch the train. They were wearing their heavy coats, carrying their suitcases, plus the bag of gifts, and it made walking a bit of a challenge. Normally they could take the bus to the train station if they did not want to walk or if it was bad weather, but they had spent so much money on gifts that Emma did not have enough left to pay for the bus and the train tickets. It was starting to sprinkle snow, and the cold wind was howling, making it even more difficult to walk.

After getting on the train, Frederick took the window seat so that he could look for interesting things to take pictures of with his new Brownie camera. He was anxious to take pictures, but he was also afraid that he would use up all of his film, and he wanted to make sure that he had enough file to take a picture of his grandmother, Henrietta, and Uncle Charlie. He was hoping he could get his uncle Charlie to make one of his goofy faces when he took a picture of him.

As usual, they could smell food cooking as they walked up the sidewalk to their grandmother's house. Even if you were not hungry, you would still want to eat when you smelled the food cooking.

As usual, Henrietta had been watching for them and ran out to meet them, and Uncle Charlie came out to help with their packages.

After dinner, they went into the living room, and their grandmother gave everyone their gifts. Mary had baked her granddaughter her favorite strawberry rhubarb pie. She had baked some ginger bread men for Frederick and Henrietta. She told them they could eat them or hang them on their Christmas tree. Of course, Frederick immediately took a big bite out of one of his, but Henrietta took one of hers and hung it on the tree. Mary got thank-you hugs from everyone. She told all of them that the hug was the best gift they could give her.

Henrietta had bought her mother a beautiful scarf that would match her coat. Emma gave her grandmother a blue- and white-spotted roasting pan. It was what Mary had wanted for a long time.

Uncle Charlie was the most surprised with his gifts. Mr. Spencer had helped Frederick and Dave carve a little train, and Frederick gave his train to his uncle. When Emma gave her uncle his socks, you would have thought that she had given him a hundred dollars. He immediately pulled the ones off that he had on and put the new socks on. He said, "I have always wanted a pair of knitted wool socks because they are so warm, and the winters up here are brutal, especially as I get older." He was only fifty, but by the way he talked, it made him sound much older.

Uncle Charlie went over, kissed Emma on the cheek and shook Frederick's hand. He then gave Emma a Bible that he had bought for her, and Mary's gift to her granddaughter was a handmade cover with handles to go over her Bible. In the Bible, Mary had written all of the family names with their birth dates and the death dates of the ones that had passed away. She included all of Emma's children.

Uncle Charlie pretended that he did not have any other gifts for anyone else. After a few minutes, he reached behind the couch acting as though he could hardly pick up whatever it was behind there. Finally, he brought out a hatchet with a bright-red handle and gave it to Frederick. He told Frederick that he was so good at cutting wood that he thought he deserved his own ax. Frederick looked at his uncle and asked if he could take it home, and his uncle told him that he could take it home with him or leave it there, whichever he wanted. Frederick told him that he would like to take it home with him so that he could show it to Dave and his father. Frederick ran over, hugged his uncle, and thanked him for the hatchet. His uncle took his knuckles and ruffled Frederick's hair.

No one had yet given Henrietta a gift except for the cookies, and she was looking a little huffed because every one had received a gift except her.

Uncle Charlie went back to the couch and pulled out a wooden box with a lid. He had made Henrietta a jewelry box. He had even carved a flower on the top and put her initials inside the center of the flower. When Henrietta opened the box, there was a heart necklace inside. She immediately ran over to her uncle Charlie so that he could show her how she could open it and put a picture of herself or a picture of her boyfriend when she got one. He had not told anyone, but he had originally bought the necklace as a gift for Michelle but never had a chance to give it to her before she ran off with the sailor. When he took it out of the drawer where he had it stored, he opened it and took Michelle's picture out of it and then put it in the jewelry box that he had made for Henrietta. He knew that his mother did not wear jewelry, so he thought Henrietta should be the one to have it.

You could hear Henrietta's squeal of excitement all the way down the street. She told her uncle that it was the best present in the world. Frederick told her no, his present was the best. This made Uncle Charlie's chest swell with pride. He had never given a child a gift before. By the look in both their eyes, he knew that he had done well with his gifts to Frederick and Henrietta. Now he would have to start thinking about what he might give them next year. He would figure out something. After all, he had a whole year to work on it.

Henrietta opened her gift from her grandmother. It was a dress with a bonnet to match. When she opened her gift from her mother, it was beautiful lace top socks and a small purse.

Henrietta could not wait to put on all of her new things. She immediately ran to her bedroom and changed clothes. She had gotten a new pair of shoes when she started school, so she polished the shoes so that they would look good with the new socks her mother gave her for Christmas. When she walked out of her room, she was beaming with pride. She asked Frederick if he would walk around the block with her so that everyone could see her new clothes.

It was not exactly what Frederick would like to do, but he agreed to go with her. He would rather go into the backyard with Uncle Charlie and chop wood with his new hatchet, but he went anyway.

Emma told them not to take too long because they would have to leave in about an hour to catch the train home. She would like them to get home before it was too late. Frederick put on his coat, but Henrietta did not want to put on her coat over her new dress. No one would be able to see her new clothes if she wore a coat. She took her coat when her grandmother handed it to her, but she told Frederick that they would go out the back way. When she got to the kitchen, she hung her coat on one of the coat hooks beside the back door and walked out without it.

It was about thirty-five degrees outside, and you could see little chill pimples on her arms, but Henrietta pretended that she was not cold. Some of her friends either came out or waved to them as they walked by their houses. As soon as they got to the end of the street, she told Frederick they were going to take a shortcut home. They did, and they ran all the way. When they got to the back door, their grandmother had warmed blankets and put them around each of them as they came through the door.

Mary had seen Henrietta's coat when she took her new roaster to the kitchen, and she knew what Henrietta was going to do.

The walk back to the train station was not as bad as the walk from the train station because they were not carrying heavy packages. When they got on the train to go home, Frederick wanted to sit up front. He also wanted an aisle seat. He wanted everyone to be able to see his hatchet. Several men had commented on it as being a good-looking hatchet especially with that red handle. Their remarks made Frederick swell with pride.

It had snowed a couple of inches after they left home, and it was now more difficult to walk in. Frederick was much too big for her to carry him now; it was all she could do, to walk home carrying the bags. Emma was tired by the time they got to the apartment. She had to go to work the next day, but Frederick would have the next week off as Christmas holidays. Frederick pulled his shoes off and crawled into his bed with his clothes on, and his hatchet lay on the floor beside his bed.

Emma dressed for bed and laid out what she was going to wear to work the next day. She went to bed and was probably asleep within five minutes. When the alarm rang the next morning, she hated to get out of bed. It was supposed to be in the low thirties, and she did not look forward to going out in that kind of weather.

When she put on her coat, she picked up her scarf that Henrietta had given to her. She put the scarf over her head and then wrapped it around her neck. It was very warm, and she loved it. If she had something just as warm to put on her feet, she would be happier.

When she met up with Sophia and Vera, they were just as cold as she was. Sophia laughed and said, "We complain about the warm weather, and we complain about the cold weather."

An older man that was walking behind them laughed and said, "Complaining is what women do best." Sophia gave him a mean look as he passed them, but the older man just smiled and tipped his hat.

57

Boots

It was much nicer working in the plant while the weather was cooler outside, but the winter was turning brutal, making it difficult to walk to and from work, go to church, or go to the grocery store. The men were not going out as much to smoke because it was so cold outside. However, when they asked their supervisors, who also smoked, if they could smoke inside, he told them he would talk to Mr. Woodie or the plant manager about it. Mr. Woodie did not smoke, so the men were thankful that he was not in his office, so their supervisor talked to the plant manager. The plant manager understood the men's problems because he occasionally enjoyed smoking cigars, so he gave the men permission to smoke inside the men's facilities but not in the plant. The women, however, did not get the same privileges.

One day as they were walking home from work, there was about a foot of snow on the ground. Sophia and Vera had on boots, but Emma had not bought any. She actually hated to spend money on boots when she thought the war might end any time, and she would be without a job. Every week when they received their pay, she would put something into her savings account even if it were just a quarter. With a few more deposits, she would have one thousand dollars saved. It really made her feel good to have a nest egg like that. Not many people in their complex had savings accounts because they barely made it week to week on what they made, but she and Frederick had learned to live on less than she made. She made sure that Frederick had boots and a coat, but she would not spend the money to buy herself a pair of boots. She was hoping the weather would improve, and she would not need them.

The weather did not improve! It actually got so cold that one older man came into the plant one day with icicles on his beard. Schools closed because the buses could not get through some of the roads because of the snow piles where they had tried to clear the roads.

When Emma started to work one morning, Frederick came to her and told her to wear his boots to work. He said that their feet was about the same size, and it would be a lot better than walking in those tiny shoes that she had on. She tried his boots on, and they actually did fit. They were fur-lined and very warm. Walking to work in the boots made a big difference.

That afternoon, she gave in and stopped at a shoe store. She bought another pair of boots. She bought them a size larger than Frederick's boots were. She thought if she bought them a size larger, they would probably fit him by the next winter, and if he needed his boots, she could wear the new ones. The next year, she could take the old ones, and Frederick could wear the new boots.

The next morning, she stuffed a pair of socks in the toe of the new boots and wore them to work. The socks made the boots too tight, and they rubbed her toes and made them sore. She was happy when she got to work and could take them off.

That afternoon, she only put one sock in the toes. They were a little loose, but they did not rub her toes, but they did rub her heels. The next morning, she decided to experiment with putting on extra socks instead of putting them in the boots. That worked much better, and they did not rub her heels or her toes.

As she walked up to the entrance door to the plant, they were putting newspapers into the stand. The headline news had to do with foreign countries. She could not figure out why they rarely read anything about the United States in the headline news. It was always about some a foreign country. She would like to know what was happening with US troops.

For some reason after she climbed up to her seat on the crane that day, she could not keep her mind off of Sly. She prayed daily that he would come home safe. She still wrote him letters, and some of them she would mail and some she would not. The ones that she would write at night would be the ones that she would usually tear up and not mail. At night, when Frederick was sleeping and everything was quiet was when she felt so lonely and would write letters to Sly. In the letters, she would tell him how much she missed him and how she dreamed of the next time he would take her in arms and kiss her again. Before she would mail them the next day, she would read them and feel embarrassed as to how they sounded. She thought they made her sound like a lovesick teenager. Even when she would tear up the letters and not mail them, she knew that she really felt what she had written in the letter. She had never had anyone that affected her the way Sly did.

The letters she wrote to him on Sunday afternoons she would mail. She dreamed there would be a day when the war would be over and he would return home, hopefully to her. She knew that he was probably teasing her when he told her that he had fallen in love with her, but she still kept the remark deep in her heart.

She did not know if she was just in love with love, or if she had actually fallen in love with him. Either way, just the memory of him as he held her in his arms when they slow danced made her hopeful that one day they may be together. She might have to accept the fact that he may possibly be just a friend to her when he came home, but to have someone like Sly for a friend would be wonderful.

It would probably be difficult for Sly to become serious about her because she was a good bit older than he was, and she had a son. She also had other children that he knew nothing about. She wondered what he would think about her if he knew that she had abandoned three other children.

When she thought about her children, sadness would overcome her. Sometimes she felt that the pain was almost unbearable. Many times at night when she would be alone in her bedroom, she would cry. She would try to visualize what Patrick looked like or what he would look like when he grew up. She would think back to the times they were all together. The way Donald would crawl on her lap with his blankie, sucking his thumb, was the sweetest memory she had of him. The grief of not having her children was deep in her soul, and she knew that most of it would probably remain there. Giving up her children was probably the hardest thing she would have to do in her lifetime.

She had no hopes of ever getting Patrick back because she had signed those stupid adoption papers, thinking she was signing a permission form for them to take him to a doctor. However, she did not sign any adoption or any other papers for The Preacher. She knew that Donald was still going by The Preacher's last name, and Patrick's last name was now Timmons. She felt there was nothing she could ever do about Patrick, but she hoped that one day Donald would come home to her.

58

Terminally Ill

It was now March, and the winds were howling outside. It was too windy for Frederick and Dave to play outside, so they were in Frederick's room playing. Emma could hear them laughing about something. One of the happiest things in a mother's life is to hear her children laugh. She was so thankful that Dave had become a part of Frederick's life. Mr. and Mrs. Spencer had also said that the boys were good for each other

About 3:00 p.m., Emma heard someone knock and went to answer the door. She had gotten so comfortable with the citizens' patrol that she had quit worrying when she opened the door.

When she opened the door, she was very surprised to see that it was Harry's parents. They just stood there looking at her, and she was probably looking at them the same way. She was so startled by their visit that she just held on to the doorknob and did not say anything for a few seconds. When she did speak, she just said hello as she walked outside, out and closed the door behind her. After the door closed, she asked Mr. and Mrs. Carswell what they wanted.

Mrs. Carswell told her that it was very windy, and it would be much better if they went inside. Emma said, "I know that it is windy, and I don't want to be rude, but would you tell please tell me why you are here?"

Mr. Carswell moved Mrs. Carswell close to the wall and then stood in front of her to protect her from the cold air. He then told Emma that Mrs. Carswell was very sick and she would like to see Harry's children.

Emma looked at them with a very stern look and started to say, "Where were you when we needed you after Harry left?" However, she did not; instead, she told them that only Frederick was there, but they had to agree not to tell him that they were his grandparents before she would let them enter the apartment. When they agreed, Emma opened the door and let them go in.

Mrs. Carswell could hear the boys' laughter from the bedroom, and it brought a smile to her face. She said, "Harry almost never laughed when he was a young boy. When he was a teenager, he became distant, cold, and cruel. I hoped after his marriage to you and having a family of his own, he would change his attitude, but evidently, it has not because we have not seen him more than a few times since your wedding day and that was mostly when he was moving his things out of our house."

Emma had asked Harry why his parents never came to visit, and he told her that it was because they did not like her. She told him that she would love for all of them to be close, but that was not what Harry wanted, so it never happened.

As Emma looked at Mrs. Carswell, she guessed that she must be very sick and possibly terminally ill because of the way she looked. She was very frail looking.

Emma told them that Frederick and his friend, Dave, were playing in his bedroom. She then asked them to have a seat and she would get him. When she walked into the bedroom, she told Frederick that they had some relatives visiting and she would like to introduce him to them.

Frederick said, "Sure." He and Dave then walked into the living room with Emma.

Emma introduced Mr. and Mrs. Carswell to Frederick. She was so proud of the way Frederick stuck out his hand to shake theirs and told them that it was nice to meet them.

Mrs. Carswell said, "We are your relatives from up North, and we were down this way and just decided that we would look you up and say hello."

Frederick thought that was great because he thought the only relatives he had were his mother, grandmother, Henrietta, and Uncle Charlie.

After introducing Frederick, Emma told the boys that they could go back and play. They came out about five minutes later and told Emma that they needed to go to Dave's apartment to get something and wanted to know if it was okay. She told him that would be fine.

As soon as they door closed behind them, Mrs. Carswell started to cry. She said, "He looks just like Harry did at his age, and he has such nice manners."

When they asked about Harry, Emma told them that the last time she and Frederick had seen him was when he beat them both so severely that she lost work and Frederick had to stay out of school for a week because of the injuries.

Mrs. Carswell said, "Beatings! Did he actually beat you and your children?"

Emma said, "Yes, and he tried to kill our unborn child because he did not want any more children."

Even Mr. Carswell did not know what to say about that comment. Many things from his past were coming back to haunt him, and he did not like the feeling.

When Mrs. Carswell spoke, she said softly, "Harry beat his cousin Dale so severely one time that it caused him to lose vision in his right eye. He beat a cat to death because it got fur on the legs of his pants and a neighbor claimed that he killed their dog." She then held her head in shame because she always prayed that the stories about Harry were not true, but evidently, they were.

Emma walked over to the window and told her to look where she was pointing. Emma told them that the men she was pointing to were tenants who were patrolling the apartment complex. "They formed a citizens' police to protect us from Harry. The only place we are safe from Harry is in our home. Teachers are watching out for Frederick at school, and our neighbors walk home and to school with him. They all know that Harry is capable of killing Frederick and me just for the sheer anger and joy of doing it. I do not know what we would do without our neighbors and friends. The police kept watch until the ship that Harry was sailing on left port, but they have now turned everything over to the naval authorities because it was taking too much manpower just to protect us from Harry."

Mrs. Carswell started crying again. She said, "How did we raise a boy to be that cruel?" She then looked at Mr. Carswell with a deep sadness in her eyes but did not say anything else. He just cleared his throat and turned his head as though he had no idea as to what she might be thinking, knowing that he had beaten his own wife and son many times.

As they stood up to leave, Mrs. Carswell told Emma that she and her children would be in her prayers. She then asked what the names of her children were.

Emma told her they were Henrietta, Frederick, Donald, and Patrick but did not tell them that Donald, Patrick, and Henrietta were not living with her.

Mrs. Carswell then said, "Three boys and a girl. That is a good family."

She then said, "I will probably never see you again, but it has been great visiting with you and meeting at least one of Harry's children."

As they left, Emma actually felt sorry for Mrs. Carswell. She felt nothing for Mr. Carswell. She had a feeling that he was the person responsible for Harry's anger issues

Later Frederick and Dave came back, and neither of them spoke of the Carswells. They went straight to Frederick's room and continued playing.

59

USS Brooklyn

Emma could not believe that it was already May, and school would soon be out. Frederick and Dave would be going into the third grade when they started back to school in the fall.

She and Frederick were both getting antsy about staying in the apartment all of the time. She had not heard anything about Harry since his parents came by that day. About a month after that, she got a letter from her grandmother telling her that Harry's mother had passed away. She read her obituary in the paper, and it only gave the date she passed away and that the memorial would be private.

That was sad! She knew it was probably because they were ashamed of Harry or that they had no family or friends who would attend. She was thankful that the obituary did not mention her children. She could imagine what The Preacher or the Timmonses would say if they saw their names in the newspaper. She had to admit that she would not have wanted Henrietta's or Frederick's name mentioned. It would be fine if neither of them ever saw Harry again. He had caused shame and fear to all of his family. How could one man destroy so many lives?

However, she did wonder sometimes what he would do if he found out where the children were. He never wanted them in the first place, so he probably would not be concerned for their welfare. It was sad that Harry had never gone to see his parents after they were married. Mrs. Carswell had always been nice to her and her grandmother while they were planning their wedding. She felt sure the problem was Mr. Carswell and Harry.

When Emma started to leave the plant on Monday, she saw a newspaper that someone had thrown away. She picked it up and started reading. There was a front-page article about the USS *Brooklyn*. It gave her heart a warm feeling because she had heard Sly talk about the USS *Brooklyn* being his ship. The letters she wrote went to an APO address, but she had no idea if he had ever received any of them.

That evening after they ate, she picked up the newspaper and started reading the article about the ship.

The USS *Brooklyn* built at the New York Navy Yard, commissioned in September of 1937, was the first of a group of seven cruisers in the mid 1930s to counter the Japanese Mogami class cruisers. The features in the Brooklyn class were so persuasive that later US Navy cruiser designs borrowed much from her. This class came fitted with a hangar aft and catapults for their SOC aircraft for spotting and observation.

The ship participated in the New York World's Fair in the spring of 1939 and served as base ship during initial rescue and salvage operations on the sunken submarine Squalus in late May and early June 1939.

The USS *Brooklyn* cruised to the south Pacific in March 1941 and then went back to the Atlantic for a few months later. For the rest of the year, she made Neutrality Patrols, supported the occupation of Iceland in July, and participated in the "short of war" operations that accompanied the steadily worsening relations between the United States and Germany.

Once the war formally began in December 1941, the USS *Brooklyn* continued her sea control missions in the Caribbean area and later in the north Atlantic, where she escorted convoys between the United States and the British Isles. In September 1942, she rescued more than a thousand men from the burning transport Wakefield. The cruiser provided gunfire support during the North Africa operation during October and November; she then returned to convoy service. While operating in the Mediterranean after mid-1943, the USS *Brooklyn* took part in the invasion of Sicily in July, the Salerno landings in September, and the Anzio Campaign during January through May. She participated in the bombardment and then carried out exercises in preparation for the invasion of southern France. *The Brooklyn will now come home for extensive overhaul.*

The last sentence made Emma excited. Reading about the USS *Brooklyn* made her feel as though she was reading about Sly. She put the paper down and sat there wondering where home would be for the USS *Brooklyn*.

60

Sly Comes Home!

The last Saturday night in June, Sophia and Vera were trying to talk Emma into going to the dance with them. They told her that she had stayed cooped up in that apartment long enough. She was still cautious and would not venture far from her apartment, especially in the evening, but she finally agreed to go with them.

It was the first time she had dressed up, except to go to church, in a very long time. She asked Mrs. Spencer if Frederick could spend the night with Dave, and she told Emma that he sure could. Mrs. Spencer said, "Dave has spent the night at you apartment so many times that he could call it home. It is time that we play host to Frederick." She told Emma to go with her friends and have a good time.

Emma took her time getting dressed. She was excited, but she was also leery of going out at night. About 7:00 pm, someone knocked on the door. Thinking that it was Sophia and Vera coming early, she automatically opened the door. Standing there was the most handsome sailor that she had seen in a long time. Sly stepped inside, closed the door with his foot, backed her up against the door, and planted the most delicious kiss that she had ever experienced on her well made up red lips.

When he pulled away, he told her how great she looked and then asked if she was going out.

Emma said, "I was just going to ask you the same question because of all the red lipstick you have on your lips."

Sly smiled at her and then kissed her again.

She told him that she let Sophia and Vera talk her into going with them to the dance, and Mrs. Spencer told her that she would let Frederick spend the night with Dave.

Sly pulled her close, kissed her again, and said, "If I had not found you at home, I would have looked for you at the dance." He then asked her if he could be her escort for the night. After she said yes, he said, "I think you should probably go fix your face before we leave." Emma laughed and told him that he may want to go wash his face also.

While Emma was fixing her face, someone knocked, and Sly went to the door. Sophia and Vera could not believe their eyes. Sophia said, "Sly, are you wearing lipstick?" He laughed and told her that it was about twenty minutes earlier and that Emma's face was in much worse condition than his was.

He told the girls if they did not mind, he would like to go with them to the dance. He said, "Many of my friends are going to be there, and they will be so envious when I walk in with the three most beautiful women there."

When Emma came out, Sly went into the bathroom to wash his face. All three of the girls were beside themselves with excitement.

When they walked into the dance, it sounded like all of the sailors were giving wolf whistles. Two of Sly's friends came over and immediately asked Sophia and Vera to dance. Sly led Emma out on the dance floor, twirled her around and then pulled her up close, and told her how much he had missed her, and then he kissed her. Emma realized that she had wasted her time putting on fresh lipstick.

The next few songs were fast, and Emma could hardly keep up with Sly. They danced the whole night. On the slow dances, he held her so close that you could not have stuck a pin between their bodies. Emma could feel his heart beating against her chest, and they had eyes for no one except each other. As the last song ended, Sly held Emma in his arms, swaying as though the music was still playing. He looked into her eyes and said, "Emma, I have never felt this way about anyone before." He then bent down and kissed her. The only reason they stopped kissing and swaying was that all of Sly's friends were whistling and clapping. Emma's face turned red, and it was not from the red lipstick because Sly kissed all of that off during their first dance.

After the dance, Sly and his two friends walked them home. When they got to Emma's apartment, she gave Sly the key to unlock the door. After he opened the door, he picked her up and carried her inside the room and then reached back and closed the door with his foot.

Emma was so thankful that Frederick was spending the night with Dave.

61

The Proposal

Over the next few months, Sly came home two to three times a month. He would visit with his parents for a few hours, then he would go to Emma's or he would go to Emma's first and the next day they would take the bus to his parents home to eat Sunday dinner with them.

When he was there on Sundays, he walked to church with them. Emma introduced him to Reverend Charles and his wife. Everyone liked him immediately. Reverend Charles leaned over and whispered to Emma, "Will there be wedding bells in the future?"

The remark embarrassed Emma, but she just smiled and said, "Maybe."

Sly and Frederick had formed a tight bond. He would take both boys and their friends out to play ball, hiking, or anything they wanted him to do with them. Emma had seen them on many occasions walking back to the apartment after playing ball. Sly would always be teasing and playing around with Frederick and Dave.

When they went dancing on Saturday nights, Sly was just as sweet to Emma as he had been the first night that he was with her. They danced only with each other, and when they did sit out a dance, Sly would sit facing Emma, holding her hands together, and kissing the tip of each finger, or he would have his arm over her shoulder. He would take the back of his other hand and gently smooth it over her face or caress her back and neck. With every touch, Sly was igniting a fire between them that both of them knew, would never go out.

One Saturday night, Sly excused himself and walked to where the band was playing. Emma thought he was going to make a request for a song. What they did after the next slow dance while Sly still had Emma in his arms was to start a drumroll. When the drumroll stopped, Sly kissed Emma, bent down on one knee, pulled a ring out of his pocket, and proposed to her right in front of everyone. The crowd was ecstatic. Everyone was cheering, whistling, and hollering to Emma to say yes, which of course she did.

That night after they got back to her apartment, Sly asked her what that look on her face was all about. He said, "You haven't already changed you mind, have you?" She told him no, but she knew that she and Sly were going to have to have a very long conversation about her situation.

Emma reached up and touched his face. She told him that she was in love with him and wanted to spend the rest of her life with him.

Sly said, "But?

She laughed and told him that they needed to have a long conversation. They sat down on the couch, and she told him everything about her life. She did not leave anything out. She wanted him to know everything about her and the problems she may have ahead. She told him about how the neighbors at the apartment complex stood guard near her apartment every night to keep her and Frederick safe.

Sly did not interrupt her with any questions. He let her talk about everything that was bothering her. He felt as though she needed to get it all out, and he was going to do his best to keep her from ever having to go through anything like that again.

When she finished, Sly just looked at her with total admiration. He said that any woman who could go through something like that had to be a very strong person. He told her that the first thing they should do would be to work on getting her divorce from Harry, and then they would get married anywhere she wanted, but he would like for his family to be involved also, and he would like Tony to be home so that he could be his best man. He was not sure exactly when his next leave would be, but he would try to contact him to try to find out.

He barely got the last word out of his mouth when Dave and Frederick came over to get something from Frederick's room.

Sly asked Frederick to please come over and sit with them because he had something that he would like to ask him.

Frederick came over with a very quizzical look on his face. He knew something was up but had no idea what it was.

After Frederick sat down, Sly said, "Frederick, I would like to marry you and your mother. Would you and your mother consider being my wife and son?" Frederick's face was beaming as he looked up at his mother, then to Sly. He had read a story in a book in school about a man asking his girlfriend's father for her hand in marriage, and he tried to imitate what he remembered the man saying. Frederick looked up to Sly and said, "Yes, sir, you have my blessings to marry my mother, and I would love to have you as my father." He then gave his mom and Sly hugs. It was so precious that Emma could not help but cry.

As soon as the boys walked back into Dave's apartment, he immediately told his parents that Sly had asked Emma and Fred to marry him.

Emma and Sly did not have to tell anyone because Frederick and Dave had already told everyone before they left for church.

Everyone was excited about the engagement, and that was all anyone talked about walking to church. Repeatedly Frederick described every detail to everyone.

After the service, Emma heard Sly ask Frederick to come with him. She saw them talking to each other, and Frederick was grinning from ear to ear, so she knew they were up to something.

Sly and Frederick were holding back until all of the people in the church had left, and then Sly took Emma's hand, and they walked over to talk with Reverend Charles.

Frederick said, "Reverend Charles, Sly has asked for my mother's hand in marriage, and I gave him my blessings. Since Sly is a visitor, we have discussed this and feel that I should be the one to ask if you will marry them."

Reverend Charles had been expecting this to happen, but he had not expected it to be Frederick that asks him to marry them. He looked at Frederick and told him that he would consider it an honor to marry his mother and Sly. Everyone that was still standing out in the vestibule heard everything and started clapping their hands.

When Sly and Emma came out of the church, it seemed that everyone came over to shake their hands and tell them congratulations.

The first chance Sly was able to come home, Charles, he, and Emma went to the courthouse so that Emma could file for a divorce from Harry. When the lawyer and clerk heard that Harry had abandoned Emma and her children, they told her that her divorce would probably only take thirty to sixty days.

They had to notify Harry of the impending divorce procedures. They would have the proper papers delivered to him by his chief officer, and he would be required to sign them. He would be able to keep a copy, and the chief officer was required to send the receipt back to them. Because she was not asking for anything from Harry for herself or her children, they did not see why he should have any issues with the divorce.

62

Frederick Meets the Intruder

After playing ball with Frederick and Dave one Saturday afternoon, Sly took them to get something to drink at the little café a couple of blocks away. They were sitting on stools at the counter talking about everything that came to mind. Frederick had been talking a mile a minute when all of a sudden, right in the middle of a sentence, he stopped talking. He was looking at a man that was coming through the door.

Sly turned around to see what had caught Frederick's attention. All he saw was a scruffy looking man, so he asked Frederick what was wrong.

Frederick told him that the man who just came in through the door was the man who broke into his house when he was a little boy. Sly remembered Emma telling him something about a man breaking into their house, and if he remembered correctly, the man cut one of her children.

The man sat down in a booth. When he looked up and noticed that Frederick was staring at him he said, "Boy, what do think you are looking at?" Frederick walked over to where the man was sitting, stood there for a second, and then confronted the man.

Frederick said, "Why did you break into our house when I was a little boy, and why did you cut my baby brother with a knife? I tried to protect them, but you knocked me down and then jumped out our window."

The man laughed, gave a big smirk, and said, "You must be Harry Carswell's boy." When Frederick said yes, the man smirked again and told him that Harry paid him to break into the house. When Sly walked up behind Frederick, the man dropped the smirk from his face. The man then said, "Boy, that was a long time ago, boy, and you should forget that it ever happened."

Frederick looked straight at the man and asked him why Harry would want him to break into their house.

The man told him that Harry needed his birth certificate because he wanted to join the Navy and could not do so without his birth certificate. He said that Harry told him that he and his wife had a fight over him wanting to go into the navy to serve his country while the war was going on, but he felt like it was his duty. Harry told him that he would give him twenty dollars to get it for him, and when he brought it back, he would give him another twenty. The man said that he was without a job, and the money would come in handy while he looked for work.

The man said that it was an honorable thing for him to do, so he told Harry that he would get it for him. Harry gave him the first twenty dollars and told him exactly where the birth certificate was and how to get to it, without anyone knowing he was there.

The man said, "It appeared to be a simple thing to do when I got to the house. I knew there was a light on in one bedroom, but what I needed to get was supposed to be in a box in the living room. Everything was going as planned until your sister started screaming when she saw me. I still had the knife in my hand that I used to cut the screen so that I could unlock the window. Your sister's scream startled me, and I did not see the little boy when he bumped into the knife. I promise you, boy, I did not intend to hurt the kid."

The man looked at Frederick and then asked, "Are you by any chance the kid that hit me with the baseball bat?" When

Frederick said yes, the man told him that he broke his leg with that bat, and he had to wear a cast for six weeks. In addition, he said, "When I gave the birth certificate to Harry, he laughed at me, punched me in the face, broke my nose, and stole the twenty that he had given me plus all the other money that I had. He told me if I reported him, he would come back and kill me, and I believed him. He was one mean dude."

He told Frederick that he felt bad about scaring him and his family. He had come by their house later to tell his mother what had happened because he thought that crazy man might try to hurt her and her kids, but the neighbors said that you had moved, and they had no idea where you had moved. He said that he thought they knew but would not tell him.

The man looked at Frederick and said, "The person you should be angry with is your old man, not me."

Frederick looked at the man and then said, "How is your leg and nose?"

The man looked at him, smiled, and then said, "Everything is fine now, but if I ever see your dad again, he is going to pay for what he did to me. I have been watching the navy yard looking for him. If I ever find him, I am going to be ready for him this time." The man pulled back his shirt and showed them his gun.

He then said, "Boy, I don't have a fight with you. If you will, tell your mom and your brothers and sister that I said I am sorry for scaring them. I would greatly appreciate it. I am not the kind of person that hurts women and kids. I was just a homeless man with no money, needing a job."

Frederick nodded his head in acknowledgment, and he, Dave, and Sly left.

When Frederic told his mother about the man that was their intruder; she could not believe what he was telling her. She was glad that they could finally have some closure to that situation, but it was hard to believe that a man with a wife and children would hire someone to break into their house. With everything else that she was finding out about Harry, nothing surprised her anymore.

Sly could not believe what Emma and her kids had been through because of one sorry man. Not only was that man looking for Harry, but Sly also like to have a chance to talk to him.

When it was time for Sly to go back to his ship, he did not feel comfortable leaving Emma and Frederick because he knew it would be several weeks before he would have a weekend leave again.

63

Are the Russians Coming to Get Us?

It had been over a week since Sly had gone back to his ship, and Emma had already received two letters from him, but it was not the same as having him around. She held out her hand admiring her beautiful engagement ring that he had given her. She still could not believe how lucky she was.

Everything seemed exciting and fun when Sly was with them, but as soon as he left, she felt sad. Frederick came up behind her t and gave her a big hug and said, "Mom, I miss him too."

Everyone at the munitions plant wanted to see Emma's ring, and they all told her how pretty it was. After Sophia described Sly to them, some of them looked a little jealous. Of course, Sophia had gone overboard a bit with her description, but it made Emma proud to be her friend. The only thing Emma did not like was that she had to wear her ring around her neck while at work because of the machinery. It was against their rules to wear any type of jewelry, but she kept it well hidden behind her clothing.

It was Saturday evening, and Emma and Frederick were home alone. The Spencers had gone out of town to visit Mrs. Spencer's parents. Emma had picked up a paper on Friday before she left the plant but did not get a chance to read it until she sat down after their meal. The headline news was all about the war. Allied troops had liberated Rome, and the British and the US troops had successfully landed on the Normandy beaches of France, opening a *Second Front* against the Germans. The Soviets had launched a massive offensive in eastern Byelonissin, destroying the German Army Group Center and driving westward to the Vistula River across from Warsaw in central Poland. Anglo-American forces broke out of Normandy beachhead and raced eastward toward Paris.

The non-communist underground Home Army rose up against the Germans in an effort to liberate Warsaw before the arrival of Soviet troops. The Soviet advanced halts on the east bank of the Vistula. The Germans accepted the surrender of the remnants of the Home Army forces fighting in Warsaw.

Allied forces had landed in southern France near Nice and advanced rapidly toward the Rhine River to the northeast.

Frederick leaned over Emma's shoulder looking at the pictures in the newspaper and asked his mother what all of that meant. Emma said, "Our whole world is at war, Frederick."

He walked around the sofa, sat down beside Emma, and said, "Are the Russians coming to get us? That is what one of the bigger boys told us."

Emma said, "For now we are safe, and I hope that we will never have to experience what those poor people overseas have had to endure."

Frederick looked serious and asks in which direction was Russia. Emma told him that they were east of them and asked him why he wanted to know.

He said, "Reverend Charles preached a sermon one Sunday about a nation from the east shall rise and rule all nations."

Emma rubbed her hand through his hair and told him that she did not think that Russia was what Reverend Charles was talking about; he was probably referring to incidents that happened in biblical times. "We really do not have to worry because we have two great, big oceans to protect us from anyone," Emma said.

Frederick then said, "What about Pearl Harbor?" Those few words brought a fear deep inside Emma, but she tried not to show it. She told him that Pearl Harbor was in Hawaii, not in America, and that their military was much stronger than any other nation.

Emma hoped that what she had just told her son was the truth. She did not want to tell him that she did not understand anything the paper said about the war either. She also had no idea where any of those places were located.

64

Divorce Papers

Around eight o'clock, someone knocked on the door. When Emma opened the door, this she had another surprise visitor. It was Harry, and he was waving some papers around asking her exactly what she thought she was doing.

Emma tried not to look afraid, and she was going to do her best to stand up to him. She said in a firm, controlled voice, "If you will stop yelling and show me the papers, I may know what you are talking about."

Harry held the papers straight up so that she could look at them. It was the divorce papers, and he said, "You know very well what I am talking about."

He wanted to know what she thought she was doing by saying that he had abandoned them. He joined the navy to fight for his country, and right in front of all of his shipmates and everyone else on the ship dock, they served him with those papers.

Emma firmly told him that he did abandon her and the children. He said, "Get all of them out here, right now. I dare either of them to say that I abandoned them. I am sure they remember what will happen if they talk back to me, and so should you."

Emma could see that several of their neighbors were trying to get someone up off the ground. It did not take her but a minute to figure out what had happened. Evidently, Harry had overtaken the neighbor that was standing guard outside their apartment. The neighbor that she had seen out there earlier was the person they were trying to get up.

When Harry saw where she was looking, he tried to shove Emma back inside, but it did not work this time. She was out the door and pulled it closed behind her.

Everyone was now looking at the sailor standing at Emma's door. One of the women whispered something to one of the young boys standing there, and the boy took off running.

Everyone that met Sly liked him and was used to seeing him around on the weekends. They knew that this man was not Sly. He was probably the man the police were looking for who had beaten Emma and her son.

In just a couple of minutes, the boy and his father came around the corner of the apartments. When Harry saw him, he immediately took off running, but before he left, he warned Emma that this was not the last of this. He also yelled back that he would teach her a lesson for embarrassing him the way she did.

No one pursued Harry, and thankfully, the man that Harry had beaten up was going to be okay. Emma found out later that he had to get stitches on his face where Harry hit him.

While at the hospital, the neighbor told the hospital what had happened, and the hospital alerted the police, and before they left the hospital, there was a police officer there to take a report about what had happened.

65

Very Cruel Person

The next day when Emma heard someone knocking on the door, she was almost afraid to open the door. When she peaked out the window, she saw that it was Mr. Spencer so she opened the door.

He told her how sorry he was about what happened while he was gone. They thought they had everything covered, but evidently, when Harry saw the neighbor standing there alone, he came up behind him, beat the neighbor over the head with a stick, and broke the neighbor's nose when he knocked him down.

Frederick perked up and asked, "What happened?"

Emma told him not to worry, that she would talk to him about it later. He shrugged and went out to talk to Dave because he had not seen him all day. Of course, the boy that ran to get his father had already told Dave what happened, and he and Dave filled Frederick in on all the details.

Emma told Mr. Spencer that she felt as though she was putting everyone in jeopardy by living there, and for that, she apologized. Mr. Spencer put his hand on Emma's shoulder in a very fatherly way and said, "Emma, none of this is your fault. Harry Carswell is the culprit, and eventually, he would get what he is due."

As soon as they were both back inside the apartment, Frederick wanted to know why she did not tell him that Harry had come back.

Emma told him that it was because she did not want to alarm him. She then told him how Harry had run like a scared rabbit when he saw Alex Mund coming around the corner of the apartment building.

Alex had been a former baseball All-Star; he still kept himself in good physical condition, and he could be very intimidating to someone who had something to fear from him.

Emma told Frederick how scared Harry looked when he saw Alex. She said, "He will probably be too scared to come around here again."

Frederick did not say anything for a couple of seconds but then looked up at his mother, smiled, and said, "Have you ever seen Mr. Mund throw a baseball? He and Sly were passing the ball one day, and Mr. Mund threw Sly one of his fast pitches. Sly told him that he thought it was going to break his hand when he caught it. He said that he had caught many fastballs, but he had never caught a ball coming as fast as Alex's did."

Emma laughed at Frederick and told him that Mr. Mund's son Charleton was probably going to be a good athlete himself. She told him how a neighbor had whispered to Charleton to go get his father, and it was only a matter of seconds until they both reappeared around the corner of the apartment complex. Alex would probably have gone after Harry had the neighbor not been lying on the ground bleeding so profusely. He felt like the neighbor's well-being was more important than catching Harry. They all know who it was, and they said that they would deal with him later.

66

Do Not Answer the Door

All day the next Saturday, Emma was very anxious and nervous. She had gotten a letter from Sly telling her that he would be home for the weekend. She knew that he meant that he would be coming there as soon as he possibly could. He said that he was going to his father's birthday dinner first, and he would like for her and Frederick to go with him, but she had sent him a letter and told him that she would not be able to. She had to work until 6:30 p.m. all week because Judy Hornet, one of the crane operators, was sick, and she and Gail Snowman, the third shift crane operator, had to cover her shift.

She had to walk home alone that evening, and she did not feel safe doing so. When she turned the corner to her apartment, she could have sworn that she saw Harry leave her apartment building, but she did not think he or whoever it was paid any attention to her. It had been a little windy, so she kept her scarf on her head that she had to wear while working. She put her head down so that he would not be able to see her face. With the pants that she was wearing and the scarf tied on her head, no one would probably recognize her.

When Frederick knew that Sly was coming, he would not stay overnight at Dave's. If Dave wanted to be with him, he would have to sleepover at their apartment.

Around 10:00 p.m., Emma heard a slight knock on the door. She was sure that it was Sly and opened the door without looking out the window. To her surprise, it was not Sly; it was Harry, and he pushed his way into the apartment and dared her to say a word. He told her if she screamed or made a noise, he would kill her and all of the kids. He then asked her who were there. She told him that the boys were in the bedroom. She did not want to open up an assortment of problems with Harry if she could avoid it. She knew that he would probably not care where they were or who had them as long as he did not have to be responsible for them.

Harry then shoved Emma down on the couch and had his hand around her throat. He told her that he had been thinking about those divorce papers, and the longer he thought about them, the madder he got. He wanted to know why she felt like she was entitled to file for a divorce anyway. If he wanted to come home after serving his country, he should be able to. After all, he was the head of this household, and he made all the decisions that involved him. He told her that she had no rights at all when it came to him.

Emma was trying to think of something that would calm Harry's anger. She spoke very softly, mainly because he had his hand around her neck. She also did not want to make any sounds that would set him off or alert the boys. She said, "Your parents came for a visit. They wanted to see you and the children."

Harry let up on his grip and asked her to repeat what she had just said.

She said, "Your parents came to visit because your mother wanted to see you and your children one last time. Your mother was very ill, and she passed away shortly after they were here."

Harry squeezed her neck and said, "Emma Patton Carswell, if you are telling me a lie, I will make you regret it until the day you die, which might be sooner than you anticipate."

Emma said, "No, Harry, I am not telling you a lie."

He turned loose of her neck and stepped back. He demanded that she tell him everything about his mother. She told him that his mother met Frederick, but none of the other children was there. Shortly after they were there, her grandmother contacted her and told her that his mother had passed away. Evidently, she had been sick for quite while.

Harry did not know what to say. He had always thought that even as a grown man, if he did not have anywhere else to go, he could always go home. He totally hated his father for the cruel things he did to him as a child, but his mother was one of the sweetest people he had ever met. It did not matter what he did or how much trouble he got into, his mother never said one harsh word to him. His father made up for it. He gave him a whipping with his belt almost daily.

He sat down in a chair and tears came to his eyes and said, "I don't understand how something like these stupid divorce papers could get to me, but news about my mother's death could not."

This was the first time since Emma had known Harry that she had seen tears in his eyes or him have a look of sadness on his face.

He got up slowly and walked toward the door. When he got to the door, he turned around and told her that he would not sign those divorce papers. He and his fiancée were planning to get married, and he had intended to file for a divorce from her for abandonment because she had moved out of their home and got rid of all of his belongings while he was in the navy serving his country.

He told her that she was actually the one who abandoned him. When he left, it was because they had a little argument. He felt that it was best thing for him to do was to leave her alone for a little while so that she could think things over and realize how she had hurt him by running around on him and getting pregnant by other men and expecting him to work and support all of those kids.

He told her hesitantly that he had gone to stay with a friend. When he came home, she had left and taken all the kids with her. When he asked Charles and Sara Mollenix if they knew where she had all gone, they told him that they had no idea where they she moved to.

He told her not to even think about causing him any more trouble because Lorenda, his fiancée, did not know that he had ever been married nor did she know that he had children, and he intended to keep it that way. He told her that they were her kids, not his.

He then looked at her in total disgust and said, "Why did you not try dressing like that when we were together? Maybe I would have stayed with you. All I ever saw you in were sacks that your grandmother brought for you to wear while you were pregnant. Of course, you were always pregnant and had those ugly brown spots all over your face. What man would want to stay with a woman who looked like that and always smelled like messy diapers? It was disgusting the way you let yourself go."

Emma had heard this type of talk from Harry for years, and she was not going to let it bother her now. She stood her ground, looked straight at Harry with the same disgusted look, and said, "Harry, you have worn out your welcome. Please leave!"

Harry acted very aggressively as if he was going to attack her, but Emma showed no fear.

He had never seen Emma act brave before, and he did not particularly like it, but he did not have time to show her who was the toughest. He just looked at her and made one last threat. He said, "You just remember what I told you about the divorce. Do not tell these lies again! Lorenda does not deserve to be hurt. She isn't part of this, and I have to protect her."

He pointed his finger at Emma again with a very mean look and told her that she had best remember every thing that he had just said. If not, she would be sorry, and he was sure that she knew what he meant.

For some reason, Emma just looked at him and smiled, and Harry acted as if he did not know what to do or say next, so he just huffed to himself and walked out the door.

Emma closed the door and stood with her back to the door smiling. This was the first time she had ever been able to rattle Harry like that, and she liked her newfound strength.

67

Way to Go, Sailor!

E mma was starting to feel a little down because the last two buses would be running soon, and Sly was not there. Around 11:00 p.m., there was a soft knock on the door. Emma went to the window to look out to see who it was this time. It was a sailor, but this time, Emma knew for sure that it was Sly and opened the door with great enthusiasm.

Sly grabbed her up, swung her around as if she was a little doll, and then planted one of those delicious kisses on her lips.

There was no comparison between Sly and Harry. She felt so much love for Sly that she thought her heart would burst with happiness. It was not very long until she forgot all about Harry and his threats about the divorce.

The next morning, Emma and Sly did not go to church because he was going to have to take the ten o'clock bus back to the ship. Frederick went with the Spencers', and finally, they had some time alone, so she told him about what Harry said about the divorce and what he had done to the neighbor.

Sly got angry about Harry's threats and the things he had done to hurt Emma. However, she wanted to handle the situation by herself, so he knew that he should not try to tell her what she should do. He did not want to appear domineering to Emma because she had already gone through enough hell with one man that was like that. He could not help but feel protective of her and Frederick, because they were going to be his family, but he did hope that one day that he would get the chance to have a face-to-face with Harry Carswell.

Sly told Emma that she and Frederick could go live with his mom and pop. They would love to have them. He could send money home, and she would not have to work in the plant or anywhere else if she did not want to. He told her if she did not want to do that, he would help her find another apartment, and he would pay the rent, but Emma said no.

She told him that she appreciated the offer, but she would not feel right moving in with them. In addition, she did not know how well Frederick would feel about moving somewhere else and leaving Dave and his school.

He asked her what Frederick would do when they got married, and she told him that she was already breaking it to him a little at a time so that he could get used to the idea.

Sly sat back on the couch, drew her up close beside him, and asked her how she would like to have a boat.

Emma sat up and said, "Talk about changing a conversation! What would I do with a boat?" After looking at his smiling face for a moment, she settled back down beside him to listen to his dream.

He told her that there was a boat for sale by the name of *The Admiral*. It was a boat that was anchored away from the docks, which took the admirals back and forth from the docks to their ships. The navy was going to replace *The Admiral* with a newer boat, and he had a chance to buy it.

He could leave it at his mom and pop's and work on it when he would be on leave. He wanted to restore it, get a captain's license, and turn it into a fishing boat. This was an idea that he had dreamed of for a long time, and he hoped that she would go along with the idea.

Emma told him that she had always dreamed of owning her own restaurant, but she was not going to go out and buy one.

Harry looked at her and said, "Why not? We could find a place where you could open a restaurant, and I could dock the boat." He told her that he could take parties out to fish, and she could feed them before and after they went fishing.

He told her that he would probably just do it on the weekends until he had his business built up, and he and Mom and Pop could help in her restaurant during the week.

Emma had no answer for Sly's offer. It sounded wonderful, but she did not know how they could make a dream like that come true.

Sly asked her where she had thought they might live when they were married and what she would do when all the men came back from the war wanting their jobs back.

She told him that she had not really thought about where they would live and what they would do after the war. She was just enjoying being engaged to Sly Bandowski.

He told her that if she did not want to work, she did not have to. They could find a place close to the ocean, and he could still have his boat.

Emma then asked him when he thought he would be getting out of the navy, and Sly told her that he was not sure. His time would be up some time within the next few months but with the war, nothing was certain, but he thought it would be a good idea for them to make some plans for their wedding and where they would live and where Frederick would go to school after they were married.

Sly told Emma that he had a couple of places in mind where he could dock his boat, and there were areas around each place where they could either build or buy a house. They could possibly buy a house big enough that they could have the restaurant downstairs, and they could live upstairs until they made their first million.

They continued their conversation until around 9:30 p.m., when he had to get ready to leave.

Sly squeezed her so tight that she thought he could break her ribs with his last hug before they left the apartment. She was standing at the bus stop with him; she knew everyone on the bus, and the other passengers waiting on the bus saw him when he bent her over and planted one of his delicious kisses on her lips before he hopped on the bus.

Someone on the bus yelled out, "Way to go, sailor!" And everyone started laughing and cheering them on.

The bus driver was used to Sly's antics and did not say anything to him when he stayed on the bottom step to the bus, hanging on with one hand and waving 'bye to Emma with the other until the bus crossed over the hill and out of sight.

Emma walked back to the apartment feeling both happy and sad. She could not believe how much love she felt for Sly. She had never felt anything like this for Harry or anyone else.

68

The Question

At work on Monday, everyone was teasing Emma about the way Sly kissed her 'bye; everyone had heard about it. She was embarrassed with their teasing, but she was also the happiest that she had ever been in her life since she was a small child before her parents passed away.

Sophia came to her and told her that she had received a letter from Tony and he would be home in a couple of weeks and he wanted to see her. She said it would be great if he and Sly could be home at the same time.

Vera spoke up and told her that she would not like that. She would feel left out or like a third wheel. She did not have anyone that she was dating on a regular basis. Delmas, an old friend, was asking his sister Ann if he thought she would go out with him. Their families had been friends since they were children. They would sometimes go on vacations together, and they would stay in small bungalows near each other.

She told them that Delmas was very creative, and he and his younger brother Darrell were always building things, and they were good at it, but she had always thought of him more like a brother or family member than someone that she would date. However, he was very good looking, and she had not seen him in a long time, but she did not know how she would feel going out on a date with him. He had tormented her and Ann to death when they were kids.

Sophia said, "Don't all boys act like that when they are young and want to get a girl's attention?"

Vera laughed and said, "I guess so, but I have never really thought about dating him, but I told Ann that I would go to a dance or to the movies with him sometime."

Sophia said, "A bird in hand was better than two in a bush."

Vera laughed again and said, "I might just go out with him to see what he is like all grown-up."

Sophia said, "Attagirl, Vera! Besides I have seen him dance, and I know you will like dancing with him."

On Thursday, Sophia got a letter from Tony. She had not been able to open it until her lunch break. He was telling her that he was not sure if he would get to come to see her anytime soon. He said that he was sorry and hoped that she had not made any plans for them.

He then he said, "When I get home, I would like to ask you a question, but I will not ask you to commit to anything right now. When this war is over, there will be time for us to have some fun and enjoy ourselves without worrying about wars."

Sophia sat down hard on the bench and let the letter fall to her lap. Vera and Emma immediately wanted to know what was wrong.

Sophia said, "I wonder if Tony is going to ask me to marry him." Both women looked at her with total amazement and wanted to know if he said anything about it to her before. She told them, "No, but in his letter, he had told me that he had something to ask me when he got home. Doesn't that sound like he may ask me to marry him when he gets home?"

Neither of them knew what to say because every time they had seen Sophia and Tony together, they were either dancing or kidding around with each other. They acted as though they were just good friends having fun.

Sophia looked at both of them and sheepishly said, "Do you think it would be okay if I went to the dance with Dalton Moodie Saturday night? After all, Tony hasn't asked me to marry him yet."

Vera and Emma both laughed. It sure did not seem like Sophia was too serious about anything except having fun.

69

Child Support

On Monday, Emma got a letter from her grandmother telling her that she had contacted the government and that Harry was going to have to pay child support for Henrietta.

She said that after he was served the order, he dropped by her house one weekend while he was on leave. He was surprised to find out how beautiful Henrietta had become. He also wanted to know why she was up there with her instead of with her mother.

Her grandmother said, "Henrietta wanted to go to school here, instead of where her mother lives. She is going to stay with me until she graduates from high school, which will be a long time away, and that is why I am filing for an allotment for her. I do not have the money to pay for her education, and neither does Emma."

Harry said, "She probably doesn't want to live with Emma because she is ashamed of her." He then tried to play on Mary's sympathy by saying, "Emma filed for a divorce while I was away fighting the war. I will probably never get to see any of my children again, because of that. She actually claimed that I had abandoned her and the children. She was only able to do that because I was away fighting in the war and was not here to defend myself. By me not being able to see my children, surely you don't think that I should have to pay child support for them?"

That did not set too well with Mary. She told him that from what she had heard, he had abandoned his family and left them without food or money and joined the navy as a single man.

Mary then said, "When I checked with the government, they told her that Harry Carswell was a single man with no dependents, and I told them that he was a married man with four children and that I had custody of his daughter and wanted to apply for benefits for her. It was me, Harry, that filed for support for Henrietta, not Emma. All they told me to do was to send them a birth certificate with your name on it identifying you as the child's father. It did not take long after I mailed the birth certificate that that they contacted me. They told me that Henrietta would start receiving monthly allotment checks from you and that you would be responsible for her support until she reached the age of eighteen. If you fail to do so, they will put you in jail."

Harry told her that he did not see how they could do that to him because he was not even Henrietta's real father. He told her that Emma had run around on him since the day they were married, and he was sure that he could find some neighbors that could testify to that because he knew that some of them saw men coming and going from their house while he was at work.

That comment caused Mary to go ballistic on Harry. She told him that Emma did no such thing. She was a good girl and a good mother and that he was a poor excuse for a husband and a father.

Harry said, "Oh yeah! If she was such a good mother, why did she give her children, away?"

Mary was startled for a couple of seconds and did not know what to say. She had no idea that Harry knew about Donald and Patrick.

Evidently someone told him about her giving Donald to The Preacher and adopted Patrick out to a couple she did not even know.

Her grandmother said that she had taken all that she could from Harry and in a loud voice called him a low down, good for nothing, wife beater, and she told him that he did not deserve a family.

Harry walked up to her and gave her a very mean look and looked as if he was going to say something until he saw Charlie walk through door to find out why his mother was talking so loud. Harry immediately clammed up, walked out of the house, and did not even say 'bye to Henrietta.

Mary then told her that she should also try to get support for Frederick. Then she surprised Emma by telling her that Henrietta and Donald were becoming friends. The Preacher has actually allowed Donald to come home with Henrietta from school several times to study together.

She thought the two of them were up to something because Henrietta told her that she wanted Donald to walk around with her so that all of her friends could see him. However, they did not go toward walk in the direction of Henrietta's friends lived; they walked in the direction of the Timmons' house.

When she asked Henrietta later about where they had been. Henrietta told her that she had told Donald about the Timmons adopting Patrick, and he wanted to see him and see what he looked like now.

The Timmons had Patrick out in the yard playing, but when they saw Henrietta walking up their street, they took Patrick back inside the house, so Donald did not get a good look at him then, but he walked back by their house about a week later by himself and got a good look at Patrick.

From what she understood, Henrietta and Donald had made an agreement that they were going to tell Patrick about his adoption to the Timmons when he got older. They are making their plans as to how they will do it, but Henrietta would not tell her about their plans, and she knew there was no need questioning Henrietta further. Mary told her that she hoped that they would forget about doing it because she did not see any benefit in telling the child. If he loved his adoptive parents and they love him, that was all that mattered.

Emma felt sad for all of her children. They all lived within about ten to fifteen miles from each other. It was a big city, but she knew that some day they would probably meet. Whether they would recognize each other was another question.

Emma knew that she could probably file and get support for Frederick, but she did not know if she wanted the hassle that she knew that she would have to go through with Harry. She would give up any support just to have him leave her and Frederick alone and never come around them again.

She wished that when he got out of the navy, he would get married, go to Missouri, and live with his new wife happily thereafter. She did not need or want anything from him.

70

She Loved Him Enough to Let Him Go

Emma panicked when she skipped a month with her menstrual cycle. She was even worse when she skipped the second one. What would she do if she were pregnant? What would Sly think if he found out? Would he be like Harry and accuse her of being with other men?

Shortly after she missed the second month, she went to see a doctor. She did not think that she actually needed a doctor to tell her that she was pregnant because she had all they symptoms, but she knew it was better to be sure. Because of the problems, she had delivering Patrick, she feared for any other children she may have.

After the doctor examined her, he asked her to come into his office because he would like to talk with her. Emma could barely get dressed because she was shaking so much. Finally, she took a few deep breaths and walked into his office.

The doctor was writing some notes when she walked in and he did not acknowledge her for a few seconds. He then asked her to have a seat because he needed to discuss some things with her.

When the doctor started talking, Emma was more shocked by what he was saying than she had been when she thought she was pregnant.

The doctor told Emma that she had several health issues going on. One was that she had a thyroid problem and the other was that she had several large tumors on her ovaries and in her cervix, and they were probably what was causing her to have symptoms similar to pregnancy. She also had some serious scarring from some possible injuries or other pregnancies.

He advised Emma that she should have surgery immediately to remove the tumors. He did not know if they were cancer, but there was a 50 percent chance that they might be. She should not put it off any longer than possible. In fact, he told her that he should be sending her to the hospital as they spoke.

Emma did not know what to do because she was so nervous. She had gone to the doctor after work, and it was starting to get late, but she chose to walk all the way home from the doctor's office instead of taking a bus. She needed to clear her mind and think about what she was going to do.

The munitions plant provided their employees with health insurance. What would she do about her job and Frederick? She needed her paychecks, and she could not ask Judy Hornet and Gail Snowman to cover her shift for six to eight weeks. It could cause her to have to spend all the money she had saved for her and Frederick, and they would be broke again.

When she got close to home, Frederick and Dave saw her and ran out to meet her. Frederick's greeting was enough to make her feel better. She at least had a son because according to what the doctor said, she may never be able to have any more children because of the scarring and the tumors.

She wondered what Sly would say when he found out. He was Catholic, and his family was expecting grandchildren.

She knew that she had to put her health first because of Frederick. She would have to deal with Sly when he got home. She could not believe that he would behave the way Harry did about things that did not go his way, but she would just have to wait and see.

The doctor had scheduled her surgery, and she needed to start making preparations to be out of work for six to eight weeks plus having Frederick taken care of and fed.

She went to talk with Mrs. Spencer that evening and asked her if it would be at all possible that she could watch Frederick, while she was in the hospital having surgery.

Mrs. Spencer seemed offended that she would even think she would not do that for her. She gave Emma a hug and told her not to worry about Frederick because he could stay with them while she was in the hospital and at home until she was able to take care of him again. She told her that she would also help prepare her meals and help with her housework.

Emma could not believe anyone could be so nice to her. Mrs. Spencer was a true friend. In fact, both Mr. and Mrs. Spencer were almost like family. They always seemed to know what she needed before she would even ask, and they were always there to help in all situations.

Mr. Spencer told her that they had another person that could run the crane. He would talk to her supervisor and Mr. Woodie about transferring him to operating the crane on her shift while she was out with her surgery and recuperation.

True to his word, Mr. Spencer had already talked to her supervisor before she had a chance to. When she told him about her health situation, he was very sympathetic and told her not to worry. Of course, they could not pay her while she was out, but they would hold her job open as long as they possibly could.

That was really a big weight lifted off Emma. Now she had to prepare for her surgery and her recovery.

She also intended to write Sly a long letter telling him about everything. She hoped that he would understand about the fact that she may never be able to have any more children. He was good with Frederick, but she knew that he wanted at least one child of his own, and if he had his way, he would like a whole house full of children.

The night before Emma's surgery, she was very nervous. She hoped and prayed that she did not have cancer. She knew that her grandmother would take Frederick in if something happened to her, but she would love to live and see him grow up and have a family of his own and her become a grandmother.

She supposed that everyone that ever had a serious illness felt the same way she was feeling. No one wanted to die and leave their children behind without a parent to take care of them. She did a lot of praying that night. She went into Frederick's room and lay down beside him. She finally went to sleep sometime after midnight.

She had set the alarm to give her plenty of time to bathe and fix Frederick's breakfast. She did not have to check into the hospital until ten, but she wanted to make sure that she had everything taken care of before she left.

Around 8:00 p.m., Reverend Charles and his wife Kedra knocked on the door. Mr. Spencer had told him on Sunday about her going to the hospital for surgery. He had stopped by to have prayer with her and to drive her to the hospital if she needed him to.

She was very thankful for that because she would have to take a bag with gowns and a robe in it, and she hated to have to carry that much on the bus.

On the way to the hospital, Reverend Charles asked her if she had been able to let Sly know that she was having surgery.

She told him that she had written him a letter, but she did not know if he would receive it while deployed, but she was sure that it would be waiting on him when he got back home.

Kedra looked at Emma and told her that she thought that Sly was a wonderful person and she was sure that he would do right by her. She told her that she felt like he would make a great husband for her and a great father figure for Frederick.

In Emma's heart, that was what she wished. She was sure that Sly would be very supportive of her, but was it asking too much of him to give up the chance of having a family of his own? He was a good person and deserved the best that life had to offer.

She also knew that she loved him enough to let him go.

71

Life-Changing Situation

E mma knew that this surgery could be a life-changing situation for her and Frederick. It could also mean life or death if it was cancer.

Reverend and Mrs. Charles assured Emma that they would stay at the hospital with her as long as she needed them. Just before they took Emma to the operating room, Reverend Charles and his wife held each other's hands and each took one of her hands, and he prayed the sweetest prayer, saying, "God, if it be your will, please guide the surgeons' skilled hands as they operate on Emma. We know of many miracles you have performed, and we know that you have the power to heal Emma. Thank you for bringing her and her son Frederick into our lives. As we remove our hands from Emma, we know that you will extend yours to her giving her peace and your grace through her surgery. God, in your tender mercies, please hear our prayers. Amen"

Emma was not afraid of death, but she was concerned for Frederick. She did not want him to have to live life without her. The poor child deserved much more than life had dealt him.

As they were taking her to the operating room, peace came over Emma. She felt that whatever happened would be okay.

Before they put her to sleep, the surgeon talked to her to telling her exactly what they would be doing. If the tumors were not malignant, he would try to remove them, but if they were malignant, he may possibly have to do a complete hysterectomy, removing her ovaries and uterus as well as the tumors, and she would not be able to have any more children.

Emma told him that she understood everything that he had discussed with her during her office visits and what he was saying to her now.

The doctor patted her hand and gave the okay to start her IVs to put her to sleep.

72

Reverend Dolan and Reverend Charles

R everend Charles and his wife, Kedra, sat patiently in the
waiting room while Emma was in the operating room.
They had done this for many of their church members.
When there might be a situation of life and death, Reverend
Charles felt as their pastor, he should be with their members and
their families during their time of need.

As they waited, other ministers were coming in an out of
the waiting room. Several of them stopped to talk with them
wanting to know if they had family or a member of their church
in the hospital.

Reverend Dolan came in with his son. For some reason,
Reverend Charles did not particularly care for this minister. He
also did not trust him, and he had heard many questions about
the boys that lived with him.

When Reverend Dolan said hello and asked him if he had
someone in the hospital, Reverend Charles told him that one
of his members was in surgery. She was possibly facing a life or
death situation or many months of chemotherapy treatment for
cancer. "We are praying that God will heal her and bring her
through this and restore her to good health."

Reverend Dolan asked him who was the patient, and Reverend Charles told him that her name was Emma Carswell, a wonderful young woman, well respected by them and all of the other church members and her friends and neighbors. Reverend Dolan looked like he had just seen a ghost by his expression, and his hands shook so much that he spilled some of his coffee.

Reverend Dolan's son was standing beside him and with tearful eyes said, "That is my mother."

Reverend Charles thought maybe the young man had misunderstood him, and he asked Reverend Dolan's son if he knew Mrs. Carswell. The young man looked at his father and then at Reverend Charles and said, "Yes, sir, she is my mother." He then left the waiting room.

Reverend Charles looked at Reverend Dolan for answers, but he gave none and immediately walked out of the room to find his son.

Neither Reverend Charles nor his wife knew what to say about what had just happened. This was a very startling revelation for them. They knew that Emma's son Frederick was probably a little older than Reverend Dolan's son was, but could Emma Carswell be Donald Dolan's mother?

About thirty to forty-five minutes later, Reverend Dolan came back into the waiting room with his son. He sat down in a chair, and his son sat in the chair beside him. The young man looked like he may have been crying.

Reverend Dolan told Reverend Charles that he felt that he owed him an explanation about what just happened.

He began by saying that when he heard about a young woman with children who lived in his church district, he decided to go by and invite them to come to his church. The mother could never come because of her work schedule. He volunteered to go by each Sunday and pick up the two boys and take them to church with him.

He said that every time it came time for Donald to go home, he would start crying. Donald told him about a man who had broken into their home and cut him. The main thing he could remember was peeking out from under the bed and seeing the man fall to the floor. Before he hit the floor, the man looked straight into Donald's eyes, and it really scared the poor boy to death. He said that he had nightmares about that man looking at him and thought that maybe he would come back and hurt him again.

Reverend Dolan then said, "When Donald was just a little boy, he witnessed his father beating his mother. Donald said the last beating his father gave his mother, he beat a baby out of her, or at least that was what Donald thought at the time. He never saw his father again after that. Evidently, every time his father got angry, their mother or one of the children would be punished severely by their father."

Reverend Dolan told them that at first he thought that the mother was out running around town leaving her babies at home alone, and they really were just babies. However, he found out that she worked the night shift at a restaurant.

Mostly what Donald remembers is that he and his brother and sister being alone, and they were always cold and hungry. He also remembers crying when someone took his baby brother away and never brought him back home again. He was afraid that they might come and get him. He loves his mother, but he is afraid to live with her.

When Reverend Charles looked over at Donald, he could see anguish in the poor boy's face, and tears were pouring down his cheeks.

When Donald saw Reverend Charles looking at him, he bowed his head and said, "I love my mother, and I don't want her to die. I am sorry for everything that I said and did to her. I hope that she will not die before I can tell her that I am sorry."

Donald's statement brought tears to Mrs. Charles's eyes.

When Donald and Reverend Dolan told them how they both had treated Emma, Reverend Charles was angry and sympathetic at the same time. He could not believe that a fellow man of God could treat anyone like that and still call himself a minister, but he knew that he would need to pray for Reverend Dolan and his son, not judge them.

Reverend Charles, his wife, and Reverend Dolan and Donald all bowed their heads in prayer. Reverend Dolan was asking God's forgiveness because of the way he had treated Emma and Frederick. He said that his heart was full of shame because he tried to turn Donald against his mother so that he would never want to leave him. He knew that it was wrong, but he loved Donald, but he knew that it was a very selfish act on his part.

Donald prayed, asking God's forgiveness because he had hurt his mother and his brother. He also thanked God for bringing him and his sister back together. He also prayed for God to please heal his mother and give him the chance to apologize to her and Frederick for all the nasty things that he had said and done to them.

Reverend Charles was praying for God's healing power for everyone involved.

Several people came to the waiting room as they were praying, but everyone respected their privacy and went elsewhere.

After the prayer, Reverend Dolan told Reverend Charles and his wife that God must have sent them to the hospital just so they could make amends with Emma.

Reverend Charles shook his hand as well as Donald's and then told them what he knew about Emma's health.

73

God Works in Mysterious Ways

When Emma woke up, her doctor told her that she did have cancer. He told her that the choice of treatment for her type of cancer would be chemotherapy. It would probably make her lose her hair, but it was the best treatment that he knew of for her type of cancer.

Emma did not know what to think or say, so she just nodded her head yes. After the doctor left her alone, she wondered why God had not cured her of the cancer. She felt a little angry with him because she had felt like he was really going to take care of her especially after the prayer Reverend Charles prayed before she went down for surgery. He told her to have faith that God would heal her, but he did not. Instead, she had cancer. She knew that cancer was one of the worst illnesses anyone could have. She and Frederick were finally in a good place in their lives, and now she would have to deal with the cancer and the treatments or possibly death.

When they took her to her room, Reverend and Mrs. Charles came in shortly afterward. The doctor had already told them about Emma's prognosis. They knew that Emma would probably struggle with her diagnosis and may even lose some of her faith, but they would be by her side, whatever her fate.

Mrs. Charles sat by Emma's bed, and Reverend Charles sat in a chair across the room. When Emma was fully awake, they told her that they had some news that may cheer her up.

Emma said, "Is it about Frederick? Has something happened to him?"

They told her no, that Frederick was just fine, but they did have someone that would like to come in for a short visit, if she was up to it.

She told them that she was sure that she looked awful and was not ready for company, but Mrs. Charles told her that she thought she would enjoy seeing her visitor.

Emma told her okay, so Reverend Charles walked out of the room and a short while came back with Donald. Reverend Dolan stood outside the door because he did not want to do anything else to separate Emma from her son or to add any more stress to her life.

When Emma looked up and saw that it was Donald, she did not know what to say. She immediately started crying and so did Donald. He went to her bed and sat down in the chair that Mrs. Charles had been sitting in and laid his head over on his mother's arm telling her how sorry he was for all the bad things that he had said to her and Frederick. He raised his head, looked into his mother in the eyes, and said, "Mom, I really do love you. I hope you can find it in your heart to forgive me for all the things that I have ever said and done to you."

Although Emma was still in great pain, she pulled herself up and put her other arm over her son's shoulder, in a way that only a mother can do. She told him that she had already forgiven him, and she then asked for his forgiveness for the life he had to live when he was just a baby and all the pain that he must have experienced in his young life.

After leaving Emma and Donald alone for a while, Reverend Charles brought Reverend Dolan in. Emma looked up a little surprised to see him. Seeing her son and forgiving him was one thing, but she did not know if she had it in her to forgive The Preacher.

Reverend Charles asked Emma if she was okay with them all being in her room. Emma would rather it just be her son, but she told him that it would be okay. However, in her heart, she really did not want The Preacher in her room.

When Reverend Dolan came over to her bed, he put his hand on Donald's shoulder and then began to ask Emma for forgiveness. He knew that it was wrong to try to turn her son against her and his siblings, and he knew that it was a very selfish thing for him to do. He said that he let the devil enter his heart and turn him into someone that he sometimes did not recognize when he looked into the mirror. He knew that he would probably never marry, but he had always wanted a son. He told how it made him feel good to take Donald and Frederick to church with him. When Donald told him that he would like to come and live with him, he thought it was a blessing from God. He had tried to convince himself that it was all because he thought she was not taking good care of Donald and he thought he would be better off with him, but from what he had heard, he knew that she was actually an exceptional mother and very well thought of by all who knew her.

It was a very joyous reunion with Donald, but it did not take long until Emma grew tired. When a nurse came in and saw how she looked, she suggested that Emma's visitors leave and let the patient rest.

They all agreed. Donald told his mother 'bye and promised that he would visit her again in the hospital. He paused for a while but then said, "When my father comes to visit other sick people, I will come to visit you."

Emma smiled at her son and told him that she would really like that.

After they all left, Emma said a soft prayer thanking God because she now knew that her illness was God's way of bringing her son and her back together again. She knew that God did work in mysterious ways. She had heard that comment all of her life, but she knew that she would be willing to go through anything to get all of her children back together.

74

Hair Loss

E mma was in and out of the hospital during the next three
months. When her grandmother found out about her
illness, she, Uncle Charlie, and Henrietta went down
and moved her and Frederick up to her house. Frederick had no
objection because he knew that his mother was sick and needed
someone to take care of her.

When possible, Vera and Sophia would visit her for a few
hours on either a Saturday or Sunday. When they left after their
first visit with her in the hospital, both of them were in tears all
the way home. It broke their hearts to watch Emma suffer.

It was not long after Emma started the chemotherapy that her
hair started falling out. Her grandmother got some of Emma's
scarves that she had worn in the plant and tied them around her
head. Each time they took them off, they were full of her hair.

Sophia and Vera decided to pay Sly's parents a visit one
weekend and tell them about Emma. His parents asked them if
it would be okay if they went to visit Emma, and they told them
that a visit from them would probably cheer Emma up.

About two weeks later, Sly's parents knocked at the front door.
Uncle Charlie let them in and asked them to have a seat and that
he would check to see if Emma was up to having company.

Frederick was the first to go to the living room. He hung his head as though in great thought and then looked at them and said, "Will Sly still love my mom when he sees that she doesn't have any hair and because she is sick?" They both reassured him that their son loved his mother and that he would love her with hair or without hair.

He told them that sometimes his mother got very sick. He and his sister were walking home from visiting one of her friends one day, and they could hear their mother throwing up from several houses away.

Mom, as everyone called Sly's mother, walked over to Frederick. She told him that she had cancer about ten years ago, and she lost all of her hair. Sometimes she threw up a lot, because that was some of the side effects of the medication, but she was cancer-free now and all of her hair had grown back, and Sly and Pop, as they called Sly's father, loved her just the same with or without hair.

They had only visited with Emma for a short while that day because they knew that she needed plenty of rest, so they told Emma that they should be leaving after they had spent about thirty minutes with her. Emma thanked them for coming all that way to visit her. As soon as they left, she went back to bed. It did not take much to make her tired, especially right after one of her treatments.

Frederick really liked Mom and Pop. They reminded him of Sly; it also made him lonesome for Sly, and he knew that his mother probably felt the same way. Even though she was sick, he would sometimes see his mother writing letters to Sly.

He also missed Dave. He had not seen him in months. His grandmother had written Mr. and Mrs. Spencer a letter inviting them to come up for Thanksgiving, and they told her that they would love to.

Emma was feeling a little better by Thanksgiving and was able to join them for the Thanksgiving meal even though she did not eat very much. She was very tired by the end of the meal, so her grandmother told her that she should go lie down while she and Mrs. Spencer cleaned up the kitchen.

Before leaving the room, Emma commented about how great it was to watch Frederick with Dave after not seeing each other in a long time. She told them that she hoped that Mr. and Mrs. Spencer would stay for a while and let the boys spend more time together. Mrs. Spencer assured her that they would and told Emma to go lie down. She told her that they would come in before they left to tell her 'bye. She also told her that she knew that the boys needed time to spend together catching up on everything that had happened since they had last seen each other.

Mr. Spencer told them that they would come back during the Christmas holidays and visit them. They were going to visit Mrs. Spencer's family during Christmas, and they would stop off there for a few hours to visit them. Frederick and Dave loved that idea.

Mr. Spencer, Sophia, nor Vera mentioned Emma coming back to work, and Emma never said anything to them about it. The insurance, which she had with the munitions plant, had paid most of her medical bills. After they found out that she would be out of work for a long time, employees at the plant chipped in each week to pay Emma's premium. What they lacked, Mr. Woodie paid.

75

The Divorce Was Final

About a week before Christmas, Emma was feeling a little stronger. Uncle Charlie took Frederick out, and they cut down a beautiful tree and brought it home. They all drank hot chocolate and decorated the Christmas tree.

The mail came and there was a letter for Emma from the court. The letter notified Emma that Harry Frederick Carswell was filing for divorce from Emma Patton Carswell on the grounds of irreconcilable differences. The letter told her that she had thirty days to dispute the divorce. There was no property to divide, and Emma Patton Carswell would have full custody of Henrietta Carswell, Frederick Carswell, Donald Carswell, and Patrick Carswell, children born to Harry Frederick Carswell and Emma Patton Carswell. Harry Frederick Carswell was seeking no visitation rights to the children. The divorce would be final on January 18, 1945.

Emma looked at Frederick and told him that they had just received the best Christmas present ever. He asked his mother what the Christmas present was, and Emma told him that in just a few weeks, she and his father would be divorced.

Frederick asked his mother what a divorce was, and she told him that it was an agreement that she and his father would no longer be married. He looked at his mother and asked, "Does that mean that Harry will not be my father anymore?'

She told him that the divorce gave her full custody of him. She did not mention the names of her other children. He said, "Does that mean that I am divorced from Harry also?"

Emma looked at her son and said, "Yes, you and I both are divorced from Harry." She did not say his father that time.

Frederick wanted to know if that meant that Harry would not bother them again, and Emma told him that the papers did not say that, but that was what it meant.

Frederick jumped up and shouted, "This is the best Christmas present ever!"

Mary and Uncle Charlie came running into the living room wanting to know if something was wrong. Emma told her grandmother and uncle that everything was wonderful. Frederick cheerfully told them that he and his mom just got divorced from Harry.

76

They Saluted the Dead Soldiers

Three days before Christmas, Mr. and Mrs. Spencer stopped for a visit on the way to visit with Mrs. Spencer's family. Dave immediately reminded his mother that she was supposed to ask them a question.

Mrs. Spencer smiled and then said, "Since we are only going to be a short distance from here, Dave wants to know if he can spend a night or two with Frederick."

Mary told them that Dave could stay as long as he liked. This was another great Christmas present for Dave and Frederick.

Frederick had his own room now. He and Uncle Charlie had turned half of the attic into another bedroom for him and the other half a play and study area for Frederick and Henrietta. He had put bookshelves all along the back wall, and they were full of books. Uncle Charlie and Frederick had carved more animals, and they were on the shelves in front of the books.

Frederick told Dave that he did not need a heater in his room because it was right over the kitchen, and his grandmother was always in the kitchen cooking, and the heat from the kitchen kept his room warm.

When they got up to Frederick's room, Dave told him that he was jealous. He would love to have a bedroom like his, but in the apartments, you could not do anything except store a few things in their attic. They divided the attic storage areas with chicken wire for each apartment. You could see what everyone had stored in his or her attics. His father was afraid someone might cut the wire and be able to get into the other apartments through the attic door that you pulled down from the ceiling of their linen closet. His dad put a board over their door and put locks on it. The only problem was, when you wanted something from the attic, you had to go to a lot of trouble taking the board down before you could get in the attic.

Mr. Spencer had driven his truck so that they could bring Dave's bicycle with them. Dave had convinced them that Frederick had many places that they could ride their bikes, so they gave in and let Dave bring his.

That afternoon Frederick and Dave counted the money they both had to see if they had enough money between them to buy some film. Then they got permission to go bike riding, and they rode up to the little store that was only a couple of blocks away. Between them, they had enough money to buy two rolls of film each and a big candy bar, which they broke into two pieces.

That evening they made their plans. Frederick asked his uncle Charlie about the airport, and he also asks him how to get there from their house and how far away was it.

The next morning bright and early, the boys jumped out of bed to pursue their plans. Emma was still asleep when they left, so Frederick told his grandmother that he and Dave were going to go bike riding and that they may not be home for lunch.

Mary wrapped up a couple of sausage biscuits, gave them each a jug of water to drink and told them to have a good time.

They got lost a couple of times, but they knew they were close to the airport when they saw some planes coming in so low that they looked like they may take the tops off some of the trees.

The boys rode to a place called Look Out Point, where Frederick's uncle told him people went to watch airplanes come in and take off. There was a huge rock close to a fence, and it looked like it was the perfect place to sit and watch the airplanes. They parked their bicycles and climbed the rock with their brownie cameras with them, hoping they would get some great pictures from than vantage point.

They had taken what they thought would be some good pictures of airplanes, so they sat down for a while just to watch the planes land and take off. All of a sudden, a big green airplane flew over them. It scared them because all of the other airplanes they had taken pictures of were mostly white with numbers written on them.

The green airplane was bigger and a lot louder than the other planes. The boys stood up on the rock to see if they could get a better look at the airplane after it landed.

There was no writing on the plane. They saw no numbers or drawings like those that they saw on the other planes.

Dave said, "Boy did we pick a great time to come up and take pictures of airplanes."

It seemed that there was something constantly going on around the airplane. Men in uniform were going in an out of the airplane, bringing things out and putting them in a green truck that was almost the same color as the airplane.

All of a sudden, the men in uniform formed two lines near the back of the airplane. The boys then saw the men stand at attention and salute long boxes brought out of the airplane.

Frederick said, "I wonder what is so important about those boxes that they have to salute to them?"

Dave said, "Frederick, I think those are coffins! I will bet you those boxes contain the bodies of men who were killed in the war."

Dave immediately stood up straight just like the men in uniform did, and he started saluting the boxes also. When Frederick saw what Dave was doing, he stood up and did the same thing.

The boys stood at attention until they took the last box off the airplane. They did not stop saluting until they saw the men stop and walk behind the coffins.

Uncle Charlie had a feeling that he knew where the boys were going that day, so he drove up to Look Out Point to watch for them. He had parked his truck out of sight and watched the boys through the shrubs. He had never felt as proud in all of his life as he was when he saw his young nephew and his friend saluting young soldiers brought home in coffins. Just as the boys did, he stood at attention and saluted. He was so thankful that he brought his camera with him, because he knew that his mother and the boys' parents would be proud of what they were doing and would enjoy the pictures.

Uncle Charlie did not leave until the boys started for home. After they got out of sight, he got into his truck and drove home. The whole time that he served in World War I, he was never more impressed with any situation as he had just been with his nephew and his friend.

77

I Love You Truly

When Mrs. and Mrs. Spencer came to pick Dave up on Christmas Eve, they asked him what he and Frederick had been doing. Dave shrugged and said, "Just riding our bikes and taking pictures with our cameras."

Dave then asked his parents if they could loan him and Frederick enough money to have some film developed. Uncle Charlie immediately spoke up and told him that he was getting ready to go to the drugstore, and he could drop the film off to be developed, and he would pick them up when it they were ready and then mail Dave's pictures to him.

Mr. Spencer told him that he would pay for the film developing, but Uncle Charlie told him that was not necessary; he would be happy to have the film developed for the boys.

He wanted to have the film developed because he wanted to put some of the pictures that he had taken together with the boys' films. He could just imagine their surprised looks when they saw the pictures of them saluting the coffins.

The boys gave Uncle Charlie the films from their cameras. He told them that he would ask the store to develop the film as fast as possible, but it would probably be a week or so before they would be ready. He promised them that he would mail the pictures to Dave just as soon as they came back.

After Mr. and Mrs. Spencer left with Dave, it seemed very quiet around the house. Emma was amazed as to how different Frederick was when he was with Dave as to how he was after Dave left. He was always a respectful and good boy, but he just seemed to come alive when the two of them were together.

After dinner, they heard people outside their house singing Christmas carols. After they were finished singing, Mary asked them in for hot chocolate or hot apple cider. After they left, Frederick was very tired, so he went to bed and did not even appear curious about what was in the packages under the Christmas tree.

Henrietta was excited about her gifts under the tree and did not want to go to bed. Finally, her grandmother let her open one of her gifts and then told her to scat up to bed.

The next morning, Henrietta and Frederick were both sitting on the floor next to the Christmas tree. Uncle Charlie was teasing them telling them that they would have to wait until nighttime before opening their gifts.

Mary and Emma were coming down the stairs just as he said that, and Mary said, "Charlie, are you kidding?" She then laughed because there was no way those two would last another minute, so she gave Henrietta and Frederick the go-ahead to open their packages.

The first gift that Frederick opened was from Uncle Charlie. In the box were six rolls of film for his Brownie camera. He got so excited after seeing what was in the box that that he ran over and jumped up in his uncle's arms, giving him the biggest bear hug he had ever given anyone and thanked him for the film.

Uncle Charlie had never had that to happen to him before, and he was a little embarrassed, but he just grinned and told Frederick that he could take many pictures with that much film, but he would have to rob a bank to pay for the developing.

The next package that he opened was from his mother. She had not been able to go shopping nor did she have any money to shop with, so she boxed up the boots that she had bought the year before and gave them to Frederick with a dollar tucked inside.

Mary gave both Frederick and Henrietta a big plate of ginger bread cookies, and of course, both of them had to eat one before they opened another package.

Frederick's next package did not have a name on it saying who had given it to him. All of them looked at each other wondering who had put the package under the tree. Henrietta was jealous until she saw a package under the tree for her wrapped in the same color of paper with her name on it.

As they tore into their gifts, Frederick got his opened first. He could not believe his eyes. Someone gave him a gun and holster set that was like the one that he saw one day when he was with Sly. Some boys were playing cops and robbers, and when they fired their guns, the caps would go off, causing a big popping sound.

When Henrietta opened her present, it was a beautiful necklace with her birthstone. She looked at her mother, then to her grandmother, and then to Uncle Charlie. Each one of them shook their heads, letting her know that neither of them had given it to her.

Frederick saw a small package under the tree with the same wrapping on it. He picked it up and saw that it had his mother's name on it, so he took it over to her. When she opened her package, she knew immediately who had given her the present. The gift was a music box with a heart on top. In the heart was her name and Sly's name. When she opened the music box, it played "I Love You Truly."

Frederick jumped up and said, "Sly bought us these gifts." His grandmother smiled and told them the last time Mom and Pop came up, they brought the gifts, and she had hidden them until they put up their tree. Sly had contacted his mother and told her that he had some gifts for them, as well as for Emma and her children, that he had hidden under his bed and asked her if they would take the gifts to Emma and her children for Christmas if he did not get home. He had them wrapped so that no one would know what they were getting until they opened their packages at Christmas.

Emma wound the music box and let it play so that everyone could hear the music. When Sly left, he had thought enough of her and her children to make sure they had a gift from him for Christmas, even if he could not be there.

It was so sweet and endearing that Emma could not help but cry. Frederick walked over to his mother and kissed her on the cheek. He said, "You got a divorce from Harry, and Sly sends you a gift that says, 'I Love You Truly.'" He laughed and said, "This really is the best Christmas ever."

Uncle Charlie raised an eyebrow at Frederick. Frederick rephrased his statement and said, "This is the second best Christmas that we have ever had. I forgot that I said the same thing last year."

They all laughed at Frederick, but inside, Emma feared what may happen between her and Sly when he got home and saw how she looked with no hair and what her health situation was. For now, she was going to play the music box and dream of what their future could be together and not worry about what it might not be.

78

Battle of the Bulge

It was now March, and the weather was cold, windy, and nasty. Thankfully, Emma was near completion of her treatments, and her doctors had giver her hope that her cancer was in remission.

Uncle Charlie brought a newspaper home, but he did not know whether to let Emma see it or not. He was not one to hide anything, at least something this important, but he did not know how all of this would affect Emma. She was doing so well with her treatments that he did not want to cause her any stress, so he decided to ask his mother if he should show the paper to Emma.

Mary was in the kitchen preparing dinner when Uncle Charlie went hunting for her. He showed her the paper first and then asked if she thought that it would be okay to let Emma see it.

Emma said, "Let me see what?"

Mary and Uncle Charlie turned around at the same time, and neither knew what to say.

Uncle Charlie said, "Emma, there are some things printed in the newspaper today, and we did not know whether you should read them or not."

His comment really scared Emma, but she stood firm and asked him to let her see the paper.

The headlines read, "Germans Executed American POWs."

Emma sat down in a chair not knowing what she would read next. The article stated that the war had been the bloodiest in history, and it had consumed the entire globe. It had predominately been fought in Europe and across the Pacific and eastern Asia and pitted the Axis powers of Nazi Germany, Fascist Italy, and Japan against the Allied nations of Great Britain, France, China, the United States, and the Soviet Union. While the Axis enjoyed early success, they were eventually beaten, falling to Allied troops.

The Germans have launched a final offensive in the west, called the Battle of the Bulge in an attempt to reconquer Belgium and split the Allied forces along the German border.

After the initial surprise of the Allied lines on the Western Front, the Germans were able to achieve a breakthrough in possibly six locations. For two weeks, it did not look as though they could stop them. They hoped to achieve a penetration of more than seventy miles into the lines. This has resulted in a significant Bulge that the 58th Panzer Corps and the forty-seven corps poured through, creating the collapse of the 106th and 28th infantry divisions.

After conferring with General Omar Bradley at headquarters in Paris, the Supreme Allied Commander General Dwight D. Eisenhower decided to order General George S. Patton on the south of the Bulge (salient) and General Hodges on the north to pivot the Third and First Armies respectfully and to focus on cutting off the Bulge at its base. Additionally, he deployed the 82nd and 102nd Airborne Divisions and committed all US reserves in Europe to fight.

The 101st Airborne Division has control of Bastogne, which is vital to the allied lines surrounded by the Germans.

The US 2nd Armored Division led by General James Collins stopped the German Panzers three miles from Meuse.

It has been stated, but not confirmed, that the Germans have executed a number of American POWs at Malmedy in retaliation.

It seems as though Adolf Hitler's decision to conduct the counteroffensive instead of the smarter military move of delaying action with defense focus resulted in the Germans losing the last of their vital reserves.

On the Soviets' front, they have now launched a new offensive liberating Warsaw and Krakow, capturing Budapest. It seems that their intention is to drive the Germans and their Hungarian collaborators out of Hungary, forcing the surrender of Slovakia.

The devastation caused by this war is so great that the full extent is hard to measure. More than fifty million people have lost their lives, and nearly half of them were civilians. Economically, the war has cost over a trillion dollars and has severely disrupted peacetime production.

One major difference between this war and earlier wars was the extent to which it affected the civilian population, specifically the Nazi regime! They targeted and killed an estimated eleven million European civilians solely out of political or racial motives.

One of the underpinnings of the Nazi regime has been a demented belief, the superiority of the so-called Aryan race; Hitler's idea of a pureblooded German people destined to become the world's masters. People, who did not fit his mold, were sent to concentration camps, where some were put to work and others were murdered in the camps' infamous gas chambers.

The primary victims of this Holocaust have been European Jews; although the Nazis also targeted non-Jewish Poles, gypsies, disabled people, homosexuals, and political opponents, and the Holocaust has numbered over five million.

It has been heard that the Nazis devised the "Final Solution to the Jewish Question," a specific plan to round up Jews from around Europe and exterminate them in Nazi death camps. By far, the country whose Jewish population most suffered was Poland, with 90 percent being killed in the Holocaust.

Many other countries, such as Hungary, Holland, Yugoslavia, Greece, Belgium, France, and Italy also saw their Jewish populations decimated. The Holocaust was responsible for killing over 60 percent of all European Jews, about a third of the world's overall Jewish populations at the time.

One of the most startling revelations is that Hitler's wife, Eva Braun, may have been of Jewish descent through her maternal line, which was *strongly associated* with Ashkenazi Jews.

After reading the newspaper, Emma's grandmother became silent. When they asked her what was wrong, she said, "Mom and Pop, Sly's parents, are from Poland. They told me that they still have many relatives in Europe who were not able to flee before the war started, and some of them may not have survived. I had no idea about what they were talking about until I read this article."

Emma asked what this would mean for Sly and Tony if they were Polish. Her grandmother said that they were of the Catholic belief, and they were born in America, so this should not affect them personally, but I am sure that they are mourning the loss of many of their family members and friends.

79

Hitler Commits Suicide

Uncle Charlie brought home a newspaper at the end of May. Top headline news: "Hitler commits suicide." Hitler decided to remain in Berlin for the last siege of the war, fifty-five feet under the chancellery, which was his headquarters. The shelter contained eighteen small rooms and was fully self-sufficient, with its own water and electrical supply. He rarely left the shelter. He spent most of his time micromanaging what was left of German defenses and entertaining such guests as Hermann Goering, Heinrich Himmler, and Joachim von-Ribbentrop. At his side was Eva Braun, whom he married only two days before their double suicide, as well as the death of his dog, an Alsatian named Blondi.

His officers warned him that the Russians were only a day or so from overtaking the chancellery and urged him to escape to Berchtesgarden, a small town in the Bavarian Alps where Hitler owned a home. The dictator instead chose suicide. He and his wife both swallowed cyanide capsules, which he tested first on his beloved dog and her pups. For good measure, he shot himself with his service pistol.

They buried the bodies of Hitler and Eva in the chancellery garden. Russian troupes recovered their remains. Even though the persons responsible for Hitler's and Eva's cremation have sworn that the ashes belong to Hitler and Eva, the German courts have not officially declared either of them as dead.

Some speculate that Hitler and Eva escaped capture and fled Germany. No one really knows for sure. He could possibly be in another hidden location.

The next news story was about The USS *Brooklyn*. The USS *Brooklyn* (CL40) is once again in port for repairs. The USS *Brooklyn* was a light cruiser, the lead ship of her class of seven and the third United States navy ship to bear its name.

She launched on November 30, 1936 by New York Navy Yard, sponsored by Miss Kathryn Jane Lackey, the daughter of Rear Admiral F. R. Lackey, and commissioned on September 30, 1937.

The USS *Brooklyn* joined the fleet in the Panama Canal Zone during the later part of 1938. She attended to routine duties until April 1939. In mid-April, she returned to the United States where she participated in the opening of the New York World's Fair on April 30, 1939.

On May 23, the USS *Brooklyn* aided the USS *Squalus* disaster south of the Isles of Shoals, New Hampshire. She acted as a base ship during the salvage and rescue operations.

The *Brooklyn* then steamed to the west coast, where she joined the Pacific Fleet and participated in the opening of the Golden Gate International Exposition.

She served on the west coast until she departed on a good will and training tour of the South Pacific. When she left Pearl Harbor for the east coast, she joined the Atlantic Squadron. She escorted the convoy carrying marines to Reykjavik, Iceland. The *Brooklyn* engaged in convoy escort and Neutrality Patrol.

With the entry of the United States into World War II, the *Brooklyn* got underway from Bermuda to patrol the Caribbean Sea.

She served as escort duty between the United States and the United Kingdom. During one of the trans-Atlantic crossings, the USS *Wakefield* caught fire, and the USS *Brooklyn* rescued

1,173 troops, which had been embarked onboard the *Wakefield*, although severely damaged by the fire.

The *Brooklyn* departed Norfolk, Virginia, for North Africa where she bombarded shore installations to cover Fedhala landing of Operation Torch. While engaged, she was hit by a dud projectile from a coastal gun, which damaged two of the cruiser's guns and wounded five of her crew. Following the Naval Battle of Casablanca, the Brooklyn departed Casablanca for the east coast.

From January until July 1943, she made three convoy escort voyages between the east coast and Casablanca and then steamed to the Mediterranean where she carried out screening and fire support during the invasion of Sicily.

The Brooklyn furnished part of the heavy navy gunfire, which preceded the landing of Allied troops on the coast of southern France. She remained on duty in the Mediterranean until she departed Sicily for New York.

The USS *Brooklyn* is now home at the New York Navy Yard, where she will be undergoing extensive overhaul and alteration. She will then exercise along the eastern seaboard and then will report to the Philadelphia Navy Yard for her preinactivation overhaul while waiting for further orders.

If Emma had ever needed a boost, this would certainly do the job. This could possibly mean that Sly would be coming home soon, unless he was one of the unfortunate ones that would not be coming home.

The first thing Emma did was to go to the bathroom, take her scarf off, and look at her hair. It had started growing back, and she was no longer bald. Her hair was short, but she would take that over being bald any day. What was hard to believe was that her hair was coming back curly. She had never had natural curly hair in her life.

She then looked at her body. She had always been petite and small, but her body looked like a skeleton with skin draped over it. She knew that she needed to gain back some of the weight that she lost. The thought of Sly coming home may give her an incentive to try to eat more.

She was thankful that the chemotherapy treatments were behind her now, and the doctor told her that her cancer was in remission. He said that by catching it in the early stages, she could possibly live a long healthy life, but he also told her that she would not be able to have any more children.

This thought saddened Emma, but as soon as she went back to the kitchen and saw Frederick and Uncle Charlie playing a game, with the excitement of beating each other, her mood became much better.

80

Spiteful Jealousy Brings Consequences

Emma was turning thirty on Sunday October 13. Sophia, Vera, Mr. and Mrs. Spencer, and Dave were coming up to celebrate it with her. This was going to be a big milestone for her. Beating cancer was a big issue, but turning thirty really made her feel old.

Her grandmother talked her into going shopping to buy her a couple of new dresses. All of her clothes were too big for her now. She hated to spend the money because her savings were dwindling down fast, and she had no other means of income, and she was not strong enough to go back to work yet.

Thankfully, her hair had grown out to about two inches, and the curls made it easier to take care of her hair and keep it looking nice.

As she tried on clothes, Emma realized that she had dropped two dress sizes. She was now a size 4 instead of 6.

Uncle Charlie, brought them shopping in his pickup truck. He had taken Frederick shopping for some new jeans, shirts, and shoes. His jeans were getting too short, his shirts barely met the waistband on his jeans, and by the way he walked, you could tell that his shoes were getting too small. She had offered Uncle Charlie some money to buy the clothes, but he told her to wait, because he did not know how much they would cost, and she could pay him when they got back.

Emma chose three dresses, and her grandmother had talked her into buying a new pair of shoes and underclothes also. She could not believe it, but her shoes also seemed too big.

When they got to the checkout counter, her grandmother would not let her pay for anything. Emma was somewhat embarrassed, but she gave in and let her grandmother pay. She did not know what she would have ever done without her grandmother and her friends. She and her cousin would have probably wound up in an orphanage or been adopted out had it not been for their grandmother.

Her birthday party was wonderful. Emma did not get as tired as everyone thought she would. After eating breakfast, at her grandmother's insistence, she laid back down for a little over an hour. She wore one of her new dresses for her party.

When she came out, Uncle Charlie whistled at her. Emma knew that he was just trying to make her feel good, which it did. Uncle Charlie was forever teasing her, so she walked over and gave him a big hug. He acted as if it embarrassed him and acted as though it was a big deal for someone so beautiful to hug him.

Emma had another big surprise when she went into the kitchen to offer to help her grandmother. Her cousin and her husband had come for a visit. She had not seen or talked to her cousin since before she and Harry were married, and it was a little awkward.

Margaret married Gerald Finch immediately after graduating from high school, and they only lived about thirty miles north of where her grandmother lived, but they never came to visit.

Gerald and Harry had gone to school together, and Harry had always bullied everyone in school, so Gerald had no love lost for Harry. Gerald was a very smug person himself and tried to appear as though he was more affluent than everyone else was, and he had taught his son Dwayne to be the same way.

Margaret had always appeared to be jealous of Emma because Emma was petite with beautiful dark hair and fair complexion, and Margaret had reddish mousy brown hair and was always overweight. She was much heavier now than she had been the last time Emma saw her, and she even was more jealous of Emma now than she had been as a child.

Margaret was two years older than Emma was, and she had always felt that their grandmother favored Emma because she was the youngest.

When Emma brought Harry home to meet their grandparents, Margaret was jealous and vowed that she would get even with Emma, if it were the last thing she ever did.

Margaret only had a very few dates before finally meeting Gerald Finch. When he asked her to marry him, she said yes immediately, because she thought he might be her only chance for marriage.

Gerald worked in a plant that made helicopters, and he had always made good money, and they always had nice things, but Margaret was still jealous of Emma marrying Harry.

A number of years after Margaret and Gerald were married, she saw Harry out one day when she was shopping. It made her feel good when he spoke to her. She started to turn her nose up at him, but it thrilled her so much to have him speak to her that she told him hello and asked how he was doing. Harry immediately said, "Much better since seeing you." Margaret was very flattered by his remark.

Harry asked her if she would like to have coffee with him. Margaret did not care if he was her cousin's husband or that she was married to Gerald; she was not going to turn him down. While having coffee, Harry asked Margaret if she heated with coal, and Margaret told him that they did. He smiled and told her that he delivered coal, and there were times when he would have some extra and asked her if she would like to have it.

Margaret was not exactly sure if he was flirting with her or was actually being kind enough to bring her extra coal. Gerald made more money than Harry made, so it could not be that he was having sympathy for her. She decided to call his bluff and told him that they purchased their coal from the Kistner Fuel and Ice Company, and either Jim or one of his sons, either Ben or Jeremy delivered their coal, but if he had extra that he needed to get rid of, she would be more than happy to pay him for the coal. Harry smiled and said, "It would be a gift, because it would be my pleasure to bring the extra coal over to your house." Harry then winked at her and asked for directions.

Margaret was so excited that she almost spilled her coffee when he winked. She had never had a single man in her whole life to wink at her, not even Gerald. She felt flush all over and could feel beads of perspiration on her neck and especially on her body. She had never been this excited about anyone or anything.

Margaret told him that Gerald worked until around six. If he wanted to wait until Gerald was home, he could come around six-thirty. If he needed to make the delivery earlier, she would be home alone.

Harry saw the excited flush on Margaret's face and knew that she fell for that line just as all the other women did. He winked and told her that it would be nice to come earlier.

When he went to her house the next day, it was about two in the afternoon. He did have to deliver a truckload of coal that morning, but he held some of it back to take to Margaret. It was not much, but it was enough to make a showing, which he really did not have to worry about.

When Harry knocked on her door, Margaret came to the door in a real frilly see-through robe. She had been preparing for Harry all morning, and she was ready for him.

When Harry saw her, he almost laughed because she made no pretense of vanity. If she only knew how she looked with all those bulges underneath that sheer fabric.

Margaret came alive when she was with Harry. Their affair was the most exciting thing that had ever happened to her in her life. When Harry told her that Emma had turned into a slob, she knew that she had finally paid her cousin back. She was taking her cousin's adorable, handsome husband away from her. Revenge was sweet.

One day after Gerald left to go out of town for a few weeks on business, Harry came by and told her that he was going into the navy. He was disgusted with Emma and wanted to get away from her. He said that he had planned on going straight into the navy, but he was going to have to wait about a week or so before leaving. He could not stand the thought of going back home to Emma, and he was going to have to find a place to stay until he could leave.

Margaret told Harry that he could stay with her if he liked because Gerald was going to be out of town. He grabbed her and said, "I do like that idea."

Margaret could not believe that she finally had Harry all to herself. She knew there would be no way that he would go back to Emma after a week or so with her. He was the lover that she had always dreamed of, and she was not giving him up for Emma or the navy. She would follow Harry to the ends of the earth if necessary. They were going to be the perfect couple.

When the day came for Harry to leave, he did not say anything to Margaret until just a few minutes before he had to leave because he did not want to see any of her theatrics, for which she had plenty.

Margaret was devastated when Harry told her that it was time for him to leave, and she started crying. He told her not to cry. If he did not get killed fighting in the war, he would be back one day, because he had enjoyed his time with her more than he had any other time of his life. He told her that because he did not want to burn any bridges just in case he needed her help in the future.

Harry caught the bus down the street from Margaret's house. She begged him to let her take him to the naval yard, but he told her that he did not want to put her to any more trouble than he already had. He said it would be more romantic holding each other as they said good-bye, instead of him having to jump out of the car where people were hustling about and only have time enough to reach over and give her a peck on the cheek. He told her that he would rather tell her a good-bye like this. He then put his arms around and gave her the long, luscious kiss he knew she was waiting for. He then told that he would be back one day, and they would be able to be together forever, just the two of them. He kissed her again and walked out the door.

He smiled, knowing that he deserved an Oscar for that performance. He did not want to take the chance of anyone seeing him in a car with her. He knew that everyone would wonder why in the world someone as good looking as he was, would be riding around with someone that looked like her. She had served her purpose, but now he only wanted to get away from her as fast as he could. He thought he was going to throw up when she tried to stick her tongue down his throat. It made him nauseous just thinking about it.

He was thankful that he did not have to wait long for the bus. He had no idea how he had stayed with Margaret for over a week. He had quit his job delivering coal as soon as he decided to go into the navy. When he went to the recruiting office, he thought he would leave from there, but instead he had to wait for processing and assignment. He found himself without a place to stay or a vehicle. Staying at Margaret's gave him a place to live until he could get out of that town. Margaret treated him like a baby while he was there. There was nothing too good for Harry Carswell. It was a shame that she could not have been better looking.

When she told him that he could stay at her house, he thought, *What the heck, I can handle anything for a week or two.* She almost proved him wrong. Everywhere in that house that anyone would sit, stand, sleep, walk, or eat on would have Harry Carswell's germs all over it. For some insane reason, he actually hoped that old Gerald would find out that he was there, supposedly enjoying his wife, his home, and his food while he was away on business. What a sucker.

After Harry left, Margaret felt like she was floating on air. She now had the man of her dreams, and she could not wait until they could be together permanently. She dreaded for Gerald to come home. Just the thought of his hands on her made her feel sick. Of course, the thought of Harry Carswell's hands on her gave her another feeling.

When Gerald did come home, she played as if she was sick so that he would leave her alone. After she missed one cycle, she just knew that she was expecting Harry's baby because she had not been with Gerald in months. He asked her one day what she was eating because she sure was getting fat. She immediately started gaining weight, and he told her that she looked like a whale

She felt like he was not a good one to talk about someone gaining weight because he was a doughboy himself. After missing the first month, she started getting scared about what she should do if she was pregnant. She thought about contacting the navy and trying to find out if she could get in touch with Harry. She was sure that he would want to know that he was going to be a father.

He had several children with Emma, so it would not be his first child. She was not his wife, and she had no way to prove that Harry was the father. *What if he denied it?* It would be her word against his.

She had never been able to conceive with Gerald and thought that she would probably never get pregnant and threw all caution to the wind with Harry.

She knew that she would have to give in to Gerald soon. If she were expecting a baby and something happened to Harry, she would need someone that could support her

She decided to take the bus to see her grandmother and talk with her about her situation. When she told her grandmother that she thought she was expecting, her grandmother raised an eyebrow and wanted to know whom the father of the baby was. Margaret did not know what to say, and she asked her grandmother why she would ask something like that.

She was almost positive that no one saw Harry coming or leaving her house. They were very careful about that, especially after he came to stay with her before going into the navy because Gerald had a lot of pull in the community, and he could really cause problems for him.

Mary told Margaret that a rumor was going around about her having a lover. Everyone was talking about how a man would come to her house almost every day through the week and would stay for an hour or so and then leave. They also knew that she had a man staying with her when Gerald was out of town.

Margaret got so upset with her grandmother that she walked out the back door, slamming it behind her. She swore that she would never step foot in that house again.

Gerald had come home early that day, so she did not have any time to be by herself. She decided to do a 360 and act as if she was feeling better and had gone to visit her grandmother.

When Gerald started making suggestions that night, she allowed him to do whatever he wanted to, hoping she would not throw up while it was going on.

The next morning, she felt like the first thing she needed to do was to go to the doctor to find out if she was pregnant. He confirmed what she had feared. She was pregnant, and she was almost certain that she knew who the father was, but there was no way that she could prove it.

When Gerald came home from work, she told him that she had been to the doctor, and he told her that she was pregnant. The doctor told her that she might have problems because of her delicate condition and that she should not be with her husband again until after the baby was born. She told him that it hurt to tell him because she knew how much he wanted a child, but she was afraid if she did not listen to the doctor, she might lose the baby. The doctor gave her a date that the baby may be born, but she said that he told her not to be surprised if it came a couple of months early because of her delicate condition.

She hoped this lie would buy her some time with Gerald. It had been a long time since she had been with him before he went out of town.

Gerald was so excited at the thought of having a child, hopefully a son, that he began immediately petting and pampering her. He did not want her cooking or cleaning or doing anything that may cause her to lose the baby, so he hired a full-time maid to do all of that, and the lack of activity caused her to gain even more weight.

Thankfully, she gave him a son, or to be exact, she may have given him Harry's son. Nothing seemed to matter to Gerald except that he now had a son. The date he was born nor the fact that he did not look premature, never registered with him.

Margaret had not seen or heard from Harry since he left. She thought it was probably because he was afraid to send any mail to her house. She had felt sure that he would try to arrange to see her when he came home on leave.

She was constantly thinking about what she would take with her when she left Gerald. She thought about taking some of their savings out of the bank so that she could get an apartment until Harry could get out of the navy, but she just did not want the responsibility of taking care of a apartment, cooking and caring for a child by herself.

Daily, Margaret was anxiously awaiting Harry's return, but day after day, he never showed up. One day she took Dwayne on a bus trip uptown. He needed some clothes because he was growing so fast. Gerald offered to take her on Saturday when he would be off, but she told him that she could take the bus and not cause him so much trouble. She actually wanted to get out of that house, and she did not want him with her. She would have loved to leave Dwayne with the housekeeper, but she knew that would not go over well.

She had to carry Dwayne most of the time. He was barely walking, and it was easier to carry him than to have him walk. He was beginning to look like Harry and nothing like Gerald. She hoped that no one else noticed.

As she was looking at clothes in the children's department, she saw Harry on the other side of the store. She was so excited to see him that she ran over and tried to hug him, but he put up his hands and pulled away. At about the same time, a very attractive woman came out of one of the dressing rooms, walked over to Harry and asked him which dress he liked best.

The woman was petite like Emma. Margaret had gained a lot of weight with Dwayne, and when she went back to the doctor after he was born, she only weighed eight pounds less than she weighed just before he was born. The woman told her hello when she saw Margaret trying to hug Harry. She thought that Margaret must be a relative or old friend. She then began admiring Dwayne. She looked up to Harry and asked him if he was a relative because the little boy sure looked like a miniature version of him. Harry pretended that he did not hear her.

Margaret could not believe it when the woman asked her if she was expecting again. She told the woman that she was indeed expecting again, and the baby was due any day now. She did not want Harry thinking that she was that fat for no reason. Harry looked at her and told her that she must be going to turn out like her cousin, popping babies out, one right after the other. His last remark really hurt Margaret. He had the nerve to say, "The only difference between you two is that you get fatter and she got skinnier with each baby."

His remark devastated Margaret, but the woman with Harry, actually laughed at his asinine remark. She gave him a fake smack on the arm and said, "Now Harry play nice." With the bruises on the woman's arms, it looked like Harry or someone else had not had been playing very nice with her.

Margaret had some of the same type of bruising after being with Harry because he said that he liked it rough, and she went right along with it, even though she thought it was a bit over board.

Margaret gave them her customary huff and walked away. She could hear Harry's laugh until she was out the door. She had no interest in shopping now and headed to the bus stop. All the way home, she could barely hold the tears back. All of her dreams crumbled in that one single day. What was she going to do now? Every day since Harry left, her dream was that once the war was over, he would come back and take her and their child away from this place. Her real dream was that Gerald would die. They would have all of his money, and they could live wherever they wanted.

For now, she had no other choice but to stay with Gerald. She knew no one else would want her; they never did.

She had not been back to her grandmother's house since the day she told her that she knew about her lover. It was all that she could do to come to this birthday dinner for Emma. Uncle Charlie had come to her house and personally invited her and her family. He told her about Emma's illness and made it sound as if she may die from it any minute and told her that he would like her to be there to celebrate with Emma because she may not be here to celebrate another birthday. That was a good reason for Margaret to celebrate. It was not exactly a lie because Emma and Sly would be married before her next birthday, and they may not live around here. Whatever it took, he was going to cook this girl's goose for always being so cruel to Emma.

Margaret thought that she would find Emma to be an ugly, withered woman consumed with her illness. Instead, she was smaller than she had been as a teenager, and it made Margaret feel like an elephant when she stood beside her. She could not believe that Emma had finally cut her hair, and she could not believe how great, short curly hair looked on her.

When Dwayne and Frederick stood beside each other, they looked like brothers. The entire time they were there, everyone was making over Emma. They would ask how she was or tell her how good she looked. No one said anything to Margaret. She did not know any of these people, and she did not want to get to know them. She could not figure out why Uncle Charlie had invited all of them. It was probably just to make her miserable. She had always known that he liked Emma the best. When he asked her to stand beside Emma so that he could take their pictures together, she wanted to grab his camera and throw it away. She did not want anyone taking a picture of her, especially beside Emma.

No one mentioned Harry. Margaret had worn her new mink coat to let him know that she was doing much better than he was, and that he was of no loss to her. She could not believe it when the distinguished-looking couple asked Emma if she would consider her and Sly getting married in the Holy Ghost Ukrainian Catholic Church.

Margaret asked whom she was marrying. She said that she thought Emma was married to Harry Carswell. Fredrick politely corrected her and told her that they were divorced from Harry, and he and his mother were marrying Sly Bandowski, a sailor in the navy.

When they showed her a picture of him, she could not believe how much better looking he was than Harry. This really made her angry.

Margaret did not say another word except to Gerald, telling him that she wanted to go. He asked her if she was not going to stay and help her grandmother clean up. She very impolitely told him that her grandmother could clean it up herself. She took Dwayne's hand and picked up the gift she had bought for Emma and walked out the door, swearing once again that she would never step a foot in that house again, and she meant it with all her heart this time.

Emma had no idea what made Margaret mad, but Uncle Charlie was smiling like a cat that had just swallowed a canary. Margaret had always been a drama queen, and Emma had learned a long time ago to ignore her dramatics, so she turned back and continued talking to her friends as though nothing happened.

Mary Byrd was embarrassed because of her granddaughter's behavior, but she also had grown tired of Margaret's behavior. If Margaret chose to be jealous and go on one of her tangents again, she was not going to let it hurt Emma, and she was not going to dignify it by making a comment, not after all that Emma had been through.

As Mary was cutting Emma's birthday cake and putting the slices on dessert plates, she could not help but feel sad about the two girls. Both of Margaret's parents died in a train accident a year before Emma's parents died during the flu epidemic. She had taken both girls in and raised them as her own, just as she was doing with Henrietta. How could two people, raised identically, be so different? Those two girls were nothing alike.

However, Mary did notice how much Dwayne and Frederick looked alike. She now wondered if Harry could have been the man everyone had talked about seen going into Margaret's house most afternoons during the week and staying at her house when Gerald was out of town on business. She had always known that Margaret had a crush on Harry when they were teenagers. She had thrown away many notes from Margaret when she cleaned her room. All of them written to Harry. Some of them just had his name written on them and others had her name written as Margaret Carswell. Others told Harry how much she loved him.

Neither Mary nor their grandfather wanted to see either of the girls involved with Harry. When Emma came home announcing that Harry had just proposed to her, she remembered Margaret's nasty reaction. She seriously doubted that Emma would have reacted the same way if Harry had proposed to Margaret. She wondered if, he would have proposed to Margaret to had he known she received a larger inheritance.

There had been lots of gossip about Harry during the years that he and Emma were married, and none of it was good. Mary remembered crying the day her beautiful granddaughter married him, and she had shed many tears for Emma since then. She was so thankful that Emma was finally going to marry someone who would be good to her.

81

Last Hired, First Fired

Two weeks after Emma's birthday dinner, Sophia and Vera came to visit Emma, and they were both upset. Sophia said, "Some men who had previously worked at the munitions plant came home expecting their jobs to be waiting on them, and naturally, they had to be crane operators."

Vera said that Mr. Woodie called her and Sophia into his office and told them that he was sorry, but he had promised the men that they would hold their jobs for them while they were away fighting for their country, and he had to honor that promise.

Vera said, "I guess we were the last hired, so we were the first fired."

They were going to different sewing plants applying for jobs, but no one would hire them because the government had cut back on their orders for uniforms, and local companies had not yet started ordering regular clothing to put in their stores. Several places told them that they would contact them when they had job openings.

With their termination, they did get two weeks severance pay, which they hoped would last them until they could find another job. If not, both of them would have to move back home with their parents, which neither of them wanted to do.

Emma said, "I will probably not get my old job back either. I wonder how that will affect my medical benefits."

Vera told Emma that some women were still working, but they had no idea how long their jobs would last. They heard that Germany had surrendered to their western Allies and the United States and Allied troops conquered Okinawa, which was the last island stop before the Japanese island.

Sophia said, "I think we should do to the Japanese exactly what they did to us. We should go sneaking in and bomb them."

Emma told Sophia not to talk like that. From what she had heard, many of the Japanese, just like the Germans and civilians from other countries, had suffered enough. She said, "I think we should pray for world peace instead of talking about bombing more countries."

Sophia said, "You are right, but it just makes me angry when I think of all the blood that has been shed in this war, and I am sure there is much more than any of us have heard about. I have heard that this war, which they are now calling World War II, has been the bloodiest in history."

82

President Franklin Delano Roosevelt Dies

Franklin Delano Roosevelt, President of the United States, passes away after four momentous terms in office, leaving Vice President Harry S. Truman in charge of a country, fighting in a Second World War.

President Roosevelt sat in the living room of his Warm Springs home in Georgia with Lucy Mercer, with whom he was having an extramarital affair, two cousins, and his dog Fala, while artist Elizabeth Shoumatoff painted his portrait.

About 1:00 p.m., the president suddenly complained of a terrific pain in the back of his head and then collapsed unconscious. One of the women summoned a doctor, who immediately recognized the symptoms of a massive cerebral hemorrhage and gave the president a shot of adrenaline into the heart in a vain attempt to revive him. Mercer and Shoumatoff quickly left the house because they expected the president's family to arrive as soon as word got out.

The doctor phoned first lady Eleanor Roosevelt in Washington, DC, informing her that FDR had fainted. She told the doctor that she would travel to Georgia that evening after a scheduled speaking engagement. By 3:30 p.m., doctors in Warm Springs had pronounced the president dead.

The first lady delivered her speech that afternoon and was listening to a piano performance when summoned back to the White House. She told someone that the ride to the White House was of dread as she knew in her heart that her husband had died.

Once there, one of the aides told the first lady of the president's death, and she and their daughter, Anna, immediately changed into black dresses, displaying their mourning for President Roosevelt.

The first lady then phoned their four sons who were all on active military duty. At 5:30 p.m., she greeted Vice President Harry Truman. She informed him that the president had passed away.

Vice President Truman asked if there was something he could do for her or her family. She replied, "Is there anything we can do for you?"

She said, "You are the one in trouble now, Vice President Truman, you have rather large shoes to fill."

President Franklin Delano Roosevelt presided over the Great Depression and World War II until his death on April 12, 1945, leaving an indelible stamp on American policies that will probably last for decades. Truman had to make a difficult decision as to whether or not to continue to develop and ultimately use the atomic bomb.

Shockingly, President Roosevelt had kept his vice president in the dark about the bomb's development, and Vice President Truman did not find out about the bomb until President Roosevelt's death. It was also not until President Roosevelt died that the first lady learned of her husband's affair with Lucy Mercer.

The first lady was able to put personal things in the background. She swallowed the shock and anger about Mercer and threw herself into the president's funeral preparations. Thousands of Americans lined the tracks to bid President Roosevelt farewell while a slow train carried his coffin from Warm Springs, Georgia, to Washington, DC. After a solemn state funeral, they buried President Roosevelt at his family's home in Hyde Park, New York.

President Roosevelt had a positive character of an optimistic and national spirit. All they can wish for now is that President Harry Truman will handle all affairs of this war with the fortitude that President Roosevelt did and keep this war away from America.

Emma sat back in her chair after reading the newspaper article. She assumed that most Americans who had read the newspaper today or hear about the president passing were feeling the same way that she was feeling. She was sick of the war and all of the fighting and lives lost. She was sure that she did not understand all that had transpired during this war, but from what she did understand, she knew that it was bad for all countries involved.

What would happen if President Truman used those powerful bombs to which the newspaper was referring? So many people would die if he did. It was a terrifying feeling knowing that their nation was in the middle of a World War and then to have their president to pass away.

83

Surprise Visitor

Emma went into the kitchen to make sure that Frederick was ready to go to school. Uncle Charlie was sitting at the table reading a newspaper. She could see an article on the back of the paper. It was talking about the devastation caused by World War II. It was so great that its full extent will be hard to measure for a very long time.

Emma was so involved in reading the back page of the newspaper, when Frederick jumped out of his chair; it startled her as well as Uncle Charlie. When she turned to ask what was wrong, she thought she was going to faint and backed up to the table to hold on.

Ready to knock on the screen door to the kitchen was Sly Bandowski. Emma and Frederick both were excited to see him. Uncle Charlie put the newspaper down and looked at Emma. He told her to go give that good-looking sailor a welcome home kiss. Emma did exactly that.

After Frederick opened the door and let Sly in, he gave Sly a great big welcome home hug. Going right in behind him was Emma. She was so small now that Sly picked her up as if she was a small child and gave her one of his delicious kisses right in front of everyone.

Mary came running into the kitchen to see what was going on. When she saw that it was Sly, she ran to give him a hug also. When Henrietta came through the door to the kitchen, she saw Sly, and went over and gave him a hug. Uncle Charlie laid his papers down, went over, and told Sly that all he was getting from him was a handshake and a welcome home.

Sly's parents had come with him, and they wanted Emma to drive back to their home with them because Sly had something he wanted her to see. They told her that they would bring her back later in the afternoon.

Frederick immediately started jumping up and down. He wanted to stay out of school and go with them. Of course, Henrietta was saying that if Frederick stayed home from school, she should be able to also, but Mary told her grandchildren they would have to go to school as usual; they could see whatever Sly was going to show their mother later. Frederick did not like it, but he gave Sly and his mother a hug, and he and Henrietta got in the truck with Uncle Charlie and headed for school.

Emma told Sly that she was not dressed to go anywhere, and Sly told her that she would look good in a sack, but if she wanted to change, they would wait for her. She was excited and ran back to her bedroom to put one of her new every day dresses. She was not sure what they wanted her to see, but since they were not dressed up, neither would she.

The trip down was a lot of fun, and every time Emma would start to say anything, especially to ask what her surprise was going to be, Sly would reach over and give her a kiss.

Mom and Pop both laughed at them, enjoying the easy rapport between Sly and Emma. They had known that this was the girl for Sly. He told them that he had found the love of his life, and they sure believed that now. They had never seen Sly behave toward anyone the way that he did toward Emma, and he had dated quite a few beautiful women, but they both knew for some reason Emma was different.

They had told Sly about Emma's cancer, but he told them that Emma had already told him. He said, "I love Emma! I would not be the real deal if I ran away from her when she needs me the most. I feel that if it I had cancer, she would be there for me."

When Emma seemed a little shy about her hair, Sly told her that he liked her hair long or short. He actually found her short hair to be cute on her, and he was sure that it had to be much easier to handle, especially while she was sick.

Sly did think that she was little too thin, but he did not comment about it. After what she had been through, he thought she looked great. She had to be a strong woman to have endured all the physical abuse she went through with Harry and then her battle with cancer. He loved her, and she was the person with whom he wanted to spend the rest of his life.

84

Miss Emma

When they got to Sly's home, Emma saw a huge boat in the backyard. When she turned and looked at Sly, he was smiling from ear to ear. He told her that while he was gone, Pop bought the Admiral, brought it home and has been working on it and had it refinished on the outside to where it looked almost like new.

Sly took her hand and led her to the back of the boat. He told Emma that he was recommissioning the boat and naming her *Miss Emma*, which was already written in beautiful letters across the stern. Emma said, "Sly, I am so honored. I don't know what to say."

He told her that he wanted her to know how serious he was about their relationship. If he did not intend to be with her for the rest of his life, he surely would not have put her name on his boat. Emma did not know what to say. In fact, she did not think that she could speak because of all the emotions she was feeling.

Sly gave her a hug, kissed the top of her head, and then took her hand, and the four of them got back into the car and drove a short distance from their house to where there was a dock for fishing boats and leisure boats.

About two hundred feet from the dock was a strip of small buildings. On the front of the first building, there was a sign that said, "Mom and Pop's Fishing Supplies."

Sly said, "My parent's have always wanted to own their own little store, so they thought if I was going to put my boat in the water here, it would be a good place for them to start their business." He then told her that he had discussed everything with his parents as to what his intentions were when he got out of the navy. While he was away, they went to check on the status of the boat and submitted a bid for it. He had told them what he could afford to pay for the boat, so they submitted a bid for that amount, and it was accepted; now the boat was his.

After purchasing the boat, they came up with the idea of opening a fishing supply store where Sly and all the other boat captains could purchase their fishing supplies before going out.

Emma caught Sly looking at his parents and grinning. He told her that he had one more surprise to show her. A short distance behind the store was a beautiful house that sat back from the dock, and it had a pier right in front of it. A porch wrapped all the way the front and both sides of the house. There was a small balcony upstairs in front of a door that would overlook the water. On the top of the house, there was something, which looked like another balcony or a viewing area that had the same railings around it. Sly told her that they called that a widow's walk. A sailor's wife could stand up there and watch for her husband's ship to come in.

Emma just stood there in total surprise because she did not know what to say. Sly took her hand, and they started walking toward the house. When they got to the front yard, Emma did not notice the sign on the front of the house because she was looking out at the pier. When she turned back to say something to Sly, she saw the name on a sign in big blue letters, "Miss Emma's Restaurant."

The sign stood out beautifully against the white of the house. She could not hold back the tears this time. Sly and his parents were beaming with pride. Sly took her around to the side of the house where there were steps leading to the upstairs. When they started to walk through the door, Pop hollered out to Sly, telling him that he was supposed to carry the bride over the threshold.

Emma's face turned red and said, "But we aren't married yet." Sly told her that he would take care of that as soon as he received his discharged from the navy, but for now, he would still carry her over the threshold to their new home as his intended wife. There were so many things that he wanted to show her. He was almost like a child in a candy store.

When they walked into the house, the first place he took her to was the living room. It had a big bay window where you could sit in and watch the ships coming in and out of the dock. It had a small kitchen to the side of the living room. There were three bedrooms. He told her that the one he had chosen for Frederick had the same view as the living room. Theirs would be the master bedroom at the back because it had its own full bathroom. The middle bedroom would be for Henrietta if she would like to come and visit with them, or if she wanted to, she could move in with them.

When the tears started to flow, Sly picked her up, swung her around, and told her not to cry because she was going to have to run the little restaurant downstairs in order to help him pay for the house and the boat. The entire bottom floor was a restaurant. There was a huge kitchen, and booths were lined on each wall and two rows back to back down the middle, plus a counter with bar stools in front of the windows so that people could eat while they looked out over the ocean.

Emma told Sly and his parents that if this was a dream, she did not want to wake up. Sly was beaming at his soon-to-be bride. He told Emma that she could decide on what side dishes she wanted to serve, and they would stock the food pantry. After that, all they would need would be the fish, which should not be a problem because his boat would take anglers out to catch the fish, and they would bring them back and take them to Tony's Fishery. Sly pointed to another building that looked like another fishing shack with an apartment behind the building, and it had its own pier.

Pop gave his famous laugh and said, "What more in life could you ask for? We have our fishing supply store, Sly has his boat, Tony has his Fishery, and you, Miss Emma, have your restaurant."

Sly told her that almost everyone had their home over or near their business. That way they never have to worry about being late for work. "I love having our family living close together. It will keep us close, and we can look out for each other."

Mom told Emma if she did not like the furnishings they had put in the house, they could change them later. She told her that they had so many things in their big house and not all of it would fit in their little home above their store, so they furnished all three houses with the furniture from their home.

Sly spoke up and said, "I forgot to mention, we have two guest bedrooms in Mom and Pop's place, ready for your grandmother and your uncle Charlie, should they ever want to visit or come and live with us, and we have a little guest house behind Tony's place, if the Spencers or Vera and Sophia want to visit. We have our own little Town of Bandowski."

85

Tony Lost a Leg in the War

When Emma's doctor gave her the okay, she started making plans to move into the house over the restaurant. When Sly was home on leave, he moved some of Emma's furniture to their new house. She had stored her furniture in her grandmother's shed when she and Frederick moved in with her. She did not have a lot of furniture, but with what Mom and Pop had already put in the house and what she had, it looked very cozy.

When school was out, Uncle Charlie and their grandmother helped them pack their personal things so that Emma and Frederick could make their move to the shore.

Uncle Charlie moved most of their things the first day, and the next day, he took everything else. Henrietta staked claim to the middle bedroom, calling it *her bedroom*. She even made signs for her door and Frederick's door with their names written on the signs.

Teasing her as he always did, Uncle Charlie asked Henrietta if she was afraid she could not remember which room belonged to her. She said, "No! I just want everyone to see that I also have a room at Mom and Sly's house. I will bring some of my things down here and leave the rest at Grandma's house. That way I will have two homes."

Uncle Charlie said, "When we get tired of you, you can go bug the rest of the family. When they get tired of you, I guess they can ship you back to us."

Henrietta had grown quite fond of Uncle Charlie and knew that he was just teasing her, so she went over and hit him on the shoulder and then gave him a big hug. True to her word, Henrietta divided her things. Half of it, she left at her grandmother's house, and the other half, she took to her mother and Sly's house.

Sly only had a short time before his discharge from the navy, and he was now able to come home almost every weekend. Sometimes he would get home on Friday and go back on Sunday. Other times, he would come in Saturday evening and have to leave to go back right after lunch on Sunday. At least Emma was able to see him more often.

They had to make a decision as to where they would like to have the wedding and if Sly's priest or if Reverend Charles would perform the ceremony. Before their wedding, the priest wanted to counsel Emma and Sly, and Emma wanted to talk with Reverend Charles about their upcoming nuptials.

When the priest found out that Sly was coming home on weekends and staying with Emma, he said that he would not marry them unless they ask for forgiveness because they were living in sin, and they had to agree to live apart until their wedding.

He told them that the sacrament of penance, commonly called confession, was one of the seven sacraments recognized by the Catholic Church. The Catholic Church believes that Jesus Christ himself instituted all of the sacraments.

He said, "Sly, you should know that the sacraments are an outward sign of an inward grace. In your case, the outward sign is the absolution or forgiveness of sins. Reconciling of man to God is the purpose of confession. When we sin, we deprive ourselves of God's grace. In addition, by doing so, we make it even easier to sin more. The only way out of this downward cycle is to acknowledge your sins and to repent of them and ask God's forgiveness. In the sacrament of confession, grace can be restored to our souls, and we can once again resist sin."

He told them that marriage was one of the seven sacraments of the Catholic Church. As such, it is a supernatural institution as well as a natural one. The priest therefore restricted sacramental marriage until they met certain requirements.

He told them that he could not marry Sly to a non-Catholic. Being that Emma had received her baptism about a year and half prior in a protestant church and she had a certificate of proof of that baptism he said, "That shall suffice for me to assist your protestant minister with the wedding ceremony."

The priest told them that they should not partake in immoral behavior. If they were living together, even if it was out of economic necessity, it would be considered a sinful act, and they should acknowledge their sins and to repent of them and ask God's forgiveness and agree to live apart until their wedding.

Sly told the priest that when he came home on leave, he would stay with his parents until they were married. He confessed his sins and asked for forgiveness. Emma was not exactly sure what being a Catholic involved, and besides, she was enjoying going to her church, so she decided to talk with Reverend Charles. She met with him alone the next day. The first thing she told her pastor was that Sly's family wanted them to get married in their Catholic church, and she would prefer to be married in his church.

Reverend Charles took hold of Emma's hand and told her that the first thing they should do was to pray together. After the prayer, he talked to Emma about what she expected out of their marriage, children they may have, and how her children fit into the picture.

After she told him about their living accommodations, Reverend Charles was very pleased with their decisions and that he agreed with the priest. Living together out of wedlock is not following the scriptures of the Bible. "I think both of you should ask for forgiveness, for any sins, that you have committed, whether they be known or unknown and sin no more."

They talked for a long time about her health. He wanted to know if she thought God healed her or did she think that it was skilled doctors who performed the miracle on her.

Emma stopped for a second before responding. When she responded, she said, "Reverend Charles, I think it was God who healed me, and I think he did so by guiding the hands of the skilled surgeons who performed my surgeries."

Reverend Charles told her that was a good way of putting it. He said, "You know, as I have preached many Sunday's about how God works in mysterious ways, possibly all the things you have been through have led you to where you are now. We must learn to always give God the glory for all things that happen because all things happen for the will of God."

Finally, Reverend Charles told Emma that he would try to work something out with Sly's priest, if she and Sly would give him permission to talk to him, which they did.

After they had received all counseling necessary from Reverend Charles and Sly's priest and had lived up to their confessions and attendance, the priest told them that they could set their wedding date, and he and Reverend Charles would perform their wedding ceremony together.

Sly's discharge date had been the middle of July but would not be official until August 1, 1945, because of the war, so they set their wedding date to go along with his discharge.

Sly had fought in this war since the beginning, and he was ready to get out of the navy and live a normal life again. Every time they went out on maneuvers, something violent normally happened. He had seen enough death and destruction to last him a lifetime.

Poor Tony had seen worse that Sly had. He lost one of his legs and received an early discharge, and he was in a very depressed state of mind. He hated the fact that he had once been an excellent dancer, and now all he could do was drag a wooden leg around.

Emma had not even known that Tony was out of the navy until the day that Sly and his parents took her down to see the boat and their new house. She knew that Sophia had not talked about him being home, so she automatically thought that he was still in the navy.

One weekend when Sophia and Vera came to visit, Sly's parents and Tony were in the process of bringing kitchen items to the restaurant to see if Emma would be able to use them.

When Sophia saw Tony, it broke her heart. She had lived for the day he would return home. Vera had Delmas, Emma had Sly, and she really did feel like a third wheel. She had always hoped for the day the good-looking sailor who told her that he had a question to ask her would return home.

Even though she had not heard from him in a long time, she never lost hope that he would someday knock, and she could hear his playful laughter as she opened the door.

When Sophia and Vera had gone down to see Sly's parents to tell them about Emma, they had no idea that Tony had gone to his bedroom in order to hide to keep from seeing them or them seeing him. Tony had asked Sly not to say anything to anyone, so he had not even told Emma about Tony until she went to see the boat that day. Sly asked her then not to say anything to anyone else because Tony did not want pity from anyone.

As Sophia looked at Tony, he put down on the counter what he was carrying, turned around, and started walking out the door. She called to him, asking him to wait because she would like to talk to him, but Tony in his depressed state of mind kept walking, pretending that he had not hear her call out to him.

Sophia ran to catch up with him, calling out his name as she ran, and he finally turned around to acknowledge her. When she got to him, she did not know what to do or say. She wanted to give him a hug and welcome him home or do something, but he had an invisible wall built up around him, and he was determined not to let anyone in.

She asked, "Tony, why do you not acknowledge me?" She then asked him what was wrong.

He turned around and said, "Just look at me! You know very well what is wrong. I do not want to embarrass you or me by pretending that I am just like I was when I left for the war. My body has changed and so have I. I don't want you or anyone else feeling sorry for me."

Sophia told him that she did not feel sorry for him, but she was angry with him because he had not told her.

Tony said, "Sophia, the reason you were attracted to me was because of the way I looked and the way I danced. Now I am neither of those things, so please just leave me alone and go find yourself another sailor to be your dance partner."

Sophia said, "Tony, you said in your last letter that you had something to ask me. I would like to know what that was."

Sophia thought that Tony was going to ask her to marry him, and she knew that she would say yes, even if he did not have but one leg.

Tony turned around, looked at Sophia, and said, "Sophia I was going to ask you to be my partner at a big dance competition. Just after mailing my letter, they sent our ship into hostile fire. I was injured and lost my leg. What kind of a dance partner would I be with a wooden leg?"

Sophia asked him if they could at least be friends, and Tony told her that he did not need her pity or her friendship and walked away. As he walked away, Sophia did a reality check. Did people actually think that she was so vain that she would turn her back on someone she cared for because having a good time was more important than friendships?

Sophia knew that she was in love with Tony. She loved him for who he was, not because he was the best dancer on the dance floor. The wall that he had built up around himself would be hard to penetrate. However, she knew that she was going to try.

86

Harry and Lorenda's Wedding

Harry Carswell and Lorenda Collingwood's wedding took place in a private ceremony in front of a Justice of the Peace because she was looking very pregnant, and her parents did not want to parade her down the aisle of their big church in front of all of their family, friends, and local dignitaries.

The very thing that Harry hated the most about Emma was her popping a baby out every time that he was with her; now he was getting right back into the same situation again. Lorenda's father was a large figurehead in their community, and he saw to it that Harry would not bring scandal to his family. He had threatened Harry with his life if he let his daughter down. They had given Lorenda and Harry a house as a wedding present. The house was just down the street from theirs. Harry could not get out of this marriage and probably would never be able to.

It would be nice if he could divorce Lorenda and get half of the money from the sale of the house and leave her and the kid and move somewhere else, where they could not find him, but he was too afraid of her father to try anything like that. Speaking of divorces, his divorce from Emma was official about two weeks before he and Lorenda were married. He would not even take leave from his ship when it was in port because he was afraid of Lorenda's father finding out that he was married. If the old man ever found out that he had four kids in another state, he would probably find himself hanging from a tree. How in the world had he gotten himself in this situation?

When his divorce from Emma became final, he went to her old apartment to let her know that it was final and that he was finally free from her. When he knocked on the door to the apartment, a lady opened the door and told him that she had been living there for months and had no idea where the people that had been living there had moved to. He was not about to ask any of the other people around there because he was afraid of them. At least they did not have the rent-a-cops standing guard at her door, but he still did not wear his sailor's uniform when he went to the apartment.

It was depressing because he had just known that it would have broken Emma's heart to know that she no longer had a chance with him. He knew that she loved him, and he had felt warmness for her; if not, he would have never married her. It was her having all those kids that messed up their lives.

His life was now set in concrete. He had no choices. He did not go to college, as his parents wanted him to do, so he really did not have any work skills except delivering coal. The plants were hiring men when they would come back from the war, but since he had no previous experience, he had trouble finding a job.

His father would not let him live at his house because they could not stand the sight of each other. He had heard his father say plenty of times that his mother had gotten pregnant by someone else and only married him so that she could claim that the baby had been his. He knew that his father had never recognized him as a true son, and that was probably what he had done with his own children. The way he was, was entirely his father's fault.

When Lorenda found out that she was pregnant, she told him if it was a boy, she wanted to name it after him. She did not like

Jr. after a boy's name, so they would reverse his name. That was exactly the same thing that Emma had done with Frederick. Now he would have two sons named Frederick. The name would haunt him for the rest of his life. Why did women have to be like that?

When he received his discharge and came home, he looked around at the city where he had lived. No one was there to welcome him when he came home from the war because no one cared. All the women that he had run around with were happily married and had homes and children. If people in the community had shown him more appreciation, it was possible that he would have never done some of the things that he did. He never had a chance from the beginning. The whole world was against him.

As the door closed on the bus that was taking him to catch a train to Missouri, he struggled with the fact that he had a gun in his pocket that could end it all, and it would free him from the life that he had no desire to live. It was much easier to kill other people, as he had enjoyed doing, while fighting the war, but he was too much of a coward to take his own life.

As soon as Harry arrived in Missouri, the ceremony took place. As he looked down at his new bride with her bulging stomach, he felt the same repulsion that he did with Emma every time she got pregnant. Only this time, he was the one trapped with no way out. Why did all of this have to happen to him? He had always been a good person and did not deserve the life he had been dealt.

87

Sly and Emma's Wedding

Sly and Emma stood before their family and friends as the priest performed the rites of marriage and Reverend Charles performed the Protestant wedding ceremony, as he would have done had they been married in his church.

Instead of being married in either church, they decided to be married on the beach in front of their home. Frederick was giving her away, Henrietta was her maid of honor, and Sophia and Vera were her bridesmaids. Sly's father was Sly's best man. Delmas was with Vera and Sophia stood alone.

Just before the wedding ceremony began, everyone could hear a noise as Tony walked down the boardwalk to join the wedding. Cane in hand, he walked through the sand over to where Sophia was standing. He held out his arm to her, and she placed her hand in the crook of his arm. He looked down at her and gave her the sweetest and most loving look anyone could give someone.

After Sly's and Emma's marriage vows, Reverend Charles said, "By the powers vested in me, I now pronounce you husband and wife."

The priest said, "Amen." He then looked at Sly and Emma smiling and said, "You may now kiss your bride." Sly looked at Emma, and she looked at him.

Sly then put his hands to each side of Emma's face, held it very gently and said, "Emma Patton Bandowski, I love you with all my heart, and I have since the night we first danced together." He then kissed her with the sweetest of all of his kisses.

Reverend Charles asked Sly and Emma to turn around. When they did, he said, "I present to you, Mr. and Mrs. Sylvester Bandowski."

On their first night of being husband and wife, Sly and Emma sat in their home looking out over the ocean. They had no desire to go anywhere for a honeymoon. Home with each other was where they wanted to be.

Sly turned the radio on to soft music, and extended his hand to Emma, asking her to dance with him. When the song, which they had danced to when they first met, came on, Sly pulled her close. Just as they started to dance, the music stopped. The announcer came on with a special announcement.

> We are interrupting our normal broadcasting for a special news announcement from President Harry S. Truman.
>
> On August 2, 1945, there were some 6,600 tons of bombs dropped on several Japanese cities, and the city of Toyama has literally been destroyed.
>
> On August 6, 1945, approximately 80,000 cicilians died when the United States dropped an atomic bomb on Hiroshima, Japan.
>
> On August 9, 1945 approximately 25,000 died as the United States dropped a second atomic bomb, this time on Nagasaki, Japan.
>
> On this day August 11, 1945, the Japanese have surrendered.

The announcer came back on, saying, "It looks like our nation has gone wild. In New York, two million revelers have poured into Times Square to watch the new flash. In Washington, 75,000 people massed in front of the White House. Pillow feathers showered down from office windows after the ticker tape and

378

shredded paper ran out. We know that everyone is celebrating this day in history."

As the music and celebrations came over the radio, Sly pulled Emma close, holding her tight. What a great time to celebrate their first night together as husband and wife. They had thankfulness in their hearts for their country and for their new life together.

Emma's battles began with a day of infamy and sadness when the Japanese bombed Pearl Harbor and she received her almost fatal attack from Harry. However, it was ending with ecstasy for the United States and for her.

The Japanese people must now bear the unbearable and endure the unendurable as will Harry with his new wife, Lorenda.

CPSIA information can be obtained
at www.ICGtesting.com
Printed in the USA
LVOW04s2057120816
500060LV00016B/281/P

9 781681 874708